Too Much
LOFT

MICHAEL J. STOTT

To George:
A champion in
golf and life!

Mike

SECOND PRINTING

Too Much Loft
Published by The Match, LLC
403 Lakewood Drive, Richmond, Virginia 23229

This is a work of fiction. The literary perceptions and insights are based on experience. All names, characters, places and incidents are either products of the author's imagination or used fictitiously. No reference to any real persons is intended or should be inferred.

Print ISBN: 978-1-09837-190-6
eBook ISBN: 978-1-09837-191-3

Acknowledgments

For the real Mrs. Peck who was the inspiration for this book.

With heartfelt thanks to my son David whose constant urging and belief in the story helped bring this trilogy to fruition.

PART ONE
MRS. PECK

1

PART TWO
MR. O

67

PART THREE
THE PRO SHOP

205

Too Much
LOFT

PART ONE

MRS. PECK

CHAPTER ONE
1960

As long as my rear end faces south, I'll never forget the best summer job I ever had. It was sociology at its best, loaded with life experiences and provided by pragmatic professors who had earned the right to pontificate. To this day their words, spoken directly to me or passed on through others, still resonate as I recall how they shaped my world. Those voices gave meaning and foundation to an adolescent on the cusp of manhood. Being a caddie also proved to me the immutable wisdom of Mark Twain who observed that people were only human, so they couldn't be any worse.

The beauty of this summer school was that class was taught outdoors, so right off you knew this was something special. Now Spring Willows Country Club will never be confused with Augusta National, though the snob level of certain members was right up there with those other captains of industry, but what it could have been with just a little more work was a top-notch ladies' championship course. Borney and I often talked about that. "Yes sir, with some vision, topsoil, bulldozers and an extra million, this course could be an LPGA stop," he'd say. Even though he was a first-class malcontent, Borney knew what he was talking about; last I'd heard he'd set up shop as a landscape architect in Tell City, Indiana.

Back then, Spring Willows' layout at 6,218 yards was a tad long for the ladies. The shrubbery and vegetation on our hallowed 200 acres were mature. Trees, the bane of classic courses grown old, were elms as stately and massive as the white clubhouse on the hill and ancillary to play thanks to architect

Donald Ross. Those willows for which the course was named? They vanished long ago thanks to a season of ice storms. Bunkers? For damn sure, we didn't need any more traps.

All in all, Spring Willows looked magnificent, especially in the horizontal early morning and late afternoon light. Sometimes coming in after raking traps, I'd look back at the second green toward the tee. The shadows and striations may have been asymmetric, but the Zen-like pastoral effect was one of respite and sustenance.

What was not peaceful and quiet was my round with Kaufman and Stroud. Even though it was a double bagger, no amount of cash could make up for my sore shoulders, their bloated egos and grinding personalities. They were always at each other. When all else failed, they got after me. Me, who carried their nine-ton bags filled with extra shoes, extra clubs, umbrellas, range balls and stocked stills.

These boys traveled on heavy fuel: as in whiskey flasks. The kicker was that the flasks had refills in the form of Old Forester bottles that I had to lug along. I don't think these guys ever broke 100. Stroud once shot a 101, but that was far and away the worst round for all concerned. He's still looking for the strokes he thinks Kaufman added to his score.

I was fresh out of that hurt locker and into the caddie shack when Al hit me with the pairings for the club championships. "Hey Looper, who do you like in the D Flight?"

"Old Lady Peck, 4-and-3," I said.

"4-and-3, over who?" asked Al, the caddie master.

"Whom," I said. "Over anybody. She's hot."

Sixty-seven years old and hot. That was a hoot for the caddies, most of them rough and tumble Catholics from Chicago's North Side. But Al knew I was on to something.

"You want to tote for her on Thursday when you're done with your groundskeeping shift? She doesn't tee off 'til 2:40."

"Kind of late, isn't it?"

"Yeah, but there's a Chamber of Commerce bash at Iroquois Woods, so most of the men will be gone."

"Thursday. That's first round. Mrs. Peck has a first-round match?"

"Yes sir."

"She's a former club champion and she doesn't get a bye?"

"Looper, that was 44 years ago. She's not top-flighted anymore."

"Al, I'm telling you, that isn't right."

"Her handicap is too high, so she gets no first-round bye."

"You know handicap doesn't mean squat at match play. That means she'll have to play more matches than most people," I said indignantly. "You know she's better than most in the field."

"That's if she wins, which she won't. If she's as good as you say, she'll handle it."

"Man at 67, I don't know. Who's her first-round opponent?"

"Mrs. Newby."

"You're kidding. The winsome Emily Newby? Why don't we just mail in the results now? Peck, 4-and-3."

"No way. Newby's much too young to fade like that."

"And vulnerable," I said. "She hits some great shots. About two a round, Al, but she doesn't do well in the clutch. You should have seen her last June in a Sunday four-ball scramble. Duck-hooked a putt on Seventeen to lose the match. But I'll give you this, she's great to watch. The guys hate to forecaddie on Four because they miss her centerfold stretch. Isn't that right, Red?" I said to the dweeb dealing cards in the corner.

"Nubile, nubile, nubile," said his poker playing buddies.

"Watching Newby play is like having a driver in your pants for eighteen holes. What's really fun is when she helps you look for lost balls. Comes into the woods, bending around the brush looking for her Maxflis. Her halter is pretty small, Al."

"That's Mrs. Newby to you, and don't you forget it," he said.

"Al, you want me to carry Mrs. Newby's bag on Thursday?" Red asked.

"Sorry, she's already requested Marconi."

"She just likes his looks," Red shot back.

"I think she really likes his manners. You guys could learn something from him," Al said.

"I still think Peck, 4-and-3. I've been watching her, Al. She's doing all right, real consistent and she even took a private lesson from Starza last week. I think she wants to prove something to herself."

"Looper, she's got eleven woods for Chrissakes. They don't make matched eleven-wood sets and yet she's got one."

"They're hand-made."

"No manufacturer in his right mind would make more than one of those sets," said Al.

"Hand-made. In Sumeria or somewhere. That's what she said. Saw them in some catalog."

"What else does she have in her bag?"

"A 5-iron, a sand wedge, a pitching iron and a putter."

"That's fifteen clubs; that's illegal. She can only use fourteen."

"Yeah, but she rarely uses 8, 9, 10. Those clubs are just confidence builders. Insurance. Besides, remember whom she married. Hugh Peck made a mint in stocks and insurance. But 8, 9 and 10 she just rotates through her bag depending on the wind and humidity."

"If she's got a pitching wedge, when does she use the 11-wood?"

"Sometimes with traps, sometimes with water. Depends on her mood. Just blasts it in from 40 yards. Though once I saw her lean on it to get a ball out of the water. On Sixteen I think it was. The only time it gives her problems is when it gets windy and she hits from high ground. A good gust can knock it down. Then the ball only goes 30 yards."

"Jeez, an 11-wood. It must have the loft of an airplane."

Al was right about that. Almost all of Mrs. Peck's shots spent forever in the air. But the thing I liked was that she hit it straight. A lot of people forgot that.

In fact, a lot of people had forgotten Mrs. Peck, period. The wife of a successful stockbroker and financial planner, she'd been a good athlete in her younger days, even one-time club champion. But a succession of four children and her role as homemaker took her off the fairways for a long time. Babies and bridge became her thing, and she didn't take up golf again until four years ago when her husband died in '56. And even then, she muddled around with her granny group. Played mostly on Wednesdays just hacking at the little white pill. The first time I ever caddied for her she carded a 106. But you could see some good mechanics. She was rusty, real rusty.

What she needed was some motivation. That came from Melissa, a nice-looking San Diego girl, who was California junior champion. As a bonding thing Grandma decided to dust off the sticks and have something in common with her athletic granddaughter.

Mrs. Peck's comeback and I arrived at Spring Willows at about the same time. As a rising college freshman, I got talked into a summer of caddying to supplement my job as a grounds crew member. My neighbor and former high school classmate Dave Trope introduced me to Al and offered to show me the ropes.

Al liked me because I was smart, polite and I kept my mouth shut. He also liked that I wore nice clothes, collared shirts and said "yes ma'am" to all the female members. At a la-di-da country club on Chicago's North Shore that counted for something.

Trope took me out and taught me the basics: how to carry two bags, anticipate club selection, hold the pin, wash balls, rake traps and forecaddie. My shoulders hurt a lot those first few weeks, but the $7 a bag I got was worth it. On any given day I didn't mind making multiple loops or rounds on the course, hence, "Looper."

It was August of my initial season when I caddied for Mrs. Peck for the first time -- a Ladies' Day Wednesday and she was out with frumpy Mrs. Reynolds, Mrs. Grant and Willow Wisp Wilson. The golf wasn't really good and certainly not powerful, but every now and then Mrs. Peck hit a crisp shot that made you think that with some practice she could be a contender. Didn't putt well, but she was a stranger to the rough because of her accuracy.

Four days later, Al surprised me in the caddie shack. "Looper, how'd you like to go twilight tomorrow with Mrs. Peck?"

"No thanks, Al. I'm going to the beach."

"Looper, I had a request for you. Plus, there's an added surprise. Mrs. Peck is going nine with her 18-year-old granddaughter."

"So?"

"So, the girl is California junior champion and a helluva looker. She's here for two weeks. This is a double bag you might want to reconsider."

"Why does Mrs. Peck want me?"

"She likes your manners, and she likes those gadgets you carry. Didn't you retrieve her ball from the pond on Seventeen with an extender or something?"

"Yeah, so?"

"Well, she also likes your resourcefulness in raking traps. You got some gizmo that does 'em fast?"

"It's a retractable sand rake that fits on your grip. Saves you from running all the way around the damn trap."

"Well, she liked that. And she thought you'd be the type of caddie she'd want to have around her granddaughter."

"Does this granddaughter have a name?"

"Melissa." As it turned out, it was not the last time I was to hear her name.

"Just nine holes, right?"

"Nine holes. Tee off at 5:30. You get their bags and meet them on the putting green at 5:15."

"Just for you, Al. Just for you."

* * *

For a picture without words, I'll give you Mrs. Peck -- Margaret Rutherford as Miss Marpole. Physically a tad small, slightly overweight, thinning white hair. Verbally very direct, very witty and pretty damn proper.

Melissa, on the other hand, was tall, relatively reserved and whacked the hell out of the ball. She was every bit the looker Al said. The play was pretty straight forward with most of the ball confined to the fairway. And since we played only the front nine, there was no water to speak of.

I decided to forecaddie the fourth hole, a 211-yard par 3. It had a mean swale, three strategically spaced greenside traps on the left and trees on the right. Mrs. Peck sent her brassie about 130 yards straight. Melissa, practically scratch from the blues, teed up a 1-iron and split the fairway at 170. Kind of short I thought, but then she hit a wedge 39 yards dead on and putted six feet for par. I hadn't seen many, except Mr. Howard, the men's club champion, play the hole that well. Not to be outdone, Mrs. Peck played a solid 5-wood to the fringe and got down in two.

As it turned out, the whole soiree took two hours and left some lasting impressions. For starters, I saw some precocious golf. Melissa played the front nine in 1-over, no mean feat for someone swinging sight unseen, and her grandmother hung tough with a bulldog-like 44.

I also recall the coral blouse Melissa was wearing. The high collar teased her short brunette hair and flirted with her ears while the shirttail bled through her white shorts capturing my imagination -- big time.

Alas, two weeks didn't give me enough time to establish the traction with Melissa I would have liked. While I suspect there was some mutual attraction, a fortnight fraught with her pre-arranged social obligations limited our liaisons to a couple evenings of pizza and movies.

But I did get pretty close to Mrs. Peck. I don't know what it was. Maybe I was the grandson she never had, but I caddied for her almost exclusively, even when higher flighted members called my number.

CHAPTER TWO

I had sweated through my pink polo and was headed for a Nehi when Al came around the corner. "Who won?"

"Mrs. Peck, 4-and-3, just like I told you."

"Any anxious moments?"

"A couple, before we got to the water. Mrs. Newby hit some well-placed shots. She's much better than in June, but the worm started turning on Killer Ten and Eleven. Mrs. Newby found the drink on both holes. Then she started talking to her clubs. By Fourteen she was talking to herself and I knew it was just a matter of time. Mrs. P's 7-wood broke Mrs. Newby's heart when she hit it 60 yards over the fronting trap on Fourteen..."

"A 7-wood went 60 yards?"

"Well, she took a little off it. Listen, they had identical lies almost side-by-side. Mrs. Peck is away and nudges that honey so it just clears the trap, catches the fringe and rolls to within five feet. Mrs. Newby puts hers on the beach, a deep screamer into the lip and took four to escape the trap. By then she'd lost the hole and the match.

"On Fifteen Mrs. Newby got so lost in the first fairway trap that by the time she reached the green, she picked up and shook Mrs. Peck's hand. I wish all the members were that gracious."

"Never happen," Al said, shaking his head. "Mrs. Peck is on a roll, huh?"

"I wouldn't say that, but she's got some confidence. If her health holds up and the heat holds off, she's looking tough," I said.

"She's got health problems?"

"Well, you know. She's 67 years old. Plus she takes medication for this arrhythmia that acts up every now and then. Mostly when life gets tense. When does she play again?"

"Any time after Thursday. She'll go against the Van Horne-Pate winner."

"I like Van Horne."

"Me too," said Al.

"Too bad the club doesn't have a Calcutta on the women's lower flights like the caddies do. Someone could make a bundle on Mrs. P."

"I still think you're dreaming. Van Horne will hammer her. Then you can go back to raking traps full time."

"Later, Al. Give me a call if Mr. Howard wants to go nine after work. Otherwise I'll be cutting grass at Mrs. Burns."

* * *

For a college kid I worked too damned hard in the summer. Almost all of it was for school. Sometimes I saved a little out for movies and the Dairy Queen, but that was about it. You have to remember, even in the well-to-do suburbs, not every kid had a car like they do now. Oh, I had access, but the begging and pleading required to get the keys was unbelievable. I saved my salvos for special occasions. Not having a car was a curse and a blessing. The limited mobility stifled my social life, but it kept the dating expenses to a minimum.

Grounds crew work at Spring Willows at my level (grunt) was as demeaning as it sounded. In the mornings, seven days a week, I hand-raked traps from six to eight. Today practically everything is done by machine. I would have welcomed automation, but I probably never would have gotten as close to the earth as I did by going manual.

I usually took the left side of the course, holes Two through Eight, plus Thirteen, Fourteen and Seventeen. Borney took the others. Of the 74 traps on the course I had 41, but he had the monsters on Fifteen, Sixteen and Killer Ten.

Man, Ten was a mother. Elevated tee, 163 yards across a pond to an elevated green that sloped toward the water. The littoral enhancement consisted of four traps around the green, each six feet minimum from bottom to lip clearance. And let me tell you, the topographical problems were compounded by the Halfway House at the tenth tee where the doctors and lawyers grabbed cold ones before starting the back nine.

On hot days, members would get two 'medicine balls.' They'd pound one before striking the ball and tote and sip the other. One day Old Man Farnham plunked two Spaldings in the drink before landing his third in the right trap. Then he took eight, I'm not kidding, eight more shots to reach the green. He just blasted back and forth over the green left, right and center until he finally got one on. Then he rolled in the putt for a 14. Nobody said a word.

On a normal day, after raking traps I either weeded traps, weeded the clubhouse phlox beds or pulled sod duty, replacing mortar-sized chunks of grass that the rich and famous were forever digging up. Occasionally I retrieved balls from the ponds at Ten, Sixteen, Seventeen or the creek between Fourteen and Fifteen. Usually Rossi got the ball responsibilities. And if I may say so, he made a nice side income from selling used balls to the Pro Shop. Especially from what he got on Ten and Seventeen, the par 3s. Today, well-run clubs wouldn't allow a monopoly like the one Rossi had. They'd be doing the bottom fishing themselves, literally raking thousands from those black lagoons.

If it rained, me and Borney, usually Borney, got stuck with the lowest job on the course, picking up sticks. Not that the work was that hard. You just hated everybody knowing that you were the one doing it. It was like wearing a badge that said "Hello, my name is peon."

Once I even drove a tractor, but that job opportunity ended soon after I jumpstarted the rear loader in fourth gear. It took off on me and I barely missed two pin oaks and the superintendent's shed. I thought I was at Darlington without a seatbelt headed for the thirteenth green. The guys working the greenside trap hauled ass. Me, I was dumbstruck. What brakes? I didn't know where they were. Finally, I killed the ignition. Well, me and my 90-mile-an-hour heart cut it off. The tractor rolled to a stop right by the trap edge. Was I scared?

Wolfgang and Domingo sure weren't. They were laughing their buns off. But Mr. Olson, the greenskeeper, wasn't amused. In fact, he dressed me down, publicly. "Don't you ever drive another thing while you're out here," he blustered. Mr. O was an asshole, but he was dead solid perfect on that call.

Borney still calls me Fireball Roberts for that one.

One job I did like was trimming weeds by the tennis courts or the pool. The courts were the best because there wasn't as much activity there, and often I found Emily Evans hitting balls off the backboard. Emily was a former classmate of mine, another looker, who'd gone to New England for private school for her last three high school years. We even dated once and she was always friendly. So, I could steal a few minutes to talk and stare at her complexion and full body. Emily did a tennis dress justice.

The only problem was when Helga the pro, was around. She'd run me off in a heartbeat. "Weeds. You supposed to do weeds, no talk to girls," she'd say. On the days that I had to water and sweep her courts, she'd sing the same song, "water courts, no talk to girls," even when there were no girls around.

But the lifeguards were the worst. Stud swimmers from my high school that lorded it over us hoi polloi and then made up to all the honeys -- and even some of the mothers. Talk about a soft job. The only calluses they had were the yellow ones from sitting on their butts or the brown ones on their noses, if you get my drift.

* * *

True to my prediction, Mrs. Van Horne put Mrs. Pate away, 5-and-4. She broke on top early, winning two of the first three holes with double bogeys. Mrs. Pate was real nervous and the few times she had good holes (like bogeys) Mrs. Van Horne did too. The ax fell on Fourteen when Mrs. Van Horne lashed her third shot, a 4-wood, to within 12 feet and two-putted to close Mrs. Pate out. Probably just as well. Mrs. Pate would have been hash at the hands of Mrs. Peck.

The Peck-Van Horne match didn't draw much interest because, of the remaining sixteen golfers in the D Flight, these two were considered intruders. Oh, they had all the social credentials, they just weren't viewed as contenders.

Mrs. Van Horne was 48 and had been a tennis player. She took up golf when she was 46 and while she was a competitive sort, she was still learning the game. Inconsistency was her strong suit, and I didn't see her staying with Mrs. Peck, the 1926 Spring Willows club champion. The thing about Mrs. Peck was she'd never forgotten how to win, even during the decades-long hiatus spent raising her family.

CHAPTER THREE

Mrs. Van Horne proved to be a handful. I had seen her taking lessons from Starza, the head pro, and didn't think much about it until the draw, but the truth of the matter was she was intent on bouncing Mrs. Peck. She began the round by hitting her drives a ton, starting with the first hole, a 535-yard par 5 that was testy even for the men. Mrs. Van Horne negotiated the slight left dogleg nicely, was on the green in four and two-putted for a 6, leaving my lady lying 8 and down one.

Life got worse at the 426-yard second hole where Mrs. Van Horne hit long and straight and carded a 5 to Mrs. P's 7 to go 2-up. Two is the second toughest hole on the course, so things weren't looking too rosy here.

And to compound matters, Mrs. Peck was really skying her balls higher than normal. I usually kept my mouth shut when my players were struggling, but in the second fairway, after another cloud scraper, I said, "That's in the ozone, Mrs. Peck." It really was, 20 yards high, 60 yards long. I was frustrated because she was giving away so much distance that she couldn't recoup unless her opponent went astray.

What saved Mrs. P were the several visits to the adjacent backyards (more on them later) that Mrs. Van Horne took on Three and Five. In fact, for a while there, she was a dead ringer for the wandering Aramean. Nasty underbrush caused her to lose two balls and we came out of those holes with two halves.

A great pitch on the long par-3 Four gave Mrs. Peck that hole, but a lost ball on Six and another half on Seven had us down two going to Eight.

On the next two holes Mrs. Van Horne nailed two long drives and two great approach shots for bogeys as we headed to the Halfway House down four.

At this point Mrs. Van Horne was playing A-Flight golf and things weren't looking too hot for the home team. Then the miracle of the Halfway House happened. Bernard Van Horne, 24-year-old son of, arrived to cheer on his mom. Loud and demonstrative, he was the very last thing his mother needed.

Did I tell you Mrs. Van Horne played much better unappreciated? She really was the Greta Garbo of Golf. She'd much rather have played in obscurity, so Bernard's arrival was bad news for the missus. When I saw him stride up in his azure Izod and beige Brooks Brothers pants, I turned to Mrs. P and said, "You've won it." And I honestly believed the worm had turned.

With the honors, Mrs. Van Horne faced the yawning pond and those greenside traps at Killer Ten. It was there she hit what was unquestionably her strongest shot of the day. What a case for adrenaline. She was so pumped up, she airmailed a 3-iron six miles over the pond, the green, the road, the shrubbery and into the pool on Judge Gleason's estate that looks just like a David Hockney painting. Next, she raised her head on a 5-iron that strafed the pond, hit the bank and bounced back into the drink. Her third swing got her to the fringe. With a nifty up and down she holed out in 7.

Casual observer that she was, Mrs. P lofted a 4-wood almost above the trees. "It's in the rarified. Unbelievable," I said. And it was. As always, she was just short of the right trap. From there, Mrs. Peck chipped up and two-putted for an impressive 4. We were down three with eight holes to go.

Eleven is Spring Willows' equivalent of the St. Andrew's road hole, the difference being our road is on the left. On this day that 335-yard par 4 produced the best laugh of the afternoon. Eleven still retains the earmark of classic design where architects put hazards where they belong, in the middle of the hole. Ours has a mean perpendicular creek running across the fairway about 170 yards out. Men think nothing of it, but women visit this hazard like they're going to the beauty parlor -- and pay just as dearly.

Mrs. Peck skyed her 3-wood into the rarified again, but this time with some distance -- about 160 yards, just short of the creek. Still shaking from Ten, Mrs. Van Horne shanked her drive into the passenger side of Eldredge Wankum's moving green Jaguar. The ball ricocheted off the door handle and shot back onto the fairway. Later inspection revealed only the slightest chrome damage to the car, but the shot did nothing for Mrs. Van Horne's self-esteem, and we left Eleven down two. When Mrs. Peck sank a 20-foot uphill job on Twelve, she was back in the match.

The ladies halved the next three holes. I'm certain it was because Bernard, with much bowing and scraping, bought his leave, creating some much-needed psychic space for his mother. Mrs. Van Horne was clearly regrouping. The good news was that Sixteen ran by the tennis courts where her buddies were lining the fence to cheer her on. Both players had good drives off the tee and second shots that skirted the pond, but when the tennis ladies began to shout encouragement, Mrs. Van Horne's game went south. The green on Sixteen lay west. Detours into the deep rough spawned cries of dismay from the courts. When Mrs. Peck won the hole with a curling ten-footer we were even for the first time since the first tee.

Seventeen is probably the most scenic hole on the course. It's a 153-yard par 3. From an elevated tee it faces a pond situated to the right and front of the green. It's faintly reminiscent of Seventeen at Sawgrass except that it doesn't have all the fancy bulkheads. Half of Rossi's retirement income came from this hole. Traps are never an issue for decent bunker players. Water is. Most golfers would give anything to be in the far-left trap, or even long, because either place is a safe alternative to the drink.

If anything, Seventeen is pure theater of the mind. Mrs. Peck's mind was to hit a 5-wood 110 yards and to loft a 40-yard 11-wood, only her second of the match, onto the green. But again, her drive was a mile skyward, and I said so.

"Now Looper, that's the third time in the last five holes you've used the words 'ozone' and 'rarified' to describe my drives. They all look like the same shot to me," said Mrs. Peck.

"Well, they are not the same. You hit all your shots high, Mrs. Peck. When one is in the 'ozone' that means it is way up there but out of control. 'Rarified' means it's way up there but will have a happy landing -- as if God is giving it a guiding hand. So, you'd rather be in the rarified than in the ozone."

"If you say so," she said, shaking her head.

It all made sense to me. So did Mrs. Van Horne's approach, a 5-iron layup. But after perfect execution, she shot herself in the foot by sculling her Titleist into the pond. Four more swings got her into the cup, but by then she'd lost the hole. Mrs. P two-putted and we were up one with one to go.

Eighteen is 452 yards uphill, a slight dogleg left. There's an inconsequential (unless you go right) lagoon 260 yards from the tee. Trees are minimal and traps are poorly placed. The green is expansive and flat. All in all, not a great finishing hole, but people always underestimate how hard you have to hit the ball to get it home.

Not Mrs. Peck. Four shots, all straight, got her to the dance floor. Mrs. Van Horne did her one better and got to the fringe in three. But then she sent her chip skittering 20 feet past the flag. Both ladies drained their second putts for halving sixes and Mrs. P went to the clubhouse the winner, 1-up, to the surprise of many.

Not me. Mrs. P was on a roll and I knew it. Al was getting complaints.

"About what?" I asked.

"About you and Mrs. Peck."

"Why?"

"Well, it seems the other members think she's got a regular caddie."

"She does, sort of. That's not against the rules, is it?"

"It's highly unusual. D-flighters don't usually have regular caddies."

"That's because most loopers don't want to caddie for double-digit handicappers. Mrs. P and I just understand each other. Besides, she hits it straight."

"Just watch yourself. They're starting to get scared of you two. They know none of the other caddies know the course like you do."

That was for sure. I lived only three blocks from Spring Willows and I had traversed Eleven through Fourteen on my way home from high school every day. Since I walked my dog on Two though Six, and worked on the course, I knew distance and terrain. I knew the course wet, dry, hot, cold, calm, windy, up and down -- as well as anyone except for maybe Mr. O, the superintendent, and Mr. Howard, the club champion.

And one other thing, I could read greens like Tarot cards, something I never let on to members when I was caddying. Generally, I just let them size up putts and stroke them offline, but I could see the day coming when I might have to impart a bit of advice.

Did I tell you I played a lot of golf up until the time I was 16? Public courses mostly, but I got to where I could stop balls on rock hard greens and granite kitchen countertops. I was really good at pitch and run too, a must for any muni player worth his saltpeter. Some summer days I'd ride my bike over to Evanston's flea-bitten 5,400-yard track and tee off at 5:45 a.m. By being first off I could play multiple balls without anyone complaining. I developed a good putting stroke. Being self-taught helped my game -- and those I caddied for.

In me Mrs. Peck did have an advantage, but her biggest ally was that the younger D-flighters underestimated her.

"Al, you know me. I just go out there and hand the members the clubs."

"Yes, you do, Looper. You also shoot lower numbers than 90 percent of the people you club for. What you really are is a confidence-builder. The D-flighters are coming to see you as an unfair advantage."

"B.S., Al."

"Just don't go reading greens for her, OK? That's when it will hit the fan. I can take all the complaints, the remarks, the jealousy because that's what it is. But no member at Spring Willows has a caddie reading greens for them, not even in the men's Championship Flight. Don't start now."

What he was saying was, "Son, you got a good thing going, don't screw it up." I decided to chill out for a few days and stay low profile.

That didn't mean I couldn't accept her invitation for supper. Two nights later I donned my blue blazer and light charcoal slacks, borrowed the family sedan and headed for her big house in Hubbard Woods. It was a pleasant evening. She even offered me some sherry. We talked about her grandchildren and I asked about her early days on the links, especially the glory years that included the 1926 club championship.

She still had the trophy. "I'm getting ready to put some polish on it," she said. That told me a lot right there.

"You're getting serious about this thing, aren't you, Mrs. P?" I said.

"No, Looper, we're getting serious about this thing. For years I lived my life for others. Now I remember how it feels to be good. I like to win. Once, before I die, I'd like to win again."

"Seems like you're a winner now. You've got a great family, ten grand-daughters. It's not like you're poor or anything. What more could you want?"

"A championship," she said with a determined gaze.

It was a look unlike any other I'd seen. This was important, I could tell.

"How's Melissa doing?" I asked.

"She won the California collegiates as a freshman, playing number two for Stanford. Beat that Polly Sue Bryant from Cal Poly San Luis Obispo by four strokes. Earlier this summer she qualified for the U.S. Women's Amateur and advanced to the quarterfinals."

"She going to visit this summer?" I inquired hopefully.

"No plans to. She's got tournaments until school starts."

"Yeah, I'll bet," I said, trailing off into thoughts of Friday's match.

Normally when you reach the round of eight, you're looking at reasonably decent golfers, even in D flight. But Mrs. Cabiness was another story. Blessed with a bye and two defaults, she cruised into the quarters against Mrs. Peck without ever swinging a club. Too bad for her. Not that Mrs. C couldn't play, it's just that her motives and focus were suspect.

I'm not sure Mrs. C ever wanted for much in life. When you are well-fixed, sometimes your ambition isn't what it should be. And if you've got money, a lot of times you can will things to happen and they do. Willing the ball in the hole without practicing is another deal altogether. That was the good news.

The bad news was summer had returned with a vengeance. The weather gods cranked up the heat and humidity and left for a late August vacation. As we hit the links for the Friday match with Mrs. Cabiness it was 94 and heading higher.

When I met Mrs. P on the putting green she was already sweating. "We going to be all right, Mrs. P?" I asked.

"We'll see, Looper. I wish I were 35 like Cindy Cabiness."

"Maybe they'll let you take a cart. Club rules say that's OK until the semis. You see if Mrs. C is agreeable and I'll check with Leon. Maybe we can still get top dollar if we carry and you ladies ride."

I didn't think Mrs. C would mind riding. She liked to play quickly. In fact, I'm not sure golf was all that held her attention that day. Word was she'd developed a thing for Devin McDevitt, the assistant pro (known as Divot to the caddies for obvious reasons and for his penchant for plowing the membership.) It seems she was in the process of getting him to give her a few private, private lessons that were scheduled to start around 3 p.m. If that were true, I figured she was looking past Mrs. Peck.

As it turned out, the golfers rode and the caddies walked briskly. The match was like playing pinball on two different machines. Mrs. P played on the old straight and narrow 26" field, and Mrs. Cabiness on the 30" model. That 30" model made for a rough round.

A lot of times you hear golf announcers talk of players hurling balls at the flag. That never happened here. Our players hurled balls at the traps, the rough, the woods and the water, but rarely, if ever, at the flags.

Mrs. C. was able to drive the cart to most of her errant shots, which was a good thing because she was a good distance woman. I heard a pro football player describe a babe as a good distance woman if she looked fabulous across a room. I hear tell that Mrs. C was not only good across a room, but good across a bedroom. She was also long off the tee. Not straight, mind you, but long. Driving deep into the woods to look for lost Titleists ran up the score and gave Mrs. P some time to rest.

I think Mrs. C. would have been happy to have been closed out 8-and-7, but Mrs. Peck wasn't cooperating. For one thing the wind sprang up, and anything hit into the wind played havoc with Mrs. Peck's lofted woods. Mrs. Cabiness was hitting low, lethal screamers into the stiff breeze. Only her low, off-line shots kept Mrs. Peck up by two as we made the turn.

On the way to Killer Ten I said, "No more high shots, Mrs. P. With this wind, high shots mean high numbers."

"I'm in the ozone today, Looper. I'm trying, but this heat and wind make me tired. I'm getting under the ball on every stroke."

"Play it more off the instep and you can drive it lower and longer," I offered.

That advice worked for three holes and we went to Thirteen up five with six holes to go. Thirteen is as far away from the clubhouse as you can get on the back nine. I guess Mrs. Cabiness decided she ought to play tough back to the clubhouse. My watch said 12:45 when she hit a driver 175 yards that cut the traps just seven yards shy of the green. A muffed chip left her 25 feet short of the flag. Mrs. P hit a 3-wood 130 and took an 8-wood and a chip to lie three from just 14 feet. Mrs. C putted to within two feet and tapped in. When Mrs. P pushed her 14-footer badly to the right we were back to 4-up.

Fourteen is the hole I know best because Curly, my dog, and I ran the dense woods on the left three nights a week. But it wasn't the forest that did Mrs. Peck in. It was her putting. Pushed a three-footer wide right again to lose the hole.

The match mercifully ended on the long-left dogleg Fifteen, the toughest hole on the course. At 565 yards, length wasn't the problem. It was the diabolical fairway traps. The day Donald Ross designed the hole he must have had it in for mankind in general. There were four fairway bunkers strategically placed to catch the first and second shots of every golfer, regardless of ability. And these things were yawners. Whenever I raked them I felt like I was in the Empty Quarter of the Sahara. And if it's true that a full one-fifth of the world is desert, I'll bet most of Spring Willows' share was in the right-hand trap 60 yards from the tee. From there it went another 50 yards, easy, and had the heaviest sand imaginable. So buried lies, not uncommon, often required two strokes to resurface. In fact, the fastest way to get out was to forget length and hit perpendicular back to the fairway. General Sweeney, a major jerk, taught me that one, but the competitive golfers never seemed to want to give up the yardage.

Anyway, Mrs. Cabiness got her dander up trying to escape the traps. With Mrs. P hitting five short, straight ones to put her on the fringe, Mrs. C conceded from the second fairway trap. It was a surrender of convenience I guess, but she was gracious about it -- and anxious to get on with her agenda. Not even standing on ceremony, she sped away in the Club Car back to the ladies' locker room.

Mrs. Peck was visibly tired. On the way back to the clubhouse I thought she looked like a Bataan death march victim. "Kind of shaky out there on the back nine, Mrs. P."

"I know, Looper. Even with the cart. I need to take some more medicine before playing next time. My putting has me worried."

"Me too."

"I just don't feel comfortable with this model. Melissa gave it to me for Christmas, but it's not the answer. The best putter I ever had was a 34" wooden Patty Berg. If I had a wooden putter, we might have a chance against that Whippet woman. Do you think Stan or Divot would have one?"

"Let me check it out and I'll call you," I said as I hoisted her bag off to the Pro Shop.

Starza and Divot hadn't seen any wooden putters in years. "They used those things to burn Joan of Arc," laughed Starza. "Nobody's got 'em anymore."

"Not that it matters," Divot said. "Whippet's going to close Peck out by lunch."

"I'll bet you $10 against that new MacGregor driver you got there that Mrs. P wins," I said.

"What do you say, Stan? It's a promo."

After a nod from the head pro, the cocky assistant said, "You're on, hot shot."

"McDevitt, one other thing," I whispered when Starza went to the back, "keep it in the road this afternoon."

My basement was like that of most homes built in the late Forties. Dank, dark and dirty. Traces of water and moldy cardboard everywhere. It took about 20 minutes, but beneath the rubble was the Excalibur, the first putter I ever owned. My neighbor Mr. Beich gave it to me, a 34-inch wooden Louise Suggs model made of pure hickory. The aging varnish gave it the feel of an old library. But once I took steel wool, sandpaper and put furniture polish on it, the shaft gleamed like a beacon. Trouble was the tattered and torn grip wasn't quite ready for show time.

The next morning I gave the pro his wake-up call. "Mr. Starza, think you could regrip this for me by Tuesday?"

"Son of a bitch, kid, where'd you get this relic?"

"Amazing, huh?"

"Friggin' A amazing. You want leather or slip-on rubber on this thing?"

"Leather."

"That'll be $3 cash and I'll have it ready by tonight. I'll get Divot to do it," said Starza. "He owes me for slipping out early yesterday."

* * *

Mrs. Peck wasn't a great one for practice, but when she hit the semis she agreed to meet me Monday afternoon on the putting green. Officially the club was closed Mondays for maintenance, so after my grounds crew shift I ambled up to the deserted putting green with my Sunday bag.

"Got something for you, Mrs. P." I produced the Louise Suggs. "It's not Patty Berg, but it's awfully close. I checked an old catalog and it's practically cut from the same cloth. Might help cure those putting ills."

"Looper, where'd you get this?" she asked, as excited as I'd ever seen her.

"You'll never guess, Mrs. P. From me to you."

"How much do I owe you?"

"From me to you. Let's stroke a few."

There is a saying that a caddie earns his keep when a player's game was going poorly. Praise (however faint), cajolery, even lying, were all acceptable as long as the bag toter got his golfer going. Mrs. Peck and I both knew the putting was a problem. I believed it was half mechanics and half confidence. If we could iron out the stroke, I was sure her confidence would return.

Happily, the putter helped her stroke, but a little tidbit I got from the women's club champion was even more helpful. "Mrs. P, when you stroke you've got too much right hand. When you get tired, your right hand takes over. That's why you had your problems with Mrs. Cabiness. Hold the club more firmly with your left hand."

She must have putted for half an hour. Then we went to the practice tee to work on swinging through the ball to cut down on the loft. "No high shots, no high numbers," I began. "Remember to work the ball forward off your foot and get those hips through."

The second lesson didn't take as well as the putting, mainly because she seemed to be getting bogged down by the heat. "That's a wrap, Mrs. Peck. You've got to go get some rest and I'm going to bag some groceries. Just think about your swing and ball placement and the excessive loft will disappear by Wednesday."

* * *

Wednesday was going to be something else. Mrs. Peck was paired against Susan Whippet, a mean-spirited snob the caddies called Snidely Whiplash. Whippet was a 51-year-old former private schoolteacher who had married well. Here was a woman who liked her advantage early and often. When she stooped to conquer it wasn't with good intentions or fair play.

Rumor had it that she'd falsified scores that summer to raise her hand icap for the sole purpose of winning the D-Flight championship to compensate for her many C-Flight semifinal failures. Winning wasn't everything to Whippet, it was the only thing. Vince Lombardi would have loved her intensity -- and loathed her ethics. I know I did.

After weeding traps I stopped in to see the caddie master. "Al, what's the deal on regulation balls in club championships?"

"USGA rules, Looper. Same laws that apply to ball composition and size. No small British balls, no liquid centers, nothing deviant."

"Anyone check for irregularities? You, Starza, Divot, anyone?"

"We're on an honor system."

"The system's gonna be tested tomorrow -- by Mrs. Whippet."

"Come off it."

"You know her. She looks for the smallest loophole. Anything to get a leg up." I paused for a moment. "I hear Whippet plays, let's just call them, 'irregular balls.'"

"I haven't heard that," Al said, mincing words ever so slightly through his thin mustache.

"Well, I have. I thought those were illegal for championships."

"They are. There's been a lot of talk about that, and the competition committee voted again in April to ban the use of non-conforming balls for this year's championships. But if enough people want them, they could be legal next year."

"So, they are out for this year?" I asked.

"Only USGA-conforming balls and equipment. Period."

"And the penalty if you're caught is?"

"Disqualification," Al said.

"Just checking," I said.

"Well," said Al, "looks like the weather may be in your favor. There's a front coming through tonight: rain and high winds expected. That ought to drop the temperature. Cool and clear tomorrow. Could be a perfect day for scoring. That should help your buddy."

CHAPTER FOUR

The front blew through just as Al said it would. Absolutely hammered the course. Borney and I picked up a lot of sticks Wednesday morning. Even had to get out the chain saws to clear some debris on fairways Three, Five and Seven. Water sat in the traps almost until noon when the sun baked them dry. All of this was good for Mrs. Peck, whose short, no-roll drives wouldn't be hampered by the soggy course the way Whippet's line drives would.

The downpour also discouraged the usual Wednesday afternoon medical crowd, so the D-flight semifinal would be played in relative anonymity. That's not to say there wasn't considerable interest in the match in the clubhouse. Judge Gleason and Billy Sauers, an arbitrager, each approached me asking about Mrs. Peck's health and the general condition of her game. Questions arose such as, "Looper, if you were a betting man..." and "Son, how'd you like to make an extra $10?"

Actually, I wasn't surprised. I'd caddied for both men. They liked to wager, and I got the feeling they were trying to get their "fair advantage" as Lombardi put it. I told them the same thing I told Al. "I like her chances fine if she stays out of the rough, is steady on the green, and if Whippet plays fair."

But I didn't expect Whippet to play fairly and I told Kelly Wright, her smart-ass caddie, that I wasn't going to put up with any B.S. from either of them. I really didn't expect trouble from Kelly, but I didn't want him abetting the enemy, either.

Clubhouse sentiment was leaning toward the old lady. When I went to get Mrs. P's bag from the Pro Shop, it was already on the outside rack, shoes shined, clubs gleaming. By the same token Kelly had to search for Whippet's clubs. Seems they had gotten misplaced.

We teed off at 2:30, and it didn't take long for the dirty tricks to start. Whippet was smart enough to wait until Mrs. Peck's downswing on the second tee to create a racket with the ball washer. I don't think it bothered Mrs. P all that much, but it bugged the hell out of me, and I told Kelly that as we took off down the fairway.

I was hoping that Whippet and Mrs. P would both generally keep the ball in play so I could keep an eye on Snidely. She had some bad habits that I felt I could mitigate if their balls were in the same neighborhood. I didn't figure I could keep her from smoking on the course, a habit that I despised since I always had to do next day clean-up, but I felt I might be able to enforce some specific club rules governing championship matches. Improving lies, improper drops from hazards and grounding clubs while in the traps were subject to penalty strokes, add-ons that I felt Whippet wasn't inclined to take.

Of the two par 5s on the front nine, Three was the cruelest to a golfer with a hook. Whippet had a tendency to go left, which on Three meant she was a distinct candidate for the Spring Willows Good Neighbor award. All along the left side of the fairway were palatial homes. One backyard was protected by a fancy fieldstone wall, another by an elaborate privet hedge while a third property, Governor Wylie's, was guarded by daylilies and various perennials. It was the Wylie's that accepted Whippet's duck-hooked drive, a fierce shot that rattled around his gazebo before coming to rest thirty yards from the fairway.

"OB," I said to Kelly. Whippet teed up another Titleist and barely kept it in bounds, 170 yards out. Mrs. P sent her ball 140 slightly to the right, just short of the leading fairway trap and then proceeded to reach the green on the 505-yard hole in four strokes. Nothing fancy, just straight. Two putts and a bogey 6 put Mrs. Peck 1-up as we entered Four, the long par 3 that Melissa had played so well.

Four was one of the few holes we could actually forecaddie. I was a little apprehensive because once out of sight I wasn't sure what shenanigans Whippet would pull. She might take the opportunity to switch to an illegal ball, a move that I was sure was going to come.

I didn't trust Whippet. By now she'd figured Mrs. P was the main obstacle between her and the D-Flight championship. I think she thought she could beat Rhoda Charles or Jocelyn Price, the other semifinalists, so this was the match she had to have.

Nothing fishy transpired on Four. They both carded fives and moved on to the 420-yard par-4 fifth. This was another fairway bound on the left by houses. Again, Whippet lashed her driver left, into Ambassador Austerlich's backyard. Whippet had a good line back to the fairway, but rules are rules. OB is OB. Visibly pissed, Whippet powdered another Titleist. This one went 191 yards, just trickling into the trap I'd raked that morning. From what I could tell, she was the first visitor all day.

"On the beach," I said to Kelly as we went into the ambassador's yard to retrieve the first ball.

"Yeah, she's getting hot, too," Kelly said. Whippet made the green in five.

Lying three and faced with an 80-yard shot over sand to the green, Mrs. P hit a 9-wood for the first time in three matches -- to within 16 feet of the flag. Using a sturdy right hand, she lagged within 18 inches and knocked it in for her bogey six, one better than Whippet. Up two going to Six.

Six is typical of Donald Ross holes found on some of his pre-World War I courses. The tee is recessed into a chute of elms that fans out onto a dark, narrow, often soggy, fairway. Sun seems to shine on this hole early in the morning and about an hour before sundown. Otherwise it has a chilly and foreboding feel to it. The houses on the left don't help. You'd swear the Addams family lived in the first home, the one that caught errant tee shots. Getting to the green was easy if you stayed right, but stray left or anywhere long and five manicured traps (like Morticia Addams's fingernails) would ensnare the ball. I just never liked the hole. Maybe my golfers sensed the vibes too because they invariably played it poorly.

Wouldn't you know it? Whippet was straight off the tee, a really nice shot, while Mrs. P got generous and pushed her drive into the edge of the woods on the right. A second wimpy effort by Mrs. P landed in a bog.

The play from the bog would have been to take her chipping iron and move the ball 50 yards up course.

"Mrs. P, that's casual water there. You're entitled to relief," I said.

"It looks like a puddle to me."

"Believe me, it's casual water or, as the rules say, 'a temporary accumulation of liquid that's visible before and after you take your stance that's not a water hazard.' You're permitted relief without penalty."

She didn't listen and went for her 5-wood. Normally the 5 is her best club, a magic wand, but the magic wand didn't work on water. What we got was a splat that demolished the puddle, barely moved the ball, and lost the hole. Mrs. P got wet big time. The mud on the opaque hose she always played in looked like chocolate pudding on a newly screened porch.

Emboldened by her success on Six, Whippet bogeyed Seven to tie the match. On Eight she won on the strength of a well-timed cough on Mrs. P's backswing. The intrusive sound caused Mrs. P to produce a chunk of sod that only a Kansas farmer could appreciate. Down one.

Nine was a standoff, except that Whippet threw her 5-iron noisily into the bag again on my golfer's third approach shot. By then we were on our way to an etiquette breakdown and a confrontation.

Brewster, the Halfway House manager, greeted us as we mounted the elevated tee at Killer Ten. His drink business was slow because of the same cool weather that was a godsend for Mrs. P. Whippet bought Kelly a cream soda while I gulped an iced tea and waited for the melodrama to unfold.

Killer Ten was always a gas, what with the elevated tee and green, the fronting pond and those diabolical traps. Even the experienced players had mental diarrhea here. The only regulars who seemed to have a method were Mr. Howard and Mrs. Peck. Mr. Howard liked to play a 6-iron to the back fringe and let the ball roll back to the hole. Mrs. P always bailed right to the patch of grass over the water that allowed an unobstructed pitch to the green. It was a dicey shot, but perfect for her 4-wood. I can remember only once when she ever recorded a score higher than 4.

I'll give it to Whippet: she played a beautiful 3-iron shot 170 yards to the very back fringe. We'd have been in big trouble if she had holed her dangling conversation of a putt. As it was, it missed by a hair and went to the lower fringe, 23 feet away. A hellacious lag and tap-in gave her a 4 to match Mrs. P. We were still down one.

It remained that way until we got to Fourteen, a 440-yard par 5. Bounded by heavy woods on the left and the thirteenth fairway and a deep creek on the right, the secret is to hit long and slightly right. That takes the left side fairway traps and a large ash tree out of play and allows for a straight second shot to an expansive, undulating green.

Fourteen is a forecaddie hole. On a hunch I volunteered to be the advance scout. I traipsed to the usual spot, standing like a sentinel on the edge of the woods. Whippet still had the honors and launched a rocket that took a severe left turn ten yards from my face. Back on the tee I saw some agitation and hoped Mrs. P would stroke her brassie and let me get on with the delicate art of locating Whippet's ball. True to form, Mrs. P sent a soft liner to the right of the thirteenth tee in good position for her ensuing shots.

I headed into the woods. From the rattle among the hardwoods I imagined the ball to be 15 to 20 yards in, conceivably with a play back to the fairway. I grabbed Mrs. P's pitching iron and began to move shrubs and leaves. Of all the woods on the course, I knew these the best because Curly and I came here looking for squirrels. And guess what, boys and girls? I found

Whippet's ball -- a smaller, heavier, non-conforming rogue missile. Actually, my right FootJoy found it. That same FootJoy buried it four inches down a rabbit hole. The left FootJoy covered it with three inches of acorns.

My reasoning was this. If I produced the evidence, it would be grounds for disqualification, but it would also be my word against Whippet's. Kelly, that dumbo, probably hadn't noticed she'd switched balls. So, I did what any self-respecting vigilante would have done: I took justice into my own hands. And feet.

With Whippet 1-up, I knew she was going to insist on a search-and-destroy mission to protect her lead. I was prepared for that and ready to lead the party, but first I moseyed over to my golfer. "Mrs. P you look a little tired," I said. "I think we're going to be at this a while since Snidely here can't afford to lose the ball. Why don't you grab that 11-wood of yours and take a 10-minute siesta out of the sun?"

Mrs. P went to gather herself, while Dumbo, Snidely and I diligently scoured fairway, rough, woods and clearing for her ball. "What kind was it, Mrs. Whippet?" I asked again. "A Titleist 4?"

If the English lead lives of quiet desperation, you can imagine how Whippet was feeling with her golden opportunity gone sour. Ten minutes later she trudged back to the tee and hit another ball, a nice, even-tempo swing that catapulted a genuine Titleist 180 yards. If she'd hit all her shots that way, we wouldn't stand a chance. In fact, I heard several years later, Divot gave her lessons on that very point. She went on to be a B-Flight semifinalist.

But I'm getting ahead of myself.

The lost ball and the penalty stroke were too much in the face of Mrs. P's relentless short, straight strokes. Mrs. Peck's 6 won the hole. "How's the heart doing, Mrs. P?"

"Much better after that lost ball, Looper."

"Need any more medicine?"

"Not now, my boy," the old warrior said.

I've heard loving couples talk about "being locked in heavenly transport," moose being "locked in mortal combat" and "battles of the bands," but what these ladies did next was extraordinary. For starters, neither quit despite playing alternately some of the best and worst golf of the tournament. They took turns giving holes away, halving holes, winning and losing. Kelly and I couldn't believe it.

Next, we trudged on past the Empty Quarter of Fifteen with halves, a hole I'd have bet my life savings that we were going to lose. Sixteen provided an unbelievable break for our opponents. Going for the throat, Whippet duck-hooked a fairway 4-wood into a huge cottonwood tree. Instead of careening onto Fifteen, the ball rebounded back into the fairway, setting up a perfect pitch to the green. Two putts for a winning bogey.

On Seventeen, the island hole, Mrs. P laid up, 11-wooded her second shot to within two feet and tapped in. Whippet drove the backside of the green, then shanked her second shot off a large locust tree. Her two-putt bogey put us all even. "The game is on, Looper," Mrs. Peck said, with renewed vigor.

The marathon continued to the long, uninspiring eighteenth, where in the distance I could see the flag limp against the clubhouse mast. Both players struggled to the green. Whippet dribbled her putt away to the right. Mrs. P knocked hers firmly to the hole for another half.

The members were obviously surprised to see us trudge off Eighteen headed for the first tee. With that Billy Sauers came out to survey the situation.

"We're all even, Mr. Sauers. It's been a helluva match. Who you got? Mrs. P?"

"Can she hold out?"

"Maybe. In any case, I don't think we're going past Four," I told him.

"How so?" he asked.

"Whippet's gonna win this thing on One or Two with her length if she can stay straight and/or Mrs. Peck gets tired. Though I have to tell you, this weather and that par on Seventeen have lifted her spirits."

"That's it?" asked Billy Sauers.

"Oh no. With the other options Mrs. P wins because Whippet thrashes around Three like a house of horrors. If it gets to Four, my guy wins because she plays the hole like Paganini. So, take your pick."

"Looper, you won't believe how much money is riding on this match. It's more than last year's Ladies' A Flight. I could get WGN out here for this right now."

That was saying something, because last year's Championship Flight was a match between old and young, senile and fertile, good and evil. It was *High Noon*. And so many WGN executives were members of Spring Willows that they really could have had a team of reporters on hand.

"Son, bottom line. Who wins?"

"Jeez, Mr. Sauers, you're asking a lot."

"Looper, what's a semester's tuition where you go to school?"

"We're talking serious money, aren't we, Mr. Sauers?"

"Serious money, son. Your best guess. From the gut. No obligation, but let's call it a finder's fee if you're right."

My ass has only puckered twice in my life. The other time was when I was six and my Dad caught me watching television at 12:30 a.m. I really wanted to be right this time.

So, I hedged. "Mr. Sauers, this match is in a different dimension right now. The smart money has to be on Whippet. But here's five from me on Mrs. P. You decide."

"I like you, kid," he said. "As they say, 'No balls, no blue chips.' You've got both. I like that."

Chugging a glass of water and grabbing two ice teas for the ladies, I hustled to the first tee. "What was that all about?" Kelly asked.

"Sauers was curious how the match was going."

"What'd you tell him?"

"That it wouldn't go past Four."

"You're right. I think Mrs. Whippet's gonna win it here."

"Maybe so, but don't let me catch you dropping that flag again when Mrs. P putts like you did on Twelve."

Kelly and I had some tired warriors on our hands: two heavyweights heading into the waning rounds. Whippet drove the right rough off the first tee, negating what could have been a decisive advantage. Leaving the tee I saw a wall of faces, like bettors at a cockfight, pressed against the clubhouse glass,.

Ten minutes later, Whippet struck again. This time it was an accidental spike track she left over Mrs. P's putting line. It wasn't even subtle. But God bless her, Mrs. P took a strong right-hand grip and bullied the ball over the scar to halve the hole.

"Did you see that, Looper?" she said in private, on the way to the second tee. "What a witch."

"Stay cool, Mrs. P, and a word of advice. I noticed when we left Seventeen that the sprinklers were on early at the second green. Don't know why. They're off now. But should you get on the back fringe, really push that putt downhill, stronger than you think. That Bentgrass will be really slow from last night's storm and this recent sprinkling. Hit it really hard."

If things hadn't been so tense, I think I could have enjoyed the Kodachrome glow and the deepening shadows. The second tee lay bathed in gold while the elms cast a muted and ominous pall well past the rough into the fairway. Our players staggered like sagging sentinels awaiting a yet-to-be-determined verdict.

Two frightened me because I could see Whippet ending this thing with a good drive and a strong third shot to the green. And wouldn't you know, Whippet had another coughing attack as Mrs. P addressed her drive. Didn't matter. She pushed it ever-so-slightly into the right rough but recovered with a firm 4-wood. Whippet, on the other hand, took the scenic route, crisscrossing the hole one too many times, so she was laying four from 18 feet when Mrs. P strong-armed her fifth shot, a 7-wood, to the back fringe.

"Whippet's got it," said Kelly. "Two putts and you can kiss your ass goodbye."

"Tell you what, asshole, you better hope this match doesn't go to Three because your player is going into the gazebo again."

"Fuck you," he said.

Being away, Mrs. P had to putt first. She was starting to sweat profusely. There was water on her face. She took her club rag and wiped her cheeks. I'd never seen a woman do that before. Wordlessly, I handed her the Louise Suggs a little harder than usual. Quietly, I held the pin, not behind the cup but three inches to the right side just in case she needed help reading the break. I don't think Dumbo or Whippet understood.

While Mrs. P walked to the ball I thought about Billy Sauers and all those wealthy men back at the clubhouse. They had more riding on this match than my old man made in a month. I just hoped Mr. Sauers would forgive me.

The first sound I heard was the hard thunk of putter on dimpled orb. The second sound, an echo almost, was Mrs. P's ball dropping into the center of the cup. I thought I'd shit. And I think Whippet and Dumbo actually did. The only other noise was an emphatic "yes!" from my golfer who retired to the fringe to await her rival's putt.

Sports fans, it never had a chance. Whippet left it three feet short and then had to hole a rather routine, but by now scary, second putt to tie.

Off to Three, or should I say, King Solomon's Mines. There Whippet strafed the gazebo again and Mrs. P found the treasure by playing a succession of steady woods down the fairway. I'll give Whippet credit: she was a stingy bitch. She airmailed her second tee shot over the first fairway trap, no mean feat for a woman, only to die on the beach when her fifth shot rolled into the left greenside bunker. Mrs. P two-putted from 15 feet. Surrendering, much less conceding, wasn't Whippet's style. But when her second sand shot failed to negotiate the green, the fat lady was singing.

Shaking Mrs. P's hand was probably the hardest thing Whippet had to do that summer. I know for a fact that she left half of her face and all of her lower lip in that trap. As for that asshole Kelly, he was kind enough to tell me that Whippet had been using non-conforming balls on all the par 5s and long par 4s. The reason I didn't catch it was because Whippet paid him an extra $10 to hold the pin on those holes. I never did get around to telling him what I found on Fourteen.

We were four whipped puppies when the match ended. We'd left adrenaline and perspiration on every hole and by this time we were in the furthest reaches of the course. That's when the most charitable act of the tourney occurred. As we were walking off the green, three golf carts headed our way. I could make out Starza's emerald green pants in one, Judge Gleason's silver hair in another and the navy polo of Billy Sauers in the third.

"Want a lift?" Starza asked.

"Why, thank you," Mrs. Peck said.

"Kid, you come with me," Billy Sauers commanded. "Mrs. Whippet and young Wright can go with the Judge."

As we whisked along the serpentine cart paths I reflected on the drama of the afternoon. Billy Sauers broke my reverie. "That looked like a concession there at the end. Am I right?"

"Yes sir, Mr. Sauers. It ended on Three."

"Just like you said."

"I said a lot of things."

"Your money said it all."

"Who'd you have?"

"I had Mrs. Peck for five grand."

"Wait a minute!"

"Yeah, five grand and that's not counting the Calcutta."

"What Calcutta?"

"The Judge and I organized it in the grill a month ago. We've got one for each flight, but the Ladies' D has the most interest by far."

"Why that one?"

"Personalities. A dark horse. Plus, I dated Mrs. P years ago."

"Go on."

"No, it's true. But these bets today were just side wagers. You've made me a happy man, kid. Mrs. P too, I can tell. She's told my wife all about the difference you've made in her game. That's a good quality to have, kid, making women happy. That's worth a lot in life."

"All I know is we've got one more match against an unnamed opponent. How'd you guys get out here so fast?"

"We've been following you via field glasses and walkie talkies since you came through Eighteen. We sent Governor Wylie home to track the match from his yard there on Three."

"Hell of a putt on Two, huh?"

"I'll say."

"I warned her about the wet green after I saw those sprinklers going from Seventeen."

"You'll go far, kid. After we talked, I doubled down."

"I guess that putt on Two really made you happy?"

"Not near as happy as that duck hook on Three. I had to laugh. Wylie was sitting in his gazebo when the ball nearly cold-cocked him. Almost lost his hair piece."

"It's been a long afternoon, Mr. Sauers."

"Maybe so, kid, but very profitable. I especially like dealing with those military types like General Sweeney. They think they know everything. Military intelligence, my foot. What he really needs is some native intelligence. That's why I like talking to you."

After leaving Mrs. P's bags at the rack I went into the Pro Shop. "Divot," I said. "I want to thank you for the great grip you put on Mrs. Peck's putter. That handle really works well."

"Glad she liked it. She'll need it for the final."

"Who's she got?"

"Charles. She beat Price, 2-and-1."

"That's too bad," I said. For two reasons. Charles was a streaky player, very tough when she was on, and right now she was playing like a B-Flight man. Too bad also because Jocelyn Price, her semifinal opponent, was without a doubt the finest specimen of pulchritude the club had, bar none. At 31, she was a killer on the courts, the course and the ballroom. I had really hoped Mrs. P would meet her in the finals.

"Roadhouse" Rhoda was something else. She earned her nickname thanks to some public improprieties in her single days. While she had married a man of position and was an extremely effective fifth grade teacher, her earlier reputation clung to her like a dress without Scotchgard. Most of the members didn't say much, they just smiled the smile, but the caddies all knew, thanks to a slip of the tongue by General Sweeney one day after two brews at the Halfway House.

"All matches need to be finished by a week from Sunday, but Starza doesn't want anyone but the Women's Championship Flight and the top men playing into the weekend."

I felt sure Mrs. Peck would need four days minimum to recover. Her nerves and her constitution needed a break. "Talking out of school here, Divot, but I'd guess Mrs. P would prefer Thursday, a week from tomorrow."

"I'll bet that suits Charles fine, probably after 11. I think she's got a teachers' meeting earlier that day."

"I'll ask Mrs. P and we'll let you know," I said.

"No hurry," said the assistant. "Also, no hurry either on that promo MacGregor I now owe you. I'm going to test drive it tomorrow. After that it's yours. I'll even throw in the head cover."

"You're all heart. Just get it to me in one piece."

CHAPTER FIVE

Tuesday proved to be one of the worst days of the summer. Not only did the temperature top out at 97 degrees, but a Mason-Dixon semi loaded with fertilizer rolled in about 11:30. Otto Olson, Jr., Mr. Olson's jerk-off son, drove a tractor out to Seven where I was weeding traps.

"Get in, asshole. The manure truck's here. We got to unload it now so the driver can run back to Kankakee. Kenny says everybody's got to help."

"Even you?" I asked.

"Yeah, even me. Ain't that the shits?"

There was a certain justice here. If Mr. O had been around, Little Otto and his college roommate would have been exempt, even though they were probably the two strongest members on the crew.

"No lunch 'til we're done."

"Real nice," I said.

"Eighty-pound bags. Can you believe it?" he said.

"How big's the truck?"

"Huge, longer than Divot's dick." (The assistant pro's sexual feats were legendary). "The real pisser is that the truck is half empty, so we have to go all the way back into it and manhaul that shit out. And it's hot in there. Real hot."

We were like African porters getting that stuff out. It was backbreaking, arduous work. We formed a line and pulled, passed, dumped and restacked the bags in the damp storage shed. Hardly a word was spoken except for an occasional "God, it smells," "pass the jug" or "hand me that towel." We finished at 2 p.m., totally drained.

"OK," said Kenny. "That's it, take lunch, go home, whatever. Thanks, I know that was no fun."

From a meteorological standpoint the heat was just beginning. The long-range forecast promised no relief until Sunday. Wednesday's weather was predicted to be 97 degrees and rain with 98 degrees scheduled for Thursday. Not good for Mrs. P.

"Mr. Starza, any relief on this Thursday commitment? Can't we go off early on Saturday or Sunday?"

"You know the custom, Looper. We don't want lower flights out on the course championship weekend."

"But Jesus, the weather's gonna be a killer."

"Deal with it. Mrs. P has a big golf umbrella. Hold it over her when she's not hitting."

I thought that sucked. Mrs. P was 16 years older than Rhoda Charles. "Some concession should be made for age and health. I suppose you're going enforce the no cart rule too, right?"

"Rules are rules. I don't make 'em."

That night I called Mrs. P to check in. "I'm feeling great," she said. "Muscles aren't sore anymore. I've been putting on the rug. The stroke looks fine. I'm rested and ready to give that Charles woman a run. Say, why don't you come over for supper tomorrow and we'll talk strategy?"

CHAPTER SIX

Mrs. Peck greeted me at the door with the change in plans. "Have you heard? We don't play tomorrow. Seems Mrs. Charles had a mandatory staff meeting. We go off Friday at 11 instead."

"How do you feel about that?" I asked.

"Suits me fine. Gives me another day to rest. I might even go out and hit a few balls. I'd like to lick that loft problem."

"It's not that much of a problem now that you're swinging through the ball. You do have to watch it when it's windy, though."

"Still, I need to get out in the heat some if it's going to be hot on Friday."

Supper was simple and elegant. We started with some wine and right away it felt familiar. "What's this, the Last Supper, Mrs. P?"

"Why do you say that?"

"Isn't this port? That's Father Conklin's beverage of choice at Holy Communion."

"I never thought of it that way."

We had port, pate and a summer tuna salad with orange and lime sherbet for dessert, a fitting meal for the worst heat wave in thirty years.

"What does your family think about your run to glory?" I asked.

"All of them don't know, actually," she said. "The Ellenbergers in Idaho and the Mullens in Seattle have been in Europe for the last month, so they are clueless. I talked to Gerald after the Cabiness match, but he and his family have been on Nantucket and we haven't chatted for ten days or so."

"How about Melissa's family?"

"Melissa keeps sending me those instructional tips from the golf magazines. I got one yesterday about keeping your hands smooth on the backswing takeaway. I think the only person who wants me to win more than I do is Melissa."

"I don't know, Mrs. P, I'm rooting pretty hard for you. So is Mr. Sauers."

"Really?"

"He's had a real interest in this whole thing, especially your match with Whippet."

"I didn't think he cared anymore."

"Oh, he cares a lot. He often asks about your health."

"How thoughtful. What's his interest in all this?"

You know how sometimes the light comes on and you realize that nobody's home? Just then my light went on. I realized any discussions about Billy Sauers' stake would have to involve finances, and I could only see that as being deleterious. Mrs. P didn't need the pressure. It occurred to me that she had no idea, or, at best, only a vague sense of the gambling aspects. The thought that there was serious money on the match was a burden she didn't need.

"You and Mr. Sauers used to date, didn't you?"

"That was years ago. We were just out of college. We both went to Northwestern and had known each other for years. We spent the summer after our senior year sailing, playing golf and keeping company. He went to law school at Harvard and I started work at the Art Institute.

"We saw each other off and on through the following summer, but you know what they say about distance. Absence makes the heart go wander. The next year I met Herbert Peck, a young trader in Chicago, and as they say, 'that's all she wrote.' They still use that phrase, don't they? And 'happy trails' and 'buy the farm?' I always liked that one. 'He bought the farm.' So evocative and historical." She paused, lost in a reverie, then remembered her role as hostess. "Would you like some more sherbet?"

"No thanks. I've got to get up at 5:15. Before I go, is there anything you want me to do?"

"No, Looper. That's kind of you, though."

"How about for Friday?"

"I think I'm set. I do think I might get out and hit a few tomorrow though."

"Well, you let me know. Thanks for dinner. I'll see you at 10:30 on Friday."

* * *

It didn't take a brain surgeon to see that Friday was going to be different. For one, Mr. O released me early from the G crew so I could caddie. For another, the whole Midwest was still in the grip of a mean heat wave. When I got to the Pro Shop, Mrs. P's bag was already out and sporting a brand new Spring Willows golf towel. Divot himself was scraping her chipping iron with steel wool.

"We're with you, Looper," McDevitt said.

"How's she look?" asked Starza.

"Loose. My only concern is the heat. She's been inside most of the week, so she might not be acclimated. Other than that, she's ready," I replied. "How's Mrs. Charles?"

"She looks like she's taking this thing seriously. She came in thirty minutes ago and went to the practice tee. Some of her shots look like ICBMs, others look like duds. Hard to tell. Both ladies get up and down pretty well, so it might be decided by approach shots," said the pro.

"Fine with me," I said.

"Why does Mrs. Peck carry an 11-wood?" queried Divot.

"If you had a club you could hit 40 yards over a hazard every time, would you carry it?"

"Of course," said McDevitt.

"That's why Mrs. Peck has an 11-wood." I was on the way out the door with new tees when Starza said, "By the way, Looper, Mrs. Charles is a streaky player. She hates water, but she's really good on the beach."

"I'll remember that." Good sand players were tough to find at D level. Between skillful sand play and enormous strength, Mrs. Charles was going to be tough. Once again my player was going to be outdriven in every phase of the game. We had to keep it close and be ready to pounce if and when Mrs. Charles went south.

"May I have two extra towels for the bag here?"

"Sure, what for?"

"I'm carrying extra ice and water, so Mrs. P doesn't faint. God, it's hot."

* * *

I met Mrs. P on the putting green and we reviewed the strong right arm position and talked about the break on the fifth green that had been troubling her. Two tours around the putting green convinced me she was ready. "Looking good, Mrs. P. Want to hit a few fairway woods?"

"No, Looper. Let's save it. I've only got so many shots in me. Let's make them count."

There was something familiar about the first tee. On closer inspection I realized we'd drawn Kelly Wright again as an opposing caddie. Not my first choice, but much better than some of the bedwetter types that Al sometimes sent out. "How'd we get so lucky?" I said to Wright.

"For starters, I asked. And two, not many guys want to work in this heat. Ain't it a bitch?"

"Yup. With this humidity I'll bet the traps aren't dry."

"And look at those flags, limp against the mast. No wind. Must be a hundred out here," said Kelly.

Starza came out to greet the four of us. He tossed a coin to determine honors. "Tails" called Mrs. P. It would be the last time in eight holes we'd have the honors.

Playing with a Spalding and a yellow wooden tee, Mrs. P moved two feet inside the right marker. Her swing was picture perfect and sent her ball 150 yards into the light, right rough. No problem.

Have I described Rhoda Charles to you? Physically this woman was 5' 10", 145 pounds, reasonably athletic and utterly determined. In class, she was imposing. On the course, she was a picture of undiluted power. When it was channeled properly, the results were impressive. In this case, 220 yards impressive to the left edge of the fairway. She followed that up with a 180-yard 3-wood that was just about perfect. A spot on 3-iron traveled 150 yards to the back of the green while we were still 120 yards out lying three. Two putts for her par put Mrs. Charles on the board one up.

"Mrs. P, I got to tell you. That was a career hole for her. No way is she ever going to do that again. You hit all your shots straight. You had two nice putts for a respectable six. This stuff will cease," I said.

Mrs. Charles hit a frozen rope off the tee on the 426-yard second hole. It went absolutely straight for 210 yards. Even Mr. Howard rarely hit them that well. Farther, but not that well. "What did King Kong there have for breakfast, Kelly? Steroids?"

"Damned if I know, Looper. She's scary."

"Doesn't look like she belongs in D Flight either," I said.

Both players stayed amazingly straight and were on in four. Mrs. Charles actually passed over the green in three, but she pitched back. Both took two putts to halve the hole.

As we moved to the third tee, I wondered if Governor Wylie was in the gazebo. After last week he'd probably had enough. As I said, strong golfers and hookers have problems with Three. Too much power off the tee puts you in the cat box and too much right hand puts you in Marlboro Country. Mrs. Charles drove the trap while Mrs. P undercut her drive and failed to escape the tall and uncut rough that preceded the main fairway. "That was up in the ozone, Mrs. P. I thought we agreed to keep it lower."

"Don't worry," she countered. A high lie allowed easy egress and Mrs. P rallied to reach the green in five. Meanwhile, Mrs. Charles played an ill-advised 5-iron from the trap and skittered the ball over the lip and onto the fairway. Two more fairway shots and a clean blast from the right greenside bunker left both parties facing 20-footers for bogey. Neither came close. Second putts were contrasts in style with Mrs. Charles ramming the back lip and getting a drop while Mrs. Peck's had to do a 270 before falling. The results were the same. Two sevens and we were still down one.

I can only liken the humidity to heated wet blankets. The elements were suffocating. Mrs. Charles was still hitting it a ton in spite of the heavy air. It was hard to stay optimistic. I felt it was only a matter of time before we began getting the woodshed treatment.

I went to forecaddie on Four, the 211-yarder that Mrs. Peck owned. She was unbeaten in four matches there. If we were going to get it going, I figured it would start here. The first shot of the hole was magnificent. It landed at my feet, 170 yards off the tee. It belonged to Mrs. Charles. Mrs. Peck's lit out for parts unknown, namely on the right, in the rough, behind a tree bordering the fifth fairway. If we could have cut that sycamore down, she'd have had a great line to the green. A nonchalant pitching wedge had Mrs. Charles on the right fringe. Mrs. P played safe and smart to the left, taking two more to reach to the green and we were down two.

Going to the fifth tee I said, "Mrs. P, you haven't been that far right all tournament. Looked like that right hand slipped, am I correct?"

"Looper, between the weather and my sweaty hands, I'm losing my grip. I can feel my pulse rising, too. Any suggestions?"

"Not for the pulse. You took your medicine?"

"Yes."

"I've got a thought for the hands. Try your glove one more hole. Really concentrate on holding the right hand firmly. If it slips again, I'm going to have you try a new one that I've got in the bag. But let's not change horses if we don't have to."

We had to. Five was a disaster. Mrs. P revisited that tree with a bungled right hand off the tee. With a limited backswing, she flubbed her wedge out of the rough and we played catch-up the rest of the way down the fairway. To show you how bad it was getting, Mrs. P three-putted from ten feet.

The sun was breaking out, exacerbating the humidity. I don't want to make too much out of this, but on this day golf at Spring Willows was utterly miserable. And down three after five holes we were starting to let the proceedings slip away. "Mrs. P, you're scaring me, but I just might have the answer right here." Walking to Six I produced a new golf glove. "This should stop that sloppy grip."

"Where'd you get this?"

"Divot gave it to me. It's a sample. He owed me one." Boy, did he. One Friday I'd saved his rear end from being French-fried by Mr. Cabiness who was starting to suspect the private golf lessons with his wife were going too far. "I've tried one and it works. Use it here on Six."

The new grip held -- too well. Mrs. P was still compensating for the slip-page and yanked her drive left, into Mr. Barlow's backyard where I thought I saw the field mice running for cover. In one sour stroke we were out of bounds and out of the running on Six.

Mrs. Charles was Mike Ditka in lady FootJoys. Same temperament, same drive to win, same tongue and same dislike of the opponent. When she was winning, she said nothing, but when the momentum turned, she was brutal. She'd start by finding fault with herself and then quickly lash out at others. Presently she was enjoying the round. If I'd been up four with six holes gone, I'd have been in a good mood, too.

On the way to the seventh tee I took charge. "Mrs. P, here's what we do. This is an experimental hole. Just take it easy. Make sure you hit your 5-, 7- and 11-woods. Then we'll go to Eight and start fresh. You can still win this thing. Mrs. Charles is a streaky player. We just need to get her going the other way and we'll be back in it."

After a few practice swings, Mrs. P started reassembling herself. Her hands came back together, the roll on the right hand disappeared and she got her hips and arms in sync. She even got out of the right trap with a nice sand save to halve the hole. That bode well I thought.

We moved toward Eight and Wright met me at the ball wash. "Party's over, Looper. Mrs. Charles will have me back in the caddie shack in time to see the first pitch from Wrigley."

"You're a smug bastard, Kelly. I'd have thought you'd have learned something from the last time we looped together."

"The difference is this time my guy is playing better and yours isn't."

"This match isn't close right now, Kelly, but you won't be back in time for any first pitch. Seventh inning stretch maybe, but no first pitch."

In retrospect, Mrs. Peck gave us all a day to remember. And I can promise you, I'll go to my grave remembering every stroke.

Eight, while not a long hole, has a narrow fairway and a lot of rough. It's fairly benign unless you chilly-dip it, which is exactly what Mrs. Charles did.

The sod she moved off the tee could have redone half my front yard. In fact, the next day Rossi made a special trip to our sod farm to repair the damage before the championship flighters hit the course.

Wrong club selection for her second shot compounded matters. Too much strength and balata combined to send that little dimpled thing the length of the parking lot. And I don't care how strong you are, it's hard to be confident hitting a shot six inches from a Mercedes oil pan. Instead of being four up with ten to go, Mrs. Charles was only up three.

Wright said nothing as we went to Nine, the one really blah hole on the course. Three hundred forty-nine yards, immaterial traps and a wide fairway filled with Bermuda grass. With all the sun and the warm nights we'd had, the grass was extremely thick. Hitting into that lush greensward was like falling into a down comforter with Marilyn Monroe. The balls really got cozy down there.

This time Mrs. Charles demonstrated a lot more control on her drive. Mrs. P tried to make things exciting by getting too much loft again, but a slight downwind kept us from losing distance. We left the green still down three.

Rather than go straight to Killer Ten and the Halfway House, the ladies excused themselves and went into the locker room. Kelly asked Brewster for a Coke and I went to replenish the ice and water. I saw Billy Sauers by the side of the Pro Shop.

"Got a hot one there?" he asked.

"Too hot for golf, Mr. Sauers. And until Seven Mrs. Charles was too hot for us."

"That's what I figured. The weather, I mean. I didn't want any part of this match. I like my chances with the Ladies' Championship Flight better. Everyone's talking about this shooting star Hillary Weston, but I'll tell you something, old Mrs. Worth is going to win her seventh title. Nerves of steel -- and she putts better than Bobby Locke ever did."

"I'll remember that, Mr. Sauers."

"How's my girl doing, physically?"

"She's tired. She made a nice rally on Seven, but we've got to keep her going. I've been laying cold rags across her neck going up the fairways, but we need some help from Mrs. Charles. She could duff a few and it wouldn't hurt my feelings at all."

"Rhoda hates water -- and there is a lot of it between here and Eighteen. You might want to remind her of that in some subtle way."

Billy Sauers was sure a gamer. His idea of a fair bet was to gather the best information and then leverage all the emotional weight in his favor. Not a bad ploy, actually. And since we had water coming up on Ten, Eleven, Fourteen, Fifteen, Sixteen and Seventeen, we had islands of opportunity.

As it turned out, we could have used an aquatics director on Killer Ten. At the Halfway House I wasn't even subtle; I went for the throat. "Mrs. Charles, would you like a drink of water," I said, offering her a paper cup. "There's plenty to go around," I said, looking across the pond.

On this day, the pin on Ten was back in the left quadrant, a tricky placement, though it made no difference to Mrs. Peck who naturally aimed for her favorite spot. She gave it the old over-the-pond, short-of-the-traps, unobstructed line-to-the-green swing. The trip to the bathroom must have galvanized Mrs. P because she put her 4-wood right on the money.

For Mrs. Charles, it wasn't a hole, it was an adventure. She over-clubbed herself again and bounced one off the back fringe into the trap seven feet below.

Talk about man's inhumanity to man. The best way to escape this particular bogey dust is via hand mashie, so I kept a good eye on Mrs. Charles as she thrashed three times trying to scale the cliffs. She succeeded with her fourth flail but sent the ball over the green, almost back over the pond.

Lying six in the water with Mrs. P on in two, she picked up and we trudged to Eleven down only two.

On the tee Mrs. P was unusually flush. I figured she was either embarrassed for Mrs. Charles or overly excited, but after a sweet tee shot I didn't press the matter. Mrs. Charles hit a sugar shot too, but hers zoned in on the perpendicular creek and nailed the back bank on the fly. 'Embedded' is the term the TV commentators use. Rather than take a drop and a penalty stroke, she tried to bludgeon the little rascal over the lip and she dislodged it into the rocky creek.

Since Mrs. Charles had one of the club's nicer sets of Kathy Whitworth irons, she wisely decided to take a drop rather than risk romancing the stones. Shooting four, she got down in four more to Mrs. Peck's six and the lead was down to one.

Twelve was never my favorite hole and Mrs. Peck played like it wasn't one of hers, either. This 504-yard par 5 is bounded on the left by macadam and fence. On the right, trees and high brush protect the club's sod farm. With a notable absence of water, Mrs. Charles pounded the snot out of the ball, carded a six and humbled Mrs. P, who couldn't keep up with the teacher's length. Down two again.

Thirteen is home to some of the strongest visual images I have of Spring Willows. Partly because that is where the tractor incident ended and partly because this was the green that Buddy Bonneville cut first every morning. Since it is closest to the superintendent's shack, Buddy would roar out at the crack of dawn with his huge 42" reel mower. Throttling down, he'd rip across the Bentgrass green in a gentle and stylish manner that belied his barbaric ways.

We called him Buddy Bonneville because he drove a red, fully loaded Pontiac. Here was a 23-year-old greaser with a wife and two kids under three, who worked three jobs to pay for the bomb on which he blew every last dime to prove I don't know what.

At least somebody – or something – in the family looked good. That car always gleamed and it never had a drop of water or pollen on it. But somehow I don't think that made up for the daily newspaper deliveries from 3-5 a.m. or the bowling alley job from 6-10 p.m. He saw his wife maybe ninety minutes a day, and the only time he had to himself was two minutes and thirty seven seconds when he performed vital bodily functions or was extracting the Blue Coral from under his fingernails. What quality of life?

But damn, he did a job cutting those greens. He left them as fast and slick as the hair on his head. On this day, Thirteen, a 187-yard par 3 was so slick it yielded two bogeys. Time was starting to run out.

On to Fourteen, the heavily wooded hole on the left where Whippet "lost" her ball. This time a phalanx of ash and hickory, two of the densest North American trees, grabbed both players by the short hairs.

With the honors, Mrs. Charles hooked her drive into an ash that left her stymied in deep rough. With no direct view of the green, she played a safety. Her third shot also went left, ricocheting backward from a hickory and leaving her with an acceptable line to the green. She struggled home in 9.

With an obvious opening, Mrs. Peck sent her ball off to parts unknown. I looked hard for that Spalding, but it was gone when it left the tee. I had relocated Mrs. Whippet's non-conforming sphere, but not the Spalding. My personal theory is that they'll find the Lost Chord before they come upon Mrs. P's ball.

Breathing deeply, we spelled relief "e-i-g-h-t". We were down one with five holes to go.

Fifteen is the par 5 with the Empty Quarter bunkers. I've never spoken much about the creek that runs right of the first monster trap and behind a line of trees. That's because no one ever visits this body of water -- except Mrs. Charles. A loose right hand and an overanxious swing sent her ball wide right, off the trunk of a willow and into the winding creek -- twice. Mrs. P fared better, getting out of the gate straight and well up the fairway before Mrs. Charles could regroup. All even with three to go.

Sixteen parallels Fifteen on the left coming back with the tennis courts on the far right. It's another par 5, but this hole has a man-made pond 150 yards out on the near right designed to catch drives off the tee. Showing the way, Mrs. P played left going a modest 130 yards. Mrs. Charles went 163 yards to the right. Her ball reminded me of a poorly thrown skipping stone, two pathetic hops and a fall from grace.

Rather than risk further ignominy off the tee, Mrs. Charles chose to drop behind the pond and go with a 3-wood from a decent lie. The logic was outstanding, the execution marginal. Eager to follow the flight of the ball, Mrs. Charles failed to keep her head down. She cleared the water, but not the bank. Her low-trajectory missile found it with a resounding thunk.

Unspeakable was the language from caddie and player. Unplayable was the lie. In intrepid fashion, Mrs. P trekked inexorably to the green while Mrs. Charles tried to regain her composure. We were up one with two holes to go.

My heart was pounding. I don't think I was hyperventilating, but Mrs. P might have been. Instead of exultant, she looked pale and wan. It was still hot as hell, but she had eschewed the cold rags the last few holes. Maybe that should have been the tip off. But there was so much going on – Mrs. P going well and Mrs. Charles going to hell, Wright going mad and me going with the flow, that I didn't think to press the point.

There had been so many swings in the match, I didn't know where it was going to end. The biggest swings were yet to come.

"How high's the water, momma?" I said to Wright as we mounted the elevated tee overlooking a pond a little more than 130 yards away. "First pitch, my ass."

"Go find a rolling donut," he spat. "You ain't seen nothin' yet." And for once in his life that scarecrow was right. Going first, Mrs. Peck took, for her, a mighty poke and put her 5-wood 25 yards this side of the water. Perfect position. Briefly she tottered and steadied herself on the club. "Oh my, I'm getting lightheaded," she said.

"I'm not surprised, it's beastly out here," I offered. She did a stutter step before catching herself on the bag.

"You OK, Mrs. P?" I asked.

"It's nothing, I just feel a little weak, that's all."

"Are you sure, Mrs. Peck?" said Rhoda Charles. "We can take a break if you'd like."

"No. I'll be all right. Let's play on."

So Mrs. Charles did, smacking a fading 4-wood into a flat trap 40 feet left and back of the pin.

"Here, Mrs. Peck, let me give you a hand," I said.

"Don't touch me, Looper. I'm going to make it myself," she said. She resolutely and agonizingly moved toward the ball.

I've seen doddering old ladies before and since, but this one, my friends, looked like she was on her last legs covering her last mile. "The eleven," she said to me.

As I handed it to her, she gave me a devilish grin and then grimaced in response to some internal calling. Slowly she took the clubhead back, stopped and stroked. I'll never know if she put too much loft on that 11-wood or not. The ball went so damn high that sometimes I think it was just her spirit being set free. "It's in the rarified, Mrs. P," I said.

That dimpled marvel stayed airborne for an eternity. Then it landed five and one-half feet from the hole, bounced twice and wedged itself between the cup and pin.

The only better chip I ever saw was on television. Jack Nicklaus was playing at Doral when I was in a hospital on a morphine drip recovering from back surgery. As he hit the ball my brain dropped to 120 frames a second. Upon impact the ball rolled across the green ever so slowly and surely to within two inches. Fat Jack's was a shot for the ages, Mrs. P's was for the rock of ages.

What happened next was never in doubt. When Mrs. Peck saw the ball disappear, she let out a keening sound that rent the stifling air. She teetered on her right foot and keeled over. Lights out. Sayonara. I bolted but couldn't catch her. Wright and Mrs. Charles were by the pondside trap, dumbstruck. "Oh, Jesus," said Wright. "Call an ambulance!"

Can you picture that? Wright giving me orders? "No Kelly, beat it to the Pro Shop, fast." I always thought you got religion early in life or in prison. I think I found it that day in the fairway.

The armada of golf carts that streamed down from atop the hill resembled the great Oklahoma land rush. Soonest of the sooners was Billy Sauers and noted heart specialist Doc Tippett. Judge Gleason had the presence of mind to drive his spacious Land Rover, but it didn't matter. Mrs. P was DOA.

Play was over for the day. With Doc Tippett in charge, the temporary pallbearers carefully placed Mrs. P in the Land Rover. I was picking up her clubs when Billy Sauers said to Mrs. Charles, "Mark your ball, you'll get your chance to finish in the morning."

Obediently, Wright stuck a small oak branch in the trap and placed Mrs. Charles' ball in her bag. "Get in, kid," Mr. Sauers said to me. "Stan will take Wright and Mrs. Charles." That's when I realized that some men never quit, that pressure is always on in life. Even in death, the pressure's on. I couldn't believe someone had the presence to worry about some sorry beachbound Titleist at a time like this.

"Kid, you're going to have to trust me on this, but Mrs. P would have wanted it this way. She'd have wanted you looking out for her and me supervising. I got a call from her last night. She wanted to talk about three things – old times, the weather and this contest. This match meant a lot to her. Your friendship meant a lot. We're going to come out tomorrow to Seventeen and finish this thing for her. You, me, Mrs. Charles and young Wright. If Mrs. Charles can hole that chip of hers, and I'd bet the house she can't, she wins the match by forfeit and is the new club champion. If she can't, our lady wins."

Promptly at 11 a.m. the four of us met at the Pro Shop the next day and carted out to Seventeen to finish the match. The grounds crew had been told to leave everything undisturbed at Seventeen with the exception of cutting the green. Wright removed the oak branch and Mrs. Charles was given an identical lie. Obviously, circumstances had changed since the day before. The weather had turned much cooler and though Mrs. Charles, a very good trap player, would later deny it, she had, in fact, been hitting sand shots from the practice traps for 45 minutes before the resumption of play.

Say this for Mrs. Charles: she was no quitter. My heart stopped when her ball exploded from the trap and rolled to within 12 inches. A very fine out.

"Well done, Rhoda," said Mr. Sauers. "Helluva shot." I know he wanted to say, "but you lose," but he was too much of a gentleman. Instead he said, "Let's go home."

"No, I want to play in. Come on, Kelly. Let's find out how this thing would have really ended." I couldn't help but think that Wright and Rhoda Charles deserved each other as they traipsed off to the eighteenth tee.

I guess you know that they've since changed the regulation about using carts in club championships. It's called the Peck Rule now for obvious reasons. It's a change that would have come anyway. Members now have a choice of using a cart, a caddie or both. Some of the more competitive players do use both. On those occasions the clubs walk and the members ride -- sort of like in the rest of life.

CHAPTER SEVEN

The funeral was held Monday morning in the Church of the Holy Comforter. SRO. All the old guard was there. Father Conklin gave a great sermon, but the words that meant the most came from her old boyfriend Billy Sauers. He recalled her role as matriarch to four kids and ten granddaughters. But the part I liked best was his evocative sweet bird of youth recollection that captivated an appreciative audience. He closed with the poignant pen of Wordsworth:

> *"She was a Phantom of delight*
> *When first she gleamed upon my sight...*
> *A Being breathing thoughtful breath,*
> *A Traveller between life and death;*
> *The reason firm, the temperate will,*
> *Endurance, foresight, strength, and skill;*
> *A perfect woman nobly planned,*
> *To warn, to comfort, and command;*
> *And yet a Spirit still, and bright*
> *With something of angelic light.*

In reality, the final resting place was Fairlawn Memorial Park, a cemetery that had housed earlier generations of Pecks and Hortons. Hundreds and hundreds of cars wound their way down Sheridan Road and out to the grave for the ultimate ritual. There I ran into Melissa, this time back in black. Some things just improve with age. To my surprise she called me by name. "Looper, hi. Thanks for coming. I know it would have meant a lot to my grandmother."

"She was a special person. I've enjoyed her company. And we had a nice run through D Flight together."

"I know," she said. "Grandma told me how much help you'd been. Did you know she called me after every match? And she was so excited to beat that Whippet woman. But you know what she really enjoyed? Just playing again and having someone to share it with. She felt you two made a good team. And that wooden putter you gave her, she really cherished that."

"I felt like your grandmother was the grandmother I never had, so it worked well for me too. I'll miss her." Searching for something else to say I resorted to the obvious. "How are you doing? I heard you won the California title again."

"2-and-1. I had a good final. If I play well my junior year, I think I'll seriously consider turning pro. There aren't many satellite tours for women, so I want to make sure I can compete. That would make Grandmother proud."

"You bet."

Committing Mrs. Peck to the savior wasn't easy. I got misty-eyed. She was a fighter and had an unforgettable personality. But my theory as a good Episcopalian was that it was now in God's hands. I left the cemetery a little emptier, but firm in the knowledge that one of the Lord's finer Christian soldiers had come home.

CHAPTER EIGHT

After the funeral I left the course for the summer, returning only on Thursday to get my paycheck. At the caddie shack Al gave me a pat on the back. "You've had a good summer, Looper. Caught the attention of some of the members, too. That can't hurt in this town."

"Well, I do think I gained some life experience," I said.

"Life experience don't count for shit, son, if you ain't learned anything," he explained, "but I think you've probably gotten a good dose of both respect and experience."

In retrospect, I did learn a lot that summer, especially about relationships and big business. I got to see human beings in various stages of adversity and learned how they responded under pressure. You can learn a lot from duck hooks and buried lies. And I definitely learned about how the world goes around -- quid pro quo.

* * *

On October 7, after mail call at school, I received an envelope marked First Strike Investment Services, Suite 701, 1135 Wacker Drive, Chicago. Inside was a check for $500. On the stub read the words "For Consulting Services -- Whippet Project." Attached was a handwritten note. " Keep your eyes open, kid." It was signed B.F. Sauers.

For a while I thought about not cashing the check, but reality intruded when second semester tuition came due. I did keep $50 for pin money, though. I was certain Billy Sauers would approve.

With autumn unusually warm I played a lot of golf on my college course, often engaging in solitary late afternoon rounds. Even shot a 73 one day. But more often than not I found myself thinking not about my new girlfriend, but my old one, Mrs. Peck, and the knack she had for putting that 11-wood over traps on short approaches. I even murmured to myself "too much loft" on occasions when I'd dig too deep and sky too high. Yes ma'am, that 11-wood shot to beat Rhoda Charles was sure sweet.

But perhaps the sweetest shot that Mrs. Peck played that year was the one she executed on August 27. Notice of it didn't arrive until December 16, just after my last exam.

Again, the envelope read First Strike Investment Services. In it was a check for $20,000, a short letter and another handwritten note from Billy Sauers.

Dear Mr. Litton:

On December 10, probate was completed on the will of Mrs. Lucy Horton Peck. The enclosed check represents disbursement from her estate according to her last will and testament dated August 27. Should you have any questions concerning this matter, please contact me at the above address.

Sincerely,
Martin J. Handley, Esq.
Partner
Handley, Casaerek & Martin.

The handwritten note was less cryptic, but more telling.

Looper,

After her husband died, Mrs. Peck named me executor of her estate. She wanted you to have this check. It's her 'thank you' for your friendship during a wonderful last summer of life. You gave her back some youth and a lot of confidence. Her intent was that you use this for college, but it's up to you.

Come see me over the holidays.

Sincerely,

B.F. Sauers

P.S. If it were me, I'd save $15 grand and invest the rest. I can help you with the last part.

I felt like saying "Merry Christmas," but all I could think was "Jesus Christ. Twenty thousand bucks for carrying clubs."

Talk about rarified.

PART TWO

MR. O

CHAPTER ONE
1961

"Otto, here's the lowdown on that temporary assistant you asked for: he's got a B.S. in Ornamental Horticulture and Landscape Design and he'll have a Master's in Turf Management from North Carolina State University."

"He's from the South, that's just great. I need a Bentgrass guy, you give me Bermuda. What experience does he have?" Mr. O hollered, holding the phone away from his ear.

"Ten years actual course experience, three on miniatures, four on public, three on country clubs. He's worked two PGA tour stops. Three years Bentgrass."

"So why do I get some rebel rather than a kid from a school in my own region? What about that guy with the associate's from Southern Illinois? I liked him."

"Otto, you asked me to help you. This kid has had two GCSAA scholarships. He comes highly recommended. Your candidate took a job at Medinah."

"Goddamn, and he didn't tell me?" There was a pause and in a voice of resignation he asked, "So what else do I need to know? Any family secrets?"

"He does have a minor connection to Spring Willows."

"What's that?"

"He is Gladys Gleason's second cousin's nephew."

"Christ, that's all I need, a homer."

"This kid is good. Better than good. And it's only for three months."

"Shit. Okay. I'll see him Monday."

That's the conversation I overheard to start my second summer at Spring Willows. Mr. O was boiling. That's all I needed: a pissed off boss my first day of work. I knew I wasn't his favorite. I was a real good worker, but he resented the pressure coming from the clubhouse to keep me on. Two members of the green committee, Judge Gleason and Billy Sauers, an arbitrager, reminded Mr. O I was an asset to the crew, especially since I got on well with the members through my work as a caddie. Mr. O thought I was a suck- up.

Did you know that on golf courses supplemental hand weeding accounts for the majority of landscape bed maintenance costs? And that, when used exclusively, it can cost as much as ten to a hundred times as much as an effective herbicide program? Mr. O knew that, but on this day, Mr. O's way of venting his frustration was sending me to the clubhouse to weed the phlox beds.

"Looper, go with Wolfgang and clean up those beds around the Big House and the parking lot. Pick 'em clean... and kid," he said, separating his sausage-like fingers a quarter of an inch apart, "get them little ones. That should take you most of the day. A good way to get reacquainted with Mother Earth. Heh, heh."

Mr. O always felt like a prisoner at the Big House, so he had Wolfgang, the little kraut, take me. Once there, Wolfgang identified the phlox and then piled back into the truck. I didn't see him again until lunch. He picked me up so I could eat with everyone. Then I was sent out to weed some more.

Weeding phlox was reminiscent of my first day of freshman football practice. Both activities were done in incessant rain. For Coach Rathke we did burpees in puddles. After the second drop it was like going to one of those water parks. And it got worse. With phlox, the dirt got in your pores and under the nails. With football the dirt got in your face and down your shirt.

My knees have never been dirtier than that day in the loam at Spring Willows. The Good Earth, my ass. That ground would grow anything. The slugs and grubworms were so active they came straight from Poe's *Conqueror Worm*. And I hated being there by the clubhouse, in the rain, by myself. I hated Mr. O for sending me there. Everyone else was cooling their heels in a truck, the barn or the shelter at the sod farm, while I spent eight hours in the mud.

* * *

Last summer I spent a lot of energy trying to quantify Mr. O, a burly sort, but I never found the right words or description until a plaque at the zoo spelled it out for me.

ORANGUTAN

These simian creatures, the most solitary of the higher primates,
live alone in remote areas. Males grow to four and one-half feet
and weigh 160 pounds.

Yes, that described the head greenskeeper at Spring Willows Country Club to a T. Mr. O was about a foot taller and twenty pounds heavier, but the other traits were oddly similar. Morose and belligerent, he lived alone in a small house in Wilmette, content to spend his evenings sipping from a bottle of Hamm's beer and figuring out how to get even with all the people who were younger, smarter and stronger than he was. And let me tell you, in the northern suburbs of Chicago, there were a lot of those folks.

As a rule, apes have limited life spans. At 61, Mr. O was the oldest, most ornery primate that ever stalked a golf course. He was unattractive and could be vulgar when required. He was also a survivor. He'd lived through 35 years of politics and eight club presidents. He managed to maintain his fiefdom cloistered from clubhouse and member intervention by keeping the course green, the bunkers pristine and the tees and putting surfaces in tip- top condition. With little formal training he'd been lucky to avert major forms of fungus and blight. His self-taught methods seemed to work for Spring Willows.

Mr. O stood 5'8" with a broad, flat chest and abnormally long arms that were probably better used with tree vines than social climbing. Nonetheless, at Spring Willows, Mr. Olson, also known variously to his staff as Mr. O, the Big O, Aught, Double O or Double Aught, was very agile when it came to maneuvering.

Did you know that adult male orangutans sport large cheek pads and inflatable throat sacs? These were visible whenever Mr. O was dressing down a grounds crew member. When he got too much sun, his skin tone ranged from orange to dark brown, a fact he tried hard to minimize by wearing a Milorganite cap pulled low over his bushy eyebrows.

When he did remove his cap, always with his left hand, it revealed unkempt dark hair which he scratched with the two smallest fingers of his right hand. A luncheon staple for him was nuts, berries and trail mix except when he sent me to the clubhouse for fresh fruit. Invariably I'd ask, "Can I get you something, sir?"

The answer was always, "Grab me a banana from one of those fruit bowls in the front hall." Rather than be perceived as a pillager, I'd go into the kitchen and get one from an Italian cook we called Guano. In exchange I'd put in a good word with Marconi at the caddie shack for whose sister he had the hots.

In truth Mr. O could be a mean SOB. His most obvious trait was an overbearing personality and tacit acquiescence to authority. He didn't like kids except his son. But his passion was women. He disliked them and he set up his course to punish everyone, especially the fair sex.

He had no respect for what he called the "yellows," senior short hitters, or the "reds," women, who were the shortest hitters of all. In fact, for weeks he refused to place yellow tee markers at Spring Willows even when the GCSAA was encouraging their use. On Ladies' Days he kept the rough high on early holes to make their rounds as frustrating as possible.

Mr. O was reputed to be a relative of a serial killer but I personally doubt that. However, that summer he was damn near the death of me. I mean, what's a blue collar grown man got against a college kid? Christ, his own son Otto Jr. (Little O) had worked the course in previous years, but I'd bet the house he never worked the phlox beds. Sometimes he had to work the evening shift monitoring the automated sprinklers, but how tough can that duty be when you do it unsupervised in a Jeep with your girlfriend in tow?

* * *

Mondays were the worst. The course was closed for heavy maintenance. Trees were trimmed, brooks rerouted, traps resanded. When it rained, a two-ton truck of sand weighed four tons. Each shovel was twice as hard to lift. When it rained on Mondays, all the life went out of you. There was close supervision, no sunbathing in remote parts of the course, no weekend to prepare for, just grunt work with, or for, people who generally conceded that you were a mere divot in the fairway of life.

On the crew we had the usual caste system. Full time employees, son of the boss, other seasonal employees. At the superintendent's shed and at the top we had the big ape. There Mr. O reigned supreme and by caprice. But I'm not bitter. It was a good paying summer job. And it taught me to forever appreciate a good boss.

In his poem, *The Second Coming*, William Butler Yeats refers to a "slinking toward Bethlehem." I don't know where our new assistant greenskeeper thought he was headed, but it sure wasn't Bethlehem. Or Jerusalem. More like Dante's Inferno. There were no banners, palm leaves or hosannas. Just open hostility from his new boss.

Part of the anger stemmed from the fact that the guy he was replacing was a real favorite of the members, the crew and Mr. O. Anybody filling

Kenny's shoes was going to have to be perfect. Kenny's aneurism, while unusual in a 35-year-old, required months of rest. Mr. O had thought he'd had a replacement, but when that fell through he asked the green committee to help him. They did, but the replacement was not Kenny and therein lay the rub.

CHAPTER TWO

Jerome Gjertson, Jr. from Dawsonville, Georgia by way of Salisbury, North Carolina arrived on the third Friday in May at 7 a.m. Perfect timing because the first jobs of the day were in full swing. He planned it that way so he could have Mr. O's undivided attention for an hour before the crew came back to the barn. That was his first mistake, Mr. O told him. "You should have been here at 6 like everyone else."

Most superintendent primary expertise, particularly for old timers like Mr. O, who learned the job hands on with no academic background, is in maintaining high quality turfgrass. Spring Willows with its 6,218 greensward was an impressive expanse of grass. The course was immaculate and up until this year had been relatively free from bugs and blight. Mr. O was proud of his "big back yard," as he put it. "After 35 years nobody's got a better lawn than I do," he'd say. Not that the whole crew was happy with his management style. People rarely love bullies. And Mr. O was that in spades, but the crew of twenty did his bidding, kept their bitching to themselves and stayed out of his way.

As any mountain climber knows, good footing is essential to upward mobility. In that initial meeting Mr. O laid out all his expectations for Jerome and didn't bother to throw in any carabineers or crampons. It was mostly one man's monologue on why I don't like you. The litany was lengthy.

Jerome was from the South. He was young. He was educated and up-to-date on all the latest technology. He was well-connected at the club (though Jerome didn't think so). He was a very good golfer. Playing to a three handicap, Mr. O for years had prided himself on being one of the very best golfing superintendents in the country. He didn't need or want a rival for the employee day tourney in July. (Jerome played to a four.) And last but not least, Mr. O perceived Jerome partial to Jacobsen machinery while he himself thought Toro ruled the world.

I came in early from raking traps and caught the last bit of Jerome's employee orientation.

"And, son," Mr. O droned on, "I don't want to hear about southern grasses. This is a northern course with northern sod. We like Bermuda grass. We even have some on the ninth hole, but we love Bent. When we overseed we overseed with Bent and rye, not Bermuda. And the only thing we want for greens is Bent, the best goddamn putting surface in the world. I don't want to hear a word about Tifgreen or any of them sterile triploid hybrid cracker grasses."

"Well, at least we agree on one thing," Jerome squeezed in.

"Are you a Toro man or a Jake man, Junior?"

"I'm for whatever does the best job, sir."

"On this course we've got the latest Toros for fairway, rough and trimming. For spraying we've got a Smithco. I like their speed and safety on the slopes. As for traps, I got stumblebums like that college boy Looper to do my raking."

"The Jacobsen has the lightest footprint in the industry. Minimal compaction," offered Jerome. Mr. O's temperature was rising. He tried another tack.

"Have you ever tried the Ransome's fairway mower? In field tests it beats Toro all hollow. It's 3 mph faster, you can hand adjust the cutting heads, monitor cutting performance because the units are in front, it's got better traction on hills and it doesn't leave footprints. We had three of them at Hope Valley."

"I don't care if you had five of 'em at Christ the King. Here we drive Toros. Any other questions?"

"How about aerators?" Jerome continued. "Jacobsen has one. It's the industry's widest selection of hold spacings, convenient controls, lower maintenance costs and longer lasting tines."

"Don't you hear so good? I said no Jacobsens. Not now, not ever."

"Mr. Olson, you don't even have to change tires. That means less work for the crew."

"Read my lips, boy. No Jacobsens."

It was only later that I found out from Starza what Mr. O had against Jacobsen. It wasn't the product at all. It was the salesman, who for a very brief period and very long ago had an affair with Bernice, Mr. O's wife. I think in time he forgave her. But he never forgave Jacobsen. Jacobsen makes some great equipment. I know. I cut lawns on the side and their reel mowers are second to none. But at Spring Willows we had nothing to do with Jacobsens. That was just a natural fact.

The interview was starting to wind down.

"As an assistant greenskeeper, what's the best thing you can offer this place?" The Big O asked.

"I see my contribution as keeping things mowing, growing and getting out of the way. That means greens that drain well, movable air and cupable space, with minimal turf disturbance."

"Now we're gettin' somewhere," sighed Mr. O. "You know anything about watering, college boy?"

"I know that the quickest way to kill turf is to overwater it," Jerome said.

"The greatest problem in course management is that most courses do not drain enough for golfing needs."

"I know that, Mr. Olson."

"The basic rule for healthy turfgrass is: the lower the mowing height, the more water required for plant survival."

"This is not my first rodeo."

"What's your watering philosophy?"

"Treeline to treeline. I can run Toros with my eyes closed and I trained on golf irrigation systems by Rainbird."

"That's good, son, because we've got the Toros. We ain't got Rainbirds here, and we ain't gettin' any. Too expensive."

Mistake, I thought from my place in the hall. Initiation dues of $40,000 and we couldn't afford a Rainbird? I think what was really happening was that Mr. O was sharing his fear of what the magazines called "high technology intimidation factor." Our Toro system was fifteen years old.

"All I can tell you is that high tech equipment helps you do it faster."

"Son, we got ten miles of pipe under this course and 600 heads. I've been doing this job for 35 years and I don't need some boy from the sandhills of North Carolina telling me how to do my job. Here's a sheet. Study it. It lists the estimated man hours required to maintain this course. Everything from mowing, watering, landscaping, moving markers. Everything except the jobs we do monthly or quarterly. That's extra. Learn it. Memorize it. More than anything else, learn this course. See the course with your eyes, feel it with your hands, your feet and your bones. Two other things. I like good flat tee boxes with spaces for tee markers. We got members who play like a bunch of hackers at the muni, so we move the markers a lot, sometimes twice a day. In order of importance it's greens, tees, fairways, bunkers and rough. One more thing: I don't care who you know at this club. You work for me. I'm the superintendent and you're just the assistant greenskeeper. Now let's go meet the crew."

It was a real ragtag collection of humanity that Jerome found assembled in the barn. The krauts, Wolfgang and Hans, Buddy Bonneville, the greaser who mowed most of the greens, the Italians, Rossi, Marconi and Dominic, who mowed fairways and retrieved balls from ponds, Lackey Leeds, the black utility man, Diesel the mechanic, a few select nobodies and me. The other college hires weren't out of school yet.

"This is Jerome Gjertson, Jr.," began Mr. O. "You can call him Jerome or Junior, he doesn't care." There was a ripple of laughter from all but Jerome, who obviously did care. "He's here to fill in while Kenny's gone. He knows a lot about golf courses despite the peach fuzz and the water behind the ears. He's worked courses for ten years from miniatures to country clubs. He knows water, plants and machines. Don't give him any shit, he'll get enough from me. And help him out, he'll need it. Class dismissed."

That's about as charitable as Mr. O ever got. Faint praise and piss. Couldn't have one without the other. I extended my hand and went back to Five where I was weeding traps. I figured I'd have time later to say hello.

As it turned out, I learned more about golf course management in three days from Jerome than I did in the three months I'd been with Mr. O. The previous summer the entire membership thought the course looked great. In May of this year everyone thought it looked even better. Then we met Jerome.

One day during the second week he stopped by when I was raking traps on Six. It had been in the nineties for three days. He offered me some water. "Whaddya think, Jerome?" I asked nonchalantly.

"Free water, groundwater, weeds, grubs, even nematodes," he said. "There are all kinds of things wrong with this place and nobody thinks anything of it. Hell, nobody's got nematodes anymore." I'd opened the dike.

My ears picked up. "You serious about the blight?"

"Dead serious," he said. "First signs of it right here on this hole, back there toward the chute in all that shade. All the elements are aligning. Heat and humidity are fine for what Bermuda we got on Nine, but Pythium kills cool season grasses and that's mostly what you got on this course. If that goes unchecked, you'll have an epidemic. Got to tell the boss about that. And about the budding problem around Eight green."

"What's that?" I asked.

"Nutsedge, the most vicious weed known to man."

"What's it do?"

"Kills the collars around the green. Very unsightly, it's like scraping your garden bare. Runs wild on poorly maintained municipal courses. You probably think those bare spots around the munis are from heavy play. Hell, no. That's nutsedge. Don't want that to get going. Hard to bring an area back. With Pythium you can spray. With nutsedge it's not so easy."

"Unsightly, huh?"

"Yes sir."

"We got some important and vocal people who live by Eight green," I said.

"Well, they're in for a surprise if something isn't done soon."

"I don't think that's what the men's club champion wants to hear," I said.

"Oh, I don't think he'll hear anything, Looper. He's gonna see it before his very eyes. While we're talking, I'll tell you a couple of other things wrong with this course, the guy who places the tee markers…"

"That's Buddy and Rossi, mostly, since they cut the tees," I said.

"The guys who place these markers," he began again, "ought to be more careful because they don't always align straight. Especially on Ladies' Days they seem more askew than normal. I mean, a player could align himself with the marker, hit the ball out of bounds and not understand why."

"If you haven't noticed, Jerome, Mr. O doesn't cotton to women much. I think maybe it's all right with him if they hit a few out of bounds. And I'll bet Rossi doesn't mind at all since he's forever selling reclaimed balls to the Pro Shop. You ought to see what he takes out of the water at Killer Ten, Sixteen and Seventeen."

"Well, I tell you why mistreating women is a bad idea at a country club: they live with men, who have to listen to them. And if they decide there is merit in repeated complaints, they go to the green committee. Then the whip comes down on the super. And that ain't pretty because the super lashes out at the crew even though he's responsible."

"We all pay for the Big O's sins on this course," I said. "That's what we call him, Big O or Double O, even Aught or Double Aught, when he gets uppity. Not to his face of course."

"I get that, but I'm going to have to talk to the greens cutters about mowing the chipping areas. These greens are ringed with rough. You couldn't hit a knockdown shot on this course right now. Too lush. The rough should stop the ball from running to a worse place, not be so penal."

"Think Buddy and Rossi will listen to you?"

"They better because this course will go south fast if it stays hot and wet."

"That's the forecast."

He took a slug of water. "And the speed of some of these greens is patently unfair. What is this, Augusta National? I'll bet in the old days the Stimpmeter was five or six. But with modern technology, some of these greens are a constant 11.5. The ones with a lot of pitch like Five, Six or Ten -- especially Ten -- are damn near unplayable."

He was right. Those greens were cut at 4/32s of an inch. It was like rolling marbles on granite. Ten was a two-tiered, 163-yard par 3 over a pond. Elevated tee to elevated green with a six-to-seven foot rise from the traps to green on three sides. Ten was a killer.

"You play?" he asked.

"Some," I said. "Played more when I wasn't working G crew and caddying. Played this year at school some."

"Varsity?"

"Solo. Shot a 73 one day."

"Not bad. I shoot to a four. Wanted to be a club pro, but I think there's a better future in this. Fewer bosses anyway."

"Not at a country club," I laughed. "Every member's your boss."

"Not if you do your job right," he said. "Let's play some day. We can talk some more." He gunned the Club Car.

* * *

That afternoon I went to the caddie shack to see my other boss on the course, Al, the caddie master. I liked caddying; it was good extra money that I needed for school. Plus, it kept me in touch with some members with whom I'd found favor the previous summer.

"Welcome back, Looper. Why didn't you come see me sooner? I've got some messages for you."

"What kind of messages?" All messages went through the caddie master.

"Phone messages from members."

"You're kidding."

"God's truth. Seems that over the winter some women were thinking of you."

"Like who?"

"For starters, Mrs. Worth, Mrs. Whippet, Mrs. Charles and Cindy Cabiness. With Mrs. Peck gone they seem to think you might be free."

"I don't know. I'm going to work G crew pretty hard this summer. I don't know if I can loop for anyone regularly like I did for Mrs. P."

"Are you saying no looping?"

"I didn't say that. I just don't know about regular. Mrs. Peck was special."

Boy, wasn't that the truth. She was a 67-year-old D-flighter. She and I had worked a summer and a half together. A former club champion who gave up golf for more than forty years, we teamed up to take her to the D-Flight championship. She won the final round 2-and-1 on her final shot and dropped dead. I kid you not. Holed out an 11-wood over water on Seventeen and died. Great shot by a great lady. She'd left me $20,000 in her will for school, so I didn't need the money quite as much this year as I had last.

"Worth, Whippet, Charles and Cabiness? Worth I can see. I've worked for her and she respects me. Did she win the women's club championship again?"

"Seventh time in nine years. Took out that Weston woman 6-and-5."

"Billy Sauers was right. He said everyone thought Weston would win."

"Worth was tough. Was three under after five holes. That's good work considering the par 5s that start this course."

"I'll say. Okay, I can understand Worth, but not Charles and Whippet. Those schoolteachers, I don't even like them."

"Yeah, but you did a helluva job for Mrs. Peck against them and they think you can do the same for them."

"I had a lot of energy for Mrs. P. She was polite, gentle, a first class person. Whippet and Charles aren't nice people."

"So, call Mrs. Worth, tell her you'll carry and tell Whippet and Charles you can't on a regular basis. Loop for them a couple of times just to keep 'em happy. Believe me, it'll pay off."

"What do I do about Cabiness? Is she still seeing McDevitt on the side?" Cindy Cabiness was a mediocre golfer with a B flight personality and an A-flight body. She was a pleasure to watch.

"God only knows."

"I don't need that kind of trouble."

"A robust young man like you might make her day."

"And ruin my career here. I'll stick to college girls."

"Do what you want, but you need to call her. If it were me, I'd loop a few rounds. Do it on Sunday when she plays with her husband and the Faunces. No harm there."

"You're right."

"You had two other calls. Mr. Howard said to save some late Sundays for him and the family. You know, when the three of them go nine. Said Tinker will carry his own bag this year."

Mr. Howard, the men's club champion, was scratch from the blues. Last year I carried three bags one Sunday when Tinker, his nine-year-old, whined his way around the front nine. He showed signs of his dad's athleticism and could flat whale a 5-iron.

"And the last call?"

"Bill Sauers. Said look him up."

"Figures."

"He likes you. Stay close to that man."

"I think we understand each other."

"How's the new assistant super?" Al asked.

"I like him a lot. But nobody's listening to him except me. He's got good ideas; he's a straight shooter and he anticipates well."

"Anticipates?"

"You know about his background, right? Agronomics, landscape design, horticulture? He says if it stays hot and muggy, the Bermuda's gonna grow great and the Bent's going straight to hell. Says he's already seen signs of Pythium on Six."

"For Chrissakes, the course is 98 percent Bent."

"I know it. And here's another tidbit. He thinks he detects nutsedge on Eight around the green."

"Where Mr. Howard lives?"

"Yeah, but I don't think anybody important is listening. I'm just a grunt. Let's just say the communication around the super's shed isn't so hot right now."

"Could be Mr. O is thinking more about defending his Midwest superintendent's golf crown next month than the course," mused Al.

"Don't know about that," I said. "I just get the feeling I wasn't his first choice for a summer hire."

"Let's be honest," said Al, "you weren't. But with Borney, Otto Junior and his roommate gone, he needed an experienced worker."

"Al, all I do is talk to the weeds. 'Get them little ones, Looper.' As far as Mr. O is concerned, I'm weed man, plain and simple."

"Plain and simple, Looper, you're the telegraph to the clubhouse. 'Native intelligence' Billy Sauers calls it."

"Are you saying I'm a plant?"

"Far from it. I'm just saying that management regards you as a valuable communication tool."

"That's me all right. A tool, damn tool. Jesus."

"Look, Looper, we'll still respect you in the morning, okay? What you're worth in caddying time and G crew time to the membership can't be measured. Mr. O doesn't have that perspective. He thinks he owns the course. And to a point he does, but if he doesn't keep this course up, especially in mid-August, he'll be gone faster than a wayward Titleist. Which reminds me. I need for you to work that exhibition in August. Thursday through Sunday, 24-27."

"What exhibition?"

"Selected collegiate players versus a Swedish team. Ought to be very good match play."

"Haven't heard about that."

"Well," he said, laughing, "I hope somebody at the shed has, because it's a very big deal. The USGA selected Spring Willows over eight other sites. It's a biggie."

"I haven't seen it on the board in Mr. O's office."

"It's only May."

"I'll ask around. Any pre-Memorial Day tournaments I need to know about?"

"We're having a women's 4-ball scramble on Tuesday. That's about it."

"Okay, Al. I'll go two rounds next Sunday if you need me. Check ya." I headed out the door.

CHAPTER THREE

The Thursday before the women's scramble Mr. O seemed unusually well-organized. He took more care than normal listing the jobs on the board and following up to see his instructions were executed. "Rossi, I want you to cut as much rough as possible. Start on the back nine. When you get to the front, work from Nine on down. If you don't finish 18 holes don't worry about it. We won't be cutting rough again til next Wednesday."

"Kind of a long time between cuttings, isn't it, Mr. Olson" offered Jerome.

"We got other things to do tomorrow, and Monday we aerate and top dress some greens. The rough can wait."

"You gonna aerate, out of season, before Ladies' Day?" the assistant asked. "Man, I don't know about that."

"This is my course, you hear? Just a little aeration. I can handle the ladies."

* * *

Later Jerome said, "Where I come from we handle the ladies with kid gloves. It looks like Mr. Olson is trying to create an obstacle course."

You know how some people are just mean? That's how Mr. O could be. I didn't have the experience or the perspective to recognize what the big bully was doing, but Jerome pieced it together for me later.

On Fridays we always prepared the course for the weekend. We did all the manicuring touches, especially around the practice green and driving range where the men first see the course. When those areas were set up well the members didn't normally notice the other imperfections. And sure enough, Saturday went fine, smooth as silk. Brisk, sunny weather helped everybody's attitude and I heard nary a complaint even from Stan Starza, the pro, who was quick to pass on complaints from members.

Monday we hit the course with a vengeance, cutting fairways even closer than normal. "What are we doing that for?" Jerome asked. "It's not like we're overseeding."

"I got it under control, Junior. You do your job, I'll do mine. In case you've forgotten what your job is," he said in front of the entire crew, "it's to listen to me."

"Yessir," Jerome said clearly. "You mother," he murmured.

"Tomorrow, Rossi, I want you and Wolfgang, Gerhard and the Kaptain to add some extra sand to the bunkers on Three and Six. Dominic, you clean up the stream between Fourteen and Fifteen. Got that? Do your normal duties first, then get started on the other stuff. Any questions?" There were none. "Go to it."

"Oh, man," said Jerome as we exited the shed, "if these ladies have any balls at all, it's gonna hit the fan."

"I don't get it," I said.

"Mr. Olson is saving the heavy maintenance until tomorrow. He's already cutting the fairways skintight. He's left the rough on the front nine too long. The course is going to be hell to play and there'll be hell to pay. He must really not like women."

"You got it," I said.

Unknown to the two of us, Mr. O wasn't done. Come Tuesday he took the Kaptain aside, one of the new college hires, and assigned him the job of setting up the tee boxes. "Put them red ones back by the whites today, Kaptain," he said. "And make sure the whites are toward the back of the box. The ladies like a challenge."

Long ball city. And Kaptain was so dumb he didn't know what he was doing. Kaptain's real name was Crofton Creighton, but he was a Superman freak and seemed to have such a hard head that Jerome called him Kaptain Kryptonite. The name stuck, and Kaptain went out and did what he was told.

And the aftershock was what I heard the second most about on Wednesday when I stopped into the caddy shack. "The G crew's not in real high favor today, kid." Al called me kid when things weren't going well. "That tee marker trick ticked off a lot of people. Who set 'em up anyway?"

"Kaptain. New kid."

"Not a very smart move. Especially misaligning them on Six."

"He was under orders from the chief."

"But not near as dumb as the irrigation malfunction on the back nine. I'll bet that soaked damn near 30 percent of the players. It's not a good move to get hens wet. I thought those things were on timers."

"They are. But we got an old Toro system. Irrigation malfunctions happen sometimes."

"Got a manual setting on them, Looper?"

"Sure, they all got overrides."

"I'm telling you yesterday's performance was just stupid. Close cut fairways? Women hate that. And let me ask you what the hell were they doing dredging the creek? And doing the fairway bunkers on Three and Six was a no brainer. Mrs. Plunkett hit the best drive of her life on Three only to nail the sand spreader."

"Saved her from out of bounds at the Governor's House, I heard."

"She still didn't like hitting the spreader. I don't think we've heard the last of it. This isn't such a hot way for Jerome to start out."

"It's not Jerome, Al. He needs this job and the course hours for his advanced degree. He doesn't want anything getting in the way. If I'm supposed to be a conduit, pass it up the pipeline that this was a pretty well-orchestrated slap at women and Jerome had nothing to do with it. He opposed the major maintenance and questioned most everything you mentioned. And I guarantee he didn't know anything about the tee marker until after play started. The tee box on Six is just plain misaligned. Has been for years. Anyway, Jerome was just taking orders. That's all any of us are doing these days."

"The Germans just took orders, too, Looper. You guys need to do better than this. Keep the damage down. Nobody wins when the ladies get mad."

"I think Mr. O was just sending the ladies an early season message."

"I'm telling you, kid. Keep it up and you won't like the message coming back."

"Al, I hear you. But we need some help. The zookeeper is a baboon."

Noontime the next day produced an interesting gathering. Mr. O had gone to Skokie to get God knows what and the whole crew was breaking bread and enjoying the sun and conversation outside the super's shed. Coming from the traps on Four I heard Jerome say, "What I don't understand is if he doesn't like women that much, why piss 'em off by making the course so hard? Instead of doing all the major maintenance and moving tee markers back, why not cut the rough short, move tee markers and pins up? That way they can play quicker and get off his damn course faster."

"That's the way he is. He doesn't like skirts, period."

"He'd have loved being superintendent down at Hope Valley then. We had two women that worked the course."

"Wee doggie. You are kidding?" shouted Buddy. "Skirts raking traps, picking up sticks?"

"They did everything. They were the best drivers we had. We had this one college girl, Rita Randleman. She was a terror. She could cut rough faster and cleaner with a mini-tractor than anyone I ever saw. We asked her why she drove so fast and she'd say, 'Honey, this is NASCAR country.' She was from near Charlotte and down there they all have speed on the brain. One day she was cleaning the fairways so fast the twigs were moving before she got there."

"Well, blow my top. Was she a fox?" Buddy asked. Only Buddy. Father of two youngsters who worked three jobs to support his fancy car and poor wife.

"What do you care?" said Butch, his crony.

"Well, if she drives fast, I might've liked her."

"I tell you who you would have liked, Buddy, was her running mate Regina Rudlin. She was hot. She'd wear tight jeans just to tease the crew. And she drove a late model Chevy with racing stripes. She was fast and mean. Mr. Olson might have even liked her. I saw her run over a squirrel one day just for fun."

"Wee doggie," bellowed Buddy. "The Big O would have loved that. Mercy, mercy."

"No mercy," said Lackey.

"You'd have gotten on good with Rita, Lackey," said Jerome. "She knew plants almost as well as you do."

"Bust my tailpipe," said Buddy. "Skirts working a course. I'll bet they didn't know shit about carburetors."

"Wrong. Reggie's dad works the NASCAR pits in Charlotte. So whatever's broke she could fix faster than most. And talk about mowing. She understood cutting tolerances real well, so the fairways and rough were always just right."

"Smooth as a dog's ear, right?" queried the Kaptain.

"Just about," Jerome said. "One day the two of them wore cowboy hats to cut rough. Mr. Tait, our super, called them 'Sweethearts of the Fairway.' After that it was 'Sweetheart this, Sweetheart that.' Having women around kind of cleaned up our act a bit. To tell you the truth, we were kinda proud of them."

"I wish I had some sweetheart riding my machine," hollered Buddy.

"This place could use a woman's touch," said Jerome, balling up his brown bag. "Something else, Hope Valley members wouldn't have put up with that major maintenance shit like on Tuesday either because Reggie and Rita wouldn't have let it happen."

"We'd have lost our jobs," someone said.

"They wouldn't have."

"How could two girls get away with that?" said Buddy.

"Bigger balls, I guess," said Jerome. "See you boys, I got work to do."

"It'll be a cold day in hell before Mr. O lets a woman on this crew," said Buddy, rubbing his crotch. As it turned out that wasn't the last we were to hear of Rita Randleman.

As Memorial Day gave way to June I found time to do some caddying. I even called Mrs. Whippet and Charles, not my two favorite ladies, and went rounds with them. They were far more cordial than when they'd been vying with Mrs. Peck for the D-flight championship. Both had worked hard on their games, especially to improve their putting. I think their pride had gotten the best of them and both cited their intentions of being C-flight contenders, leaving D to the club's best lookers and lesser golfers Cindy Cabiness and Jocelyn Price. As a token of my faith, I promised each a round in the club championship so long as it wasn't against one another. Al even complimented me on my diplomacy.

Mrs. Worth gave me a real surprise. She wanted club tournament services, too, something I was happy to provide to someone who had toured the greens in only 25 putts the last time we'd walked. But what she really wanted was a Friday, Saturday, Sunday stretch in August for the women's member-guest. Seems her old Wellesley roommate, a 6-handicapper, had agreed to play and she thought they could win it all.

"As long as it doesn't interfere with preparations for the exhibition," I told her.

"I'll just ask Al for a late tee time, Looper. Any time after 2:30 you can make, right?"

"Unless we got overtime, I'm golden," I said.

Cindy Cabiness, round, firm and fully packed, was now 36 and still seeing Devin (Divot) McDevitt once a week. That had to be Spring Willows' worst kept secret. Either John Cabiness didn't know or care. As a result, Cindy went on about her flirtatious ways with men and boys alike. From me she wanted, of all things, a lesson reading greens. She was one of the few members who knew how well I really played and she remembered the help I'd been to Mrs. Peck in that regard. So one Thursday before twilight we went eighteen and I explained the nuances of grain, terrain, slope and breaks. By Fifteen she was reading the surfaces very well and I had gained increased appreciation for good-looking women. I'd thought with her reputation, she might want some other favors, but no. She just wanted to be a better putter. I'll say this, my True Temper shaft was straight for the entire loop. Paid me $14 for the round and another $25 for the lesson. Nice lady.

With the onslaught of the new college kids, I was no longer low man on the course. Mr. O even entrusted me with the Jeep to run clubhouse errands. And it was always me he sent. Maybe it was the close haircut or collared shirt, but nobody seemed to make runs to the Big House like I did. I must have made ten trips a week. It was always, "Run this to Teresa" (the secretary) or "Haul this up to Binswanger" (the general manager).

On the third wet day in a row, while playing Message to Garcia, I ran into Billy Sauers, Mrs. Peck's confidant, and my mentor from the previous summer. "You had a good talk with Al last week, Looper?"

"I'm no snitch, Mr. Sauers."

"I understand that, but you're the best informal source of communication between the maintenance staff and the clubhouse. Between the maintenance staff and the Pro Shop for that matter."

"I just want to see justice done. If everyone works hard and plays fair, we'll be fine," I said.

"Life's not fair, son. Remember that."

"Life's not being fair to Kenny, I can tell you that. We heard today it's going to be another two-to-three months before he's back. More pressure."

"Son, you don't know what pressure is if some of the water and disease problems don't get resolved. We have more standing water and undesirable weeds than I can ever remember." I had a feeling he was just warming up. "Tell Jerome to keep his chin up."

"Yes sir." And that was it. Nothing directly about the nutsedge on Eight, the casual water on Six or the hooded traps on Thirteen. Just goodbye and a cheery message for Jerome.

So why should it have been a surprise to me what happened next. On Friday right before lunch, the Kaptain, Butch and I were reworking the traps on Thirteen. You know how many tons of sand it takes to completely redo a medium size bunker? About fifteen tons. No lie, fifteen each, and we were on our third trap.

As the foursome approached we stepped aside. Three balls dropped to within twenty feet of the flag. A fourth flew the green and buried itself. Judge Gleason trudged around to Omaha Beach. "I'll be honest, sir," said the Kaptain, "I don't know how deep it is."

"I'm making a local rule," intoned the Judge. "Ground under repair," he said. "I'm taking relief."

"We don't need it," countered Billy Sauers as he firmed his first putt into the heart. "Kid," he yelled to me, "He in?" he said, pointing his putter at the maintenance shed.

"Yes sir," I responded.

"Good. You boys take a late lunch. We got some business to transact." I guess that's how they do things in the big time. Got a problem, deal with it. In person, right now.

"What's that all about?" asked the Kaptain.

"That's four members of the green committee going to talk to our boss."

"Screw it, it's time to eat," said the airhead.

"No, that's not what Mr. Sauers had in mind. I think we work on traps a while longer until the green committee is done."

"We might not get to eat at all today," said the Kaptain.

"That's right. In fact, when they're done, Mr. O might have more than enough for us to chew on."

I learned later the power lunch in the administration barn went like this. For starters, members at Spring Willows rarely went to the shed. And the green committee never did. So that was the first shock, the mountain going to Mohammed.

The grievance list was long and the visit wasn't social. It was all business and had all the trappings of a performance review. "First off," said Billy Sauers, "you need to remove the standing water. Christ, Otto, you know about drainage. Dig some trenches, put down some sand and soil. And for God's sakes get some air movement on the sixth tee. Get those fans Jerome's been talking to you about."

"You know about that?" Mr. O asked. Seems he had turned Jerome down three times on some inexpensive, unobtrusive fans.

"Second, this course is beginning to look like an intensive care unit. Signs of Pythium all over and nutsedge on the collars at Eight. Heat, humidity or no, you gotta control that now. I don't care what you do to get at those roots, rhizomes and tubers. Put some herbicide or something on them full label or this course is dead. And if this course is dead for the exhibition in August, you, sir, are also dead."

"You're the second person who's mentioned an August exhibition. Is Arnold Palmer coming or something?"

"Excuse me?" said Billy Sauers.

"Am I missing something? Three weeks ago, someone, I think it was Looper, said something about an exhibition. Exhibit what? We having an art show at the clubhouse? Heh, heh."

"He's serious," the judge said. "He doesn't have a fucking clue."

"You ought to listen to your staff a little better. Twelve collegians are playing an all-star team from Sweden at Spring Willows on August 24, 25, 26 and 27. And one reason we're here is that the USGA says you haven't turned in the forms about course dimensions and conditions."

"This is the first I've heard of it," stuttered Mr. Olson.

"It's at least the second time," Billy Sauers said. "Far Hills, New Jersey called me personally this morning because you aren't doing your job. I don't want to hear from USGA headquarters under those circumstances. Understand?"

"Yes sir."

"And while we're talking about manners and course conditions, we don't ever want a repeat of the travesty of several weeks ago. Leave the ladies in peace. Do major maintenance if you must on Monday, Tuesday and Thursday afternoons and Wednesday morning, but none of this George Patton bullshit. They're still laughing at Iroquois Woods about Mrs. Plunkett hitting the spreader. Nobody laughs at this club, Otto."

A livid Alvin Bullock broke in. "And if the green on Ten is ever – ever -- as short as it was for that day without my permission," he paused and looked at his committee, "without *our* permission, you'll be fishing balls out of the pond at midnight without waders."

Bullock was referring to the ultra-slick surface on a very sloped green. Few putts held at all and most rolled south off the green to the water's edge. Average score that day was seven. "My wife is B-flight club champion, Otto. Alice took a twelve. My wife doesn't take twelves. You remember that."

"What he's saying is that we will not tolerate even the most vocal whiner being humbled for no better motives than those that are purely sadistic."

"Thank you, Judge. I couldn't have said it any better," added Billy Sauers.

They went on for another twenty minutes, but you get the gist.

"I'll get right on it when I come back from Moline," said Mr. Olson.

"What's Moline?" asked the Judge.

"It's the Midwest Superintendent's meeting," said Mr. Olson.

"That's where they drink beer and play golf," said Karsner.

"You're defending champ, aren't you?" said Sauers.

"Yes sir, two times. Shot a 73 last..."

"Fuck your 73. You go have a good time. While you're gone you think about this conversation. But before you go, give Jerome a break and let him show you how a course should be run. Good day."

Kaptain, the dumb ass, overheard that last part and told me that Mr. O didn't speak for five minutes. When Mr. O found out he'd been listening, Kaptain went straight to the top of the shit list and pulled grunt duty for a month and a half.

"Some pit stop," I said.

"I think I'd pass on lunch today, Looper. Keeping shoveling," said Billy Sauers, stepping toward Fourteen tee.

* * *

A week later we finally figured how Mr. O missed the notification of the exhibition. It came by phone to Kenny the day he had his stroke. Subsequently all the mail the club had gotten concerning it had been addressed to the assistant superintendent and Mr. O, mental giant that he is, sent it to Kenny's home. Boy. And then with a closed mind he missed the verbal hints altogether.

Mr. O's trip to Moline amounted to an extended vacation, with every-one benefitting but the monkey himself. We heard from an informant that he did not defend his crown well. A second day 79 consigned him to runner-up behind Hal Percher of Shawnee Mission Country Club in Kansas, a fact he confirmed for himself when he called Monday to tell Jerome he'd contracted ptomaine poisoning at the final banquet.

"Like the punchline says, Junior, start without me. Ha, ha. In fact when they let me out of this hospital, I'm going to Dubuque to see my cousin and his wife. Anything comes up, you handle. By the way, get those fans for Six you want. Take care of the water and the disease. Don't mess up on the disease. I don't want no Pythium, nutsedge or brown patch when I get back."

"When's that gonna be?" asked Jerome.

"Probably a week."

"Then I need your permission for some new hires."

"We got enough people now," barked the ailing super.

"Not since Saturday. Rossi ruptured a disk lifting and Buddy damn near lost a finger adjusting a greens mower."

"How'd he do that?"

"It was still running."

"Dumb ass. How long's Rossi out?"

"A month, minimum." He paused. "So, I need a body or two."

"Get 'em, but don't spend too much."

"Yes sir. Anything else?"

"Yeah, don't screw up. And if you got any big questions take 'em to Binswanger or Mr. Sauers. You know Sauers, right?"

"I've heard of him."

"He heads the green committee. One other thing. Make sure you send those forms in for that August exhibition. Today."

"Yes sir."

"That's it, Junior. Good luck."

At lunch Jerome called an impromptu employee meeting. It was succinct and the effect was electric. "Here's the deal. Mr. O is sick; he'll be back in a week and we got lots of work to do. I know some of you have been unhappy in your jobs around here. When you come in this afternoon and before you go home, I want you to fill out this paper. It'll be in your locker. Tell me what you like about your job, what you don't like and if there's something else you'd rather do. Also say what we could do as a group to do a better job. For those of you who don't speak English so good or write so well, come see me and we'll talk about it. Any questions?" There were none.

He turned to me as the group was breaking up. "Looper, you stay late this afternoon in case we get too many talkers."

As it turned out, other than the usual pissing and moaning about the oppressive work environment, the biggest bitching had to do with the two-way radios we used to communicate on the course. Seems like half the time the workers couldn't talk to one another because the guys from the Pro Shop were yakking. "Yeah, I'm going out to pick range balls now. Should take me thirty minutes unless Mrs. Cabiness wants to see my MaxFli." Bullshit like that flooded the airwaves, making it impossible to communicate on a timely basis.

As we combed the questionnaires, it was obvious some simple reassignments would improve morale immensely. "With Rossi and Buddy gone, we need someone to cut," I said.

"How about the krauts? They're meticulous. They got the right mentality for the job." Ergo, Wolfgang and Gerhard got the jobs cutting tees and greens.

"What about roughs and fairways? We got to move someone over?"

"Let's wait on that. What we really need is another assistant type, not more stargazers. I'll call my old super at Hope Valley tonight. Maybe he knows of someone. We need a longer-term solution here if Rossi and Buddy are going to be out a while."

Jerome was right, we had a real hybrid group. Not as many transients as a lot of clubs, but a crew that clearly was in another world. Take Kaptain. He said he went to college at Illinois Normal, but there was nothing normal about him. Jerome was reluctant to let him near too many machines, especially after he tipped a cart over on Nine in front of some members. The Toro survived but the attached blower unit was a write-off. As a matter of fact, Kaptain and machines parted company altogether after he mishandled a chainsaw, nearly slicing his leg.

Every club has utility men, guys who do this, do that, do that, do this. They always get in their forty hours but doing what no one knows for sure. Spring Willows had two such men, Lackey Leeds and Lon Jennings. These aging blacks wandered the course doing work that ranged from tortuous to touch-up. Lackey's real name was Lakey, his parents were from the English countryside, but being dubbed a "dumb nigger" early on he suffered a lifelong sobriquet he despised. After a while he came to accept it, especially after Lon, a gentle, but brooding sort, suggested life would be smoother if he just lived with it.

Neither one made it out of high school, but Lon at 6'2", 240 pounds, had Fulbright strength. He lifted tractors, put mowers up in the rafters and when the fertilizer truck came, it was Lon you wanted picking up the first bags.

The two of them seemed to drift through the day doing stuff no one else wanted to do, instinctively pulling edges, picking up sticks and trash. But they were at their best in the nursery, a fact that wasn't really appreciated until Rossi went down.

Jerome broke my reverie. "You know this Mr. Sauers fellow?"

"I do."

"Think you could introduce me? I think he knows a lot more about me than I know about him. I'd like to hear his agenda first-hand, especially if I'm going to be boss for a few days."

"I'll see what I can do." Mr. Sauers suggested 4 o'clock at the maintenance shed after the trading desk closed. He screeched up in his gunmetal grey Mercedes and spent another five minutes on paperwork.

Once inside he vented. "Those bozos in the pit don't know anything. I'm Bill Sauers," he said, ignoring me and sticking a stiff mitt at Jerome. "Welcome to Spring Willows. How can I help?"

"Mr. Sauers, let me officially say how much I appreciate this opportunity. This is a fine course that can be made better. As I think you know, my roots are in the Piedmont and Sandhills, well south of here. I'm much more comfortable in my own belt than I am here. When I finish my term here I want to go back." He stopped and took a breath. "But, sir, my observation is that most of the problems on this course have nothing to do with transition zones and soil composition, it's more about management, morale and productivity. And I can help you there. So," he took another deep breath, "what is it you want?"

"I want this course to be a shining jewel. For the most part, it's always been a gem, but we need these 200 acres up and polished by that exhibition.

The USGA expects it, the membership expects it and I expect it." I had no doubt who had the greatest expectation. "If things come off like I think they can, maybe someday we can get the Walker Cup or the Women's Amateur. Am I coming through?"

"Right now, we couldn't host the Azerbaijan Open, much less the Women's Amateur."

"I know that, but when those ladies come here in August, I want this course so spectacular that Jesus himself would think about visiting. We are playing host to America's best collegiate women and Europe's best female college players, who right now happen to be from Sweden."

"Gee, it would be nice if somebody had told us sooner. We could have addressed everything earlier."

"I don't know about everything, there's still the nutsedge problem."

"There are problems on every hole."

"I see you've got some troughs dug on Six and one of those fans blowing. Nice touch. I hardly even noticed it."

"Didn't cost much, either. The others will be in soon now that I have permission to get them."

"Permission? You should have had that long ago."

"What else, Mr. Sauers? This is your course. I just work here."

"Just stay on top of things. I think Mr. O has gotten a little lax this year, but that's changing, I suspect. Anything you need? Have you enough staff with Kenny, Rossi and Buddy out?"

"I hired a turf management grad from Southern Illinois last night and I got another body coming. Both start Friday. With a couple of other changes we should be all right."

"Grad's name?"

"Ri- um, Richard Randleman."

I snorted.

"What was that all about?" asked Billy Sauers.

"The Milorganite, it's up my nose," I said.

"Milwaukee organic nitrogen," laughed Sauers. "Looper, industrialized sewer sludge is the last stuff you want up your nostrils." Turning to Jerome, he said, "When Otto gets back he's obviously in charge, but if you need anything, anything to get this course ready for the ladies, you let me know. Move tees, widen fairways, relocate creeks, resand traps, whatever it takes. There's to be no more screwing with the female membership," he said, "though I know that wasn't your fault."

"Tell that to Divot," I said.

"I've told him," he shot back.

"I appreciate your time, Mr. Sauers. Pleased to make your acquaintance," said Jerome.

"You're welcome. Keep up the good work." Then to me he said, "Looper, you free Sunday? Mrs. Worth and I are teeing off at 11."

"See you at the Pro Shop at 10:30," I said.

The Mercedes left as it came, in a cloud of dust. "Caught me by surprise there, boss."

"Yeah. Well, I'm not gonna broadcast this one too loud. Word's going to get out anyway. I want to get Richard settled in..."

"You mean Rita, don't you?"

"For now, it's Richard. I don't care what you guys call her later. To begin with, I want to get her focused on the disease and cutting problems. Then we've got some tee boxes to redo. Nine, Thirteen, Fifteen and everybody's favorite, Six."

"And the second hire wouldn't be Reggie Rudd, would it?"

"The hot rod queen. I wish. No, it's Roy, Rita's brother. He's in the turf program at Carbondale, too, so he knows northern sod."

"You didn't tell the boys everything about Rita, did you?"

"The boys didn't want to know everything about Rita, just the size of her engines and how fast she went."

"What's a southern girl doing in Illinois?"

"Her dad's an associate turf professor at North Carolina State University. With all her summer experience, he wanted her to go to school up north to learn about a different belt. Bring more job offers."

"Why Spring Willows?"

"She needs those last three hours, just like me."

"Mr. O's gonna blow a gasket."

"She's a charmer."

"He's an asshole."

"Looper, there have been major chemical advances in the last two years. He's got to change. When she gets done with him he won't care what gender she is. She may not save the world, but she'll help save this course. Then Billy Sauers will have his crown jewel."

It was almost five and I was tired.

"Here's the deal. I told Rita she's gotta act like a guy for the first ten days or so."

"Oh, brother."

"Won't be that hard with a maintenance uniform, a hat and no makeup. Plus, she's got a deep voice. The first few days I've got her doing soil samples which we have to have for the USGA. Dominic and the krauts can cut. I've told her to come in early and take lunch at 11 so she'll miss most of the activities. She can use the washroom when everyone's out."

"Where's she staying?"

"Same place I am, with my aunt. No big deal. Just play along. If we can get by a few days with Mr. O we'll be all right."

CHAPTER FOUR

Jerome did a terrific job keeping 'Richard' on the fringes. He had her in at 5:30 and leaving at 3. In between she wore a loose uniform and a faded army cap. She kept her hands grubby, face muddy and mouth shut. And when she did cut rough, she did so with none of the fast driving flourish I was expecting.

It was now mid-June and the Midwest was experiencing one of those abnormally hot and wet periods that breed disease and bring standing water. I'd come to the shed for a scythe when Jerome called me aside. "Meet Richard," he said.

I smiled. "You're good," I said. "I'm convinced."

"Another week maybe," said Jerome. "Mr. Olson's back tomorrow. If we can make it to next Thursday we ought to be golden. Looper, come on to the house tonight, my aunt's fixing supper. About six."

Turning to Richard, he said, "What you got, Doc?"

"Soil sample results. The good news is you've got no webworms, army worms, cutworms, billbugs or fire ants."

"Fire ants," he hollered. "Jesus, I hope not. Not in Illinois."

"I only mention it because they're starting to get them in Hope Valley. You've got some overly sandy spots on Five and Twelve and a strip of hardpan on Two you ought to seed."

"Anything else, professor?"

"You could fix the penal greens, pot bunkers and grassy hollows, if you've got a mind."

"What about the free-standing water?"

"Getting better on Six. Worse on Four because of a clogged drain on the left side before the swale. On Sixteen you can drain it to the pond or put down more dirt. You need a fan by Eight green, and we need to keep spraying the nutsedge. Finally, we could use less rain. Any more and Pythium will be a problem. That's about it, medically. Aesthetically, we could do a little more window dressing."

"Slow down, fireball. The fan on Eight is coming."

"Look, you asked. And as a player, if you don't straighten out the tee box on Six, the USGA will tan your hide."

"Looper, you and Rita start resculpting Six tomorrow. Take a mower and cut provisional tee boxes up the chute 40 yards. That hole will have to play short for a while."

"I'll tell you something else, Jerome. I don't know for sure since I haven't played yet, but I'd bet the yardage on this course is off. Reading the card, it looks short. From 150 in it looks about right, but off the tee, I'm skeptical. Might want that remeasured before August in case you have to reprint cards or redo signs."

"I'm sure she's right about the yardage discrepancy, Jerome."

"What did I tell you, Looper? A woman's touch."

"Richard, it's been a pleasure. I'm going to terminate some spores. See you tonight."

* * *

Later that evening it became apparent that Spring Willows was in good hands. The two turf managers had the agronomy down cold and Roy appeared to be a mechanic of Promethean proportions. "What do you think of the crew?" I asked Roy.

"Nothin' special," he said. "All crews are basically the same. You got blacks, foreigners, freaks and greasers. But that Kaptain is a piece of work. I don't believe I'd let him near anything motorized. I saw him damn near tip a cart over the other day."

"May want to ground that boy, Jerome," I said.

"Damn," said Jerome pensively, "he's not even supposed to be on machines." Pausing, he changed the subject. "Rita, with the boss back tomorrow, I think you need to work on Six tee in the morning and then work those traps on Five in the afternoon. That'll put you in the middle of the course all day and away from the roads. Mr. Olson doesn't like to stray off the asphalt a lot. Besides, some man's work will help perpetuate the illusion."

"It's a man's world isn't it, Aunt Molly?"

"That's true," said the chipper dowager, "but do you ever notice how they come sniffing around when they're really in need?"

"I'll be glad when I can quit binding my chest and let my hair down, I know that," Rita said.

"Looks pretty good right now," I said staring at the shoulder length auburn locks and generous breasts. "Look at it this way, you'll be one of the few people who gets a second chance to make a first impression."

"I just want to make the right impression. I have to graduate, too."

* * *

The Big O returned to men (and woman) hard at work. The poison and the visit with his cousin were long forgotten, but he was still steaming about the lost championship. "Those assholes don't know how to set up a course. I've never seen such slick greens and punishing rough. And the slope rating was off the chart. I don't know how that clown from Kansas won." On and on he went.

He did stop long enough to tour the course and talk to Roy who was cutting rough. "You Richard?" he began, overtaking Roy on the tractor.

"No sir."

"Be careful of that mower, son. Toros are tough, but that doesn't mean you can bronc ride 'em."

"Yes sir, I'm going gentle, cutting to within five feet of the tree line like I was taught."

"Well, that's fine for this hole, but over there on Seven, Eleven, Twelve and Thirteen, where there's a bit of road, give it 15 feet of rough so as to spare the automotive public."

"Yes sir, I'll do that, sir." The bowing and scraping went on a while longer, with Roy obsequious enough to pass the test.

* * *

The following day the super got a phone call from Billy Sauers. "Just calling to see how you're doing. Stomach all better, well rested, glad to be back? Hear you should have won the tournament. Some people just don't know how to set up a course."

"You can say that again." Mr. Olson was oblivious to the putdown. "These guys ought to take lessons from us. Some guy from Kansas won. I can't believe that. I shot a 75 on the last day and still..."

"Otto, I want to tell you the course is coming around. Jerome looks like he's got the hang of it. And his two hires, Roy and Richard, they're doing the little things that will make a difference in August. My only reservation is with that guy you hired, Kaptain. He appears a bit spacey to me. Might want to keep an eye on him."

A little gospel helps everyone and that piece of inspired verse from Billy Sauers gave us the breathing room we needed... until week two.

CHAPTER FIVE

"Jerome," said Mr. Olson, "I'm hearing good things about the staff, especially Roy and Richard. Starza tells me the members appreciate how good the rough looks and how firm the greens are holding."

"We're trying, sir. I wish the tee box on Six would green in faster before those women get here in August."

With Mr. O pauses only lasted so long.

"What do you mean women? I thought we were having an exhibition in August? Mano a mano?"

"No sir. All-American girls versus Swedes."

"Men against women?"

"No sir, this is an all-female occasion. You didn't know that? I guess life is just full of little surprises," he said.

"Sure is," Mr. O said, grinding his teeth.

The crew was washing up for the day. Mr. O stepped out of his office and addressed the group. "Do you guys know what's scary about this August exhibition? Did you know about this?" He sounded like James Cagney. "Did you know that we're doing all this fucking work for a bunch of women? We're bustin' our balls for a bunch of women?" That wasn't exactly true. "Mother of Jesus, what's this world coming to?"

Walking over to the round sink he grabbed a container of soap. "Lemon GOJO hand cleaner. Lemon GOJO hand cleaner?" Now he sounded like Ralph Kramden. "What is this? Where's the Stoko Mat 2000 or the Kresto hand cleaner for stubborn dirt?"

"I've got it here," said the Kaptain.

"Are you guys pussies or something? Lemon GOJO is hand lotion for women."

The next scene will remain with me for all time. I heard the scraping of an iron stool, the slam of a locker and the soft footfall of work boots. Richard grabbed the GOJO from Mr. O. "It sure is, handsome, and you can't have it." With that she took off the cap and shook her tresses. "And when those women get here in August, we're going to make them feel welcome. I'm just the advance guard. Get used to it."

"Wee doggie," came a piercing cry.

"Son of a bitch, don't that beat all?"

"God DAMN!"

"Are you shittin' me?"

"I don't believe what I'm seein'."

"Well, strike me blind."

"SHAZAM," were just some of the exclamations that accompanied the unveiling of Richard.

"How'd she get in here?" hollered Mr. O.

"She works here," yelled Dominic.

"Your name's not Richard," he said, staring at the uniform.

"Yes sir. Rita 'Richard' Randleman."

"Who hired this wench?" blurted Mr. O.

"I did, with your permission, sir," said Jerome. "We needed help and you gave me the authority to hire…"

"Not a woman, I didn't."

"I took the best available applicant." Jerome turned to the staff. "Anybody got any complaints about Richard?"

"Wish I'd known earlier," said the Kaptain.

"Drives a tractor better than Rossi," said Wolfgang.

"Works longer hours than the rest of us, except Jerome," said Lackey.

"Let her stay, Otto," said a new voice. It was Binswanger from the Big House. In three years I'd never seen him at the shed. "She filled out the USGA forms. Far Hills likes the answers."

"Jesus Christ, you really know how to hurt a guy. In my thirty-five years on the crew I never saw a woman."

"That's your problem, Otto," said Binswanger.

"We had two of 'em at Hope Valley," said Roy.

"Jesus, this is a shock."

"Clean up and go home," Binswanger said to the boys. "You've had enough excitement for one day." To Mr. O he added, "I want to go over these Moline expenses with you. I've got a few questions."

I knew that meeting would last until I could run for cover. I stripped off my uniform, washed my hands with the GOJO and headed for the door, stopping only to give Richard a high five.

"That was slick," I said.

CHAPTER SIX

Annual employee day at Spring Willows was always held on the second Monday in July. The staff was given run of the premises for the afternoon and was served a classy buffet. The food was always first rate. Sometimes I think Chef Raoul cared more about his fellow workers than the members. The fromage and assorted desserts were always primo.

Truth be told, Mr. O cared less about potatoes and crepes than the golf tourney. Sixteen players had signed up, including five of us from the maintenance shed: Mr. O, Jerome, Rita, Roy and me. Since the pros weren't allowed to play, the super considered only Al, the caddie master, a threat. He'd taken Mr. O to the wire several times, but it had been twenty years since Mr. O had lost this event and that was at a time when the club pros were eligible.

Al always did the pairings and since relations were still a bit strained at the maintenance shed, he did it in twosomes, pairing Mr. O with Alfredo, the athletic maître de, Jerome with Rita and me with him. At the halfway mark, Mr. O was leading with Jerome and Chuck, a big blond kid from the Pro Shop, one back. Al and I were three over and Rita was four over. Roy was plus eight thanks to trap problems. Al looked at the scores as we grabbed ice teas from Brewster's Halfway House atop Killer Ten.

"Better slow down there, cowboy," said Al to Jerome. "I'm not sure you want to win this thing. It can't be as important to you as to Ape Man down there."

"It's not, but I just want to make a point. It's stroke play. I'll find a way to lose it. You might tell Chuck to slow down, though."

"The Big O can't hurt Chuck, beyond suggesting to Starza that he pick up range balls for the next year. Besides, he's playing out of his gourd."

"Rita, you've got a smooth stroke there, lady," said Al.

"Thanks. I just try to feel the club head and follow through. Nothing magic."

"Except for the chip in on Eight from out of the nutsedge," said Jerome.

"It's going away," scowled Rita.

"She's been spending so much time over there, I think Mr. Howard thinks she's his personal gardener."

"I've fixed the problem, right? So, lay off."

"You guys getting on any better with Mr. O these days?" inquired Al.

"He doesn't talk to me," said Rita.

"He's still pissed at me," said Jerome, "but the members have been real supportive. The course looks pretty good, so we're not being hassled quite as much. If we survive the exhibition, we'll be fine. Meanwhile we can just take out our frustrations on this dimpled thing."

With that, Jerome teed up his Titleist to have a go at the 163-yard par 3. Some members referred to its bunkers as the White Cliffs of Dover traps.

"Imposing escarpments of quartzite that punish poor souls who aren't dead on or don't opt for a safer play," is what Judge Gleason calls them. Ideally, the place to be is below the pin so you can lag toward the hole. Jerome popped his ball to the lower tier to within six feet. Rita chose the safer play which Mrs. Peck always liked. She shot to a small grassy knoll just over the pond and to the right where she could bump and run close to the flag. Rita's short wedge stopped five inches from the hole.

"This stuff gets old," Jerome yelled to us back on the tee. "Can you imagine living with a competent woman like this?" Mr. O is afraid she might show him up, I thought. When Jerome holed his putt, he and Mr. O were all even.

Al and I traded stroke for stroke, enjoying the round and the company, sometimes even playing two balls, experimenting with fades and draws. On the 187-yard par-3 thirteenth Al grabbed his 4-iron. "Relatively flat green, right? Watch how I take this sucker back to the flag." With that he sent his ball ten feet past the flag where it bit like a tiger and then clawed back to within three feet.

"Looks good to me," I said, settling for a shot from the fringe. "At least I know I can count on my chipping. I'm not sure you can make that shot every time."

Much later, on the patio of the clubhouse, Mr. O held court, explaining how he won the day. Seems like he went birdie, par, par to nip Jerome by two shots and to retain his title for the twenty-first consecutive year. "I was never worried," he told Starza. "I knew your blond boy wouldn't hold up and the pressurc just got to Junior over there."

"I folded under pressure, Mr. Olson," said Jerome through a mouthful of crab dip.

Back on the putting green Rita told me how Mr. O really won it. "The cart girl came to us on Seventeen and said Mr. O was only one over. Well, Jerome was one under at that point. He then took his 7-iron and calling three 'practice' shots put them three feet right, three feet short, three feet long. All just where he said he would."

"This next shot is for real," he announced and skyed it into the drink. "That should do it," he said, playing the hole in double-bogey 5. On Eighteen, Jerome flubbed a simple pitch on purpose just in case Mr. O was watching and took a bogey. Nothing to it.

Back at the feeding trough Mighty Joe Young was foraging like the big chimp he was. Plate beyond the brim, he was in an expansive mood, basking in his tainted victory and enjoying his fifth vodka tonic. "Damn, these are good, Ralph," he said to the bartender. "We ought to do this every day."

"Couldn't afford it," said Mr. Binswanger. "You'd eat us out of house and home."

"Then I'd die a happy man," he said, belching toward the first green.

The last vestiges of light were just touching the terrace. The cleanup crew had removed the buffet and Mr. O was sucking down his last toddy. Only a few of us were left when he broke from his trance and yelled down the patio. "Rita, come here a minute."

Jerome and Rita turned. "Just Rita." With that Rita ambled over. "Sit down, sweetheart. I've never had a woman work for me and I never will," he let that sink in. "But I've been thinking. You got a degree in landscape design and horticulture, right?"

Rita nodded. "Minor in silviculture too, tree management."

"I know what silviculture is. Today I was noticing that we're foliage deficient in a decorative way in a couple of spots out here. Like on Eleven, Twelve and Thirteen where that damn road borders the course. Once we had beautiful elms all along those fairways until the Dutch disease got them. Next time we plant, we need a balanced population of something. No weed trees like poplars or hackberries, though. We could also do something on Eight and Nine. There's nothing distinctive to set off that stretch back to the clubhouse. We'll need some window dressing for the exhibition. Maybe you can give it that woman's touch you were talking about. Get Lackey to help you. He thinks I think he's just a dumb nigger, but he likes that stuff. You get his opinion."

You could have heard a butterfly talk. It was that quiet. Nobody said a word. Instead the first fireflies flickered, hanging in the stillness. "Rita, one other thing. Don't fuck up."

"Yes sir."

"See you at the shed," said the boss man. That was it. No more, no less, no goodbye, no good luck. Just "see you at the shed." He went back to the great beyond or Borneo, wherever he was that night.

* * *

Tuesday morning at six sharp Jerome stopped Lackey. "When you come back from trash and ballwash duty meet with Rita at the Nursery."

"Not me, boss, I ain't getting alone with no white woman."

"She's one of the boys. Mr. Olson said so and he wants you to meet her over at the nursery to talk about shrubs. So, change those towels, add soap and water and meet Rita at 8."

"Yes sir."

Two hours later Rita met Lackey with a Club Car.

"I understand you know about plants," she said.

"Yes sir. Who told you that?"

"Mr. Olson."

"Hmm, I thought he thought I was a dumb nigger."

"He said you know about plants. He thinks we need to get more color-ful and he told me to talk to you. Let's ride the course and talk about it. What do you think about the foliage on this course?"

"Not bad," said Lackey in a slow drawl, "but it needs help on Eight, Nine, the road holes, and the pond on Sixteen. Other than that, it's a right nice course, plant-wise."

"Right nice. You from the South, Lackey?"

"Pascagoula, Mississippi, by the Gulf, ma'am."

"Mr. Olson's thinking short term here."

"Nothin' new there. He's always thinkin' short term."

"For this exhibition I think he wants a quick fix, add some breaks, screens and color."

"I wouldn't turn the first shovel without talking to the pro and the green committee," he said. "Get yourself a little plan, get a stamp on it. Then we can make somethin' happen."

They reached Eleven and gazed from the raised tee at the generous greensward. One hundred seventy yards from the tee the perpendicular creek crossed over. To the right was a long line of trees that buffered the fifteenth green and eleventh fairway. To the left was an unsightly cinder and macadam road crying for help. Paralleling the fairway and looping right around the green, it continued another 500 yards along Twelve.

"What do you think?" asked Rita.

"Ugly," said Lackey. "This hole hurts my eyes and ears."

"Where's the visual excitement to this hole?" asked Rita.

"Motion, it needs motion. People overlook that. Different ornamental grasses can give you a different look. It's a visual thing. And Miss Rita, motion produces sound. Think about that. Would you rather have the look and sound of *Miscanthus sinesis* over there or the look and sound of Mr. Wankum's Jaguar? Personally, I'd rather have the flowers or the *Miscanthus* than the car... and I bet those Swedish ladies would too."

"*Miscanthus sinesis*? Are we talking about Japanese Silver Grass?"

"I don't know what you're talking about, but I'm talking *Miscanthus sinesis*. Likes moist soil and sun. See," he said, pointing into the distance. "It'd be perfect in the low area by the road. And the flowers from late August to frost would be a sight for sore eyes."

"Do you know Latin, Lackey?"

"No ma'am. But some *Panicum verigatum* would be a good screen and some *Ilex verticullata* would be real nice for winter. Long term the answer is *Liguster* behind the green and trees along the road, but we ain't got time for that."

"You sure you don't know Latin?"

"Miss Rita, I know specimens, clumps and screens. Though I don't see so good, feel so well or move so fast, I know color, texture and motion. The boss man, he don't think my mind or my ass is too swift."

"But you do know Latin and plants?" Rita persisted.

"When I first came north, I worked in a nursery. I got to know all them plants."

"Does Mr. Olson know that about you?"

"Mr. Olson don't know nothing' about me, Miss Rita. But I do know I been wet nursin' his flowers all by myself for a long time."

"How does a hole hurt your ears?" she asked, motioning to the void by the road.

"Trees absorb noise, right? If we had trees on Eleven we wouldn't have to hear the cars from the road like we do now."

Rita always referred to that tour around the course as "As the World Turns." She reported back to Mr. O that even though time was short, visual enhancements could be made by August -- by the truckload if necessary. She also affirmed her faith in Lackey. With Buddy ready to return, Mr. O relieved Rita of most of her cutting duties to concentrate on aesthetics, reserving final approval for himself and the green committee.

The ultimate solution to the unsightly road on Eleven was a costly combination of berm and trees. Neither came without a fight. The trees went in before the Swedes arrived and were an immense improvement by themselves. Most of the dozer work for the mounds started immediately and, of course, members bitched about hitting hooks from dirt piles. Washed sod smoothed over the biggest objections. By mid-September, after the exhibition, when the red maples began strutting their crimson autumn colors the holes looked damn near magnificent. Even the old farts wondered why "we" hadn't done it before. Mrs. Worth, one of the few respected female golfers, told Alvin Bullock that what the course had been lacking for years was a "woman's touch." And if the menfolk had been more "sensitive" they'd have probably not only had a nicer course but a more satisfying time at home. Not that that would have helped Mr. Cabiness, but Billy Sauers got the message. At the annual meeting in December, Mrs. Worth became the first woman ever to be elected to the Spring Willows green committee.

Lackey Leeds got his way too when Rita recommended that *Miscanthus sinesis* and *Panicum verigatum* be planted on the right side of the twelfth fairway as a secondary screen to the nursery. The texture and motion of the grass created such a soothing effect that the female players insisted that these same grasses border the road by the seventh tee.

How we got the trees was a master stroke by Rita. She convinced Mr. O that he needed a visual reference point behind the eleventh green. As it was, the hole just faded into the road and a chain-link fence held that back bulging bushes and privet hedges. For a course as nice as ours, one that catered to the well-to-do, Eleven and Twelve were industrial armpits. "Mr. Olson, at the very least you need a tree back there, preferably one that changes colors. You're going to have a beautiful left side when those maples take hold. Why don't you add some complementary maples on the right or at least a black gum tree or two? That way you'll have a colorful backdrop for summer and fall. The golfers will love you for it," she said.

"What we need," said Mr. O, one week later to the head of the green committee, "is a visual reference point behind the green there. I'd recommend some red maples and maybe some offsetting black gum trees so we get some color for summer, too. We also ought to line the left of Eleven with new trees to take full advantage of their heliotropic effect."

"Hell, Otto," said Billy Sauers, "you don't even know what heliotropic is. But I like the idea and I like the quality of thinking coming out of your shop. Give my compliments to the staff back there. And start planting."

* * *

I was leaving one Friday afternoon when Mr. O and Jerome were reviewing the calculations. "You mean we need 337 tons of sand for fairway traps and 187 for greenside," Mr. O said incredulously. As courses go, Spring Willows was not overly bunkered. Oakmont has what, 209? We had essentially four per hole.

"Yes, the total comes to about 524 tons of sand. Think of it this way," Jerome said, shoving the calculations in front of Mr. O, "one million forty-eight thousand pounds of beach. That's a lot of bogey dust."

"No shit, Sherlock. Need it within the week too, if we want to get it spread and settled before the Swedes come. Well, we got a supplier, I'll get on the horn and leave an order."

I've already indicated that Mr. O's communication skills weren't the best. Most supers would have phoned an order and then driven up to the clubhouse and had the confirming paperwork mailed out that day. Despite protestations to the contrary, I don't think that was done. I think the only numbers put to paper were the penciled figures Jerome handed Mr. O. Which wouldn't have been so bad had Mr. O or Jerome been the only ones in on the ordering process.

However, as fate would have it, there was an intermediary – the unpredictable Kaptain. By now the Kaptain had been involved in so many minor accidents and screwups that in his best management style, Mr. O began to shield the crew and the members from this loose cannon. The cart turnover and the chainsaw incidents had made the rounds and Mr. O was afraid to put the Kaptain near any motorized equipment. In fact, Mr. O had purposely assigned him to the more mundane and manual art of raking traps, pulling edges and picking up sticks.

Problem was, Mr. O could not fire Kaptain, who was a distant relative of Alvin Bullock. As a joke and to make the work more palatable, Mr. O referred to Kaptain as Trap Manager, a sobriquet the Kaptain willingly accepted. That piece of folderol backfired big time when Kaptain answered the phone on Tuesday.

"Hello, I'm calling from the Best Sand Corporation about the new sand order. Is this Spring Willows?" said the caller.

"Yo."

"I'm calling to confirm an order for 524 tons of angular sand. Is that right?"

"Can't tell you that right off," said the Kaptain.

"Well, is Otto Olson or the assistant there?"

"Not right now. Nobody here."

"Well how about the person in charge of traps? Is he there?"

"You're talking to the trap manager now."

"Does that number sound right to you? Is there any paperwork there you can check?"

"Let me look," said the Kaptain. And let me tell you, he found some paperwork, the blue sheet with Mr. O's hen scratchings, headed "Trap Requirements." "I got it. I see a lot of numbers here. There is a 524, but I think the number you need is 1,048,000."

"He wants a million tons of sand?"

"I don't know about that, but I do know they are redoing a lot of traps on account of the Swedes and all. And it has to be the number because it's the one that's circled in red."

"One million forty-eight thousand tons, you sure that's right?"

"It's got to be, it's the one that's circled."

"Okay, have Otto call me back if that's not right or if he doesn't want it all at once. Otherwise we'll deliver it Friday to the barn."

"Yeah," said the Kaptain. "That's a good idea, then he can tell you where to put it."

I was just coming down from the Big House on Friday when the thirteenth dump truck rolled in. Mr. O was livid. They weren't the ordinary dump trucks you see when a foundation is being dug for a house. They were the huge hauler variety. Only once have I seen so much sand and that was in a *National Geographic* special on the Sahara.

"Where am I going to put this stuff?" he asked the lead driver.

"Hell, I don't know, you ordered it. But you better decide quick because there are thirteen more just like these on the way."

"There can't be."

"Trust me, man. Thirteen more. I seen the paperwork."

"How many cubic yards in one of these trucks?"

"Like sixteen to seventeen. You should be able to do about four traps per truck. I just know it's a lot of sand."

"Too much sand. You got to be shitting me. I didn't order this much all at once."

"The paperwork says you did. Norris says he got the order from you last Friday and he confirmed it this week."

"Not with me, he didn't."

"With someone here. Your trap manager."

"I'm the trap manager and Norris didn't talk to me this week."

"Well hoss, he talked to someone who said he was the trap manager. If that's not you then you got an imposter here."

"Looper, did you talk to Best this week?"

"Not me, Mr. O. You might try Jerome or…"

"Jerome wouldn't fuck up like this, it has to be some other nitwit... Oh, Jesus," said Mr. O, "He talked to friggin' Kaptain. Oh God, I can't use this much sand all at once." Turning to Wolfgang he said, "Go find Kaptain and bring him here." Turning to the lead driver he said, "You, you stay here. I'm calling Norris."

Ten minutes later Mr. O was back. He had his sand calculations with him. "Tell the last eight trucks to turn around. I don't want them today. I'll show the rest of you guys where to dump this stuff. Looper, direct those last three trucks to Three, Five, Six and Seventeen. Rossi, when the trap manager gets back, drive his ass over to me on Fifteen. Kaptain Quartzite has got some explaining to do. And raking. In fact, that boy's gonna rake so many traps, he'll do it in his sleep."

"Bedtime for Bonzo," said Buddy.

"More like bye bye blackbird," said Rita.

We never learned for sure what happened over on Fifteen, but from a distance it was plain that the spit was hitting the sand. Occasionally we could hear Mr. O's voice above the haulers and most of the time Kaptain was staring at his shoes.

We could tell that the boss was reaming him a new one. What we didn't know was that he was conferring upon his victim enhanced responsibilities. "Kaptain, my man, I want to teach you some of the finer points of bunker maintenance," he began. "From now on you are my sand man. If anything needs to be done manually in the traps you are to do it. You got me?"

"Yessir, Mr. O."

"First off, has anyone ever told you the difference between a fairway and a greenside trap? Fairway traps are solely for direction. They tell the golfers where to go. Just like I tell you where to go," said Mr. O. "Course designers could care less if balls go in them. They are there as a guidepost. 'Go right.' Stuff like that. But man being man, he goes in traps more often than around them. And man is mortal, sort of like you. Unlike you, most men don't rake traps. In fact, that's what you're here for. I've heard players say, 'Let maintenance do it.' Those are the same guys who on the next hole put it in the bunker and bitch about the unraked traps. Now, you, as my main trap man, are going to appease these SOBs. From now on if there's a trap to rake, I want you to do it, whether it's on Four or Fourteen, your job is to see those traps are groomed manually. Get me?"

"You want me to manage traps."

"Not so much manage traps," said Mr. O, going back on an earlier promise, "as rake traps. I think you need to work your way up again."

"That's cool. When do I start?" said the Kaptain, handing Mr. O his next line.

"How about now," he said, "here in the Empty Quarter."

CHAPTER SEVEN

If Mr. O thought he had trouble communicating with the Kaptain, it was nothing like the bad blood that was building between the shed and the Pro Shop. "I thought you guys resolved that shortwave hassle while I was gone?" said Mr. O.

"We had," said Rossi, "but now those jerks are at it again. All of it is unnecessary B.S."

"I agree," said Earle, one of the college hires. "I don't need some assistant pro using the airwaves to tell Divot that Cindy Cabiness looks hot today. For one, she always looks hot. And two, Divot already knows."

"We need vacant frequencies for uninterrupted communication with each other," said Buddy, now back on the job and relegated to the role of a mechanic.

"Yeah, so, like, I can tell you when a trap is done," raved the Kaptain.

"Not quite, Kaptain," said Mr. O.

"What's with those guys anyway?"

Jerome laid out the answer for me a few days later while riding to Nine. "The problem is professional jealousy," he said. "Take my word for it. It occurs at every club in the country, public or private. And it's got to do with changing roles. For a long time, we were just farmers to them. Then we went from greenskeepers to superintendents and were college educated. We also manage the high end of the budget. And when people say the golf course looks great, the pros aren't getting any credit for it. And the topper is when they see us leave at nine on Saturday morning while they have to be around til sundown. They forget that we're here Mondays and the rest of the week at 5:30 a.m. when they're in bed.

"They're an insecure lot, too. I don't know for sure what their deal is, but they think someone is always out to get them. Most golf professionals are micro managers. For instance, they can manage to build a rack to put socks on, but they don't have the stock ordered until the racks are built.

"Or they got a tournament and everyone is teeing off in fifteen minutes and no one's registering guests. Superintendents have to do it all. Golf pros in general just stand around and wave their arms. They just manage themselves poorly and everything else.

"If they had our jobs, they'd been unemployed -- fast," Jerome continued. "For us, everything is planned -- and it's all subject to change. If a cloud blows in and it starts raining, we have to come up with a whole new scheme. The only new scheme the pros have is how to get their buddies on the back nine, especially on public courses." He was really rolling now.

"'Just nine holes that's all,' they say. I tell them they can't play the back nine because they'll get caught by the regular golfers. But they don't care," said Jerome. "They don't care about anything but themselves."

I thought Jerome was being unfair, at least to our Pro Shop guys. I didn't recall Starza or Divot causing all that much trouble. He read my mind. "It's not those guys so much as the other assistant Liggett and the bag room boys. Those bag boys end up cleaning clubs, parking carts and ride the range picking up balls. It's when they go out of the shop that the radio trouble starts. 'Sergeant Slicer to Big Bogey' and all that. 'Hey, Mordecai, you ought to see old man Flowers flailing away with his 5-wood. He can't drive his car much less a Titleist. God damn, they're aiming at me.'

"Stuff like that. And sometimes even the pros are a conduit for members' comments. Especially if they don't like how the rough is cut or how we water. They all complain the rough is taller on the left side on the front nine and taller on the right on the back nine. How many times have I heard,

'Why can't you guys get it straight?' It's a lines-and-shadows thing. The way the course is laid out, the sun falls more on the left on the front and more on the right on the back. And where will grass grow?"

"Where the sun hits it, I guess," I said.

"Where the sun hits it. How hard a concept is that? They'll really have a time when the Swedes come because the USGA has demanded that we have two cuts of rough for those matches. That means we'll be a little longer than normal in the second cut. And we'll have to go a second week without cutting the rough at all. Remember, when the bitching starts, you heard it here first."

"OK, got it."

"The watering the pros just don't understand. We have set limits for fairways, tees, greens, aprons, hills, low lying areas. It takes three minutes for a head to make a revolution. Each fairway and rough gets three to four revolutions. Then there are syringes, short runs where we don't run full cycle. And if you ask them what innies and outies are, you'll just get some obscene answer when all we are really talking about are fine tuning irrigation techniques."

We'd been sitting at Nine for five minutes. Jerome turned off the motor. "Ask me about green heights and cup placements some time. I could go on for a week about them. Oh shit," he said. "Look at this. Some bozo ran over the sprinkler head in a cart. Those things aren't supposed to be within 30 feet of the green. We ought to require a driver's test."

"They ought to be outlawed," I said. "Whatever happened to caddies, the time-tested seeing-eye dog for golfers? Carts can't read greens. Carts can't forecaddie. Carts can't clean clubs. All they can do is carry bags."

"And make money," Jerome chimed in. "Carts make money. And at most clubs, the pro gets a piece of the action. As long as there is money to be made, there are going to be carts. Look, you caddy. I caddied. We both know that carts diminish the total playing experience. Camaraderie, exercise and communing with nature are totally different with a cart. Yes, they ought to be banned, except, maybe, for the physically impaired or in real hot weather."

Mrs. Peck might be alive today if they'd allowed carts in last year's D-flight finals, I thought.

"Look at this. Bent all to hell," he said, looking at the mangled head. "Ought to make them fix it themselves."

* * *

As July rushed toward August, the course was coming along pretty well. The hot weather gave some foliage a wilted look, but morning and evening water helped most flora withstand the heat. The heat from the Pro Shop, however, was incessant, a dissonance with which we were familiar. But as we looked around, our house appeared to be in order.

Apparently, Far Hills wasn't so sure. Or maybe, I should say, wanted to make sure. I was just pulling out a John Deere when Mr. Binswanger cruised up in his late model Chrysler. "Looper, tell Mr. O and his college sidekick that he's got a four o'clock with Mr. Sauers at the House."

"But that's after hours."

"Sauers said four. It's important. It's got something to do with the Swedish girls."

Mr. O's reaction was predictable. "Look, I'm here nine hours a day. He can meet with me at six a.m. I'm up. I'm on the job."

"Market's still open til 3:30," I offered.

"That's not what I said, dummy. I'm here at six. That guy can meet me at six. One of these days I'm going to tell him to go poke himself."

As it turned out, Billy Sauers apologized to Mr. O for the lateness of the hour. "Gentlemen, I apologize for this late meeting. I'd have preferred to do this at six this morning, but the USGA called my office at eleven. I had just received a checklist and they wanted to make sure I covered these course maintenance items. There are a lot of hospitality functions as well, but those are Binswanger's problem. Here's your list. You need to review this tonight and give me a status report by tomorrow noon. What's not ready requires a status and timetable for completion."

"This reads like the 95 theses, Mr. Sauers," said Jerome.

"Well put, young man. I think that before this is over it will be a religious experience for us all. Good day."

"Jerome," said Mr. O, handing off the papers, "I'll be in the office tomorrow at six if you have any questions about any of these."

CHAPTER EIGHT

Mr. O stuck his freshly-shaven face through the office door. "Any questions, Jerome? I always like to give the staff a little homework now and then," he said.

"I've never minded long hours," Jerome said wearily, "but I think you ought to see what it is the USGA expects. There's a lot here and you'll want to communicate it to the whole group."

"I can handle it, college boy," said Mr. O, more uppity than he'd been for a while. "That's why we got underlings around here. People to carry out the shit that I give. Comprende?"

"Oh, I get your drift, sir. All I'm saying is that it isn't a one-man job. The guy who thinks it is, is in for a big surprise."

"OK, OK. Let me get a cup of java and I'll see what these birdbrains want." Mr. O plugged in his coil heater, boiled a cup of water, dumped some decaf in his 20-ounce GCSAA mug and pulled up a chair. "See, I'm even taking the doctor's advice these days. Decaf for Mr. O."

"That's the only way you've mellowed."

"So, what's the big deal with these USGA forms?"

"It's not the forms themselves that are so hard," said Jerome. "It's the compliance. They've got a 64-page handbook and a 110-item checklist requiring our attention. See here on the left there's a heading like this one: 'Fairways.' Then reading across it says, 'Present condition,' then 'Date,' then 'Condition one week out,' then another 'Date,' and finally 'Responsibility.'"

"That's all? What's the big deal about a checklist? We got a month to get ready and to check this stuff off. No sweat."

"It's not that simple. This checklist needs to go out today via Special Delivery. In Far Hills it will be reviewed. If you read all the documentation the way I have, and I think you should, you'll see that there is much to be done. And the scary part is that there are subtle checkpoints along the way. I talked to a friend of mine at Hope Valley and he says that the USGA makes personal inspections three weeks out and sends a mystery golfer to see if the course is ready. If it's not, they pull the event and give it to Baltusrol close by where they know things are done right. Mr. O, this report is important, and we got lots of work to do. Look at the checklist."

"Hope Valley is minor leagues, and your buddy don't know squat about northern courses or the USGA, so I ain't listening."

"With all due respect, Mr. O, my friend is now the superintendent at Hope Valley, and what is relevant is that he was at Oakmont when they had the U.S. Open there. He's probably more current than we are."

Deaf ears. Mr. O slugged another jaw full of decaf. "Look at this crap." The list was impressive. Comprehensive.

In addition to generalities about the venue, the "Preparing the Course" section asked for specifics about fairways, rough, greens, bunkers, water hazards, arboreal impediments, tee boxes, irrigation, disease and all associated minutia.

The hole-by-hole checklist went on and on.

"As you can see, I've filled in most of the technical stuff. What I didn't know I pulled from the blueprints," said Jerome. "And where dimensions have been altered over the years, I've made adjustments. You need to check them all though since you've been here longer than I have."

"That's for sure."

"Three weeks before the event, they want the course set up exactly like it will be for the exhibition. Pull out all the stops. Full window dressing. Everything up to snuff. My buddy said the three-week checkpoint is really important."

"When they get here I'll take them around in a Club Car and motion to 'em where things are going. They'll get the idea."

"What they'll get," said Jerome, asserting himself, "is the idea that you don't care much. And if they get that idea then this exhibition is gone and maybe some of the staff with it. Remember what Mr. Sauers said?"

Mr. O turned red. "Where'd you hear that, college boy? I thought that was between me and Sauers?"

"Rumors," recovered Jerome. "I hear things sometimes."

"You hear too much if you ask me," said Mr. O. "Let me get another cup and let's get this paperwork out of here."

For the next four hours the two slaved over the forms, searching for long-lost and misplaced records, reconstructing events and being as generally truthful as memory served. It was probably the hardest Mr. O had worked in months. Clearly paperwork was not his strength, and it was all he could do to sit still and provide Jerome with the needed information. After the third call to the Big House, Binswanger admonished Mr. O to keep better records. "I didn't need that," said the ape. "Shit, he'll probably tell Sauers. Keep working, I'm going to check the nursery."

At noon Jerome filled in the final column. "Here. Sign this," he said when Mr. O came in for lunch. "I'll get Looper to run this up to the clubhouse."

The package was thick. I didn't think anybody cared about this course that much. "Send it Special Delivery so it gets to the USGA by the day after tomorrow. And tell Mr. Binswanger thanks for his help."

I nodded at Jerome and threaded my way down the asphalt road past the fairways at Twelve and Eleven. The maples and black gums were coming in well and the sod on the berm had taken hold nicely. When the maples and gums matured, Eleven would look as nice as the second hole at Merion. I gunned the cart up the hill. Except for the tractors, our equipment seemed grossly underpowered. Somehow that seemed fitting.

I handed in the package. "Thanks, errand boy. Any problems?"

"You'll have to ask the slaves that did the paperwork."

"I need to call Jerome?"

"I didn't say that."

"You don't have to. I could tell from all the calls from Mr. O and the sideways chatter who was filling this thing in. I'll tell you, Looper, it's a good thing this is a Donald Ross course because in the end that's what's going to save this exhibition. Donald Ross. The Big O can mess with the tee boxes and screw the women all he wants on Ladies' Day, but when the whip comes down this exhibition is going to happen and happen right. As God is my witness."

Somewhere I felt the presence of Billy Sauers in all this.

"When this course review happens," droned the club manager, "Billy Sauers will be here to personally guarantee to the USGA that the queen of Sweden herself could play this course and feel she got a fair shake."

"Sounds good to me," I said. "This needs to be in Far Hills the day after tomorrow."

"Teresa will take care of it. Good day, Looper."

I've always been good at timelines. As I shuttled back to the shed, it occurred to me that visit dates from the USGA and the mystery golfer had to be very soon. Sooner than we expected. Like within the next week. I didn't know if Spring Willows could react that fast.

I was right. At 8:30 the next morning as I was loading the spreader I could hear cursing from the shed. "Who do these assholes think they are? By Thursday? No way."

Out of the shed came that pygmy head. "Hey, you," he hollered. "Go round up everybody on the south and west sides of this course. Have 'em stop what they are doing. Bring 'em here now. I got new orders for the day. We're setting the course for the exhibition. Junior here's gonna get the others. Jesus, why can't guys plan any better?"

To his credit, Mr. O appeared to have done some preplanning for this effort, but he must have done it in a foul mood. He handed out diagrams and specific instructions for each hole and I didn't see what the big deal was, but I wasn't privy to the master plan. Nor, as it turned out, was anyone else. One look at his diagram for the tee box at Six would have provided a clue, but I was consigned to setting tee boxes at Seven through Ten, checking the phlox around the clubhouse and doing odd jobs like measuring rough height on the par 5s.

At quitting time, I overheard Rita tell Jerome, "I know they're going to have to reprint the scorecards. There's no way the yardage on those cards reflects the course layout. You watch. If the women's length on Four is 211, which is actually over the maximum suggested yardage for a ladies' par 3, I'll play nine in the nude, in front of Ape Man. It's 217 or more. I haven't toured the whole course since the Chinese fire drill this morning, but I'll bet there's other things wrong as well."

The phone rang as I left. As I was hauling my sorry ass from the shed I heard Jerome say "Looper, it's Al. He wants to see you."

"I'm not so clean right now."

"Doesn't matter. He says it will only take a minute. Stop by the shack. It's important."

* * *

"I'm here, Al," I said, hot and sweaty from the drill.

"Gotta look better tomorrow, Looper," said Al. "Remember Mrs. Worth wants you to caddy for her and her college roommate. She's coming in for a trial run tomorrow. I got the three of you down for 2:40. You'll be toting, not playing. And for funsies, they'll be playing the new layout you and Mr. O put together this morning."

"At best, I'm an accomplice."

"So, I hear. 2:40. Look sharp, feel sharp, be sharp."

"I'll be here. I'll tote for anyone who gets around in 25 putts."

* * *

Thursday was hot and muggy, the way it can get in Illinois in early August, but not as bad as Missouri, say a place like Tarkio, where in August the temperature is 95 degrees and the humidity is 110 percent at 7 a.m. and continues all damn day. I spent the first five hours putting flowers, geraniums and impatiens on the tee boxes. Window dressing, Mr. O said. For a guy short on frills, he spent a lot of energy that Thursday on the small stuff. "I think the Big Kahunas are coming in tomorrow," he said. "These suit-and-blazer guys will be running around here sniffing at everything. And thanks to you boys, I think we're ready. And the added bonus is that I won't have to put up with that pipsqueak Sauers."

Remember I told you that humans were the orangutans' only significant enemy? In this case the enemy was the USGA. "Is the course ready for the Swedes and the USGA?"

"Oh, yeah, it's ready, kid. They'll have a whale of a time. Slipping and sliding, slashing and thrashing. This is going to be a tough SOB."

"I hope your setup isn't too tough, Mr. O. I don't think that's what the USGA wants."

"Kid, I did the Illinois State Amateur twenty years ago and we just had a session in Moline on big tourney sets. I got this one knocked."

I wondered. Mr. O didn't strike me as a fast learner.

"I thought Billy Sauers wanted to be here when the Far Hills group showed," Jerome said.

"He did, but his biggest client called and now he's in L.A. with no other options, so it's us vs. them suits," Mr. O said.

Not good, I thought, as I eased on up the road to meet Mrs. Worth and her roommate.

"Looper, I'd like you to meet Louise Pennington. She lives in Grosse Pointe, Michigan, and has played many of the better courses in the U.S."

"Nice to meet you, ma'am. I hear you play to a six."

"That was in May. I'm down to a five at the moment."

"You two ought to tear up the member-guest then, " I said.

"Right now, we're looking forward to testing this new layout you've prepared for us, Looper," said Mrs. Worth.

"This layout, for better or worse, is Mr. O's doing, Mrs. Worth. I set the tees at Seven though Ten. I know the course is supposed to play long and beyond that I don't know much."

"Well, we'll know soon enough, won't we, Louise?"

Soon enough came on the very first hole. Mrs. Worth went abnormally wide right with her tee shot into a first layer of rough I will politely call "shaggy."

"I don't recall the rough on this hole being quite that tall, do you Looper?" said Mrs. Worth.

"No ma'am. It appears a trifle high to me as well. I'll make a note of that."

Three had misaligned tee markers. Mrs. Pennington stayed straight, missing the tough rough on the right and left, but had to level a mighty poke to clear the trap. "I don't think the Swedish girls will have a problem with that tee-to-bunker distance," the ladies remarked.

At Four I asked if they wanted a forecaddie. "No, we want you here, Looper," Mrs. Worth said. As I gazed down the fairway of this monstrous par 3, my eye fell to the dangerous swale-bunker combination on the left. I could hear it coming. "Margaret, is this hole really 211? It looks more like 220 to me."

"Louise, to tell you the truth, I've never seen it this long. But the men's distance plays to 234, so it could be, given this common tee box."

"My god, we're almost back to the blues," said Mrs. Pennington. It made no difference to Louise. A big drive and a wedge that fell to within four feet made matters academic. She stiffed the hole with her putt and escaped with a par. "That was an adventure," she said.

But nothing like the trip to Six. The reshaped tee box had taken hold, but the markers were up to their old tricks. "Don't hit it where the markers show, Louise. Just draw it up nicely through the chute."

As I accompanied Mrs. Worth to her ball, she expressed disappointment at the haphazard presentation of the course. "I don't mind the distance, but there's something askew here, Looper. I'm almost embarrassed. I don't think Louise would ever say anything, but there's something just not right here."

The frustration continued unabated except for a moment on Killer Ten when Mrs. Pennington damn near aced one of our toughest holes. Kathy Whitworth could have been playing that day, but would not have bested Mrs. Worth's playing partner for closest-to-the-pin honors. Mrs. Pennington parked her Titleist pin high, three inches from the cup. It was almost six o'clock when we finally marched up the home hole. Both ladies lashed sharp 4-irons to the fringe and two-putted for pars, making for a sweet ending.

"Looper, you're as nice a young man as Margaret said you were. I've quite enjoyed meeting you. I hope when I come back you'll play with us. I understand you're quite a golfer yourself."

"Thank you, ma'am. I try."

Mrs. Pennington had plenty to say about the course. Not to Mrs. Worth, mind you, but to the USGA. For, surprise, surprise, unbeknownst to all of us, she was the mystery golfer. And if I live to be a hundred, her report and that of the "suits," -- Mr. O's Big Kahunas -- who visited the next day, will remain among the most incisive and scathing documents I've ever read.

We got to read them both, compliments of Mr. Sauers. "Otto," he said to Mr. O, "Binswanger is bringing down copies of the mystery golfer and the formal report for your staff. I want them to read it and when I get there at 3, Binswanger will read the report for the benefit of those who don't read well. Then we will discuss it, and the ramifications for this club and your staff."

"But my men go home at 2:30," he protested.

"Not today. And you, Otto are in deep shit."

The excrement hit the fan at 2:30 when I opened the report. As an educated guy I have to tell you, these reports were very well written. The use of understatement was outstanding. Heywood Hale Broun, the sports commentator, couldn't have done much better. The vitriol was well controlled and oozed in all the right places. Only upon reading the full reports did I understand the magnitude of Mr. O's crimes against women.

I started with Mrs. Pennington's missive. "It's one thing to take liberties with lengths and architecture," she began, "but to combine them with penal greens, pot bunkers and grassy hollows so they serve as a constant injustice to the weaker sex is patently discriminatory. I have no quarrel with long carries over serpentine wanderings of creeks or large bodies of water, such as those found at Ten, Eleven, Sixteen and Seventeen. Frankly, they add to the challenge of the game. But when they present themselves in such overwhelming numbers that every shot looms as a heroic carry, I have to assume that the architect and the superintendent are engaged in a sadistic conspiracy."

The USGA report was equally vituperative. "We were prepared for a dull and unattractive spectacle, but it was much, much worse than anticipated. Field trips such as ours, are always journeys of discovery, in this case, into previously uncharted depths of vegetative misery, human suffering and want."

I froze. These were not kind words. The report touched on every aspect of course layout from tee to green. It was as comprehensive an inventory as I ever hope to hear. It referred to the "concrete hardness of shaved putting surfaces" (from some inadvertent verticutting, no doubt), "punishing rough that exacted a stiff penalty for inaccuracy off the tee," "marginal areas of play that induced stately-to-glacial rates of play," "stands of imposing oaks and elms," and "mammoth, high-lipped fairway bunkers reminiscent of those at Royal St. George's in England." Even the dumb guys in the audience got the picture. The Kahunas were pissed.

Mercifully, the message seemed to soften as the reading of the word continued. I started to get the feeling that what was at issue was not the shape of the course, but the mindset of the guy who set it up.

"After conversing with members of the crew, it is the opinion of the USGA committee that the attitude is not a shared sentiment but the handiwork of one supervisor.

"Therefore, given the longstanding relationship with the USGA and certain members of Spring Willows, and given that a natural alternative site cannot, with assurance, be secured, it is the considered opinion of this committee that the U.S.-Swedish exhibition remain at Spring Willows with the proviso that the aforementioned problems be duly rectified."

We passed, barely. But we were all guilty by association and we knew it. That which hit the fan was sure to touch us all.

Billy Sauers was a picture of fear and loathing, not so much at the staff but at the Chief. He ripped each and every one of us a new one. He spared no one. He reached out and touched Rossi, Rita, Buddy, Kaptain, me, Jerome, Lackey, everyone in that room. I was ashamed for the crew and for myself. I felt like I let down my parents, my school, my teacher and God himself.

He reserved the biggest slice of the pie for Mr. O. "No employee body acts alone. The good ones reflect the strength of their leader. Likewise the weak. And last Thursday's performance is among the sorriest examples of human endeavor I have ever witnessed. Each of you acted as sheep led to slaughter. Meek and mild, you let this Neanderthalian gnome of a man bully you into acts against your better judgment. Shame on all of you.

"You heard the committee. This course passed; the exhibition stays here only because they couldn't get Baltusrol after all. However, you all flunked my test. And each and every, and I mean every one of you, is on probation until this exhibition is over. Mr. Binswanger has a complete list of adjustments that must be made to this course over the next two weeks. There will be daily checks by the green committee. This exhibition will come off. It will be done right, with or without your help. If there are any questions, leave them with Mr. Binswanger. You are dismissed."

In thirty seconds the crew was gone. Mr. O himself was at the door when Billy Sauers called out, "Otto, Binswanger and I would like a word with you privately."

* * *

At 6:15 my mother answered the phone. "It's for you. Sounds important."

"Looper, this is Billy Sauers. You free for dessert tonight? And do you think you can get Jerome and his buddy here about 8:30 at my place?"

"You mean Rita?"

"Rita, Richard, whatever. I want to bring a little closure to our afternoon session. Dress informally. Strawberry shortcake."

"Sure, Mr. Sauers, no problem. See you there, Woodley Road."

I knew Rita and Jerome had plans, but this meeting sounded mandatory, so I convinced them to put the movies on hold. We donned our best khakis and summer skirt and went over together.

"You guys are overdressed," said Mr. Sauers, greeting us in Bermuda shorts and a pique polo. His wife rolled out the cake, strawberries and whipped cream. She served it to us on a screened-in porch that was larger than my living room.

"To set the record straight, I'm pissed. Not at you guys so much, but at that dumb-ass boss of yours. However, nothing's changed. You're all on probation. In the first place, nobody should have let him get away with that. I also understand that he was the only one with access to the master plan. It was his for Chrissakes, so you were all operating in a vacuum. Remember, that philosophy got the Germans in trouble. I also know that many of the people who have some sense around that shed were relegated to menial jobs, so it's not like you actively participated in this suicide. But dammit, Mr. O damn near killed us all.

"After the general session ended, Binswanger and I had a little epilogue with the superintendent. I have full reason to believe he now understands the severity of his problem and what he has to do to save his balls, his job, his pension and this exhibition."

"I thought he was on probation after the Ladies' Day deal," I interrupted.

"Looper, not that it's any of your business, but the short answer is I don't have time now to change superintendents. As for you guys, you're here tonight to hear from me that I have confidence in you. I want you to be the eyes and ears of the green committee. You," he said looking at me, "are probably tired of that, but that's your lot in life right now. Over the next three or four days let the crew know that they aren't all the fuck-ups I made them out to be. I'll grant they're not all mental giants, but they're not all fuck-ups either."

We could see the fireflies lighting up the perimeter just beyond the porch, extending random points of light to a row of hedges that hid a large, well-illuminated outdoor swimming pool. The cicadas' erratic cadence served as a poignant counterpoint to the well-articulated thoughts of the arbitrager.

"What I really want out of this exhibition," he said, "is recognition for a well-run international event. I'd like to see more of these at this club because it's good for Spring Willows and its membership. I believe with a little work this course is good enough to become a stop on the LPGA Tour. I'd also like to see a member or two serve on a USGA national committee. Several of us have done yeoman service on a regional basis over the years and I'd like to see some personal recognition extended for the time and effort spent. Besides, that which accrues to the members also accrues to the club, if you get my drift."

Loud and clear. Billy Sauers was bucking for office. That was the first time I'd ever gotten a whiff of any personal aggrandizement beyond killing the competition in the stock market or lifting money each week from General Sweeney. "I may only shoot in the eighties, but I'd like to think I'm on par with any of the bozos that are currently on the USGA site selection committee."

Later Jerome told me that that status equated to free rounds of golf at the best courses in the country. Small reward, I thought, for a man who had given of himself so selflessly for Spring Willows for all these years.

The conversation wandered to what we were going to do after graduation. The other two had more definite plans than I. Rita wanted to be the first female super at a course that hosted a major LPGA event. "You're shooting pretty high aren't you, young lady?" said Billy Sauers.

"Maybe so, but I figure someone has to be first and it might as well be me. Then when I get good and famous maybe I'll go home and be the first female super at Pinehurst."

"Now that would set the golfing establishment on its ear," said Jerome. "A female at Pinehurst."

"You might want to think bigger than that," chimed in Billy Sauers. "How about running a course in the Northwest or the desert, you know, for a little varied experience, and then becoming the set-up gal for the LPGA Tour? That job is currently done by a man, but he'll be retiring in a few years. Start as his assistant and then slide in. Hell, who knows, after that maybe you could become part of that inner circle and run the LPGA itself."

The one thing that never ceased to amaze me about Billy Sauers was his vision. He always saw possibilities and answers where others didn't. I guess that's what made him such a great arbitrager and a wealthy man. I'd have never worked out a career path for Rita like that, much less in ten minutes. He reminded me of a fraternity brother who read a lot of Kierkegaard. He once plotted a career path for me as a comic book writer. I'd have never dreamed there was a market for that kind of thing, but sure enough, I checked it out. With my brother's prescience, it didn't surprise me that he got into one of the helping professions as a preacher.

"Well, I'm shoving you college guys (everyone now treated Rita as one of the boys) out the door. I've got a six o'clock with your boss tomorrow. I just want him to know I mean business. I know we can get this course ready. I just want him to feel the urgency. People respect what you inspect. Mr. O understands that. I expect to be inspecting a lot in the next two weeks.

"I almost forgot. Two things. First, for each of you, copies of the USGA manual *How to Conduct Competition*. It was written by a friend of mine in Far Hills. It offers guidelines for all amateur tournaments. You might want to share excerpts with the staff. Mr. O's got his own copy. He's going to have it memorized by the time this exhibition comes off.

"Second, course remeasurement starts tomorrow. The USGA will be taking several readings. They'll do one set for the exhibition and another for us on all our lengths so we can finally get our distances down right. I'm curious to see what the women's distance is on Four. Also, the USGA will print its own scorecard for this event. We can redo our own when the Swedes clear out." He pushed his chair back from the table. The evening was over. "Thanks for coming."

We staggered into the dark, the big stone house receding in the distance. It was nice to have a mentor even if he did kick ass and take names sometimes.

* * *

The next morning the course was hopping. Mr. O was going over his list, checking it twice and giving orders like a drill instructor. "Yes boss," could be heard frequently. We actually seemed to function better under the newly focused management.

Later that afternoon, ten days before the exhibition, Jerome, Rita and Mr. O were deep in discussion. The superintendent stretched his long hairy arms across the table, eyeing potential pin placements from a long-neglected blueprint. In truth, I doubt those diazos had been out of the drawer in years. "The way I see it, we recommend putting them here, here, here and here," he said, putting down random pencil points.

"Mr. Olson, I know the prevailing thinking. The USGA suits do not want the golfers making it putt-putt. They will give them different looks, six hard, six easy, six medium, six left, right, center, six back, front and middle. The USGA doesn't want extreme pin placements, so some of this close-to-the-edge stuff you are marking is definitely out," said Jerome.

Mr. O cut in. "It says here in the manual that we are supposed to rank the pin placements and not bias any day's set-up in favor of a particular style of play. Say," he stopped, and a quizzical look came over his furrowed, simian brow, "what style do the Swedes play anyway?"

"It doesn't matter," broke in Billy Sauers, throwing the latest Special Delivery package on the desk "because the USGA told me this morning that their field staff will take care of the set-up on the competitive venue. So, you guys can fold the tent on the pin placements. Though I am impressed you've read the manual. Very good, Otto. What they want from us is lots of grass cut right, manicured greens, two tiers of rough, aligned tee boxes and a sparkling clubhouse. This other document here," he said, waving a thick sheaf, "is for Binswanger and all his hospitality requirements. Good thing we got that women's member-guest thing this weekend so we can practice for the real deal."

"Oh, shit," I said.

"What's with you?" asked Billy Sauers.

"I forgot I promised Mrs. Worth I'd loop for her and her partner."

"Oh, yeah. That Pennington women," he said. "Ask her how she got the job of mystery golfer. I'd be interested in that."

With that he was gone as quietly as he had come. "What was that all about?" I asked.

"He's just looking in on me. On us," corrected Mr. O. "He wants to make sure there are no more fuck-ups. Right, Junior?"

"Looks that way to me," said Jerome.

I have to tell you I had real ambivalence about seeing Mrs. Pennington again. Since the USGA reports had circulated I had come to feel like a partner to a crime, a violation of trust to which I had exposed Mrs. Worth and all the members of the club.

"Don't worry about it," Mrs. Worth told me on the practice tee. "She's paid very good money to make those reports. Besides, she recognizes the handiwork of a sadistic man when she sees it. She was married to one for twenty-five years. Despite her diatribe, she really likes this course and thinks that it's highly appropriate for the exhibition, assuming the funny business can be cleared up."

"You could've fooled me," I said. "That report was pretty scathing, I thought."

"She has a marvelous command of the English language, doesn't she?" said Mrs. Worth.

"I'll say," I mumbled. "Mrs. Worth, is there a grand plan for this weekend? I know you are in the top flight. Are you two going to grip it and rip it or what?"

"No Looper, that's for guys. 'Grip it and rip it,'" she sighed. "Men are all about power. You know, Bubba may be in the woods, but he hit it 300 yards. That's baloney. We're finesse players with a simple goal, win low gross, low net and get our names on that women's member-guest trophy. Oh, and have a simply wonderful meal at Friday's opening banquet. Norwegian salmon, I think, is the main course. Would you care to dine?"

"That's awfully kind of you, Mrs. Worth, but I think not. I'm not sure your competition would like that too much, you two toting your caddie along. It's not like there will be others there."

"That's true, Looper. But my husband will be out of town, so it would be just us two women with their escort. You're a handsome young man and you know lots of the members. You'd fit right in."

"Thank you very much, Mrs. Worth, but I think it would be better for all concerned if I pass. Besides, if I went and you scorched the competition, the wet hens would never stop talking. You don't need that."

"Perhaps you're right. But Louise and I would like to thank you in some way."

"For what?"

"We've got the best caddie. We'll win this thing hands down."

Her confidence was not misplaced. On Friday, they blitzed the field. They carded a 65 for a new women's best-ball course record. On Saturday, they followed it with a 67 to lead by 12 strokes. Tempers were short. Outside the Pro Shop I overheard Jocelyn Price suggest to McDevitt "that those bitches be given a 5 a.m. tee time so they couldn't find their balls." In the locker room a weepy Cindy Cabiness, whose game had actually improved dramatically, complained bitterly for the second straight day at the unfairness of having the best caddie paired with the best players.

"If it's the caddies that bother you, why don't you get your assistant stud McDevitt to carry your balls instead of the other way around," said a peeved Rachel Haugen. "The best deserve the best. Let it rest, will you?"

Marconi nailed me at the caddie shack. "Jesus, Looper, you guys have lapped the field. Tell your ladies to ease up."

"They're in the zone. What can I tell you? I even misclubbed Mrs. Pennington and she airmails a 4-iron to within three feet. They're on automatic pilot. I'm just toting bags."

"Well, there are some unhappy women in the clubhouse."

"Let 'em talk. I think the second place awards this year look pretty good."

"Sure, but no names on a trophy."

"I can't help it. My players are good. And they're nice women. People ought to remember that."

Sunday brought no relief to the field. A 66 solidified a spot on the silver, and turned attention over the final nine to the race for second between Price-Leftwich and Whippet-Ross. A curling 23-footer on Eighteen by Whippet capped an impressive three-hole par-birdie-birdie finish to give them runners-up honors, 17 strokes off the pace.

If most of the women in the Championship flight were sore losers, they didn't show it. Applause at the ceremonies off the eighteenth green was hearty for Mrs. Worth and Mrs. Pennington. And with enough prizes and hardware to go around for the contestants in the other flights, I think grudges were few and the admiration plentiful. And if, in the gathering dusk, I identified the occupants of Cindy Cabiness's car correctly there was even some solace for the losers. I guess she had to go home fulfilled one way or another.

CHAPTER NINE

Exhibition week was upon us. No rest for the weary. Monday is usually a time of heavy maintenance, but this week the green committee was having none of that. "This course will be closed until Thursday morning," Billy Sauers declared. That meant three days of finishing touches with no ladies golf on Tuesday and no doctors playing Wednesday afternoon. It did not mean no bitching.

"It's been posted since May that there would be no play these three days," Binswanger was saying into the phone as I passed his office. "It's in your newsletter and it's been on the Pro Shop bulletin board for months. I don't care if the President of the United States is coming; he waits til Thursday."

Signage for the coming event began to appear Tuesday. "Welcome All-Americans and Swedish Champs." Foreign phrases and an impressive USGA draw sheet dominated a newly-erected bulletin board outside the Pro Shop. The assistant pros, a slick and haughty lot, were dressing even sharper than usual. The cooks had stiffly starched and pressed whites. At the caddie shack, morale was ebbing and flowing. Al had already assigned caddies. A month before he had picked only the best and brightest from Spring Willows and then went, with Billy Sauers's permission, to the ultimate extreme and invited the caddie master at Iroquois Woods to ship over his four best caddies. Billy Sauers wanted everyone displaying impeccable manners and standing on ceremony.

Even at my level, guys were wearing clean clothes. Buddy and Rossi had new hats and the entire staff took a visible pride as they finished even the most menial tasks. I couldn't believe it. Mr. O complimented Kaptain for picking up sticks after Tuesday's midday shower. Would wonders never cease.

One thing that did not change was the puerile language outside the shed. I think it had something to do with testosterone levels and wishful thinking. "Is it true that by their eighteenth birthdays all Swedish women are required to be non-virgins and that they have bozaams as large as my hands?" Kaptain asked me.

"Bozaams?" I said, stunned.

"Yeah, you know. Out to here," he said, extending his hands. "Jugs?"

And before I could recover, "Is it true that Swedish girls sleep in the same room as their fathers until they're sixteen?" The questions and comments got raunchier as the week went on. And yet, the cleanliness of the clothes never diminished.

Wednesday morning, as I was coming in from bunker duty, Mr. O beckoned me into his office. "After 2:30 today you're off duty until next week," he said. "I got orders. The house wants you scrubbed and ready for the exhibition. I know you've been scheduled to caddie and you'll be paid here as well as up there. Don't worry none. I think for the rest of the week you're needed more up there than down here. Oh, call this number in Chicago before you finish up here." Then a wry smile came over his apish countenance. "Looper, get some for me."

The number looked familiar, but I couldn't place it. Turned out it was for First Strike Investments. "Mr. Sauers's office."

"Arlo Litton. Returning."

"Yes, Looper, he's expecting you." Christ, I thought. How does some secretary I've never met know my nickname?

"Kid, hope you don't mind me telling Abigail about your nickname. She remembered you from the settlement we sent you last fall. Anyway, this is short notice, but I need you for escort duty. There's a banquet tonight for the girls and I was supposed to ask you and, frankly, with all the troubles we've had at the club, I forgot. No tux or anything, summer suit, bright tie are fine. The girls will be wearing cocktail dresses. Informal sort of thing."

That kind of thing may be informal to Billy Sauers, but that's because he moved in those circles. Last I remembered, cocktail dresses were a pretty big deal and as close to state dinner pomp as you could get without being "formal."

"Who else my age is going to be there?"

"Some of your former high school classmates, a couple of swimmers, stockbrokers' kids, people like that." In other words, people out of my social strata. "You'll be right at home. I think you'll even know one of the girls. See you at the clubhouse at 6:30."

I spent all of the third hole figuring out my wardrobe. I knew my black shoes weren't shined, but the white shirt and blue suit were freshly pressed. Hell, I even had a stylish tie that would work. And if I were lucky maybe I could talk my neighbor Mr. Brown into letting me drive his Lincoln. I'd cut his grass for the last five years and he'd often offered his "sex wagon" if I ever had a hot date. Maybe tonight would qualify.

Mr. Sauers's words kept repeating themselves. "I think you even know one of the girls." Had to be someone from my high school class because I sure as hell didn't know any Swedes. By the sixth hole I decided it must be Emily Evans, the club's best young women's tennis player and a former Algebra buddy of mine.

Mr. Brown, what a sport. "Arlo, here's the deal. I'm getting rid of the Lincoln and tonight I've got a loaner that I'm trying out. Why don't you take it?"

"I don't need a station wagon as much as I need a little style tonight," I said.

"Oh, I think this will be stylish enough. Come on over about 6:15 and I'll give you the keys."

Our family sedan looked pretty pale compared to the sporty red Jaguar. "This one's got more bells and whistles than you're probably used to. Make sure you check out the instrument panel before nightfall so you can locate the light switch. Horn's on the steering wheel," he said, motioning inside the car.

"Mr. Brown, you're a prince."

"Good things happen to good people, Arlo. Get a handful for me tonight."

What a sexist world, I thought. I'd hate to be a woman facing that crap every damn day. No wonder my mother and her friends got bent out of shape so easily. This sexism thing must have cultural roots, I decided, if even Mr. Brown talked that way.

Once in the Jag my comfort level went way up. At the club I even got an admiring look from Quinton Pierce when I eased alongside his father's Cadillac. "Coming up in the world, Arlo," said the former state champion sprinter.

"Smooth ride you got there," I said.

"Yours is smoother."

The ballroom door was crowded as invitees struggled to get past a registration table and into a receiving line. I was prepared for neither. Mr. Binswanger's secretary and Cindy Cabiness were handing out badges just a little subtler than "Hello, my name is. . ."

"We decided to do this," the secretary said, "so everyone would really make an effort to meet one another. With all the Dagmars, Hannahs, Ingrids and Annies we thought this would help break the ice."

"Here's your nametag, Looper," said Cindy Cabiness. "Once you get past the receiving line, look up Mrs. Worth. She's got a guest she wants you to meet." I was starting to feel more at home already.

"Looper, good of you to come," said Billy Sauers. "Hope I didn't upset your plans. You remember my wife Elise?" I nodded cordially and shook her hand while mumbling something about her dress. "Oh, don't get away tonight without us talking a little business. I've got a few questions you can answer." More snitching for the clubhouse, I thought. Oh, well. Quickly enough I got passed down the line and then out into the effluent, or should I say affluent, to find Mrs. Worth. I was three steps short of the bar when I felt my left arm go into arrest.

"Stop right there, young man. I've got someone I want you to meet." I squared to the right.

"Looper, I'd like you to meet 'Melissa Davenport,'" we all three said together. "Well, then you've met," noted Mrs. Worth.

"I caddied for Melissa and Mrs. Peck one afternoon. We met again at the funeral," I said. Turning to Melissa I asked, "how's the golf game?"

"Top five at eight tournaments this summer," Melissa said. "We're looking forward to this. Some people have said this is nothing more than American amateurs in a meaningless outing with foreign-born college players who already play here. I bet I played Ulrike Berenson, Annie Arneson and Grete Borg three times already this year."

"How'd you do?" I asked.

"Great golf, actually. I held my own against Arneson and Borg, but I never quite vanquished Berenson. But then maybe that's why she's a champion and I'm not," said Melissa.

"Isn't there some resentment against these girls coming here and taking college roster slots?" I asked, looking for a comfortable conversation level.

"Maybe some, but they've earned it. In truth, these are nice girls. We may try to beat one another's brains out, but off the links we actually like each other."

"Looper, I can see you don't need me so I'm going to be social," said Mrs. Worth. "We have assigned seats for dinner. You'll be at Table Five with me and Melissa. Supper is served at 7:30. Don't monopolize all her time. Meet some of the foreign girls. I'm sure you'll end up caddying for some of them."

She had that right. In fact, over the next four days I drew three of them. For Thursday's practice round I got Aimee Nilsson, a 5'6" dynamo who could flat powder the ball. She's one of the few women I've ever seen master a 1-iron. Pinpoint control whose only failings were said to be club selection and pressure. During the practice round none of that was evident. She played with another Swede, let me do the clubbing and kept no score. She toured Spring Willows like it was old home week.

During the round, I searched for the obvious course layout problems that the USGA and the mystery golfer had uncovered. I saw none. Still, I had this underlying fear that Mr. O's resentment of women might show some way, somehow during the exhibition. At Four I took a long look at the ladies' yardage. The tees were moved well front and marked "211." Gazing at the far end of the tee I smiled. No question that Four had been underestimated in the past. The hole had to have played to 217 or better for women for the last ten years.

As for the tee box at Six, it looked great. It was grown in and finally properly aligned. For once it looked actually possible to power a ball straight out of the chute.

The Swedes took no prisoners during the practice round. Occasionally Nilsson would come over for an extended conversation about a hole, but mostly she kept to herself, reading the greens and staying out of harm's way.

She was particularly tickled by the par-3 water holes. "Little deevils," she called them. Killer Ten I thought would test her mightily, but she skyed the ball so high that it burrowed into the green like a V-2 with no chance to roll. A nice lag and a tap-in for par. Not many of our men did that well. And on the 153-yard par-3 island-like Seventeen, she trickled into the trap, escaped to within two feet and stiffed the flag for another par. In fact, the only hole that presented problems was the Empty Quarter at Fifteen where she took two to get out of the massive fairway trap. Other than that, it was just your routine 73, (I kept score out of curiosity) which I thought was a hell of a feat for someone taking on the course sight unseen.

The buzz at the Pro Shop was that the Swedes had the better of the practice day with the exception of Melissa, who cracked a 69 to tie with Ulrike Berenson for the low round. As luck would have it, I ran into Melissa leaving the Pro Shop. "Nice round," I said.

"Thanks. How'd your player do?"

"Well, I don't know about the others," I said, "but this Nilsson babe looks tough to me. She's got my vote for winning something. And I'll tell you something else, when this is over, she could make some big bucks hanging around here and teaching people how to hit a 1-iron. She's scary with that club."

"How'd she do with fairway bunkers?" Melissa asked.

"She flew the ones at Three and Five, but had a problem at Fifteen. Took two to get out from decent lies."

"So, nothing's changed," she said. "That's probably the one weak part of her game. Seems to tighten up when she has to go long from the kitty litter."

"That's kind of a cold assessment, isn't it?" I asked.

"This is business."

"But you had a great round, right?"

"Looper, you've been around golfers long enough to know that practice rounds mean nothing. Let's see what tomorrow and the next day bring. Then maybe we can talk about nice rounds." And that's all she had to say on that subject. As she walked away, I could hear her spikes digging into the asphalt. Why did I feel like I'd been talking to Billy Sauers.

And then I was. Strolling from the Pro Shop to the parking lot I caught the quick strides of the chairman of the green committee.

"Looper, we never finished that business conversation from the other night." In actuality, we'd never started it. "I'm looking to diversify a few of my clients and wondered if you had any thoughts about golf stocks? Any maintenance stuff or equipment companies that may make sound investments? Nothing risky. Something even you might put some money in."

"Is this a sales pitch, Mr. Sauers?"

"Hell, no, kid. This is mano a mano. Is there anything out there that looks good to you, as an end user?" I had a strange feeling he had an eye on some of that $20,000 Mrs. Peck had left me.

"Actually, there might be a couple. From the equipment side, Jacobsen's making a comeback with their mowers and their irrigation systems seem to have found favor with the supers."

"Where'd you hear that?"

"I read the minutes from Moline."

"I bet Mr. O didn't."

"As for club manufacturers, there's a guy in California making putters that're getting some attention from club pros. I see them once in a while when I'm looping for members. You might have your analysts do some research and see what they uncover."

"If their numbers square with your gut, you want me to put you down for couple hundred shares?"

There it was, the pitch. I really didn't want to say "no" to this guy. I decided to buy some time. "I don't even know that the guy's company is public. Maybe he needs some investment capital."

"Good thought, son. I want to move on this. Early birds and all that. Changing the subject, which side do you like in this exhibition?"

"Got a Calcutta going?" I asked.

"Betting on women's college golf is uncharted territory. We're just running minor wagers on the girls who will do the best and worst. Who'll win or lose the most matches, that sort of thing."

"Did I get invited to that reception so I could be a betting agent?"

"No. Your dinner invitation was Elise's and Mrs. Worth's idea. They thought there would be value in the staff meeting the guests, especially if you were going to caddy for some of them. And I thought maybe you could be of some help to those of us in the backroom."

"Quid pro quo," I said, remembering my lesson from last summer.

"Something like that." He stopped talking while General Sweeney and Ambassador Austerlitz walked by. "So, who do you like?" he continued.

"I don't know them all yet, but from what I've seen, of the Swedes I like Kreutzer, Berenson, Arneson, Nilsson and Borg. Of the Americans I like the Lindley sisters, Alison's probably a stroke better than Lindsay, and Mrs. Peck's granddaughter Melissa Davenport."

"Well that's helpful, Looper. With this better ball and foursomes formats they're playing Friday and Saturday, the gaming committee has an option for separate puts and calls for Sunday's singles matches. I think the action will be heaviest if these matches are close. You want in on any of that?"

I thought back to the previous summer when Billy Sauers made piles of money off the Peck-Whippet match thanks to a casual conversation we'd had before the match went extra holes. He'd even sent me an unsolicited check for $500. "Consulting Services -- Whippet Project." Quid pro quo.

I wondered if I was starting to think like him. "Not right now," I said.

"Don't go anywhere the next few days. The club green committee might have a few questions for you." The course was perfect. I decided he must have meant his green committee.

* * *

Friday dawned hot and muggy. I hit the caddie shack for a few extra towels before getting my assignment up top. "You drew the Berenson girl for a morning match," Al said.

"The best Swedish player and I'm pulling her bag; how do you know that?"

"I just know," he said with a smile. "I'm the caddie master, right? It's my job to know these things."

"I suppose the men's grill knows it, too," I said, giving him a hard look.

"I don't know what the men's grill knows, but I know that you've got a 9:38 date with a Swedish girl who is expecting you to have her bag at the practice tee at 8:45. You better get lost."

For the first time all summer I was in a fog. I'd been able to straighten all the crap out about Mr. O and Jerome and Rita and Kaptain, but I was having serious ambivalence about my role as a caddie. Usually I just got the bags, said hello, walked ahead, found balls, clubbed my fare, read greens and took the bags back to the shop. Now I felt like I was supposed to do all of that and glean intelligence on my player. I knew people wanted to know strengths and weaknesses, especially weaknesses. Does she twitch in the rough, blink over water, choke in sand, fade on Fourteen, go to the restroom after Nine, take a drink at Ten? Where is she in her cycle? No one was really saying that, but I had a feeling that if I laid all of that at the feet of the green committee someone would find a way to make money off of it. That's not really where I wanted to be. What I really wanted to do was tote some bags and look at attractive women for three days. Hell, I'd already seen some pretty good stuff at the opening night dinner. So, that's what I decided to do. Forget the green committee.

* * *

Ms. Berenson had a big damn bag. A big, heavyweight bag like the one Mr. Stroud carried. She also had a big, big smile. "You're Looper?" she said.

I wasn't ready for that. "Uh, yeah. I'm Looper."

"Mr. Starza and Melissa told me you were the best caddie out here. And since I'm the best, I get the best," she said.

Made sense to me, but that was a little overwhelming so early on a Friday. "They're kind to say that. You want to go to the practice range or putt?" I asked.

"Range," she said.

There is absolutely nothing tough about golf when you hit the ball the way Ulrike Berenson did. Upright stance, easy backswing, proper weight transfer through the hips, smooth follow through. Nothing to it. Two hundred yards every time, 220 when she reached back. She hit sixty-five balls and then we went to the putting green. There she dropped three colored balls on the fringe and rammed them all into the nearest hole ten feet away.

"Not white," she said. "When the green gets this crowded I can always find my balls. I get them from a manufacturer in Europe." After fifteen minutes of one-putts we adjourned to the first tee.

Man, this may be my fastest round since going solo with Mr. Howard a month ago, I mused.

Berenson's playing partner was Petra Kreutzer from Malmo. I remember Malmo because the ferry stops there. Petra played for the University of Gothenburg. Petra sounded a bit Teutonic to me, and Ulrike explained that her father was a German industrialist who married a Swedish beauty queen. Follow the money, I thought. Why does everyone follow the money?

I hadn't met the Americans. One was Kerry Pierce, a long-legged blonde from SMU, and the other Lisa Newman from Stanford. All but Petra had played extensively against each other, so there didn't promise to be many surprises among them.

The caddies were another story. I knew Ransome and Walker, Pierce's and Kreutzer's caddies from Spring Willows, but I'd never seen Lance Wilson from Iroquois Woods. Turns out he hadn't done a whole lot of caddying but had played some at Spring Willows and his well-connected dad prevailed upon someone to let his son spend the weekend hanging around girls.

The guys at the shed would have been disappointed in the Swedes we got. Oh, they were attractive enough and very athletic. But the bozos on the G crew were going strictly by stereotype and they envisioned these dames as 5'10, blonde and filled out. Ours were in the 5'6" to 5'7" range, a tad burly and extremely well-muscled. We had athletes, not models, which suited me fine because if I were to be going 36 holes in this heat, I wanted to be chasing the ball of a jock and not some calendar girl who couldn't hit a lick.

Early on the round was uneventful. Scoring was low and moments of high adventure were limited, mostly because the girls stayed out of trouble. Both the Swedes drove into the trap on the 505-yard third hole, but Kreutzer crushed a 4-wood from the beach and recovered for a halving par.

We were all even and all sweating profusely walking up Nine toward the clubhouse. Now I've heard varying theories on course layout, one being that Nine and Eighteen should circle back to the clubhouse. And most modern architects agree that walking upgrade on the home holes is a sorry way to end a round. On this particular Friday the Illinois humidity hung like Spanish moss, almost as bad as in Tarkio. There was no air movement whatsoever. Rain wasn't predicted until nightfall, but we were already soggy, practically swimming. I also knew that at least two of the bag toters were headed for double duty. It looked like a long day.

It was iced tea all around at the turn, except for the Swedes who produced some Swedish concoction they called Effernass. With the honors still being carried from a nice birdie at Five, Newman approached Killer Ten. She stroked it just offline so that it bounced on the fringe and dropped six feet into the right trap. She was facing a hairy out. Pierce didn't do much better. She made the green, but was on the back, high and away, facing a slick downward putt.

The Swedes' accuracy to the elevated green was unbelievable. I don't know what was in that Efferness, but Berenson bashed her ball to within four feet and then slid the ball in sidehill for birdie. Kreutzer holed from eight feet for par while Pierce three-putted for four and Newman played out for a seven. She left for Eleven visibly shaken.

In the distance I could see the USGA posting tallies on the massive scoreboard. One official on a ladder was taking orders from a man on a walkie-talkie. After receiving a result, he scurried up seven or eight rungs and hung a new number. If the other matches were going as ours was, there were going to be some tension-filled final holes.

Eight sets of spikes crunched across the asphalt to get to Spring Willows' road hole. It already looked much better given the landscaping down the left side and behind the green of this 335-yarder. The maples looked good and went a long way toward shielding the course from the traffic that wound its way to the clubhouse.

The spike sounds jerked me back into reality. I was still curious about my morning assignment. Why had I drawn the best Swede? Was it because on Sunday, when the singles matches were played I was going to draw her again -- or her opponent? I didn't know how the USGA set these things up, but knowing Spring Willows, the mole scenario didn't seem beyond the realm. I took one last sip of the iced tea, pitched the cup into the hunter green container by the ball washer and vowed to concentrate. I handed Berenson her driver.

I noticed everything about the stocky body, the flex of the club, the strike of the ball and the demeanor of the player from that swing through the rest of the round. I decided she was a machine with a cause, which was to split fairways and lag putts. That's not to say there wasn't some adversity, there was. She found the left woods on Fourteen where the hickories and ash were. All the players, and I mean all, that I have caddied for who have ventured in that forest negotiate the hole sideways. Once in they go perpendicular, taking the safe play and then venturing down the fairway. Not Ulrike Berenson. We foraged a bit for her Titleist before rediscovering it hard by a hickory. At best she had limited visibility toward the hole. Even a sideways play back to the fairway looked tenuous to me.

"Three-iron, Looper," she said.

"Yes, you have one," I said.

"Bring it here, please, we're going to hack out."

I remember 'hacking' being a horsy term for taking an adventurous ride. If she were serious about playing this thing then I was along for the ride. Actually, it made sense. Kreutzer had pummeled another drive and was in decent shape. If Berenson could pull off a miracle shot maybe they could put the Americans down two.

Prospects for a backswing were minimal. It looked like a punch was all she could muster, a choked 3-iron at an 18-inch opening through a phalanx of trees. "Here goes." The 'thwack' of club meeting ball had a crisp sound to it, like a perfectly struck shot from the perfect lie. I waited for the inevitable ricochet that always followed the plight of my D-flighters in trouble. But no, smooth sailing all the way.

I don't know how she generated the power, but with a superb piece of shot-making she cut off the dogleg and lay two on the fringe of this 440-yard par 4. Rejoining the fairway, I saw Pierce's shoulders droop. She turned to Newman, "where'd that shot come from?" Newman got her par, but the match was effectively over when Berenson chipped in to hole out for birdie. The Swedes were up two with four to go.

It was still that way when we reached Seventeen, the 153-yarder with water front and right and a trap on the left. Most of the members at Spring Willows hated this hole. It's a tester with little tolerance for wide right, wide left or short. Long lets you sneak in the back way, assuming you aren't long right into the huge oak, which serves as a delayed route into the drink.

The Americans won this hole. Newman clanked her 6-iron off the flag and dropped the residue, but the real learning for me was the way Berenson handled adversity. Her shot burrowed into the narrow trap left of the tiny green. The quintessential disappearing ball trick, I thought, the kind that *Golf Digest* always shows with articles entitled "My Favorite Shot -- The Buried Lie" by Kathy Whitworth or "Birdies from the Beach" by Cary Middlecoff. This will be one tough mother, I muttered.

I handed Berenson the heavy club with the "S" etched in the bottom. Kreutzer came over to watch. "Ulrike loves these," she said. I would too if I could always put them one-half inch from the cup the way she did. Pierce's heart was halfway up her esophagus when the ball stopped. Newman gave the Swede a hard look before stroking her two-footer home.

Eighteen is a 452-yard lazy dogleg left, all uphill. Down one, Pierce reached back for some extra length and got the right-to-left movement she needed, but the sweeping curve was 40 yards early and into the second cut of rough. I almost started singing "keep on the sunny side," since the grass was longer on that half of the hole, but thought better of it. Newman, now really pressing, pushed a driver right. She was still in the fairway, but added 15 yards to the approach. No getting home in two from there. When she left her 3-wood 40 yards short and her pitch 25 feet from the hole, the match was over. Four pars left the Swedes 1-up. It had been a tight, well-played contest, with victory going to the shotmakers. The girls shook hands, turned their cards in at the tent and headed for the women's locker room. I stopped at the board outside the Pro Shop.

"Hot out there, ain't it, Looper," said Starza.

"I'm dripping. That bag was heavy too."

"You got another heavy one this afternoon. You're off at 2:20 with Janna Jorgensen. "

"That doesn't give me much time."

"Change your shirt. I'll get McDevitt to grab you a couple of sandwiches and run Jorgensen over to the practice tee. He's been wanting to get close to those babes all day. I'll have him meet you at the tee at 2:15."

The ham sandwiches tasted mighty good. A nice cold Coke pumped some life back into my legs. The air still hung like heavy oxygen in a rain forest. My right shoulder was a tad sore and I decided that I'd go the afternoon round with the bag on my left. I changed my socks and my shoes, putting on an older, drier pair of Foot Joys. I also donned a white, soft cotton polo shirt, not because it looked stately and formal, but because pique shirts and heavy bags exacerbated the chafing. "Al, who ordered this weather?" I asked.

"Won't be any better tomorrow. There's a front coming through and you boys and girls will be playing in the damp."

"Maybe they'll postpone it," I said.

"Doubt that. More than likely they'll just dodge raindrops. Besides, you've got only one bag tomorrow. How bad can four hours with beautiful women be?" he asked.

"I'm looking at function more than form. Those girls can hit."

I swept through the Pro Shop on the way back to the first tee. "Swedes are up, 5-3, after the morning in case anyone's keeping score," Starza said, looking in the direction of General Sweeney who was fingering a fall line of sweaters.

"Form follows function," I said, grabbing two pencils and a scorecard.

In appearance and demeanor our club starter Tom McAfee reminded me of P.G. Wodehouse's oldest member. He was a sage sort and smart enough to keep his mouth shut. He confined his conversation to such bon mots as "head down, fast round" and "just punch it, sweetheart." He was getting ready to announce the pairings when I appeared.

"Thanks, Divot. I appreciate the sandwiches and the help."

"Anytime, and I do mean anytime you need help this weekend, just call me. This is a line of work I can do all day." McDevitt's hormone levels were up again.

"Did you get a date?" I scoffed.

He lowered his voice. "As a matter of fact, we're going dancing."

"Congratulations, Stud." I wondered what Cindy Cabiness would say about that.

"Representing Sweden by way of San Jose State University," intoned Tom McAfee, "Janna Jorgensen." Two minutes later we were underway.

For the Swedes' sake, I hoped Jorgensen was the worst of the lot. She sprayed the ball all over the place, leaving most of the work to her partner Annie Palka. Not that Palka needed much help. She was 1 over on her ball alone through Twelve, and down only two to the American duo of Willard and Wallace.

At Thirteen, the 187-yard par 3, Jorgensen surfaced, hitting a rocket to within twelve feet, draining the lag for a bird and her only contribution of the day. It was obvious by Sixteen we were on our final hole. As I handed her a 3-wood for her second shot, she asked, "Mr. Looper, is Mr. Devin a nice man?"

I stopped; the mechanisms locked. "McDevitt? Devin McDevitt? I don't know what to tell you."

"Does he have good manners?"

And an excellent bedside manner, I thought. "I don't know what to tell you."

"Is he charming, at least?"

"Yes."

"Good," she said. "Then that will make up for my golf today."

So that's where her head had been. I wondered if Palka had known that. Apparently she had. At the scorer's tent she practically threw the card at the officials. Outside, the Swedes met their coach. "We're here to play golf, not screw around," Palka said angrily. "Tomorrow she plays with someone else or I play for the Americans." The glare she gave Jorgensen was scary. The venom reminded me of something insidious, reminiscent of Bette Davis vs. Joan Crawford. Billy Sauers would be interested in that. So would the guys at the shed, I decided.

CHAPTER TEN

The front stalled over the Mississippi Valley and was trapped in our neck of the woods by a "strong area of low pressure in the Tennessee Valley," said the weatherman. Intermittent drizzle, thunderstorms and heavy rain were predicted for Saturday. Great weather for golf. Yeah, right. All the players had to do was walk. Caddies had to contend with rain gear and umbrellas for players and ourselves. I had the added burden of the heavy Swedish bags.

The good news was we only had to go one round.

While my team, the Americans, were now up 7-5, I was curious to see if one side played better than the other under adverse conditions. Friday night I had half expected to hear from Billy Sauers, but the phone never rang, so I set off for the course Saturday in clinging, cloying humidity. Tarkio again, without the sun.

"Unless there's a flood or standing water, they'll play," said Al. "They want to start the singles on time on Sunday. I hear Wide World of Sports will be here for that."

"That's all this course needs, Al. More theater. What next?"

"TV, I guess. This may be your ticket to the big time, kid. Maybe some seniors or LPGA players out there need a caddie. Don't forget old Al when you hit the big time. Don't forget your 9:42 with Anneliese Kleiss."

Ah, yes. Anneliese Kleiss, another top-20 player. The book on her was great long irons and a devastating short game. I heard that if she got off the tee reasonably well, she was a threat to win any match. Certainly, that was the case Saturday. Play started in a faint mist. By Three we had a light drizzle, by Six a steady water curtain. Play was erratic, with the golfers exchanging matching pars, bogeys, birdies, and "others" on each hole so that neither side gained a significant advantage.

I'd never been in a match so even. After a brief conversation with her partner on Nine tee, Kleiss unleashed a cannon. When it caught the right rough, her partner went conservative. Kleiss subsequently recovered and we went to the Halfway House all even.

It was raining harder now and even the "water repellent" jackets the girls wore looked like they were being tested. "Play on," said the tournament director. I kept the bag cover over the clubs and worked three towels to keep them dry. Twice the girls changed gloves. We could have been in church as quiet as it was. Friday's galleries had given way to eight solitary soldiers. Marchers in the moist, trudging to a monotonous beat.

Fifteen with the traps did not bring the change of pace I expected. Everyone cleared the pond at Sixteen, setting the stage for drama at Seventeen. At last. One of the Americans found the drink because of a wet grip, but a Swede found the sand and in her escape from the waterlogged trap she flew the green. They both bogeyed, the others parred, and we were still tied. When the players matched cards on the home hole we were still all even after Eighteen.

The discussion at the scorer's tent centered on whether to continue. All the other matches, those which had started earlier and those which followed, had finished. Berenson and her partner had won, 10-and-8. Wallace and Davenport, first off on the day, blasted two blondes, 6-and-5. The Swedes had won most of the others, giving them a one-match lead. However, by prior agreement, the captains had decreed that for Saturday play if any match were tied after 18 holes, play would continue until one side won a hole.

"I'm not continuing this misery into tomorrow," said Alison Lindley.

"I'm already wet," concurred Kleiss. They each grabbed some sandwich fingers and trudged to One. Tom McAfee was nowhere to be seen. He'd probably gotten lost in the moist himself.

For the last three hours the match had been played on auto. I'm sure there was emotion, but I wasn't seeing much, just witnessing unbelievable golf. Mrs. Peck's match with Whippet had gone 21 holes, the longest I'd ever seen. I was hoping for a quick finish here. Now after 27 holes and still tied I was wishing for any finish. We started the long climb to the elevated tee at Ten again. It was raining much harder. Under normal circumstances the course would have been closed.

"Come in," yelled the captains. "We'll resume tomorrow."

"No," Kleiss hollered back.

"Stay dry," bellowed Lindley. Then she turned to her partner, "We end it here."

The Swedes glanced at each other and took the challenge.

The gauntlet was down, the gloves off.

Were the green not so slanted, it would have held standing water. Kleiss went first and found the right back fringe. Probably a par, I thought. Lindley's partner plunked it 18 inches over the pond onto the fringe. Under normal conditions that shot would find the drink. Today it was a 26-foot lag. Lindley didn't bother with a tee, but dropped her ball on the box, took no practice swing and plugged it 12 inches above the hole. Game, set, match?

"Maybe, baby," said Lindley to no one. The other Swede slipped on the tee box and damn near skewered herself with her 7-iron. It ended once and for all when Kleiss was four inches short on a game effort from the fringe and Lindley trickled the pill into the cup. Six hours, eighteen minutes and 28 holes of miserable weather and memorable golf was over.

The banquet that night was festive and cordial. The dominant topic of conversation was the marathon in the mist. I counted 92 pars in 112 holes

-- absolutely amazing. Hell, I was even interviewed on Sunday by Wide World for my views. "The secret was that when it rained, they let it. The match was testament to human will and international relations," I said, "and the most even I've ever seen, except for the Whippet-Peck contest last year." Had to get a plug in for my buddy, Mrs. P.

Billy Sauers was at the banquet as well, and I heard all about it when he got home. I was already in bed, asleep, when he called.

"Wake up, kid. This is a business call. Front's blowing through and we got work to do." I hadn't seen him in two days and now 'we' had work to do?

"First off, great call on Karsten. It appears they may have interest in some investment capital. You might have an aptitude for this."

"Wish I had some capital to go with it," I mumbled, trying to brush away the licentious dream I was having about Janna Jorgensen.

"Don't worry. I am considering some discretionary dollars for you."

"But I don't have any money," I said.

"Don't give me that," he shot back. "You and I both know better. This looks like a win-win kid. That's what it's all about. Now, about tomorrow, I need some skinny."

"Mr. Sauers, with all due respect, I don't know how I can help. I don't even have the pairings."

"I got 'em at the banquet."

It figured.

"I'm most interested in the people you've seen personally."

"I feel a little uncomfortable here."

"Does a finder's fee improve your comfort level?"

"That's not what I mean."

"I know it's not, but bear with me here. We've got captains of industry counting on you."

I was awake. "Let me go to the bathroom. I'll be right back." I propped the pillow up behind my back and turned on the light. I thought I saw a tote board at the end of the bed. "Would we be having this conversation if the matches weren't tied?" I asked.

"Absolutely," he said. "But the deadlock ups the stakes and the sphincter factor."

"For whom?"

"For everybody. Look kid, no balls, no blue chips, right? I'm teaching you stuff you'll never get in school. This is OJT of the best kind."

"OJT?"

"On the job training. And you're learning from the best."

"Okay, I believe you. Who we got?"

"These are all single matches. Let me go down the list. You talk and I'll listen. If I'm not interested, I'll tell you. Willard vs. Keisling."

"Willard, one up in 20."

"I didn't ask that, for extra holes."

"Okay, but I thought it might be good for a side bet."

"I like your style, kid. Keep talking. Pierce vs. Kleiss."

"Hmm. That's a toughie. Today was a long day, but Pierce can be erratic. I like Kleiss."

"Cargill vs. Kreutzer."

"Take the half-kraut in Fourteen."

"Wallace vs. Jorgensen."

"Did you see Jorgensen tonight?"

"Sure. I remember big tits and Divot hanging all over her."

"Anything else?"

"She seemed pissed off at the end of the evening."

"Wallace in 11. Jorgensen won't be in it."

"A. Lindley vs. Erikson."

"I'd take Alison Lindley over King Kong. She's got gonads of steel. If her golf career doesn't work out you ought to hire her."

"Grisham vs. Sorensen."

"Sorensen in a walk."

"I'm not interested in any others except this last one."

I caught my breath. "Davenport vs. Berenson," I said.

"They save the best for last, don't they, kid?"

"Is this the order they go off in the morning?" I asked.

"Ten-minute intervals, starting at 10."

"That's why I got a noon start time," I said. "I better get some sleep. Good night."

"Whoa," came the roar out of the phone. "Good night nothing, pal. We're not done here."

"Oh yeah, the match."

"Right, the match."

"Tell me, Mr. Sauers, are any law enforcement officials going to see any of this?"

"Looper, the local constabulary will get exactly as much of my revenue as I am willing to give them."

"In other words, nada."

"Correct. Now who do you like?"

There was a long silence. I added it up mentally. Strength and weakness analyses are classic marketing techniques.

"I give Berenson the advantage in driving distance, iron play, short game, average strokes per round and sand saves. Davenport's the better putter, is more accurate off the tee, knows the course better and has the edge in intangibles. They are essentially even in greens in regulation."

"I don't want an essay, just an answer."

"Who's asking and how much?"

"Everyone is curious. I'm the only one asking and I don't know how much or which side yet."

"You didn't ask about tiebreakers."

"Too dicey," said Mr. Sauers. "Plus, if it's close, I figure one of these two will decide the competition. So, who is it? After three days you've got to have an opinion."

"Berenson's the best player. Davenport's got more to prove. I'd take Mrs. Peck's granddaughter on this course and see if I couldn't get 1½ to 1, or however you do it."

"Like baseball. Just like friggin' baseball. Nice wrinkle, kid. I might try that."

"Mr. Sauers, I hope my name doesn't come up in any of this."

"Only in my dreams, Looper. You are lily white, son, and a damn saint. Oh, Al told me to tell you to bring shorts tomorrow. Seems like the club has bought the caddies coveralls like the tour loopers get. Don't know why they weren't ready when this competition started. Probably some screwup at the clubhouse. Anyway, the coveralls have the players' names on the back. And yours says..."

"Davenport," I interjected.

"You got it. I was hoping for Berenson, where you could have a little more control, but the powers that be felt that might be a little unfair since you've looped for her once already this weekend."

"Don't they know I caddied for Melissa last year?"

"I don't think so. Ought to be interesting."

I was so wide awake I knew I'd never get back to sleep. "Mr. Sauers, I didn't need this call."

"I know, but I did. The good news is that you don't have to be at the club until 10:30... for TV makeup."

"You're kidding," I said, feeling the blood pound away.

"Have a beer and another hot shower; that should do it."

I never drink beer at home, but I went to the fridge, grabbed one of my dad's cold, golden Budweisers, drained it, drew a hot bath and promptly fell asleep.

CHAPTER ELEVEN

The next morning, I walked to work. I live five minutes from the shed and eleven from the clubhouse if I hoof it hard. I was nearing the shed when a pickup pulled over. "Get in, college boy."

It was Jerome. "Was that you I saw sloshing through the monsoon yesterday? God Almighty, some people don't know when to quit."

"Man, I was tired."

"I'll bet you were. It took us a while to repair the green where a plugged ball dug up the putting surface on Ten. I was tempted to cut the hole right on that dimple."

"What did you do? Set up the course for guerilla warfare?"

"Mr. O was planning to. Apparently he had a very unpleasant exchange with Mr. Cabiness at the reception and was planning to misalign tee markers or some shit this morning. But the USGA set up guys intervened and gave him an on-course tutorial."

"Is he in hot water?"

"I think the USGA guys are keeping quiet for now. Mr. O was actually helpful in suggesting pin placements and some other things, so his misstep might be dismissed as poor judgment."

Whew, disaster averted. Good thing, too. This sabbath was a gorgeous, cool sunny day, more like weather we get in late September. A little windy, but just right for drying the course.

"We've missed you around the shed," said Jerome in his southern drawl. "Oops, excuse me, administration barn. Even the super, though he won't admit it. Mr. Sauers did a nice thing and invited him to the banquet last night and had him take a bow. Shocked the old bugger, but he took it as a sign the course came together pretty well. Of course, that was before the dust-up with Mr. Cabiness."

"From the perspective of a guy who has walked a lot of it for the last three days, I'd say it's tip-top with the possible exception of a clogged drain on Fourteen-Fifteen creek."

"Got that this morning. Rossi fished out a bent 7-iron and a bunch of leaves. Who you got today?"

"Davenport v. Berenson."

"Who do you like?"

"You're the second person in the last twelve hours to ask me that."

"Who do you like?"

"I'm not a betting man," I said, "but I like Davenport in a long match."

Jerome let me out at the caddie shack. "One word of advice today."

"What's that," I asked.

"Be photogenic. You'll see why shortly."

A photographer and local reporter were just concluding an interview when I stepped into the shack. "Looper, here are your coveralls," Al said. "Like these green names on the back? We get to keep these things after the exhibition. If you're a nice guy, I might let you keep yours."

"Al, you know I'm always a nice guy."

"Of course you are. And the members appreciate it. Especially the influential ones."

I let the comment slide. "How do I look?"

"Like you're ready for TV. Go get 'em, Tiger."

The main parking lot had turned into a circus. On Friday, a local film crew had been the only visible electronic media. Today I saw three Chicago TV stations, including a WGN truck and a large Wide World of Sports transport.

Before I got to the clubhouse I could see print and electronic personnel clamoring for access to the players. A besieged USGA media staffer abruptly announced there would be no access to the athletes until conclusion of play. That sent a few enterprising journalists scrambling for other sources.

"Whoa. I know this is just an exhibition. But where would we be if this course weren't right?" I said softly.

"Shit's creek," said a passing Mr. Binswanger. "Don't forget that, Looper."

I dodged the parking marshals and eased into the Pro Shop. McDevitt looked a bit harried. "You okay, McD?" I asked.

"Yeah," he said, "just some women problems."

"Of the international variety?"

"Yeah," he said, running down a request for scorecards.

I looked at his stooped shoulders and thought about the domestic spillover with Cindy Cabiness. I wondered how it was affecting Janna Jorgensen's play.

"First match is coming in now," said General Sweeney from the porch.

"First match was Willard vs. Keisling," I said. "That looks like Wallace and Jorgensen, fourth match out."

The players trooped to the tent. Two minutes later Liggett, the other assistant pro, said, "Wallace, 9-and-7. Only went eleven holes."

With that Divot disappeared toward the practice tee. "Taking Davenport her bag, Looper."

Hmm, I thought, 9-and-7. That sounds remarkably like something I said last night.

"Don't you look like cock of the roost," said Starza. "First, the course gets all gussied up and then we beautify the caddies. What's this place coming to?" he said to Sweeney.

"It's coming apart," said Sweeney "nobody should lose 9-and-7. That's a crime against your country to lose 9-and-7," he ranted, acting an awful lot like a man who'd just lost something himself.

I wandered to the practice tee. I didn't hurry because I knew McDevitt was taking care of my bag and fare. No way was he showing his scalp around the clubhouse as long as Jorgenson was on the loose. Poor Divot, some day he might learn about mixing business and pleasure. But not this weekend.

* * *

I could tell Melissa was striking the ball exceedingly well. Draws, fades and straight ahead. I just stood at a distance and watched. That's when Wide World found me and started asking about the Marathon in the Mist. "I think that's what we'll call it," the commentator said. "Has a nice ring, and God knows, you went to great lengths to decide it." I gave them the full skinny and then excused myself, easing over to the practice tee. "Want to putt some?" I asked.

"Been there, done that," Melissa said. "Let me get some water and let's move to the first tee." Tom McAfee was presiding for the press, pontificating like the oldest member himself. Several men were standing by the course marshals listening to walkie-talkies.

"Nothing new," Angus Malthaus said to a denizen of the men's grill. "Swedes are up in seven of the remaining ten matches, but Alison Lindley is killing Erikson. She's four under after six holes and is up by six. Oughta call her 'Lights Out' Lindley," he said.

There was stone silence except for the Wide World announcer while our players were introduced. As I strode to the front of the tee box, he grabbed me and asked, "And here's Melissa Davenport's caddie Arlo Litton. Arlo, you've seen both women play, how do you handicap this match?" This I do not need, I thought. Who was this guy, Billy Sauers? I needed to get a driver to Melissa, and I was starting to stress. At a loss for words, I blurted out, "I'm packing for the winner."

"And there you have it, from a man who has caddied for both women in the last year. Arlo Litton, alias Looper, says his gal's got it won." And that's the way the caption ran on the screen when they did a segment on it later in the week on *Inside Golf.* "Looper Litton." It took me quite a while at college to live that one down.

* * *

From the outset it was obvious that this was going to be a Take No Prisoners match. What you have to remember is that tournament golf, even chauvinistic exhibitions like this, are not uniformly graceful occasions. And the truth is, despite the camaraderie at the banquets, on course the players don't always like each other. I think it's an instinctive thing. There can only be so many winners, especially when it gets down to singles matches, and everyone has something to prove.

Both players hit rockets off the first tee. When Berenson detonated one, you could hear an authoritative *crack!* For her part Melissa played persimmon woods and seemed to have little trouble this day matching the Swede off the tee.

The stiff breeze was also to Berenson's liking. I noticed she poked her fairway irons just a little farther and was a tad crisper with her short game. If Billy Sauers had been out here he wouldn't have been surprised at all that the early match followed my scouting report. However, much like a basketball game where one team is just a bucket away from taking charge, my impression was that one big move by the Swede could blow it open. The round progressed quickly and we went through seven holes true to form. Berenson was up one having birdied the 420-yard par 5.

From the tee something appeared amiss at the short par-4 eighth. And then I saw it. Off to the left of the green were two lawn chairs containing Mr. Howard, the reigning club men's champ, and his ten-year-old son, Tinker. "Best seat in the house, Looper, except for yours. What's happening here?"

"Berenson's up one. Davenport's struggling a bit. With this wind dying down, it should help my player."

"Anybody tired, hungry?"

"I'm beat to death after yesterday."

"I didn't mean you. When they putt out, ask them if they want any water. Tinker and I are acting as a water station."

"A water station with a walkie-talkie. That's a first."

"Don't want to miss any calls," he said.

The women halved the hole and came over for some water. I made introductions. Melissa and Mr. Howard had already met. "How you hitting them?" he asked. "OK," said both girls noncommittally.

"Straight," responded Walker Wilhelm, Berenson's caddy.

"That right?" Mr. Howard asked me.

"That's right. Look, neither player is saying much right now. I think it's about to get intense."

"I can see that" he smiled. "Enjoy the round."

As we trudged to the ninth tee, I gazed back in time to see Mr. Howard pick up the walkie-talkie. I knew where that call was going.

Berenson was still 1 up after Nine when Melissa left her birdie putt on the lip from forty feet. Miffed, she flipped her putter to the fringe in the first display of emotion I'd seen since the practice tee. "Looper, go inside the clubhouse and get me some of that Swedish sports drink. Raoul's got it in the refrigerator. The Swedes won't share theirs with me. I'll see you at the Halfway House."

Going into the clubhouse was the last thing I wanted. There was enough tension around without the added pressure of running into someone who wanted to know what the body heat of my player was. Luckily, I saw no one except Raoul. He seemed to know I was coming. "Good luck," was all he said. I smiled back and grabbed a small pack of raisins.

The tenth tee was a madhouse. Old Tom had taken station up top. "Everybody off this box except players and caddies. You there, Sweeney. Step back," he said to the general.

"Swedes are up two with four matches left," someone whispered. I hadn't wanted to hear that. This whole event had gotten too big, too public, too crazy and too rich for my blood. What happened to the spirit of exhibition? I wondered. A friendly match between amateurs? I'd never seen restraining ropes at Spring Willows, ever. Reminded me of a communications professor who once told me that to guarantee publicity all you needed were dogs, children or pretty women. Here we had men acting like both dogs and children gawking at pulchritude. And then there was the underlying scent of money. Everywhere.

Both players hit the green with six irons. I took Melissa's club and headed down off the tee. As I was breaking my way through the crowd, that same Wide World announcer stuck a microphone in my face. "Looper," we must have been old friends at this point, "what's it like out there?"

"Mortal combat," I said, pulling away to catch my player.

"There you have it," he intoned, "from the Melissa Davenport's caddie. You heard him, 'mortal combat.' Looks like a fight to the finish. Robert Taft reporting from the tenth tee at Spring Willows Country Club." The ladies both two-putted and made their way to the tee at Eleven.

In the last two months this hole had begun to assume a character of its own. Both the berm and trees on the left and the foliage behind the green were beginning to have their desired effects. The additions alleviated some of the unsightliness of the road so that now this 335-yarder had the potential, someday, of being as picturesque as any in Illinois.

Frankly, I was getting annoyed with the crowd. They were pressing the tee box at Eleven, there was no rope to keep the unwashed masses back and I didn't see any marshals. Walker and I looked at each other. I turned to the crowd. "All right, stand back. Give the players some room and some quiet. This is a golf match, not a girlie show."

Immediately I wished I hadn't said it. WGN and Wide World both had it on film and, damn if that wasn't the lead for the Sunday evening sports. "It may not have been a girlie show for the twenty-four players involved, but for those who showed up at Spring Willows Sunday…"

For the first time all day, Berenson hit something other than a crisp tee shot. It was a "thunk." The club hit sod; the sod hit the ball. She still muscled it a solid 170. Unfortunately, that's where the creek crosses the fairway. Surprisingly, the crowd had the decency to confine their reaction to audible gasps rather than raucous cheers. Melissa's eight-footer for par won the hole.

At Twelve we had most of the fairway to ourselves. We had a few spectators with us, but most were content to mill about the holes contested near the clubhouse and watch the players finish at Eighteen.

Our respite was short-lived when a marshal on a cart stopped me between Twelve green and Thirteen tee. "What's the score?" he demanded.

"All even," I told him.

On the other end of the radio I heard a familiar voice. "Tell Looper that Nilsson eviscerated Lammers and Wickham and Borg have gone extra holes. Arnesson is about to eliminate Newman, so if he's counting, the Swedes are up one with three to go. Tell him he's got to win his match."

"Mr. Sauers said…"

I cut the marshal short. "I heard what he said. You tell him that's a 'Roger.'"

"He's got the picture," said the marshal.

I braced for the onslaught. I figured that if you had any interest in these proceedings and were at Spring Willows, you'd be in one of three places: at command central near the eighteenth green, on the first tee for extra innings or headed towards us.

"What was that all about?" asked Walker.

"Tight matches," I said. "They wanted to know if we'd be done by 4:00," I lied.

"Dunno," he said, "someone needs a home run."

Didn't get it at Thirteen. Berenson drove the trap, but saved par to no one's surprise and Melissa coaxed in a six-footer to halve the hole. At the fourteenth tee the marshal was back and people were moving down the adjacent fairway at Two.

"What's all this noise?" I said.

"Wickham and Borg have gone to Twenty," he said. "And he said to tell you to strap in because Arnesson left Newman for dead."

"He said that?"

"That's exactly what he said."

"And..."

"And 'don't blow it.'"

I remember a time when caddying was fun. Last year it was fun. Looping around with Mrs. Peck, handing her 9- and 11-woods, just enjoying her straight, short 60-yard lofts. No pressure there. Oh, a little, at tournament time, but nothing you couldn't put in perspective. But here and now, one year later, I felt like I was in a whole other league. People, TV, money. All invading golf, a game best played alone in the long lines of fading sunlight, not in the white glare of publicity.

Melissa was set to tee it up when a roar erupted to our left. A throaty alto "Yessssss" punctuated the chaos. There followed another roar and another, longer "Yyyyeeeessss." I recognized the voice and the upward thrust fist and putter of Alice Wickham.

"What was that?" Melissa barked.

"Match must be over," I said nonchalantly. "Come on, tee off, we've got holes to play."

"Wait a minute," Berenson said to Walker. "Find out the score."

Walker stood her bag next to the ball washer and headed through the woods. He didn't get twenty yards before the first hoard practically trampled him. "What happened?" he blurted out. There was a pause as he listened, turned left and half-sprinted to the tee.

He told us what I already knew. "Wickham won it 1-up. This is the last match on the course and Sweden is up by a point." With that Ulrike Berenson broke into the broadest grin I've ever seen in a competitive woman. I could almost see the endorphins rising. She looked straight at Melissa and asked, "Do you know who Charles XII was?"

Melissa stared blankly.

"Tee time," I said. "Marshals, will you please control the crowd?"

Melissa took a measured backswing and deposited her ball 210 yards out dead center. Berenson's was ten yards farther. Melissa appeared agitated. "Who was Charles XII?" she asked.

"Sweden's last great conqueror. He's up there with Gustavus Adolphus. In the end, he fought the Danes, Poles and Russians. He finally got beat," I added hopefully.

"Well, I'm not Polish," she spat. "Give me that 3-wood."

"That's not your best club from here," I said. "How about a 2-iron?"

"How about keep quiet and give me the 3-wood?"

I wrestled with his one. Good caddie-player relationships are forged on mutual respect and trust. And there are times when a caddie should assert himself.

"The three, dammit."

This wasn't one of those times. "Look, Looper, I'm going to win it with or without you. What will it be?"

"Looks like a 3-wood," I said.

And it was. I read golf magazines when I can and occasionally I see the term "sneaky long," but I have never, never, seen it applied to women. But Melissa found something that day and just about reached that Sunday pin setting 230 yards away. She flat out whaled the ball and got a fortuitous kick off the right mound to send it within nine feet.

"Right. 3-wood," I said, putting the head cover back on. Berenson reamed her shot into the right-hand bunker, which truth be known, is where she preferred it. Get ready for the sand saver, I told myself. And that's another thing, you don't see many sand saves for birdies. Berenson recovered to within three feet.

The crowd was growing. I've always wondered how well-bred people with so much money can be so ill-mannered outdoors. Berenson's birdie was a foregone conclusion and Walker already had her driver out for Fifteen. What the world was really waiting on was Melissa's nine-footer. "Looper, over here," she called. It was the first time she asked my advice all day.

"The putt is against the grain and the ball will die left at the hole. I'd say aim two balls outside the cup, but hit it firm."

"You'd give the hole away?"

"Yes, ma'am, on this one I would." She stepped up smartly and ran that sucker into the heart... the heart of the cup. My heart, her heart, Berenson's heart and probably Charlie XII's heart for all I know. I'll tell you, I caddied some after that match, but I never bagged for another female eagle-maker.

If I thought it was loud after Wickham won, I needed earplugs after Melissa holed out. There was bedlam. "Yesss, yyyeeesss," went Alice Wickham. "Yyyeeesss." The press of the crowd got worse. It was so bad crossing the creek to Fifteen tee that Walker almost got pushed off the bridge. I saw a pickup beating a path to Seventeen. It was loaded with stanchion and chain. Too late for Fifteen, I thought, but Seventeen with its small tee and green promised trouble without some sort of law and order.

If we were going to salt the match away I thought Fifteen was where it would happen, since Berenson didn't like fairway bunkers. But I guess my guy couldn't stand prosperity. Each hit, for them, pathetic tee shots. Berenson ended up in the sand, but recovered nimbly and Melissa hit an impressive 4-wood moments later only to find a greenside trap. After the drama at Fourteen, unsteady putting by both parties produced only the third bogeys of the round. We marched to Sixteen.

For her part, Berenson appeared perturbed at Sixteen after a cameraman tripped and emitted a distracting yelp, which caused the Swedish star to lift her head. Her dimpled projectile rocketed 140 yards toward the small fronting pond, took two skips off the glassy surface and skittered back onto the fairway 190 yards out. What luck. The growing gallery roared. They were applauding every shot now as the two boxers traded heavy blows. Two more pars.

Melissa grabbed a 2-iron for her second shot. We were still up one. There's no pressure here, I thought, just national pride and thousands of dollars at stake.

At Seventeen, the crush of humanity was staggering. Ropes encircled the small, rectangular elevated tee, holding back a crowd four deep. I gave Melissa her 6-iron and took my place at the back of the box.

"Hey, caddie, move over, I need this shot for TV." I looked behind me to see the stumblebum cameraman from Wide World again.

"Melissa, stop," I said. "We're going to straighten this out. Marshal," I yelled. Two aging gents appeared. "Please position the cameraman beside the tee," I said.

"You're having a bad day, aren't you, son?" the marshal said to the cameraman. "There's a perfect spot down here for you."

"But I need to..."

"You need to be down here, man, out of the way," said a third militiaman.

Disaster rarely strikes the good players on Seventeen. Par is relatively easy as long as you stay out of the water. Melissa's adrenaline must have been running because she drove ten yards past the flat green. Berenson was on the left corner with a 15-footer and a slight break toward the water. Melissa pitched and ran to four feet. Berenson's ball stopped two inches short. Murmurs from the crowd accompanied both putts for par. America still led the match by one with a hole to go.

From a superintendent's standpoint, Eighteen looked damn good. It wasn't the greatest finishing hole in golf; I always thought Fourteen and Seventeen had more drama in the important matches where I looped, but on this day, with its brilliant sunshine and broad fairway lined with mobs of people, I thought it would do just fine.

After the Charles XII comment on Fourteen the players avoided each other, so it was up to the caddies to keep lines of communication open. There was no mystery as to what was at stake. Well, the Wide World cameraman probably didn't know, but the rest of us were wired in. I went over to Walker and shook his hand. "I don't know where it ends, but I've enjoyed it."

"Me too. Gonna be interesting," he said.

The gallery stretched from tee to green. A slice or duck hook by either player promised instant injury, but by now the golf was too good, the moments too golden, for some flub. I became contemplative. I felt sure there was a logical conclusion to this crazy summer that started with Mr. O and his hate for women. I just didn't know what it was. Could it be that this was the supreme irony, that the man who had spent the better part of his professional life trying to punish women had crafted a course in America's heartland that was now playing host to an international field of some of the world's best women golfers?

Did he really hate women, or was it his wife? Or himself he hated, I wondered on Eighteen that day. He sure didn't hate the course. It was his life. And maybe he was an ape and an oaf, but he did know greens and tees and equipment, even if he could use some continuing education. God, Mr. O, you almost blew it.

I thought of Jerome and Rita and what drama they'd added to the last ninety days. What's life without conflict? Maybe that's what I'd learned. Last summer it was about relationships and quid pro quo; this season it was anger. Origination and resolution of anger. I wondered if I had any anger.

I liked my dad and sister, loved my mom. I liked my roommates at school. I liked Al and most of the members. I did get pissed off at Mr. O sometimes, but that was about it. I was sure I was angry about something. I'd have to think about it.

I didn't have to wait long. The Wide World goon was back, muscling his way to the front and getting ready for a ground level shot four feet from the box. "That camera moves or I pull the plug," I said.

"Look, I'm Ryan Wilson and this is Wide World of Sports, fella," said the cameraman.

"May I have some help here?" I asked a marshal. "This man is bothering the players," I said. "He can get the shot he wants from back there," I said, motioning to the back of the box.

"I'm a working journalist," he huffed, "and I'm not taking orders from a caddie."

"This camera moves now, or I move it with a sand wedge," I told the official.

"I want a closeup," he whined.

The gendarmes were closing in. The cameraman settled for a ground shot from 20 feet. And he got two good ones when the girls powered screamers to the prime landing area 220 yards away.

"Hey, thanks," Ryan Wilson (aka Bozo) said. "This is my first golf assignment and I'm trying to make an impression."

"You're making an impression, just don't try so hard." I was running to catch Melissa. Ryan ran hard to catch up. I stopped him cold. "Okay, you want the perfect ending shot, here it is. At the green from the fringe, get opposite the Swede so she putts toward you. Follow that first putt as it curls to the hole and then, regardless of the putt, rack focus on the girl. That's your shot. Because if it's in, she ties and they win. If she misses, she's disbelieving. Action, reaction, sport. That's sports photojournalism in a nutshell."

"On the fringe, huh?"

"On the fringe."

"What's the deal there?" said Melissa.

"First day on the job. I'm making him a hero."

"How about me?"

"You're already a hero. Want the 3-iron?"

"Yes. I'm not the one that needs a birdie." The 3-iron was short by 40 yards, but perfectly placed. Berenson's 3-wood was left, pin high 35 feet from the green. In between was a bunker.

"We lucked out," said Melissa. "If she had found the trap, I'd have picked up. She doesn't miss from the sand."

As it was the Swede had a dicey chip from medium rough. Between the beach and the green were three feet of heavy and then light fringe. From there she faced thirty-one feet of downward, left-breaking terrain.

Melissa took a wedge and dropped it twelve feet below the hole. Not great, but on the green. Berenson grabbed a pitching wedge, studied the ball, took her stance, and backed away. "Sand wedge, please."

Heavier club for taller grass. Good call, if she hits it hard enough, I thought. With this kind of shot the trick is to swing through harder than necessary to carry clubhead momentum and spring the ball. The best approach is to imagine the pin is five feet farther away. I heard a light plane drone overhead. It had become deathly quiet around the green.

The sun glinted on the Swede's shaft as it began its downward trajectory. Powerful, smooth, sweet. Did I say light contact? The ball sprang, but too softly, clearing the trap and the heavy fringe but dying on the edge of the green. Not the desired result. She never showed any emotion and never broke stride. She stalked the green low, plum-bobbed, checked her line and squatted above it, giving it one final read. She reminded me of a tigress in nature films, pacing back and forth before the kill. I just knew someone was going to die.

Across the green I saw Bozo lining his camera up just as I said. He was on his stomach, sighting his machine like an M14. If he only focuses, I thought, he's going to have a happy boss.

Berenson stepped up, ran her left hand down her hip, steadied her wrists and head and stroked.

An instant replay, especially in slow motion, gives sports such a sense of theater. When the film is shot at 48 frames per second and played back at 24, you see each revolution of the ball, dimples kicking flecks of sand sideways, wobbling over spike marks, skidding across dried Bentgrass on a journey as long and lonely as, I don't know, a world without love. This trip was thirty-one feet of heartbreaking travel.

I've watched that putt a hundred times. The cameraman Ryan Wilson sent it to me after he got nominated for an Emmy.

When Walker pulls the pin, my throat never fails to catch as the ball goes 450 degrees around that cup. In slow motion it stays down forever, but it never goes 'thunk.' And it always comes out. Thirty-one feet, three inches that ball traveled, a journey by way of the center of the earth.

And the audio, have you ever heard recorded sound in slow motion? It's a little less garbled than 78 RPM vinyl slowed down to 33 1/3. In this case it sounds like an inexorable moan that builds to a dull unintelligible crescendo. In truth, it's not a pretty sound. In real life, at normal speed, it was a fantastic experience no matter whose side you were on. The anticipatory roar began the instant after she stroked the ball, which traveled the exact line she planned. The rumble built and swelled into near frenzy. I kid you not. Berenson pumped her fist when that ball hit the cup. Her putter rose to shoulder height, but at 1/32 MPH too fast that little white pill, all 1.68 centimeters of it, lipped out.

If I thought the explosion on Two was loud, I almost lost my hearing on Eighteen. I have a framed picture on my desk of me and Melissa right after the event. It's autographed by Alice Wickham, whose blood curdling and now famous "YYeess," has become a part of my lexicon. When things really great happen now, I say "YYeess," just the way she did that afternoon. Alice Wickham almost broke my eardrums. This cheerleader was jumping like Mick Jagger and every bit as loud. The din was incredible. As the crowd surged on to the green, Alex rack focused on Berenson. Her face looked wistful, a strand of her light brown hair gracing her eye and extending below her mouth. She looked gorgeous in defeat.

The crowd, untutored savages that they were, rolled onto the putting surface. The marshals worked hard to push them back. It looked like Times Square on New Year's Eve. People were everywhere, jumping and hollering. If Yogi Berra had been there, it would have been no big deal. Absolutely none. "It ain't over," he would have said. And he'd have been right. There was still more golf. At least three strokes I figured. Two from Melissa and one from Berenson.

My concern was how smooth Melissa's line was, what with the maniacs who'd trespassed on her line. I checked it. She checked it and the marshals checked it. It looked OK to us. Twelve feet uphill. It went eleven-six. Berenson motioned for her to tap in. When the ball bottomed, Melissa went over and hugged Ulrike Berenson. It was an honest, sincere display of friendship and respect. They held each other longer than the perfunctory pleasantries I see on TV. Then arm-in-arm went to the scorer's tent.

Walker swooped down, retrieved Melissa's ball, and tossed it to me. "Souvenir," he said. "Got mine here," he said, motioning to Berenson's Titleist that he'd just marked. We started toward the Pro Shop when yet another marshal called a halt. "Back to the green guys," he said helpfully. "Awards presentations." Shouldering the bags, we drifted to the side of the mammoth scoreboard that held the names of the twenty-four participants, some of whom I'd gotten to know quite well in a few short days. I was amazed at the number of red digits. There'd been some great golf.

To the side of the scorer's tent I saw Binswanger gesturing wildly to his assistant manager to make tracks for a floral truck fifty yards away. A sound system was being extended to the side of the green and the tournament chair Trafford Bowles was getting ready to speak. "It is indeed a pleasure for me," he intoned "to welcome you here as a part of what we hope will be the first in a long-running international golfing exchange between the USGA and the Swedish Golfing Federation." He went on about the agony, ecstasy and atmosphere of the event before turning the microphone over to the president of the USGA.

"Captains of both squads decided this morning that if there were a tie following this afternoon's rounds that no effort would be made to resolve them competitively. Their feeling was that if the teams were that well-matched then the result should stand. It is therefore fitting…" Bring on the girls, I thought. They're the ones that created the excitement, not you windbags. "… that I introduce to you Pia Nordstrom, nonplaying captain of the Swedish team, and Pauline Pickett of the U.S."

The women made complimentary noises about their opponents and in a nice display of sportsmanship took turns presenting medals to one another's teams. At the conclusion, the USGA thanked Spring Willows for a fine four-day run etc., etc. I hoped that maybe Mr. O would take some of that to heart for, sure as shooting, despite some hard feelings along the way, he could take most of the credit for the well-manicured course.

Walker and I steered for the Pro Shop until we were stopped by more marshals. "Hey, lighten up. The event's over for me," I said to the old codgers.

"Not yet, not for you two. Over here."

Damn if it wasn't Ryan, the Wide World cameraman again with the boy wonder commentator Robert Taft. "Stand right there," said Ryan as he racked in on Berenson and Melissa, who were giving their version of the shootout. It was sound bite stuff mostly. And I was trying to figure if their observations jibed with mine. From what I could hear it was reminiscent of the match I'd experienced.

"…and we'd especially like to thank our caddies for allowing us to concentrate on the match," said Melissa.

"Squeeze in here, men," said boy wonder. Addressing me, he said, "when did you know Melissa had it won, with the eagle on Fourteen?"

"Not hardly," I said in my best on-camera voice. "I had an inkling on Eighteen when Alice Wickham broke my eardrums with another 'Yyyyeeeessss.'"

"I think we've got that on tape, don't we, Ryan?"

"We sure do," he said.

"And you, sir," he said to Walker, "what was it like to watch your golfer's ball lip out on Eighteen?" I mean, what a lame question. What's he supposed to say? "I was counting on it, being that I'm an American, Bob." Or "I just wanted to run across the green and make the hole bigger?"

Instead he looked at Berenson and said "she played like the champ she is. A lesser player would have given up four holes earlier."

Walker gave her a little chuck on the cheek with his fist and Robert Taft went back to his "and there you have it," signoff. We shook hands with the girls for the first time. There seemed to be plenty of respect in that foursome and a spirit of fair play that had been lacking in some other championships I'd been in. "Well done, ladies. We'll take your bags to the Pro Shop," I said.

"If I could play that well, I'd head straight for the tour," said Walker.

CHAPTER TWELVE

On Monday I heard the superintendent say, "Looper, you didn't have to come in so early. You oughta take the day off. Go home."

"No, Mr. O, I know this course got a workout over the weekend and there is stuff to be done. Since this is my last week before I go back to school I wanted to give it a full effort. Nice job. The course really did look good. Held up well after all that rain on Saturday."

"Jerome and Rita get credit for that. It was a team thing. I can tell you one thing I learned this weekend."

"What's that?" I asked.

"Some women can flat play," he said.

My first job Monday was to inspect for signs of wear and tear on One and Two -- and from Fourteen in where the crowds had hovered during the final matches. Aside from some heavy footprints on greens and fringes the course looked amazingly good.

"Aerating and overseeding ought to take care of any residual stuff," I told Mr. O.

Wednesday Mr. O had a wrap-up meeting with Jerome and Rita who were giving him some technical manuals their professors had sent. "Basic education with an updated twist," insisted Jerome. "Nothing Mr. O doesn't know intuitively. Just something to fall back on if he needs it."

"How about the irrigation literature?" I asked.

"The Rainbird stuff? He knows where to get that. I'm not stirring that one up."

Rita left the following day for Bend, Oregon where she'd signed on as an assistant super.

"New belt," she said, "just like my dad wanted."

"First rung to Pinehurst?" I asked.

"Something like that. Looper, it's been fun. Thanks for going along with the charade. I'm sure this summer will stand me in good stead in the days ahead. Trailblazers never have an easy life."

"Stay in touch," I said.

"You bet," she said.

* * *

On Thursday I eased into the caddie shack. "Welcome stranger. What took you so long?" asked Al.

"Busy week at the shed. Rita's gone, Jerome's fixing to leave, just a lot to do."

"Just so you know, I've put you in for one of those caddie scholarships."

"Don't you have to write essays and stuff?"

"Not on this one. The national committee takes nominations from clubs. You present a great image. The model caddie, the kind most clubs kill for."

"Well, that's awful nice, Al. And not to appear ungrateful, but except for guest appearances, I may have looped my last Eighteen for the summer."

"Guest appearances?"

"If Mrs. Worth or Mr. Howard call, I'll go with them. Otherwise last weekend did me in."

"What if Cindy Cabiness calls?"

"Tell her hello. She doesn't need me as long as she's got McDevitt."

"Divot's in the doghouse now. That Jorgenson mess didn't sit too well with her. She told Hillary Weston she's through with him."

"Until she gets lonely in two weeks. Then her pride will vanish, and McDevitt will be back in the saddle again. But that's their worry. Mine is getting a real job."

"You got two more years of school. What's your hurry?"

"Maybe it's just been a long summer."

CHAPTER THIRTEEN

Mrs. Worth was out of town for the weekend, but Mr. Howard did call for Sunday, so I went Eighteen with him and his family. Tinker carried his own Sunday bag and looked like he may have inherited some of his dad's golfing prowess. "He's got nice tempo through the ball. Some adults never get that," I said to his father.

"About ninety-five percent of the men at this club are all about power," Mr. Howard said, echoing a theme I'd heard earlier that summer. "What they really need to do is control their tempo and work like hell on their short games. I may have a course in my front yard, but I've got a driving net and chipping and putting areas set up in the back. That way I can practice in private and stay out of members' way. When people talk about my game, they mention my power off the tee and my irons, but it's my short game that wins it for me.

"Watch this." We were on Seven, about 127 yards out. "This is a wedge for most people. I like a nine. I'm going to call my shots. First one will be left six feet from the hole. Second one will be fourteen feet past. Third one will be within two feet. Watch closely."

He set up for each shot the same way -- and missed his combined distances by 23 inches. "That's control. Life is about control."

The Howards toured the next nine holes in relative silence. We were each enjoying the warm afternoon air and the arboreal silhouettes. I watched monarch butterflies and tiger swallowtails dance on the zephyrs. They zipped in and out of the sunlight with a grace that only ballerinas could emulate. Meanwhile, gray squirrels sprinted between the hickories and oaks doing diligence that would pay dividends during the colder days ahead. Their claws caught the bark on the trees and created a gentle rattle reminiscent of the jangling irons in Tinker Howard's Sunday bag.

All in all, it was a great day to be on the greensward, particularly since play was light and most members had other things to do. Mr. Howard broke my reverie on Sixteen. "One of the most attractive aspects of this game for the average golfer is the beauty of the surroundings," he said, reading my mind. "When a guy is playing poorly the course may be the only consolation he has. The puny strivings of some golf architect aside, it's really the thrill of nature that brings him back, don't you think?"

His observations gave me pause. Here I was. I'd spent the last two summers groveling in the loam for Mr. O, digging up dirt for Billy Sauers and toting heavy bags for personalities large and small. Yet I returned to the course day after day in one capacity or another, as bagboy, bagman, snitch, sandman, amicus curiae. I must love this place. For sure, it had changed my life.

"Take this hole," said Mr. Howard, staring at Seventeen. "What's so hard about it? Your motion needs to be fluid. Jerky motions put you in the drink. Tinker, give me a range ball," he said to his ten-year-old. "Let me show you," he said, continuing the lesson. "Watch this, son. Stopping the swing too soon gives you that 'plop' sound there. Too much right hand will give you 'thunk' and the trap. Just right produces three feet from the pin. Nothing too it. Tinker, you can hit from the reds with Momma."

He let out the club on Eighteen and went 260 yards if he went an inch. "That's what they see at the clubhouse, but that's not why I'm a winner." In another five minutes he was putting for birdie.

"I'm in options and commodities. Do you know about them, Looper?"

"Not much, " I mumbled.

"High risk, high reward. Ballsy stuff that requires an inside knowledge of markets, trends, meteorology, instinct and no fear. I'm good at it. That's why I have that house over there," he said, motioning toward his mansion. "That's why I have that pretty woman as my wife and, in part, why I'm men's club champion. But I'll tell you one thing, for all the bravado I profess to have," he said lining up a thirty-one foot putt, "I wouldn't have wanted that putt Berenson had a week ago. A whole country on your back? When's the last time Sweden won anything international except in wrestling or canoeing? That putt was big-time pressure. That woman deserved a gold medal for that stroke. With her strength and will she'd be a great commodities broker." He left his putt short by two inches. "Great effort," he said, tapping in. As confident as he was, I knew he was still talking about Berenson.

"You coming back next summer?" he asked, as I placed his putter in the bag.

"Hadn't thought about it too much, actually," I said.

"Well, you ought to. Probably time for you to move from the shed to the Pro Shop. You'd be good up there. You know most of the members and they respect your knowledge of the course and the game. Plus, you got manners and native intelligence. Some of those pretty boys we got in there now don't know a driver from a putter, and those who do can't keep their hands off the members. Starza needs a fresh face up there. You might want to think about that. Pay's pretty good. I don't think recommendations would be a problem. Think about it, hard."

I didn't know what to say.

"You don't have to say anything, Looper. Just think about it. You all packed?"

"Yes sir, I'm leaving tomorrow after work."

"Here's some gas money. Fill up the car." He handed me a fifty-dollar bill.

"Thank you, sir."

"Think about what I said."

While he and his family walked to the snack bar, I took their clubs back to the Pro Shop. "Wash 'em good," I said to Ratchet, the ball boy. As I gazed down the hill, I could see the setting sun just brushing the treetops. Long left-to-right shadows fell over One, Eleven and Eighteen, while the final green was bathed in a rich, fading light. Kodachrome, I thought.

I ambled to the caddie shack, spun the combination on my lock, and began to clear out my locker. I threw three dirty towels behind the counter and stuffed a fourth in my athletic bag. I changed shoes, put the FootJoys in a carrying case, and dropped two smelly polos in a plastic inner lining. The last rays of sunlight barely worked their way into the dingy compound, falling on a deck of bent Bicycle cards on the beat-up card table. As I left the shack, I fumbled for the fifty in my pants and slipped it into my wallet. Maybe good things do happen to good people, I mused. That still didn't explain why Ulrike Berenson's putt didn't drop.

* * *

School was a blast. I finally had courses I wanted to take. My room-mates couldn't understand how I could get up so early, but for a G crew guy, getting up at 7 a.m. to eat breakfast was a luxury. In the afternoons I had time for studying, writing for the school paper, intramurals and three rounds of golf a week, often by myself. When I soloed, I'd play three balls at a time. One for Sweden, one for the U.S. and one for me. I'm still not sure if I was out there for the game or for that thrill of nature Mr. Howard talked about. I especially enjoyed the lingering daylight, the bustle of the squirrels and the soft breezes that accompanied me and the monarchs on our rounds.

I heard from Rita. Bend, Oregon was badly in need of a woman's touch. She was having no trouble in the Pacific Northwest implementing some contemporary methods on a neglected course. "Rogue River C.C. was great at one time," she wrote, "all it needs now is a reincarnation. That's why they brought me in. I can do this."

"Don't end up like Joan of Arc," I wrote back.

Jerome stayed on at Spring Willows through the first week of October when Kenny got back. Then he took a job at Kinston Country Club in North Carolina. "Kinston puts me back in my belt where I need to be. This place isn't as polished as Hope Valley or as posh as Spring Willows, but it's a great course for putting new ideas into practice. Besides, the people are nice and respectful of what I'm trying to do. I'm going to like it here, for a few years at least," he wrote.

He went on to say that he appreciated my friendship during the summer and that, despite the violent disagreements and occasional dehumanization at the hands of Mr. O, he thought he'd become a better greenskeeper and manager because of it. He also said his feelings were not tempered at all by the $3,000 bonus he received when he left. The accompanying note was cryptic. All it said was "Thanks for bringing us out of the Dark Ages."

I didn't get a bonus, but then, I didn't expect one. I did, however, get some correspondence from First Strike Investment Services, Inc. The first piece of mail was in the form of an account statement, one I'd never seen before. It was very formal and showed three transactions and tracked the progress of some securities purchased since the account's opening.

There were eight digits by my name, which I found odd since I had no brokerage account. And while the transactions were with familiar names, I had no recollection of ever buying any stocks. I noted, too, that there was upward movement in each stock since the date of initial purchase. At the bottom of the sheet was a line that said, "Total Market Value: $6,546.00." I was confused.

Three days later, I got a handwritten note that was obviously intended to clarify the formal papers. It read, "Looper: by now you've probably gotten your first account statement. Congratulations on your ability to pick winning stocks. Keep the monthly records on file for IRS purposes. (This is very important.) You will have to report this income. In case you are wondering, this account has been set up for you by an anonymous donor.

"Secondly, here's another check for your investment advice. Your record in the recently completed International Exhibition was outstanding, bringing joy and humility to those who deserved it most.

"Our midnight phone call produced considerable revenue sharing. In fact, I am taking the liberty of sharing some of that with you now. I especially appreciate your candor and insight into the emotional stability (and instability) of the various contestants. While I restricted my own wagering to only a few selected matches, I was able to counsel and succor other members of the gaming fraternity.

"Specifically, I took Willard in extra holes like you said. And I made a killing on Wendy Wallace over that Jorgenson girl. I bet it wouldn't go past Eleven and Sweeney lost his shirt. Alison Lindley vs. Erikson was an equally wise choice. In a show of restraint, I left all other matches alone." I was very surprised that he didn't get involved with the Davenport-Berenson contest. Then I turned the page.

"I stayed away from that Davenport-Berenson clash except for a minor side bet. I bet Stroud 5-to-1 that Berenson would convert every sand save opportunity, which you assured me she would (and did). That proved to be the piece de resistance.

"You do good work, son. But it may be time for you to move up the hill. Good, smart young people are hard to find."

He closed with, "This year make sure you come and see me over the holidays." Signed Billy Sauers.

I put the letter down. A check fell out. It looked remarkably similar to the one I had gotten a year ago. It read "First Strike Investment Services, Inc. – International Exhibition Consulting Services -- $3,000."

I was numb. Maybe I should have been getting used to it after Mrs. Peck and last summer. But this year all I did was look around and make observations. And then tell somebody what I thought. How hard was that? Well, I had to admit, getting through to that ape Mr. O was brutal some days. But Billy Sauers seemed to listen. And I had no trouble communing with nature on the 200 acres that comprised Spring Willows.

Moving up the hill, I didn't know about that. Rogue River or Kinston Country Club seemed more my style.

PART THREE

THE PRO SHOP

CHAPTER ONE
CHRISTMAS, 1961

John Cabiness was a study in human misery. He stood alone by the sweater rack pondering the spring merchandise. I couldn't help but thinking what a forlorn and tortured soul he was. If he weren't so impotent I might have pitied him. I mean, I'd never let my wife tramp around the way he did. Over, under, inside, outside, all over town and all over McDevitt, one of the assistant pros. I mean, even unimportant people like me notice stuff like that, especially in a high-profile environment like Spring Willows.

A true lost soul, last winter he looked confused and miserable at Spring Willows' Christmas bash.

The final straw came as a result of a conversation I overheard outside the men's grill. Once again I wondered why Billy Sauers was always around when the final votes were cast.

"John, you know I'm not one to mess around in other people's personal lives, least of all yours. And frankly, I don't care what that pretty wife of yours does in her spare time, but I can tell you this: it won't do to have a president-elect whose wife openly slips around with the assistant pro."

"Sleeps around, you mean," said John Cabiness.

"Slips around, sleeps around. When it gets to this level she's fucking with all of us. If it were a one-time affair we could forgive and forget, but you have to admit, John, these private lessons of hers are the ultimate dalliance.

Personally, I love your wife for all the right reasons, but you can't represent us as the host at the State Amateur next year with this stuff going on."

"But she thinks the world of this guy, Billy," John Cabiness whined. John Cabiness was sweating bullets in his black holiday attire. His festive cummerbund matched his crimson countenance. His brow was dripping. His After Six wing collar was soaked.

"I do too, John. But it's too obvious and too public. Look, I don't mean to sound harsh, but how long has your family been members of this club?"

"Since it was founded. 1914."

"And how many of your relatives have been club president?"

"My father, grandfather, two uncles and a father-in-law."

"How many were club champions?"

"All five."

"And how long have you known your wife?"

"Twenty-one years."

"How long have you been married?"

"Fifteen."

"And how long have you known McDevitt?"

"Three."

"Right. Three fucking years. And how long will it take the board to come up with another candidate for president if you don't gird up your loins and put a stop to this shit?"

"I really don't know."

"With all due respect, John, try about two minutes."

"But, that's not proper," he protested.

"But not unheard of either. If you want that post, you need to lay down the law to that sweet wife of yours."

"But Billy, it's not that easy. I love her. And she loves him."

"John, it is easy. It's like firing someone for the first time. Tough emotionally, but after that it's a piece of cake."

"Look Billy, this is the holidays. I'll take care of this in my own time. I'll do it, but on my schedule."

"All I'm saying John, is no balls, no blue chips. I can't make it any plainer than that. This relationship has to stop even if I have to confront the S.O.B. myself. No assistant pro from Dime Box, Texas, is going to make a mockery of this club and its members. And before you go on that ballot, I want your promise that that relationship ends."

"Oh, God. Jesus, Billy don't do this to me."

"For Chrissakes, John, do it for yourself. Be a man. Live up to your name. At the very least, do it for your Jennifer. No twelve-year-old daughter should ever hear rumors about her mother."

"She doesn't know a thing," he snapped.

"You can only hope."

"All right, I promise to try."

"That sounded wimpy to me. You're going to have to kick ass and take names here."

"Oh man, I don't know."

"Yeah, you do. This conversation never took place. That way you can be the lone gunman in this assassination, and everyone can rush to judgment about what a man you are. Semper Fi."

Billy Sauers turned to walk away, broke stride and addressed the wretch again. "One more thing, John."

"Yes?"

"Merry Christmas."

"Merry Christmas to you, Billy."

I headed away from the men's grill when I heard a voice and felt a hand. "Good of you to come, Looper. I see you've got that Davenport girl in tow. You're coming up in the world."

"Yes sir, I'm trying," I mumbled. "I appreciate the invitation."

"Nothing to thank me for, son. This was the club's idea. We're still hoping summer may find you up the hill in the Pro Shop. We'll need staff when Kellogg leaves for Medinah."

"I don't know. That's a lot of responsibility."

"Bullshit, Looper," he said, calling my bluff. "You know almost every damn member in this club. The caddie master brags about you, the members stand in line to have you carry their clubs, and even that dumb-ass super Mr. O thinks you're good. And Starza needs someone he can trust."

Billy Sauers didn't miss much. He'd just named everyone that mattered. I paused. "I was thinking maybe this was the year for Europe."

"Europe? Have you lost your mind? Europe will be so expensive in this summer of the undervalued dollar it will take you three years to pay for the trip."

"Mr. Sauers, it may be my last chance."

"Christ, what am I doing with you bunch of babies tonight? Looper, it's your destiny. The Pro Shop is meant for you. It's everything you're good at: golf, finance, member relations and organization. Plus, the connections are unbelievable. You'll have job offers before the summer is out. You'd be crazy not to take it."

"For one thing, it hasn't been offered."

"For one thing," he said mocking me, "you haven't applied for it. Get your ass in gear. Binswanger will be in all next week getting ready for the New Year's Eve party. Go see him. Fill out the application. See if Starza will interview you by phone. I think he's at Seminole this week. I'll get a number where you can call him."

"What about the employment committee?"

"Looper, you're talking to it. Mr. Howard and I are the only ones who count. And if you don't know where you stand with us, we're all in trouble."

He had a point. Mr. Sauers had been a behind-the-scenes mentor for the last two summers, coaching me on the finer points of country-club politics. In return, he had gotten the inside scoop on how members were performing in club tournaments and international exhibitions. He'd parlayed the information into some serious side money. Mr. Howard was the four-time defending men's club champion. And while he and Mr. Sauers didn't pal around that much, each had an overwhelming drive to win at everything as well as nurture the environment and ambience that made Spring Willows one of the most prestigious country clubs on Chicago's North Shore.

"Well, I do like this place."

"And we like you. So why not get on with it?"

"I just don't know."

"Look Looper, I just heard that phrase – and I suspect you did too, so don't make me beg. You're ten times smarter than that sap I was just talking to. Spare us all, do yourself a favor and go see Binswanger."

With his wild gestures he almost spilled his scotch. His agitation was rising. "And son, just so I make myself clear, you never heard that conversation I had with Cabiness there."

"I don't know what you're talking about, sir."

"Good man." He took a deep breath.

"I'll think about the Pro Shop, Mr. Sauers."

"Think hard." With a clap on the shoulder he sent me on my way.

* * *

Upstairs it was pandemonium. The recurrent themes seemed to be "home for the holidays, huh, son? We're looking forward to having you with us in the Pro Shop next summer." If I heard it once that evening I heard it twenty times. Where did people get the idea I was going to join them for yet another summer? The idea had been circulating since the fall when Mr. Howard raised the issue with me on a late Sunday round -- and God knows how long he and Billy Sauers had been making noises before that.

"Where have you been, Looper?" asked my date Melissa. "I thought I'd lost you."

"Not likely. I've got the prettiest date here."

"You've been neglecting her, son," said Ellis Worth, husband of multi-time women's club champion. "You can't have women golfers unescorted around me. When Margaret finally putts out, I am coming looking for a fine specimen like Melissa."

"You're sweet, Mr. Worth, but you've had too much punch. Why don't you go find your wife or send her over here and we'll talk about our 1-irons?"

Melissa looked stunning in her off-the-shoulder, ivory-colored gown. Her brunette hair was coiffed mid-length and complemented a healthy tan that hadn't quite faded from a summer of tournaments and a notable international exhibition against Sweden's best amateurs on Spring Willows' own fairways.

I'd known Melissa for several years, all on a very casual basis as a result of her relationship with Mrs. Peck, former club champion and longtime Spring Willows member. Melissa was her granddaughter and I had caddied for them when Melissa was visiting from California. She'd been junior champion at the time and now was at Stanford. Since matriculating she had steadily worked her way up the junior rankings and was now one of the nation's top young female players. Since Mrs. Peck's death sixteen months earlier, her aunts, uncles and cousins were making a concerted effort to see more of one another, hence Melissa's appearance in Illinois.

Our date? I'm not sure whose idea that was, but I'll bet the fifty-five dollars in my wallet that Billy Sauers was near or at the center of influence when that bit of intrigue was hatched. Anyway, all I know was that I received an invitation and a phone call during a six-hour period over Thanksgiving with the strong suggestion that I call a certain Melissa Davenport at 415-693-0055 to see if she wouldn't be my date for the Spring Willows Christmas Ball. "She'll be in town, I'm sure she'd love to accept," said Billy Sauers's wife, Elise. That she did, and cheerfully, considerably brightened my Thanksgiving and Christmas season.

This was only the second time I'd darkened the portals of the ballroom for a formal event. The first was as an invitee to a welcome reception for the international exhibition. The talent in the room that night had been young and breathtaking. This evening there were far fewer Swedish meatball comments. The only dirty jokes emanated from those who never missed these affairs. The surroundings had begun to feel familiar. My comfort level had improved. I guess that happens when one gets to know people. Several times during the evening I found myself thinking that just maybe I liked these folks.

As of late the club had worked hard to cultivate a small but growing base of younger members. On this evening there were two bands in the house, one for the old fogies who liked big band stuff, and one for the junior set who preferred the dance floor to the buffet line.

Melissa was clearly at home in this milieu. Members knew her as Lucy Horton Peck's granddaughter or as the first-class golfer instrumental in the U.S. comeback last summer. Others came to know her as my date. Even Mrs. Whippet, one of Mrs. Peck's archrivals, made a point to come up and ask for an introduction, an etiquette I thought diametrically opposed to the foul play and bad manners she'd displayed against Mrs. Peck some sixteen months ago.

"Looper, you are coming back, aren't you?" she said in her most grating and gravelly voice. "The club needs you."

"That's nice of you to say, Mrs. Whippet. By the way, I'd like you to meet my date, Melissa Davenport."

"Pleased to meet you, dear. I suspect you could beat ninety-eight percent of the men and women in this room."

"I don't know about that," Melissa said coolly. "There's a lot of ability here."

"Most of that is untapped, dear. In this world there are doers and talkers. Right now, talk is carrying the day. I dare say if we put the clubs on the cart there are only two in this room you couldn't beat." Susan Whippet gazed into Melissa's eyes and took a long drag from her cigarette, turned her head slightly and expelled two exquisite smoke rings.

"Who would that be?" I asked.

"Worth and Howard."

"What about McDevitt?" I said.

"First off, he's not here. Secondly, I suspect his best club is a driver. I doubt his short game is very effective." Another pause. Another drag.

"How's your game, Mrs. Whippet? You had a good run in C flight this year."

"I belong in B flight, Looper. I can be that good."

I was startled by the admission. Last year I felt sure she'd been sandbagging, but to hear it from such a strident personality took me off guard.

"But enough about me. What are your plans for next summer? Up the hill, I hope? When Kellogg leaves for Medinah we'll need an ace like you, someone we can count on. Starza can't do it all. He's got lessons to give, management and merchandise responsibilities, not to mention monetary. That shop is an $800,000 operation, Looper. We need someone like you."

"You've got McD…"

She took a drink and cut me short in a voice intended for public conversation. "I said we need someone we can count on, not some assistant pro who thinks giving private lessons begin at the belt buckle."

I was starting to feel very uncomfortable. Glances had become glares.

Susan Whippet lowered her voice. "Getting a new assistant isn't all that easy, Looper. The Big Divot has a lot of supporters. He plays very, very well. There's a lot to be said for a guy who can hit long and straight and score well with members. Bottom line for you though is that this is a great opportunity. Better than any MBA program or silly trip to Europe."

"Yes, ma'am."

"Nice to meet you, Melissa. Good luck at the Women's Open next year. I'm sure you will qualify." She was gone.

"What is this?" I said to Melissa. "Two people know about my plans for Europe next summer, my mother and…"

"One other guy," she interjected. "Sounds like somebody's been talking."

"Come on, let's get something to eat. That crabmeat looked awfully good."

The buffet line had thinned. The normal tussle for the moveable feast wasn't as frenetic. "Good stuff," I muttered between mouthfuls. "Beats what I get at home."

We went back for seconds and retired to a small parlor well away from the grand ballroom. "You know, Looper, I think there's a message here tonight. And it has something to do with the Pro Shop and your need to be in it. Unless this is some orchestrated thing, I'm hearing a lot of interest in you up on the hill next summer. Maybe it's fate."

"It's Billy Sauers," I said. "He invited me here so he could make his point. I didn't come tonight for a job interview, but I should've known that's what it would be. C'mon, let's go find a band."

One thing I'll say about the Spring Willows clubhouse, it was an imposing structure inside and out. I knew the outside intimately thanks to countless hours weeding phlox beds, cutting grass and cleaning the parking lot. A sweeping lawn surrounded three quarters of the monstrous Victorian building. The eleventh tee guarded the south quadrant, while the eighteenth green and the first tee bordered the west and north sides. An immaculate putting surface occupied the north sector. Suitably removed behind a mixture of cedar trees and tall privet hedges was an acre of macadam which served as a holding area for every luxury car known to man. And on this night there were two shifts of valet parking attendants running guests to and from the extended parking lot not far from the pool and the tennis courts.

Inside the clubhouse, ceilings, like some members, were unapproachable. In the ballroom they rose thirty feet high. Ornate rococo ornamentation highlighted their vaulted nature and the crown molding. Everything about the place bespoke lucre, especially old lucre. But here at Spring Willows money could no longer guarantee admission. Status helped. Family ties helped more. Here was another place in America, the land of decaying culture, where being a legacy mattered most of all.

Tonight's turnout was far greater than the international exhibition welcome. The din was constant, though much of the buzz rising to the rafters required revelers to roar at one another. I don't know how much listening was going on given the nature of the crowd and the presence of alcohol, but there was plenty being said.

The acoustics, on the other hand, were marvelous, allowing merry-makers to wallow in the best music the big band and sound machines could muster. "Nice tunes down the hall," said Melissa. "Let's join the fun."

To be honest, for the next ninety minutes I didn't think about next summer at all. I just enjoyed Melissa's company, the setting and the season. I had to admit I savored the ambiance. If this were how the upper class lived, I could see why F. Scott Fitzgerald was so obsessed with the lifestyle – and so worried about his St. Paul roots. Most of all I enjoyed Melissa. We seemed to share an understanding of people and a set of common values I found refreshing. I could blame the liquor I suppose, but we didn't drink any until Ellis Worth jammed some in our hands later in the evening. Up to then it was slow waltzes, fast dances and some surprisingly chummy moments from some old high-school classmates whom I thought had dismissed me years ago.

"Maybe it's because they can see you matter to some important people around here," offered Melissa.

"Maybe it's because of who I am inside," I said.

"These guys aren't dumb, Looper. They can read, too. You've got substance and are being given substantial encouragement from the highest sources."

"Yeah but when's the last time Woody Braun, excuse me, Woodard Wilson Braun, IV, said anything to me? I'll tell you when. It was eighth grade on the soccer field when I scored on him. And what he said wasn't very nice."

"What about high school?"

"He went to Choate and I stayed here. No way he'd talk to me if…"

"If what? If you weren't being noticed?"

"Yes, thank you."

We were angling toward the mistletoe when I felt a strong hand on my left shoulder. "Son, the missus and I wanted to wish you a Merry Christmas."

"Thank you, Mr. Sauers."

"I don't want you to forget our conversation, either. You seemed a bit troubled at the end. That worries me."

"It's just that…"

"Excuse us, won't you, Melissa? You and Elise give me and Looper a couple of minutes if you will." Seizing the moment, Billy Sauers began to escort me to the nearest wall. "Just what?"

"For once I'd like to get something on my own."

"Like what?"

"Like maybe a summer job."

"Let me ask you something," he said, beginning a line of questioning very reminiscent of that outside the men's grill. "How'd you get that first caddying job?"

"I applied for it."

"You applied for it. And how did you get the grounds crew job?"

"I applied for it."

"Looper, two years, two jobs. Who helped you get the first two jobs?"

"No one."

"Correct again. You got them on your own. You kept them on you own. Now, let me ask you this: how would one in your position go about getting a job at the Pro Shop?"

"I'd apply for it."

"Looper, there seems to be a pattern here."

I felt really small, bunched in the corner of the ballroom. "My point is, Mr. Sauers, I guess I don't want to be handed a job because some members like me."

"Looper, people don't just give other people jobs. Especially not around here. You have earned the right to be considered for the Pro Shop position. For two years you have been earning the respect of the membership. You have a good way about you. You have excellent manners. You're bright and you keep your mouth shut. I like that in a lad. So does Mr. Howard. The membership respects you, especially after the way you took charge on the eighteenth green accommodating that jerk from Wide World of Sports. Did you notice your well-to-do high school buddies acknowledging you tonight?"

"I did find that a bit strange."

"It wasn't because of your lovely date. It's because you've got something they don't have yet. Respect. You don't see me or Mrs. Worth or Mr. Howard or Judge Gleason talking to them, do you?"

"No, sir."

"Hell no, and they're our neighbors."

"I'm dumbfounded."

"Well, don't be. But don't be dumb either. Europe can wait. You'll get your chance. London and Paris aren't going anywhere. You are. This is the ship to be on next summer. That's all I'm going to say on this subject. But Looper, do us both a favor next week. Check in with Binswanger. It's not just me that wants you in the Pro Shop, Looper."

CHAPTER TWO

Three days after Christmas, in near-blizzard conditions, I was back in the clubhouse, visiting the club's general manager.

"Looper, good to see you," Mr. Binswanger said. "Billy Sauers said you might come by. Interested in that Pro Shop job?"

"Thought I might inquire," I said. "Is there a job description?"

"Not at present. We'll be doing some shuffling, so our staff will have to be flexible."

"What kind of shuffling?"

"Kellogg's moving to Medinah. I hate to lose that kid. He's a good one. Complements existing staff well, too. And then we have a new shop girl, Denise Long, you probably know her. Graduated a couple of weeks ago from Iowa State. In fact, she's in the shop now ordering merchandise for next season. Why don't you go see her?"

"What about the application and interview?"

"I've got your grounds crew application from last year. That's good enough. Anything you want to add? Class honors, anything like that?"

"I won a writing prize and am on track to make Phi Beta Kappa as a junior, but that's about it."

"Fine, I'll note those. Stop inside and say hello to Denise."

"What about the interview?"

"We just had it, Looper."

"I haven't filled anything out."

"Don't worry, I'll do that. But if it will make you feel better, sign this blank application. Here."

"At least tell me what you think I'll be doing."

"Taking tee times, registering guests, selling merchandise, advising members about balls, gloves and clubs. You may have to pull some starter duty if McAfee gets sick again. And, if we get really short-staffed, you might have to give a lesson."

"I'm not a pro, Mr. Binswanger."

"No, but I've seen you play, and your game is better than ninety-five percent of the folks out here. I can see you giving lessons, especially to the ladies. Oh, and from time to time you'll be called upon to play a few rounds with members, especially before the member-guest and club championships."

"That's it?"

"That's the job. Nice work if you can get it. On those lessons, most of the money goes to you. Starza clears fifty dollars per half hour; McDevitt, thirty-five– and at that he's a bargain. "You'll probably get fifteen."

"McDevitt gets thirty-five per half hour?"

"That's what he puts in his pocket. Go see Denise," he said waving his hand. "The committee meets in two weeks. You'll get a letter. Nice to have you aboard."

I passed through some backrooms and a pretentious portal into the Pro Shop. Denise was placing some ladies' shorts on chrome racks when I entered the shop. She looked twenty pounds heavier than I remembered, but still had a cherubic face and full figure. At 5'4" and slightly overweight she was still a looker. She moved with assurance among the sweaters and slacks. "You're the new shop girl, huh?"

She jumped. "Whoa, you startled me," she said, patting her heart. "Don't do that." She caught her breath. "Arlo Litton. Well, I'll be. If you aren't a sight."

Denise and I went back a long way. She was a year older than I, and as a second grader she was the first girlfriend I ever had. At the time she had bright blonde hair that gleamed halo-like wherever she went. As a result, she was always the teachers' pick for the blessed angel in Christmas pageants, a position she loved until fifth grade when she decided she'd rather be the Virgin Mary. But her hair served her like the mark of Cain. By then she'd become such a character actress that no teacher at Harper Elementary was going to give up a natural angel, especially when they already had goody-two-shoes Marilyn Forsythe as Mary. If it were any consolation, Denise's blonde hair worked at least through high school. With all her energy she knocked the guys dead as a cheerleader.

"Did you graduate early?" I asked.

"Sure did, two weeks ago. Between advanced placement and summer school I had enough credits to graduate early."

"How'd you wind up here?"

"My degree is in business and marketing with a minor in fashion. The piece that got me to Spring Willows was my knowledge of fashion. Two summers in college I worked in the fashion department at Marshall Field. I sold apparel, designed counter displays, dressed windows and went on buying trips. This is a natural progression."

"Kind of a comedown, isn't it? Sounds like you were on a pretty sweet corporate track at Field."

"It's not where I want to be right now. Maybe later."

"Who'd you know to get here?"

"Mrs. Worth. But once I applied I was on my own."

I wondered if any of us were on our own anymore. I was positive Margaret Worth had mentioned Denise Long to Billy Sauers. Prequalification from Mrs. Worth would serve as one hell of an endorsement.

"Good for you," I said.

"It'll be nice to have someone from my own background here this summer."

"I just came up to fill out an app."

"I hear, in your case, it's just a formality."

"Apparently so. I can't imagine life is always this easy."

"I doubt it. But hey, take it while you can."

"Where's the rest of the staff?"

"Starza's in Jupiter seeing friends at Seminole. McDevitt's in Texas seeing family. Kellogg is at lunch. Not many golfers today with this white stuff. When do you start?" she probed.

"I'll probably take a week after exams and then come up mid-May. Should be an exciting summer, especially with the State Amateur being run here."

"I'll probably have to order some special merchandise for that. Maybe I can get some good ideas from a PGA seminar in Florida next month."

"So, after Florida and Spring Willows what are your long-range plans? I can't see this being a lifetime position."

"It's a start. Maybe open my own shop somewhere. Carmel, Rodeo Drive, Palm Beach, Boca. I don't know. Short term I want to lose some of this," she said, pulling at her pink sweater, revealing an ample waistline. "This, I don't need. My New Year's resolution is to lose 25 pounds and get into some of those clothes I had as a freshman."

"With your drive I can see that happening. What's your second resolution?"

"You want to be my boyfriend?"

"Denise…"

"Oops, sorry. First thing's first. Do you have a relationship?"

"Denise, my mom and I are pretty tight, but that's about it. As far as dating people in the workplace, my dad tells me that's not a good idea. But I'll tell you what. It'll be good to have someone from my own background working here. Put me on your dance card for some good times this summer."

"Looper, you always were a straight shooter. You got a deal."

After some more small talk I bought my leave, checking in one last time with Binswanger. He and his secretary were at lunch, but on the way out I saw a letter to First Strike Investment Services, Billy Sauers's company. Lifting the page, I saw my grounds crew application, a retyped Pro Shop app and an additional note from the club manager to Sauers, the arbitrageur. It read, "Sauers: Looper in today. Note the Phi Beta Kappa designation and the fiction prize. Kid's a prince and a perfect balance to McDevitt. Also gets on real well with the shop girl and understands the importance of not mixing business with pleasure. He'll await your letter. Binswanger."

Is the whole world this well-orchestrated, or is it just Billy Sauers? I replaced the sheet and left the big house, turning a warm left cheek into the biting blizzard.

I think I've told you I live only five minutes walking from the maintenance shed, and perhaps eleven from the clubhouse. But on days like this, when the snow was a foot deep, even with boots it took a mite longer to plow my way home. And that was perfectly fine with me because in all of Illinois I don't think I'd ever encountered a more peaceful stretch of land than Spring Willows. Each season brought a panoply of colors, each dawn a distinct hue, each change of weather a different mood. And I reveled in it all. For four years of high school walking home was absolutely the best part of my day. The stroll down Eleven, Twelve and Thirteen was a welcome respite from the rigors of school. Sometimes, when the weather was foul and no players were out, I'd cut through Sixteen, Fifteen and Fourteen and exit by the curling rink just for a change of scene.

But today seemed special and I was happy to leave the politics at the clubhouse and turn my emotions to the cold and damp. Snow was forecast for the rest of the day and the parking lot was swollen with fluff. Given there were no functions for two more nights I doubted that the plows would hit the lot until early tomorrow. I stepped into the drifts and made my way around to the front of the clubhouse, leaving solitary footprints as I went. I gazed south down Eleven. From the terrace my vision floated over the creek to the line of red maples that was the new signature of what was once our most mundane hole. From my vantage point I scanned the distance. Horizontal layers of snow whipped the oaks and hickories, giving an even grayer cast to the aging hardwoods.

I unflapped the hood to my ski jacket and pulled the drawstrings. The wind howled into my ears until I got the cord tight. Then it was just me, the wind and the wet snow stinging my nose and exposed cheeks. I wiped the flakes from my lashes and worked my way down to the maples, whose thin tentacles were barely distinguishable against the backdrop of mounting white. I could detect, barely now, the limbs of the black gums as they edged the right playing surface of Eleven.

Skirting what I knew to be the green, I veered right and then stumbled headlong into the sunken bunker surrounding the putting surface. Moisture surged under my hood. I lay in a mass of confusion staring skyward at an ashen, almost white sky, laughing at my own stupidity. For all the times I'd raked and weeded that deep trap I should have remembered the location. I chuckled again, thinking of Mr. O, the one person who would really appreciate the humor of the moment. From my vantage point I watched some far off boughs bend ever closer to the ground. Much more snow, coupled with a hard freeze, would do some serious damage. Across the road onto Judge Gleason's property, I could see his two large tamaracks tottering forward with each gust of the wind. Overloaded, I thought. These boughs were in for a tough forty-eight hours.

Oddly, I didn't move for a full half hour. After the initial shock I reached a comfort level with the elements and lay supine, silently gazing at the sky and contemplating life and my place in it, much the way I remained motionless after the shrill sound of the morning alarm. In my wintry blanket I felt cocooned, recalling images from Conrad Aiken's epic short story, *Silent Snow, Secret Snow* and the protagonist's obsession with the white.

I'm not sure what my being in the bunker, the clubhouse or my presence in the Pro Shop meant yet. I was pretty sure I had a summer job if I wanted it. The rest of my life seemed in order. School was going just fine. Relations were good with mom and dad; even my sister and I were speaking. And my social life was on the upswing as well.

A warm feeling swept over me as I relived the Christmas party at the club. Aside from the dressing down I got from Billy Sauers, my existence was pretty darn good. The evening with Melissa had gone very well to the point where we had even gone to the movies two nights later. But even better, her family had decided to stay though the New Year. With that came plans for us to spend New Year's Eve together, a thought that almost melted the snow around me. While our plans weren't definite, it appeared that we were going to take in the dance at Spring Willows for at least part of the evening. I felt I had come a long way since my caddie days.

My reverie was broken by a blown clump of snow. Oblivious as I was, the wind had reached gale proportions. I slowly rose and steadied myself against the furious blast. I could barely see the distant clubhouse and instead focused on the tree line back to the tee. A thick white line highlighted the leeward arbors and served as massive sentinels as I turned and trudged wet and cold toward home. I passed the super's shed, or 'administration barn,' as Mr. O liked to call it. No one home this day. And with bad weather piling up, it looked like the year-round staff might be off for a couple of days, with the exception of those attending to the curling rink, paddleboard courts and the parking lot.

* * *

New Year's Eve was pretty darn neat. Melissa and I went to the dance and stayed there all night. Unlike the Christmas frolic where I was besieged with employment messages and ideas about how to run my life, we were greeted with quiet acknowledgements. The whole parent–child dynamic was almost nonexistent. Granted we didn't feel like peers or equals -- this crowd would never allow that -- but at least we felt accepted as a couple.

And this duo thing was beginning to have some interesting aspects. For a guy relatively inexperienced in these matters, even I recognized hints of romance in the air. Guano, my buddy from the kitchen, spirited us a bottle of champagne at about 11:30. We found the anteroom off Binswanger's office and broke training for a while. Neither of us professed to be drinkers, but the warmth of the clubhouse, the gaiety of the evening and the biting chill of the sub-zero night coalesced into moments of champagne-induced cuddling.

When we emerged, we were questioned by the partygoers wanting to know just where we had been when the ball fell, etc. Margaret Worth was particularly miffed that she couldn't promptly welcome in the New Year with my date, whom she considered to be next year's U.S. Women's Amateur champ. Elise Sauers took a far more enlightened view after seeing the lipstick on my collar. She merely offered, "We old fogies have been served long enough. I think it's time youth had its day. Happy New Year, dears."

Elise's husband was busy conducting business, his own and that of others, but he did make a point to give me a warm pat on the back, thanked me for visiting Binswanger and assured me the committee would be meeting shortly.

I guess I don't need to tell you I got the job. On January 13 I received the formal offer. It came in a letter from Binswanger who said that my title would be 'Pro Shop assistant' and that I would be paid $4 an hour. Some quick math told me that if I worked 40 hours a week for 14 weeks I could earn close to $2,240 in reportable income for the summer. In addition, though nowhere was this mentioned in the letter, I could probably take in more than $1,000 in tips and lessons. This information came courtesy of Billy Sauers and was subsequently confirmed by McDevitt. I waited three days to respond and sent Binswanger a formal reply indicating that I would start on May 15.

But for two notable exceptions during second semester I put golf behind me. One was my own game. I made an effort to play at least twice a week and to hit balls with Aston Williams, my friend on the varsity team. As the days grew longer, we took an early supper and then hit the links for nine or more at twilight. Aston was a lot like me, a contemplative sort, and we often let our clubs do all the talking, smoking 4-irons into banked greens while letting our minds take us to faraway places.

Most of my thoughts went to Palo Alto, where Melissa was packing her clubs for Stanford. When not getting letters from her I scoured the San Francisco paper in the college library to glean the latest results. She was having a good year, scoring well in dual matches, and emerging as a medalist in some of the more important tourneys. But as the expectations rose and pressures mounted, the correspondence became less frequent.

To her credit, Melissa had told me in early January what to expect. Relationships with college golfers aren't the best. She recounted tales of senior team members who by necessity concentrated on their games and schoolwork to the exclusion and often displeasure of potential love interests. I understood, but still found myself focused enough on the west coast and her daily routine that I began making weekly calls. At first, she was surprised and a bit miffed, but in short order she began to view the conversations as a therapeutic release from the high-pressure world of competitive golf and we grew closer as a result.

* * *

I've always enjoyed getting mail from women, so it was all the more surprising when on Valentine's Day I got a package and a note that began:

Dear Looper,

Here's a start on your summer wardrobe.

I've been looking at new lines in an effort to get the Pro Shop merchandise (men's and women's wear anyway) into the 20th century. And I'm making headway. Binswanger and Mr. Sauers have been pleased with my choices and suggested I send you these embroidered shirts so you'll look presentable on your first day on the job.

They've sent me to several PGA professional training and development seminars. The ones on merchandising and maximizing golf shop retail business gave me a bunch of ideas on how to make the Pro Shop more appealing. The merchandise show this year was first-rate. Starza has added some new manufacturers and is beginning to do a lot of custom fitting. I've been given some autonomy here so, at this stage, I don't feel as stifled as I feared.

One encouraging sign is that the men are starting to come in here actually thinking about their wives. They are beginning to buy from a gift line we now carry. Even John Cabiness (poor sap) bought a crystal Waterford golf ball for his wife. He must be miserable. His purchase aside, shop sales are already up 20 percent for the year. That increase is primarily due to gift and fashion sales, so I'm revved up.

Hope these shirts fit, and you and Melissa are doing OK. I special ordered these hues for you because they show off your coloring to best advantage.

Your fellow employee,

Denise Long (Shop Girl)

P.S. The gym trips are working. I've shed eight pounds since the holidays. Come see us when you're home.

Going home during the school year wasn't something I did much of, so I never did make a spring appearance at the Pro Shop. That didn't keep me from getting frequent updates after I made the mistake of answering Denise's initial epistle and package.

For my part, I tried to keep the letters short, dispatching just enough warmth and trivia to be pleasant but not enough to elevate the relationship to pen-pal status. I really had too much to do, and I suspect she did as well. Between studying, managing the swim team, golf and a low-level social life, I had all I could handle. And with a new job, its related travel and going to the gym, I would have thought Denise did, too.

What I found as the winter wore on was a more frequent bombardment of my campus mailbox with missives from Spring Willows. And, in truth, the contents were at once revealing and spellbinding. In Denise I now had an insider with a young person's perspective who relayed rumors and details the likes of which Billy Sauers would rarely reveal. In many ways it was like being back on site.

The big news (or bone of contention) was the ongoing saga of Cindy Cabiness and McDevitt. The relationship was over, sort of, Denise reported. Allegedly, John Cabiness wrote McDevitt and told him to stay away from his wife. Denise wondered whether the letter was ever mailed or merely submitted as evidence to Billy Sauers that, in fact, John Cabiness had taken a firm stand on this most personal matter and was now fit to follow his ancestral line to the club presidency.

All sorts of people were unhappy with this feeble attempt at leadership. First and foremost was Billy Sauers, who would have preferred John Cabiness initiate a more manly face-to-face confrontation, but with McDevitt escaping to Florida for some January tournaments the letter had to suffice. Denise did say that Billy Sauers was reported to have said, "You should have bought a damn ticket, gone there and punched him in the nose, John."

However, unspecified business difficulties were diverting Billy Sauers's attention big-time, so at a critical stage in the presentation process he and Judge Gleason rubber-stamped the Cabiness nomination and elected to live with the consequences. Denise intimated that she thought there was a Plan B but went no further. Also aiding John Cabiness's bid, she noted, was the prolonged absence of McDevitt himself who, it was rumored, was having some real competitive success in Florida and not expected back until early April. Stay tuned, she said.

She also advised that by the Ides of March she had dropped 15 pounds and was feeling better about herself. She even said some of the members' wives had complimented her on her perseverance. One, Emily Newby, had cautioned her against too much weight loss since it might be hazardous to her health. "I think there was a message in there, too," wrote Denise. "I notice that Mrs. Newby tries very hard to be checked out by the men around here. I don't think she likes the competition. But, I will press on until I get my tires slashed," she wrote.

Apparently, Emily Newby had not changed one iota in two years. She was still the one bag all the caddies wanted to tote and undoubtedly remained the talk of the caddy shack. I would stay tuned, I thought, if for no other reason than for protection in case I found myself mired in some clubhouse intrigue. Not as an eyewitness to history you understand, but more as an innocent bystander caught up in the greening of Devin McDevitt.

Through it all I wondered what Billy Sauers's take was. I surmised it was frustration at John Cabiness's resolve and indecisiveness. But as I later learned in some detail, Billy Sauers's late-winter business issues precluded virtually any involvement with Spring Willows, much less his leadership role in the resolution of John Cabiness's marital difficulties.

In fact, I only had two pieces of communication from Billy Sauers the entire semester. The first was a phone call from his secretary, with an apology from him for not making it in person, to find out my class schedule. The second was an overnight letter with an airline ticket and an expense check. A terse personal note said, "Use this for three days and nights in Florida. I want you to attend the PGA's seminars 'Dealing with Difficult People' and 'A Pro's

Guide to Exceptional Customer Service.' These will help you this summer. Any side trips to Fort Lauderdale are at your own expense. Have a safe trip. Send me a postcard. Billy Sauers."

That was it. No, 'do you want to go?' No 'Can you go?' Just 'go.' So I went, barely missing a nasty Midwest storm and picking up a little sun stolen poolside before my Sunday return.

The sessions were more informative than I expected. Most of it was applied common sense. I mean I could already identify and understand difficult people, but the behavior modification portion gave me some ideas on how to handle the drunks like Kaufman and Stroud as well as the obnoxious General Sweeneys of the world.

Exceptional Customer Service was a bit redundant given my penchant for trying to please. However, the speaker's frame of reference, and ideas on how to give quality attention to customers from a Pro Shop perspective, gave it a reality base for the summer travails to come.

After the trip to Florida, schoolwork, swimming and sportswriting became my focus. As swim team manager and assistant sports editor of the campus paper I was close to the action and wired in with the swim coach. He provided insights into the human psyche. In a way it was like working with Billy Sauers except I never got a national award from Billy like I did for an article when our team beat Kenyon for the conference title.

Not that my winter months were without reminders of golf. For one, I was getting fortnightly missives from Melissa about her game. Then there was the ever-increasing correspondence from Denise, the nature of which I was beginning to question. Her letters were chock full of detail on SKU's, shelf space and return on investment, details of which I'm sure had been overlooked by previous management. Sales for February were up thirty percent over the previous year. She attributed the increase to earlier ordering of merchandise and a mailing she undertook to the female club members. Her new gift lines were going gangbusters. I might even want to pick up an item for my favorite girl, whoever that was, she hinted.

Her notes also mentioned the continued absence of Billy Sauers. She likened his disappearance to that of a responsible absentee owner, available if you really needed him, but gone otherwise. Her contact was minimal, she said, though she recalled one phone call praising her for her fashion and revenue-raising expertise. "Stay on those mothers and kids," he said, "I think you're onto something." By the way, he wanted you to know that Spring Willows was looking for a director of golf.

A surprise note from Kinston came two days later and in my reply to Jerome Gjertson, last year's assistant superintendent pro tem, I asked why Spring Willows might be looking for a director of golf. Jerome was quite direct. For one, he said, most posh clubs like ours already had one. Generally, such men, always a man, he affirmed, tended to be aging figureheads and/ or former tour players.

Injuries, or a case of the yips, may have short-circuited mediocre careers, he said, but almost all directors of golf had some singular season or career moment that highlighted their resumes. "At Hope Valley our first director's only claim was beating Lew Worsham in a playoff at some long forgotten pro-am. Beyond that the guy was a boor and a drunk. After a season and a half (and a night with the president's wife) he was sent back to a head pro arrangement just south of Hades, Mississippi," he wrote.

Jerome's take was the Spring Willows job was big enough and that Starza was busy enough to warrant establishment of such a position. "Personnel selection is critical. I'll tell you one thing," he said, "Billy Sauers better like whoever they hire."

A week later I called Jerome on the phone. "Life in Carolina's Inner Banks suits me fine," he said. He'd bought a two-bedroom house off the water and he and Jackson, his yellow lab, were happy as clams. Jerome's only problem at Kinston Country Club was members wanting to play with frost on the greens. "The learning curve is slow here," he said. "Most of the members are retirees who don't want to hear anything that feels like a restraining order from someone years younger than they are.

"As for that Pro Shop deal, you're about as well prepared as a man can be. You're probably overqualified. Caddie, G crew, Starza and Sauers-influenced, you're the whole package, Looper."

"I'm not sure where I can add value to the current staff," I said.

"I'll tell you two spots where they need help: in the bag room and with the carts. It's not that there aren't enough people; it's the education of who and what they got. One assistant pro should handle the bag room and one should monitor the carts. Right now they've got Al trying to handle the caddies and the carts. That would be OK if he had some help from Kellogg, but he's getting ready to leave for Medinah. That bag room needs an iron hand, a Bismarck type. Nothing would improve relations faster with the Pro Shop than a good check-in and clean-up system for bags. Hell, they've got enough bag boys. Someone needs to sit on them and make them work. And that includes when they leave the bag room to get the carts. Check that out and see what goes on. Half the time it's Drag City from the cart shed to the first tee. What those boys need is a tight leash and some expectations. They're not going to get it from McDevitt."

"Probably not," I muttered.

"How's he doing, anyway?"

"I understand he's had a good mini-tour season. John Cabiness is club president this year. Divot's coming back, but for how long I don't know."

"I may not be the marrying kind, Looper, but I think I'd have more pride than to let the assistant pro poke my wife."

"I know Billy Sauers feels that way."

"There's a man with strong convictions. What do you hear from him?"

"Virtually nothing. I got those orders to go to the PGA seminars and that's about it. I hear from the new Pro Shop girl that he's been preoccupied with his own business."

"Well, he'll want to involve himself in the director of golf selection because whoever they choose will have a big ego and require supervision."

"That's why they've got Judge Gleason," I said.

"I've never met a director of golf who didn't think he was God's gift. Judge Gleason can rule all he wants. They'll still need an enforcer like Billy Sauers."

"Or Mr. O," I said.

"Mr. O's a piece of work. Which reminds me, one other thing you can do at the Pro Shop is be the liaison to the shed. I think Mr. O might have had that in mind when he recommended you for the job."

"Mr. O recommended me?" I asked incredulously.

"Yes sir, he did. On my last day there I heard him talking to Binswanger. He gave you an unqualified endorsement. Said he hated to lose you but looked forward to improved dialogue with the Pro Shop."

"You're kidding?"

"Actually 'communication' was the word he used. I gotta run. Call me when you get up there."

* * *

The director of golf issue came to a head with Starza's stroke in early spring. My notification came through Denise. It seems that around one lunch time Starza felt a tingling in his left arm as he was gobbling an egg salad sandwich before giving a lesson to Mrs. Pate. Apparently, he thought nothing of it. "Angina," he said.

"Based on his diet I'd believe it," opined Denise.

About twenty-five minutes into the lesson he complained of chest pains. When Mrs. Pate expressed concern he sat on a three-legged stool and finished the lesson. When he got up, he staggered, dug three divots, two with his knees, one with his nose, and lay motionless.

Fortunately, Denise wrote, Mrs. Pate was a nurse in her former life and CPR-trained. She administered to him while Kellogg summoned Dr. Pate from the putting green. Starza was sent by ambulance to Evanston Hospital and diagnosed with a mild stroke. Denise went to see him. "He's in good spirits but will be out of work for about three weeks. The prognosis is good, but his work schedule is in question."

I had a better spring vacation than Starza did. For once I indulged myself, took a little of that money Billy Sauers sent me for my Swedish Exhibition Consulting Services and went to the Bahamas with some college friends. We ran into some girls from Sweetbriar and drank just enough Pimm's Cup to maintain a seven-day glow. All in all, it was a good way to recharge the batteries. The return to campus life found us meditating on mid-terms and papers. While I never liked exams, the essay-writing was easy and I passed countless hours doing extra work on my compositions and classroom prep as a hedge against any faltering performance on finals.

I also found time for golf. Aston was practicing with the varsity, so I went solo late in the day, working on high fades from the fairway and chips from heavy rough. I once heard a pro say that for every 75 chips a golfer hits he should stroke a thousand putts. My putting game didn't need that kind of attention, but I did close each day stroking 100 ten-footers just to make sure the touch was still there. Turns out that wasn't quite enough to keep me from finishing second in the college intramural tournament to a transfer student from Stetson.

Thanks to Denise's constant correspondence, Spring Willows continued to be top of mind. Starza this, Kellogg that, Binswanger this, etc., ad nauseam. The good news was that come May 15 I'd be back in the loop.

The bad news was I wasn't sure I had time for all the menial stuff I would be expected to do. What was enlightening in one letter was the news that a committee headed by General Sweeney had been formed to find a director of golf. Also on the committee were Judge Gleason, Alvin Bullock, Margaret Worth, Eldridge Wankum and Billy Sauers. To hasten and facilitate the process, Spring Willows had hired a recruiting firm, Wedges & Longiron. The goal was to have the successful candidate in place by June 1.

I didn't know word one about Wedges & Longiron, but my assessment of the committee was that with the influence of Judge Gleason and Margaret Worth, Billy Sauers had his majority so my read was that the director would be a fellow who would fit in and function well.

My thinking, of course, was based upon the premise that Billy Sauers would be an active participant in the selection process. That he wasn't mystified me. In fact, it appeared that the consulting firm was calling all the shots and Billy Sauers's only official appearance was at the initial committee meeting.

I found that odd, given his hands-on approach to everything else at the club. How could a guy who meddled at the grounds crew and caddie levels, and walked among the elite at the clubhouse, not be omnipresent when picking a director of golf? Something was amiss.

Something was. Denise's next letter filled in a number of the blanks. In addition to business distractions, Billy's wife, Elise, was diagnosed with cancer. Details were sketchy, but the prognosis was not good. Since the diagnosis she had been to clinics from Anaheim to Austria and Menninger to Moscow without much luck. The news appeared to be bleak on most fronts. Elise was looking at less than a year to live. This development was known only to a select few (Gleason and Worth), and became public only when McDevitt overheard a private conversation Billy Sauers was having with Binswanger. Not being a very private person himself, Divot unintentionally spread the word.

That explains a lot of things, I wrote back. I can't blame a man for tending to life's real priorities, i.e. a wife and a business. But for a man with as much mastery and command it seemed strange not to have him in charge of the search committee.

The parade of candidates was fairly impressive, Denise wrote. The resumes read well, and the credentials looked good on paper. Her knowledge was firsthand because Binswanger had asked her to read and rank the applicants. There's even a guy who beat Snead in a GGO playoff, she said, and a couple of Ryder Cup alternates from years gone by. Interviews start May 7, she wrote.

Whomever is chosen can't come soon enough, I wrote back. Starza won't be able to handle a full load when he returns. The assistant pros were barely hanging on with the escalating amount of good play the weather was bringing. Denise said she had become almost fulltime in front, and Harley Hudson, the retired pro from neighboring Iroquois Woods, was helping three days a week.

The most telling comment came during a call from Binswanger. "Looper, when the hell do you get here?"

May 15, I told him.

"That day can't come soon enough," he said.

Other than that, things were pretty quiet, Denise noted. Surprisingly, McDevitt and Cindy Cabiness appeared to be ancient history. John Cabiness was trying to look presidential, and apparently his supporting cast was letting him. Nobody dresses better than John Cabiness, Denise wrote. He's got that great gray hair that looks smashing in all those pink polos, but underneath I think he's a very sad man.

Billy Sauers would have probably used the word "pathetic."

Take a deep breath, finish finals and come on down, Denise wrote. And speaking of down, I've another lost seven pounds. That's 22 now, if anyone's counting.

I didn't know what I was supposed to do with that information even after the letter was signed, "Warmly, Denise."

* * *

Spring was coming late to my college town. My rounds were played in heavy clothing and chilly weather. Finals were fast approaching, and I was worried about only two courses, Advanced Accounting Principles and Entrepreneurship and Emerging Markets. Both demanded utilization of untapped brainpower. I questioned whether I was up to the task. My other classes, World War, Marketing Case Histories 343, Beowulf and Astrophysics II were relatively simple. By doing optional papers and supplemental reading early in the semester I'd managed to lighten the year-end academic load. Finals were testing but rewarding and I left for Spring Willows confident that I was ready for the real world. Boy, was I wrong.

CHAPTER THREE

My appearance at the Pro Shop coincided with Starza's return. His reception was of royal proportions. Even the kitchen staff paid their respects, gestures that seemed to keep his weakened condition buoyed for the first several hours.

Starza was direct, as always. "Looper," he said, "the doc says I can only work until 2 p.m. for the first week or so. So, if I bug out on you guys it's nothing personal."

"How can I help you?" I asked.

"Your first couple of weeks will be OJT. The fastest way to learn would be to take turns shadowing Divot, Kellogg and Denise. Kellogg's postponed his departure for a month or so. Ask them what they don't like about their jobs and offer to do it. Don't ask what they like. That will be obvious, and you can learn best by watching and listening. The only thing I don't want you to do, is do what Divot likes best. Hands off the members, old and young, is the best policy. I don't know how much I'll be able to provide in these interviews, given my reduced schedule. I suggest you make a list, and once a week we can review the things on which you want clarity. That OK with you?"

"Works for me," I said. "Otherwise I'll go to Kellogg, Divot or Denise."

"On a personal note, thanks for your letter and that collection of Wodehouse oldest members stories. They made my day. You both have a way with words."

"Thank you, sir. I was just trying to spread some cheer."

"Well, I thank you for it," said the old pro.

Just then Binswanger came briskly through the door. "Stan, here's a list of candidates who made the second cut. General Sweeney wants to get it down to four, five max, so we can start interviews. He asked if you have any info good, bad or indifferent about these chaps. If so, get it to him by tomorrow. Of course, you know we've got that fellow from Arkansas coming in. He got a good recommendation from Tommy Bolt."

"Well, that says something right there, doesn't it," Starza mused. "Tommy Bolt had the worst manners of anyone in tour history. I'm sure that will carry a lot of weight," he sighed. "OK, I'll have some notes for you by tomorrow."

"I assume you'll have a say in the process," I said.

"I get to make written comments, and I've been invited to lunch or dinner to offer some perspectives. But it will be the selection committee who makes a final recommendation to the employment committee, who will extend the offer."

"Who chairs the employment committee?" I asked.

"General Sweeney."

I understood for the first time the basic flaw in the system.

"We'll see how that plays out, won't we?" Starza said.

A screen door slammed followed by a shriek. "Looper." It was a downright slim and visibly attractive Denise Long steaming my way.

"I hear a voice, Mr. Starza, but I don't see anyone I know," I teased.

"It's good to see you, college boy," she said, giving me a big squeeze.

"I didn't recognize you, Denise. You've withered away since the holidays."

"I've lost 28 pounds. And the way they've got me working I may never gain them back. How are you?"

"I think this is a perfect time for me to leave," said Starza. "See you two tomorrow."

"Get some rest, boss," I said.

"Count on it," he said, grabbing his blue blazer and director applications before disappearing out the door.

"At last, some psychic relief," she said.

"Where?" I said, gazing around the vacant Pro Shop.

"Here, dummy, you. You represent the return of real people; someone I can talk to without the fear of being hit on."

"That's a problem?"

"Sometimes. There are couple of leches in the membership and some equipment reps who aren't all that well-intentioned."

"What about McDevitt?"

"So far, he's been hands off. I think he's trying to lay low. He even seems to be avoiding Mrs. Cabiness."

"Sounds like the ultimatum worked."

"I don't know about that, but he's been a gentleman to me, and I've appreciated that."

"How's life been for you here? You got the hang of it yet?"

"Absolutely. Working for Binswanger is like not having a boss at all. He saw how I redesigned the shop and since the money started rolling in, there have been few complaints."

"None?" It didn't seem likely.

"A few. However, as the weather has gotten warmer, and I've lost more weight, the personal attention has gotten more intense. I don't know what I'll do when summer comes. I'm not wearing sweaters in 90° heat. I think I'll just adopt you as my bodyguard."

"That's flattering, Denise, but I'm the nonviolent type."

"No problem, Looper, I'll just tell them we're engaged. That will stop the members. As for the reps, I'll threaten to change lines. That might slow down the bullshit."

"If it's really a buffer you need, some guy to shoo away the squeezers and teasers, maybe I can do that. Deal?"

"You be my bodyguard; I'll be your long-lost friend. Something like that? You watch my back; I'll watch yours."

And that arrangement worked well for those first few weeks. I buckled down learning what Denise and Starza did day-to-day. I also got a daily dose from Divot who was essentially pulling double duty with his boss still on a limited schedule.

"Looper, you've got to be one of my main counter guys," said Divot one morning. "Starza can only do so much and I got my hands full with lessons. I don't know where all these kids are coming from. I can't decide if it's the Arnold Palmer phenomenon or the interest that Denise is drumming up among the parents, but it seems like I'm on the practice tee morning, noon and night. In fact," he paused, looking hard at me, "if I were smart, I might let you give lessons to some of the squirts. As it is now, I can't accommodate everybody. Hell, even my social life is suffering." He paused again. "If I got Starza's permission do you think you might give some lessons? It's fifteen dollars per half hour for kids and I'll bet the club would let you keep ten."

I looked up, half-honored and half-amused. "Correct me if I'm wrong, but doesn't all the money you earn go straight to your pocket?"

McDevitt looked down and swept the Pro Shop carpet with a putter from the rack. "That's right," he coughed, "but it all goes through the shop register."

"Meaning you still get to keep it all. It just goes to the register and on the club books as revenue?"

"That would be an affirmative, young man," blurted the bloated, imposing presence of the uninvited General Sweeney. "As a member of the employment committee, one which approved the hiring of Mr. McDevitt here, I can vouch that his income is indeed supplemented by teaching. Starza's too. But I see no reason why, if you are accorded teaching status, you can't attain a similar arrangement. Perhaps, however, McDevitt was hoping for an override. You wouldn't be that greedy, would you Mr. McDevitt? Given your probationary status?"

"General, I was just trying to offload some of the teaching assignments. We hadn't much time to discuss money," said the subdued assistant pro.

"Offload. That's a military phrase, McDevitt. I'd forgotten you'd been exposed to our armed forces."

"Yes sir, general. I was in an ROTC program in college."

"Pray tell, what branch? Army, was it? As I recall, you didn't finish. Something about a breach of etiquette, lack of military bearing. Something like that? Wasn't exactly honorable discharge, more like a mutual understanding that you and the services were incompatible. Do I have that right, McDevitt?"

A British subject at this point in the humiliation would have said, "Quite." And the commanding officer would have been done with it, but General Sweeney kept it up for another ten minutes until Kaufman and Stroud strolled in demanding an 8 a.m. Saturday tee time.

Sweeney ended the monologue with "I think young Litton here should get the full amount, McDevitt. As a member of the employment committee that's what I'm going to recommend to your boss. Good day, gentlemen." And with a grand gesture and a grope for his cigar the General disappeared out onto the terrace letting the screen door slam behind him with that irritating snap.

"Somebody should fix that door," yelled Denise, "before I scream."

"Somebody better sign us up for Saturday morning at 8:00 a.m. or the green committee is gonna hear from us," said Stroud.

"I can help you gents," said McDevitt in his most obsequious manner, "but it can't be until 8:34."

"We always have an 8:00," said Kaufman.

"Gentlemen, we've had this conversation before. You frequently have an 8:00 a.m. tee time when you have a foursome. You always want 8:00 a.m. when you don't have a group. I see no indication that there are four of you for Saturday. How about the 8:34?"

I'll give it to him; he was really trying to be diplomatic with two of the club's most difficult members. "You're still at the nineteenth hole by noon. What do you say?"

"OK, by you, Jack?" Stroud said to his long-nosed partner.

"Yeah, but put us down for 8:00 a.m. on the following Saturday. There ought to be four of us then."

"I'll make a note, Mr. Kaufman, but I'll need some assurance that there'll be four, otherwise we'll pair you up."

"We'll take it up with the starter," said Stroud, as the two strode off, letting the doors snap shut up again.

"Divot," said Denise. "Do something about that door."

Closure arrived quickly that afternoon on the two items I was most concerned about. My remuneration at the shop ended up being fifteen dollars per half hour, money that went straight through the register to me. But recognizing that the lesson spillover wasn't self-generating without the assistant pro's help, I kicked back five dollars to Divot. He responded in kind by sending more kids and even some of the beginning mothers my way, an arrangement that remained unchanged even after another assistant, Peter Timmons, arrived.

As for Kaufman and Stroud, they got their 8:00 a.m. tee time, but only because as a fill-in starter for that day I paired them with Conklin and Corbin, two equally irritating seniors. The upside was that both groups liked to wager insignificant sums on their insignificant games so the round, I heard later, was spirited and frustrating for both twosomes. Spirited because Kaufman and Stroud would sip Old Forester from their flasks while spewing gaming banter that begged for response. Tempers ebbed and flowed, according to Brewster who manned the halfway house, with Conklin and Corbin taking command only to have Kaufman and Stroud halve the match under press conditions on a lucky eighteenth hole chip-in. The grumbling continued well into the following week, with neither side happy that there wasn't a clear-cut victor. However, the two camps weren't entirely unhappy either because thereafter the group became a near-regular foursome with an 8:10 a.m. tee time.

During the course of the summer I had to pull more duty as a starter then I would have ever imagined. One reason was that Tom McAfee, the old-timer, quit early in the summer in a dispute with the new director of golf. And because we were short-staffed and I had a reputation for "people skills," I was in frequent demand for the position. Truth be told, the starter is one of the most thankless jobs in the entire field of recreation. Very few people, and I emphasize very here, are ever happy with their tee times, especially when they're assigned playing partners or required to take carts. There are occasional bonuses, but for the most part the work is as gratifying as picking up sticks on the G crew. Members are absolutely sure you are there only to serve them immediately, or sooner. Their gratitude for favors rendered, for improving their starting times, or preferred partners, is nearly nonexistent.

Guests of members, however, were always, and without fail, apprecia- tive of the most mundane services I provided. Extra towels, scorecards, ball markers, whatever it was, always brought an earnest "thank you" and often a five spot or two.

What didn't bring an earnest thank you from the staff was the hiring of the director of golf. Harrison Haynes Hennessey joined the Pro Shop staff as promised on June 1. His arrival was met with much fanfare and expectation. His playing credentials were good: three-time PGA tour winner, his last being in the 1956 Mobile Open, top 20 in the Masters twice. He had a teaching certificate and was a member of the USGA technical committee. His most recent position was as head pro at Mesa Verde Country Club in Tempe, Arizona. His portfolio contained the requisite number of recommendations, and some correspondence from Arnold Palmer, which I was told carried enormous weight with General Sweeney when final candidates were submitted to his employment committee.

The announcement of Harrison Hennessey's appointment was made in a manner I thought out of keeping with the tone and tenor of Spring Willows. Normally I would have expected a staff memo and letter to the membership signed by Billy Sauers detailing chapter and verse on our Mr. Hennessey. Instead the Pro Shop was informed by an impromptu standup routine by General Sweeney, whose description of the successful applicant evoked visions of a wandering carpenter entering Jerusalem. By the time General Sweeney was through I checked the drinking fountain to make sure the water hadn't turned to wine.

"Mr. Hennessey prefers to be called, 'Mr. Hennessey' by his immediate staff," intoned General Sweeney. "He also prefers that Pro Shop employees wear clean, crisp shirts and long trousers every day. No exceptions. He also requires that his golf shoes be polished each evening and be in his cubicle awaiting inspection pending his 9:00 a.m. arrival every morning. Furthermore…"

There was a palpable murmur in the audience, gazes went skyward, eyeballs rolled, bodies squirmed. Somehow reciting the Ten Commandments didn't seem to be the way to start a new relationship.

"General Sweeney," asked Denise. "Sir, does that long trousers rule apply to me, too?"

"Well, I would suppose so, Miss Long. You are a member of the Pro Shop, after all, and rules are rules. In the military, dress codes are hardly discretionary. We came ready to play every day, starched and stitched."

"Tarred and feathered, you mean," mumbled Kellogg.

"You were saying, Kellogg?" Sweeney inquired.

"I was saying, sir, that Denise's job entails showing and selling the latest fashion to men and women. I think the club's interests are best served by her being allowed to wear feminine clothes, not long pants. The Emily Newby's of the world are hardly playing golf in long trousers."

"Regulations are regulations, Kellogg. You don't have to abide by them, but that's only because your ass is out of here tomorrow. Everyone else, by God, is going to abide by these rules until they are amended by an authority higher than staff whim. Pro Shop protocol," he went on, "will be mandated by the new director of golf, whose experience and wisdom should considerably elevate the level of professionalism around here. Are there any questions?" asked the General. "No? That will be all. Staff dismissed." General Sweeney and his 230-pound portly frame disappeared through the slamming screen door.

"Jesus, will someone fix that door," uttered Denise through gritted teeth.

"Denise, I hope you can sell in long pants because I think you got a hard case coming tomorrow," Kellogg said.

"I'm not worried about the long pants," she said. "The minute revenues start going south that regulation will change. What I'm worried about is the stuff we don't know about, like hours and attitude. I know about pompous asses, my uncle is one, but I didn't have to work for him."

"All I can say is good luck. You'll need it."

Good luck we did not get. The hurt locker read like this. Starza was still on half days until July. Kellogg's replacement Peter Timmons was still getting acclimated to Spring Willows. An ill-chosen intern, David Klimatz, second cousin to an influential member, was trying and failing to supervise the bag-room boys. Divot was preoccupied with lessons when he wasn't being Divot. Denise's innovations were accounting for half of the Pro Shop's revenue with Starza's custom club-fitting accounting for the other half. We were being run ragged, praying like hell the new director would be an able body that might ease the load.

Instead Harrison Haynes Hennessey -- Mr. Hennessy, to you -- was a load. I knew the shoeshine routine would get old fast. Ironically, it is the one job that hyper Klimatz, who quickly became known to one and all as Climax, did well. He did it so well, in fact, that the buffing of Mr. Hennessey's shoes became known as "Job One." Klimatz had a hard time earning the respect of the bag-room boys, but, by God, those shoes were front and center every morning.

"Those shoes look absolutely fabulous, Klimatz," said the new director. "So good, as a matter of fact, I'm hesitant to wear them on the putting green, much less my round with Sweeney this afternoon. It would be a shame to get grass clippings on them."

"They'll be as good as new tomorrow, Mr. Hennessey," said Climax. "Go ahead."

"Say, you boys mind the shop while I go do some member relations work." With that Mr. Hennessey strode to the parking lot, unlocked his car and drove off.

"Member relations work. Hmm, let's see. It's 9:30. He just got here. Now he's off to do member relations work off-site? I thought member relations work was something you could do at the Pro Shop," said Denise.

"I don't know," said Climax. "Maybe he's going to see Mr. O."

"Not likely," said Divot, fresh from a lesson. "He just drove out the front gate."

"I've got shirts to put up," said Denise, "so I'm not going to worry about it."

I headed out to the starter's post, unconsciously and quietly closing the screen door behind me.

"Thank you," said Denise. "You won't have to do that as soon as the new regime gets that door fixed."

"How is the new regime doing, Looper?" came a recognizable, husky voice.

"Mrs. Worth, I see you're off at 10:10. Anything we can get you besides your bag?"

"Yes, let's get my bag," she said, heading toward the bag room.

"Martinez…" I began.

"No, you get it for me, Looper. I need a word with you anyway." After a well-timed pause came the question of the day. "How's the new regime?"

"Too early to tell, Mrs. Worth. Looks like he knows his stuff. Good playing credentials. He's got the hail-fellow-well-met part down. General Sweeney's got a new best friend, so things can't be all bad."

"For whom?" she pressed.

"For General Sweeney," I responded with false humor.

"Sweeney's an ass and we both know it. I'm just taking a pulse. I'm getting vibes that things aren't all that smooth up here."

"Mrs. Worth, things haven't been smooth since Starza had his stroke. Right now the help is a bit inexperienced and…"

"And what?" she interrupted. "Pompous? Arrogant? Lackadaisical? Self-centered? You can say it, Looper. The jury is still out on Mr. Hennessy," she emphasized with a bone chilling cynicism, "but I think his demeanor will do him in if he doesn't get results." We were almost at the bag room.

"Like what?" I asked.

"Like this State Amateur, for one."

"Well, to be honest, Mrs. Worth, it feels like amateur hour up here except for Starza, Denise and sometimes McD. Mr. Hennessy hasn't endeared himself to anyone yet. Hell, the bag boys call him…"

"Moses," interrupted Martinez, handing me Mrs. Worth's bag. "Good luck today."

"Thank you, Miguel."

"Last year I felt we had more leadership. There was more organization and Billy Sauers had his hand on everything. We miss that."

"I don't know about John Cabiness," she said. "He's got troubles I hope I never have, but I don't know how soon we'll get Mr. Sauers back. Elise is really sick. I've only seen him twice this month, but he did ask me to check on things up here."

"For a guy who's supposed to be running the show, our new director of golf appears to be a frequent no-show at the shop. I know he's supposed to play and pal around with other members, but Starza was great with that and still got his work done. I guess we need guidance and more, more of a…"

"Presence," said Mrs. Worth.

"Yeah, more of a presence would help."

"We'll see what we can do. In the meantime, chin up."

"Yes, chin up," I said, still numb from giving what felt like an honest but traitorous report on the shop.

"Don't feel guilty, Looper," she said. "We're all in this together. And we've got to solve this together. By the way, are you free Sunday? For nine, say about six?"

"Sure, I'd love to caddie."

"No, to play," she smiled. "They'll be three of us. Pack your clubs, I'll see you there."

I stumbled back to the shop, remembering to shut the door gently. Just then, Buddy Bonneville, the greens cutter from the grounds crew, appeared.

"Yo, Looper, where's that door what needs fixing? We got a call about loose screens or somethin."

"Springs," shouted Denise as she rounded the shirt counter. "That door there needs new springs. Think you can do it?"

"Sure," said Buddy, "looks like a tension and bumper thing. If I can fix pin setters in bowling alleys, I can fix that. We've got some stuff at the shed that'll do it. Be back in ten. By the way, Looper, Mr. O said for you to start supervising the cart boys up here. They're all over the walkie talkie, again. Worse than last year. We can hardly get a word in edgewise."

One more problem I thought, remembering that one of Mr. O's pet peeves was juvenile voices hogging the airwaves. He needed the frequency clear to communicate with his crew out on the course.

"I'll look into it, Buddy. Thanks for the help on the door."

The walkie talkies were just the tip of the iceberg. The real problem was the lack of supervision over the cart guys. Starza, on his limited schedule, and Divot, with his slick persuasion, kept the flow of work at a tolerable level, at least as far as the membership was concerned, but the carts were another deal.

Most clubs our size had a man who did nothing but supervise carts from maintenance to personnel. At Spring Willows that guy was supposed to be Climax, who actually knew the machines quite well. It was the personnel he couldn't manage.

Truth be told, David Klimatz had many of the attributes necessary to be a successful assistant pro. He was a 6 handicap. He was polite to members, he had an understanding of the E-Z-Gos and the Club Cars, but he couldn't supervise worth a damn. He was tentative with younger staff and seemed to lack the spine required for law and order. The job really cried for a General Sweeney with a take-no-prisoners attitude or someone with supervisory skills. David Klimatz had neither.

The cart problem came to a head one Sunday afternoon. "Looper, we're still on for six, right?" said Mrs. Worth, dropping off her bag.

"I didn't realize you were going twice today," I said.

"Two different rounds. Two different purposes; business and pleasure," she said.

"Let me guess," I responded. "Ours isn't pleasure."

"See you in an hour."

As a precaution I sauntered out to check the starter sheet. Scrawled by 6:00 p.m. in black ink in Starza's own handwriting was "Worth, Sauers plus 1." I knew who the "1" was. What I didn't know was the rest of the story, but I felt sure I would get it shortly. And I was right.

The state-of-the-course speech began immediately following my first tee shot. "Looper," began Billy Sauers, "excuse me here, Margaret. Looper, you and I both know there are a million ways to fuck off working on a golf course. You and I have witnessed countless cases of such malingering. But it's time for this shit, under the supervision of the Pro Shop, to cease. One reason I wanted you up there was to instill some law and order and, frankly, through no fault of your own, it hasn't happened. The employment committee, with no outside watchdog," his sentence was interrupted by a crisp 3-wood, "has made a series of poor choices rivaled only by Warren G. Harding's selection of cabinet members. I'd like to blame it all on Sweeney, but I can't. Normally, I'd have been around to review his choices, but circumstances have dictated otherwise. There are some things over which currently we have little control.

"Herr Hennessey, while not a part of this discussion, has a contract that will be difficult to abrogate without just cause. Given enough time, I'm confident he'll hang himself, as long as he doesn't kill us all first. So, for the short term," he paused to lash a 5-iron twenty feet from the hole, "I'm going to concentrate on the problem areas over which I can exercise some control.

"As you know," he said, withdrawing his putter from a Sunday bag, "my business has been in disarray and my wife has been dreadfully ill. I am pleased to report that as of Friday I have beaten the barbarians back from the gate and that the Elise appears to be in remission. To enhance the domestic tranquility she has asked me, no, ordered me, to worry about something other than First Strike Investments and her health. Naturally, Spring Willows came to mind. And now that I'm back here for however long, I'm going to try to make a difference. The Pro Shop is where I choose to start."

He was on a roll now. "In order to be successful I need human beings, that's as opposed to cretins, Looper, whom I can trust. Your exemplary record over the last two years and your lofty position on the hill make you an ideal agent of change. God knows that place needs change," he said, lining up a twenty-footer.

"Shit," he said as his birdie try lipped out. "Excuse me, Margaret. What Starza will tell you tomorrow is to spend part of each day monitoring Klimatz and the employees who run those carts. You'll have no problem with Hennessey because it's been suggested that he has more important duties to worry about than cart employees. I doubt he'll leave you alone completely because he gets a piece of the cart revenue. However, he has been made to understand that the membership prefers walking and he is, under no circumstances, to increase cart usage above its present level."

We were on Two now. I was staring down the 426-yard fairway. Billy Sauers was staring down his ball. "You'll have to humor the SOB, Looper. 'Yes sir' and 'no sir' him some and he'll drive off in that crappy Cadillac of his. In case you were wondering, and I know you are," thwack went the wooden head against the Titleist, "God, I love the sound of persimmon in the evening," he said, interrupting himself, "you'll spend another quarter of your day at the counter and the other quarter as starter. We'll have a new starter soon, but for the next few weeks I want you visible out front. I know you are thinking about cart maintenance. Don't. That's one area where Klimatz is entirely competent. He may be scared witless of people, but he is fearless around machines. My three areas of cart concern," he said, uncorking a 4-wood to the front fringe, "are power, driver education and defensive driving."

"Power, as in authority?" I asked.

"As in electricity. Those cart boy clowns don't always pay attention to whether or not the cart is charged. Have you observed the charging operation in its entirety?"

"No sir."

"When you go down tomorrow, notice how the carts are neatly aligned, how the power cords come down from the ceiling and are threaded through the steering wheel. In the early morning nothing will be amiss because Klimatz unplugs all of them himself after the overnight charging is completed. Where the trouble occurs," he said, running his putt six inches by the hole, "is when the cart comes in for another charge and those young bozos from the bag room drive off with the cord still plugged in. Sparks fly. It looks like the Fourth of July. Plus," he said, tapping in for par, "it's dangerous as hell. I don't think the kids do it on purpose, but they do think it's funny. The chargers are expensive to replace, and that stuff has to stop.

"Margaret, that was a nice par back there. Way to go," he said, pushing his tee shot slightly right. "The driver education thing requires a tighter rein than Klimatz can give. Those puerile young men ostensibly use the carts to dump trash. But what they do, in fact, is go past the range or to that hidden spot near the tennis courts and go four- wheeling. As you know, Looper, there are some extra sandpiles back there. The bozos build ramps and compete to see who can jump the carts the farthest. Carts have been tipped, scratched and damaged." His 5-wood from the trap left him seventy-five yards from the green. "When it rains the boys go to the far side of the range, out of sight of adult supervision, latch onto the rear of the carts and go skitching, or whatever the term is these days. In my early teens in snowy weather we would hitch onto cars and get pulled along for miles. That behavior was inappropriate then, and the golf course application is inappropriate now. This club needs neither injuries nor lawsuits. We need discipline. Am I making myself clear?"

He fluffed his lob wedge into the second cut. He had a nasty lie and I wondered if he'd be as forthright with his fourth shot as he was being with me. He never broke stride or breath. As his 3-wood cut through the thick green side collar he continued. "And on days of intermittent precipitation that is another practice that is over as of this conversation."

"Which one is that, sir?" I interjected.

"Don't talk to me when I'm putting, Looper. It's the one where the cart boys head off down the hill away from the driving-range tee, hit the brakes and skid halfway to Springfield. Tire tracks were left last Wednesday. Not only is that practice unseemly and unsightly, turf repair is expensive. So the next moron who does it will have the sod replacement cost deducted from his final paycheck and given a bill for the remainder."

"Sir, are you suggesting the culprit will be terminated?"

"Excellent use of the word. That is exactly the sentiment I want conveyed back at the shop. And you, my boy, are the one who will deliver it."

"I feel like a messenger here," I said, lining up a treacherous 18-footer.

"Messenger, angel of mercy, agent of death. I don't care what you call it, just make sure the word gets back to all concerned."

Because of my added responsibilities, I short-armed the putt and settled for bogey.

"I love this hole, don't you, Margaret?" Billy Sauers said as he surveyed the newly measured par-3 Fourth. "Some days I feel like I can land this little pill pin high and other days launch it into that swale on the left. What say we play closest to the pin? Margaret, we'll give you plus twenty yards. Loser buys drinks. Looper, don't worry, I'll put it on my tab and you can repay me."

"Good idea," I said, needing something to relieve the ever-increasing baggage I was accumulating. I had to laugh. It was unlike Billy Sauers to pick a sporting proposition where he was odd man out. My money was on Mrs. Worth. For all the times I had caddied for her, she was Mrs. Accuracy on this hole. This day she nailed her long tee shot straight down the middle.

"Nicely done, Margaret. Let's see what Captain America has for us here."

Captain America was wide right of the hole by five and three-quarter inches. We know that because Billy Sauers had a tape measure in his bag for just such occasions. We needed the measurement because with her extra 20 yards Mrs. Worth was a mere 36 inches short. I stroked my ball in for birdie mostly because I didn't hear anyone conceding anything.

"Looper, I think Mr. Howard would have envied that one. That may be the nicest shot I've seen on this hole in thirty-five years."

"Thank you, Mrs. Worth. It was probably the best shot I ever made," I said as we marched to Five.

CHAPTER FOUR

The beginning of the end for Herr Hennessey was not his bungling of the State Amateur (the final nail) but his continued ineptness in personnel matters. His situation was exacerbated by his mishandling of Spring Willows' experiment with a cart girl. In a well-intentioned strategy to boost food and beverage revenues, Kaufman and Stroud, with considerable support from General Sweeney, suggested the club needed an "attractive, young female" to zip around the course with assorted beverages (especially mixtures for the alcohol Kaufman and Stroud carried) snacks and sandwiches.

Mistake one was not consulting Harlan Brewster, the longtime employee who ran the concession stand at the Halfway House atop the tenth tee. Mistake two was not consulting anybody, anywhere, who was already running a similar operation at any high-end country club. Mistake three was not suggesting that Harlan Brewster direct the operation since he was the one person with more knowledge than anyone regarding course consumption and volume. Mistake four was Hennessey's proclamation, "I don't do underlings."

By his fourth week on the job Herr Hennessey had developed an unearned sense of entitlement that was beginning to chap certain members. When Billy Sauers heard Herr Hennessey's comment he observed, "Christ, supervise is all he's supposed to do."

To no one's surprise, Hennessey did insist on interviewing all of the cart girl candidates. For a week there was a parade of flesh through the clubhouse. A number of young adults passed through, many children of members, but the director of golf decided that hiring a member's child might engender hostility among the parents of the losing candidates. Consequently, he settled upon one Cassandra Sanders, an attractive (check the box), junior college student (check) with a predilection for revealing garments (check) undoubtedly encouraged by the D.O.G. himself.

Initially, Cassie was embraced by virtually all males on the premises, caddies and service staff included, with the exception of Brewster. His concern, and an unintended consequence of Cassie's presence, was a loss in tip revenue. The abject truth was that Brewster counted on the generosity of members to boost his meager pension. Regrettably, his voiced concerns fell upon Hennessey's deaf ears. As a result, service at the Halfway House began to deteriorate, imperceptibly, then significantly, adding one more item to a growing list of upper management concerns.

At first, female members reserved judgment, in part because they were less inclined to patronize food wagons of any sort. Old habits die hard. For the women at Spring Willows, a beverage at the turn constituted ample hydration for the back nine. But with Brewster's normally friendly nature turning sour, an undercurrent of discontent began to surface. Women began going to the clubhouse for water and bypassing Brewster altogether.

While Cassie was pleasant to the women on the course they rarely purchased anything and rarely reciprocated her friendly greetings. Once-closed mouths began to snipe and snark about her attire. While entirely appropriate for the Côte d'Azur, her apparel appeared a bit much for the reserved distaff of Spring Willows. A coterie of the concerned, including Cindy Cabiness and her cohort Jocelyn Price, arranged a meeting with Herr Hennessey that went from bad to worse. The two expressed their displeasure with "that cart girl," her dress and the unpleasant treatment now emanating from the Halfway House.

Their presentation fell upon deaf ears. Hennessey carefully explained that "that cart girl" was an experiment designed to boost revenues. He buttressed his case by citing Iroquois Woods' apparent success with a similar experience. The D.O.G. told them that in the month since Cassie's appearance, club food and beverage revenues were up YTD. Hennessey adroitly failed to acknowledge the increase was entirely due to an extra wedding reception and a debutante ball.

He also shared with the women the enthusiastic reception "that cart girl" was receiving on the course itself. Males young and old had indeed embraced Cassie Sanders and were spending considerable sums on both food and beverage, which the women should know, he lectured, were two vital revenue drivers at any well-to-do club. Males were also tipping well, another sign of satisfactory service, a fact he knew from Cassie's glowing daily reports.

The women should've known better than to bother the D.O.G. with their concerns about Cassie's wardrobe. Ultra-short skirts and skimpy tops had no place at Spring Willows, they protested, unaware their appeals were a waste of breath, given the audience.

But the women had an unexpected and well-placed ally up on the hill, an influential party who had quietly kept her own counsel for weeks until she observed a trend which spurred her competitive nature. Being pragmatic, she targeted Binswanger, who had wandered into the Pro Shop, for her opening salvo.

"For someone who's supposed to be riding the range, that cart girl is spending a lot of time in the Pro Shop," she told the general manager as he studied the latest alpaca sweaters. And with Denise it was always 'that cart girl.' "She doesn't need to be in here at all," she continued. "There's no food here, no beverages. She should be drumming up business on the course. All you've got in here are the assistants and Pro Shop staff and they're not going to be buying from her. At least not during work hours," she said snidely.

"Did it occur to you she might be trying to enhance her wardrobe, present a more upper class look to the members? What better place to start than in the Pro Shop?" offered the general manager.

"Mr. Binswanger, for starters I doubt she can afford the Pro Shop prices. Second of all, her taste in clothes runs a little on the trampy side."

"'Slutty' would be a better word," said a feminine voice emanating from the fitting room. "The girl's appearance is a disgrace to this club. It's all my husband talks about when he gets home from the course. Not how many birdies, not closest to the pin. Not even the money he won. Just what 'Cassie' wore today. I'm sick of it – and I'm not alone, not by a longshot," said C-flight champion Emily Newby.

"You need to listen to her," said Denise. "In fact, if you want some other opinions you ought to talk to Cindy Cabiness and Jocelyn Price. They took their case to Mr. Hennessey last week."

"That's news to me."

"The D.O.G. got an earful, but I suspect he kept it to himself given that 'that cart girl' was his hire."

"Why do you care?"

"Because we're better than that. Short skirts and flimsy tops belong in burlesque shows, not Spring Willows." Left unsaid was Denise's smoldering motive for moving Cassie completely out of the Pro Shop since noticing Cassie becoming more and more friendly with yours truly.

Had I known; I would've stayed out of it. Billy Sauers's advice to 'leave the henhouse to the hens' applied here. As it stood, I remained blissfully unaware of the depths of Denise's feelings for me until after the State Am, when Denise confessed them.

Feigning more pressing business, Binswanger departed just as Emily Newby dropped a pink top and golf club on the counter. "That cart girl has upset the rightful order of things around here," said a potential queen bee. "We need an attitude change around here and it needs to start with men, the real weaker sex."

"So how do we do that?" queried Denise.

"I think we use our wiles. There are more seductive woman around here than cart girls. Just saying." The nubile Mrs. Newby completed her transaction with "just charge it, please" and left flashing Denise a wicked smile.

I walked into the breach oblivious, having just completed a starter shift. "Any water in the cooler?"

"Can't say," Denise said. "Look for yourself."

"OK, thought you might know since you were standing by it."

"I'm not as thirsty as I look," she responded. "How's business out there, Tiger?"

"Pretty brisk for a Wednesday afternoon. Doctors and dentists are hitting the links harder than I would have thought, given the heat."

"And buying drinks, too, I bet."

"I wouldn't know about that on the first tee."

"But you see the beverage cart buzzing around, I suppose."

"Not really. That action seems to take place out on the course."

"You know, for someone who is supposed to be selling drinks and snacks, that cart girl spends a lot of time at Pro Shop," Denise said.

"Between being a starter, a bag-room whatever and a behind-the-counter guy, I wouldn't know about that. If I did, I'm sure I don't have time for it."

"You don't huh? Well, she seems to have time for you."

"Hadn't noticed."

"Others have."

"What do you care?"

"She disrupts things," said Denise.

"Like what? She doesn't bother you."

"She bothers others. You know, guys trying to work."

"Doesn't look like they're bothered."

"Looper, I just want the place to run smoothly, efficiently, so people like you can do their jobs."

"If I can deal with it, so should you. What do you care if she bothers me?"

After a long pause she followed up with, "You know what you really need is a little less golf. In fact, what you really need is a woman in your life."

"So, now you're my mother?"

"Men. Absolutely the dumber sex." She stormed off into the supply room.

"What was that all about?" I mumbled, ringing up a twosome.

"Dunno, I wasn't paying attention. All I know is what some women like," Divot said.

"That's going to get you into serious trouble someday."

"Already has," he said, heading out the door to give a lesson.

CHAPTER FIVE

With the State Amateur just six weeks away, Spring Willows appeared to be on track for the early-August event. Committees had been formed and the publicity machine was running smoothly. Internally, it was a different story. Hennessey had been slow to grasp the magnitude of the event and the extent of his responsibilities. He thought that he made a grand figurehead, and thus anointed, assumed that the working class, especially the club manager, would be handling the details.

Hennessey's grand awakening came from his unreturned Monday calls to the assorted food vendors and pavilion people. On Wednesday, the same calls were made to Binswanger, who was shocked to hear that the orders for their State Amateur services were normally placed four weeks earlier.

Shortly thereafter, having consulted various committee members, Binswanger approached Hennessey on his way to lunch. "Harrison, may I have a word?"

"Certainly."

"It seems you haven't reserved pavilions, much less placed food orders, for the State Amateur."

"No, no, I'm planning to do that this week. It's all according to my master plan."

"I don't think so. You are four weeks behind, my friend."

"No sir, I'm supposed to plan those ten weeks out. That puts me right on schedule."

"Hennessey," his irritation mounting, "when do think we are hosting this event?"

"Ten weeks from now. Just like the master plan says."

"Ten weeks? Ten weeks? Show me in your master plan where June 20 is ten weeks from August 1."

"I couldn't give two hoots about August 1," blustered Hennessey, "but when those State Amateurs walk in here August 29, Spring Willows will be ready."

"Mr. Hennessey, by August 29 those State Amateurs will be so far gone from here you'll be calling them for a job. The tournament starts August 1."

"You're joking."

"And if this club is not ready, you'll be history. Am I making myself clear? Spring Willows will not be embarrassed by your incompetence. If I were you, I'd start thinking really hard about what you need to catch up on and get back on track. You need more people, more resources, help with suppliers? Let me know, we'll call in some favors and make it happen."

"But…"

"Make it happen," Binswanger repeated.

I wasn't around for the aftermath, but Denise was. As she was heading toward Binswanger's office for a scheduled appointment, he bumped her in the hallway with a cryptic "not now," slammed the door and dialed an emergency number. She lingered long enough outside the doorway to hear, "Billy, there's been a fuck-up. Hennessey is damn near a month behind on the State Am. I don't know how we missed it, but we've got to go into overdrive to get this thing back on track. I'm going to do an assessment this afternoon to see where we stand, but this is a heads-up to say we may need to call in some favors. We aren't in triage mode just yet, but we may want to have an emergency meeting once I see where we really are. I'll keep you posted."

Denise was tiptoeing away when Binswanger blasted out of his office. "There you are. Sorry to be so rude. Come in and shut the door. We're a month behind on the whole god-damned State Amateur timeline. A month, a whole goddamn month. I can't believe it," he steamed.

"Mr. Binswanger, if it helps, I think we're fine on the merchandise. I placed those orders three months ago after I went to that seminar you sent me to. I ordered the recommended paraphernalia along with special Spring Willows windbreakers and ball markers. The merch should be coming in two to three weeks before August 1."

There was a long pause. Binswanger folded his hands, leaned forward on his desk, and released a wry smile. "I knew there was a reason I liked you. Denise, you just saved this club considerable embarrassment. Anything else I should know?"

"Well, I did make some preliminary calls to tent people so we'd have covered space for merchandise, and I figured we might need covered space for serving food, so I reserved some tents for that. When they asked about erecting some seating or pavilions for viewing around the first hole and eighteenth green I told them to check with the Director of Golf. I assumed it was something Mr. Hennessey was supposed to be in charge of."

"Yes, 'supposed to be' is the operative phrase. Denise, between you and me, the club is about to go into crisis mode for the next six weeks. This afternoon, when I call an all-employee meeting of the clubhouse staff, we'll be asking people to up their games and expand their responsibilities. I'll be calling on you. I want you to be prepared to accept some additional duties and responsibilities from this office outside of your normal shop duties. For this, you will be properly compensated. But for now, please keep this under your hat," he said surreptitiously, "and be prepared for whatever may come your way."

"Thank you, sir. I don't know what to say."

"No need to say anything." As she turned to go he added, "Denise, well done."

* * *

The all-clubhouse employee meeting was essentially an indictment of Herr Hennessey and the job he had not done to date. Even I was embarrassed for the D.O.G. Left alone afterward, I suspect Hennessey was contemplating his future, which appeared, in a word, bleak.

That evening, over a cold clubhouse dinner consisting of leftover luncheon salad, lukewarm bread, lemon sorbet and an assortment of liquor, a skeleton "executive committee" convened to assess the tournament status. Present were the usual suspects: Sauers, Starza, Binswanger, Judge Gleason, president John Cabiness and Margaret Worth. Noticeably absent were the D.O.G. and his benefactor, General Sweeney.

"I apologize for the sorry supper," said Billy Sauers. "Desperate times call for desperate measures. Don't worry about Sweeney and Hennessey. They'll get their marching orders tomorrow. When we're done here tonight we'll have an updated action plan that will be made to work. My main concern is the time frame.

"Herr Hennessey has put us behind the eight ball. As of now we are moving into an all- hands-on-deck mentality. Our general manager here did pass some good news to me late this afternoon in that the merchandise and pavilion/tent components are not as far off schedule as we had initially feared. We have that shop girl, Miss Long, to thank for that, is that correct, Bernard?"

"Correct, Billy," said Mr. Binswanger.

Three and one-half hours later the liquor had hardly been touched as the executive session ground to a close. "Margaret, thank you for acting as secretary tonight. A thankless but necessary job. Bernard, get the new action plan typed up first thing tomorrow and distributed to the appropriate players. Hold individual meetings as necessary with all the appropriate staff. Schedule those meetings up here at the clubhouse so they understand how important this is. I'll meet personally with the superintendent. I want to visit Olson myself so there is no misunderstanding."

CHAPTER SIX

As Spring Willows scrambled with the club's State Amateur master plan, my social life took on a new dimension.

McDevitt got overbooked and then suffered a minor medical setback. I was asked to take over McDevitt's six-session package sold to one Jessica Woolworth. As luck would have it, the comely Ms. Woolworth was an accomplished equestrian and a talented tennis player who had never lifted a club. The lesson package was a gift from her father, who encouraged all of her athletic interests. I learned much later the idea was strongly seconded by her mother who saw golf as perfect social avenue to meet the "right" kind of young man.

Turns out Ms. Woolworth, at 5'10" lithe and tan, could stroke a ball. The first forty-five-minute lesson normally covered grip, address and stance. Ms. Woolworth covered it in sixteen. The twenty balls I allotted to short game assessment seemed sufficient after she deposited the third of five shots within seven feet of the pin. On a whim I had Ms. Woolworth lash several 5-irons. They all went arrow straight. It appeared the girl could play. One initial irritant was the girl's incessant pleas to hit a tee shot.

"Jessica, let's save the woods for the next lesson. I think we've done quite enough for today; don't you think?"

"No, I don't. My father says a good drive often sets up strategy for the hole, so I want to see if I can hit a driver."

"Frankly, I think we're rushing things a bit here."

"Just let me hit one. Just one."

"All right, just one."

"The first step is to put the peg, I mean the tee, in the ground properly. You do it like this, right?"

"Correct. Put the ball on top of the tee, find a soft piece of turf between the designated markers and depress. Keep the tee a half to three-quarters of an inch off the ground. That will give you clearance and allow for solid contact when the club swings through."

Jessica Woolworth, she of statuesque build and possessor of golden-rod locks, pressed the tee into the soil. With the ball properly perched she stood at address, uncoiled her lengthy frame and unmercifully attacked the unsuspecting pill.

"Jesus, what was that?" said a passing Binswanger. The sound of club meeting ball reverberated down the tee line like a carefully muted howitzer blast. Despite all of my time around talented players, I was rendered silent.

"How was that?" asked Ms. Woolworth.

"About 220. Pretty darn good. What you say we try one more to ensure it wasn't a fluke?"

"Great. I bet I can hit it farther."

"Can we not try for distance? Just focus on mechanics. The goal is to hit it straight. Good contact trumps anything else. OK?"

"Jesus," she said impatiently, jamming another tee in the ground. "You sound like a clucking hen. I know I can hit the next one farther."

"Please, can we just not go there? People trying for distance have ruined many a swing. I'm not sure we know what your swing is yet."

"I think we probably do. Watch this." With that Jessica Woolworth swung violently, and launched another straight and narrow missile. "I told you."

"About 230. You might have a knack for this game. But to be really good you need to putt well and put in plenty of time practicing."

"Drive for show, putt for dough, right? My father says that. When's the next lesson? I think I might like this game."

"I'll check the book. Whatever you do, make sure you come out and work on those short irons."

"Yessir, I might like this game."

* * *

As lesson two evolved into lesson three, I found myself thinking of Jessica Woolworth as less of an object lesson and more of a romantic possibility.

As the lessons accrued the friendship seemed to blossom. As did the undercurrent talk. Even members who wouldn't normally bother to notice spotted the burgeoning romance. One senior member felt obligated to speak up.

"Looper, here's some sage advice from an old man. Don't get your ding-a-ling in a sling," said Billy Sauers when we crossed paths near the Pro Shop entrance. "I see you are starting to spend a lot of time around that Woolworth girl."

"Just lessons, Mr. Sauers."

"And a couple of dates, from what I hear."

"OK, and a couple of dates."

"Why do you suppose she is taking lessons, son?"

"To try a new game I guess. She's athletic."

"And?"

"And I don't know. How would I know?"

"Looper, she goes to Radcliffe. That makes her pretty bright. Think about it. These lessons are an investment in her future. Didn't your Psychology course teach you anything? That 'opposites attract' tripe is bullshit. People like those who are like them in appearance, social status, intelligence, philosophy, outlook, etc."

"I'm out of her league, Mr. Sauers."

"Don't sell yourself short. You may not have her breeding per se, but you have all the right stuff. Studies show that an overwhelming percentage of the golf-playing public is male. If you were a well-bred chick like Jessica, where would you go to find a date – or better yet, a mate? A bar? A church? A grocery store? With Jessica's complete package -- looks, breeding, money, education -- she is never going to be hard up. Stands to reason the golf course is the place to go find Mr. Right. Somebody like you."

"I don't think so, Mr. Sauers."

"Son, you underestimate your value to the human race and young women like Jessica. You aren't stuck up like those puerile, ass-kissing trust fund babies. Smart ones like Jessica know a catch when they see one. Bet she's spoken to you more than once in the last week, right?"

"Well, as a matter of fact…"

"Keep your eyes open, Looper. This could be a good summer."

* * *

Denise had become an important cog in Spring Willows' drive to get the master plan back on track. Long hours consumed the first ten days after the emergency session, and Binswanger began to lean heavily on her for master-plan implementation while leaving Hennessey to oversee the more public aspects of the tourney. The D.O.G.'s bluster played well to his hail-fellow-well-met persona, allowing him to entrust critical details to his secretary, Denise and a short list of trusted staff members.

Denise was worried, but not about the tourney. Timmons told me later, one afternoon while she was hanging the new State Am windbreakers, that he overheard her seeking counsel from an experienced member.

"Mrs. Cabiness, can I ask you a question? You seem to have a way with men."

"I'm not so certain of that, Denise."

"They sort of flock around you when you come in here, so I assumed…"

"OK, if we're being honest, I've had a way with two men around here and one of those associations is over. What's your question?"

"How do I put this? When there is a person of interest…"

"A man," said Mrs. Cabiness.

"Yes, a man."

"Someone you'd like to make your man? Anyone I might know?"

"Why do you ask?"

"The more I know, the better advice I can give."

"Uhh, OK, sure."

"Is it Looper?"

Denise's shoulders sagged, the corners of her mouth went perceptively south and moisture radiated from her hazel green eyes.

"Mrs. Cabiness, he practically avoids me. He gets along with everyone; he chats up all the women, especially that cart girl, and now he's giving lessons to Jessica Woolworth."

"Denise, that's part of his job, to make nice to members and project a pleasant aura here in the Pro Shop."

"But I wrote him this winter. I've tried to be a friend. I dress well. I'm reasonably attractive. I'm told I have a great personality. What's a girl to do? I don't want to just throw myself at him. What if he turns me down? I'd be so humiliated I don't think I could keep working here. I'm embarrassed just talking to you about this."

"First of all, don't feel embarrassed. We are addressing a dynamic that goes back to Adam and Eve."

"It was easier for Eve because she didn't wear clothes."

"Maybe you shouldn't wear clothes."

"I'm not ready to stoop that low... yet."

"Maybe you should. That is something the cart girl might do. Denise, I may not be a woman of the world, but I've been around the block a time or two. Desperate times call for desperate measures. How desperate are you?"

A tear trickled down Denise's cheek. "I don't know, I just feel... confused. I know what I want, I think, but I don't know how to get it. And that is so... frustrating."

"Maybe it's time to double down. That's a golf and gambling term. And, let's face it, we are in a sporting environment. Maybe it's time for you to be more overt, more obvious in your interest. I realize working in here you can't be but so obvious with your clothes, with the need to maintain decorum and all, but perhaps with your actions. It certainly worked with me and that devil McDevitt. Have you tried standing a little closer, you know – invading his personal space, perhaps accidentally touching him? Sometimes a sudden delight like that can ignite a spark. The accidental brush against the sleeve. And I would say your ample physical assets are sure to provoke a response."

"Mrs. Cabiness, there's already too much testosterone around here. I don't want other people getting ideas."

"Denise, all I'm saying is sometimes you have to fight fire with fire. Here's another idea. Have you thought about asking him out?"

"Girls don't ask guys out, Mrs. Cabiness."

"They do when they want something badly enough. How badly do you want it, Denise?"

"I, I just don't know. I'm just... just..."

"Where do you want Looper, Denise? In your life? In your arms? Where?"

"Cindy, if I may interject here," came the authoritative voice of Billy Sauers, "you two seem to be addressing the question Sigmund Freud could not answer: what does a woman want?"

"Billy," said a very surprised and embarrassed Mrs. Cabiness.

"There are very few secrets on the hill, my dear." Denise had gone from embarrassed to mortified. "As for you Miss Long, I applaud your taste in men. You have chosen to fixate on one of the few males I truly admire in this club. However, and this is a very important caveat, may I strongly suggest that you temper your enthusiasm for young Mr. Litton until we get through this damn State Amateur. He does not need to be distracted by an intelligent young lady such as yourself while we salvage this tournament."

Denise countered. "Mr. Sauers, I hear you. And I respect your opinion. But what about that damn cart girl and the girl he's giving lessons to? Don't you think you should have a word with them, too? And maybe while you're at it counsel the crux of the problem himself?"

"I will ruminate on that and perhaps have a word with the young man. In the meantime, I want your mind and eyes focused a little more on the state golf tournament. I need you and Mr. Litton dedicated full time to the success of this event, not each other. Got it?"

Denise blurted, "He hardly knows I exist."

"You sell the young man short. I can assure you he is well aware of your presence."

"She wants more than his presence," Cindy Cabiness interjected.

"So I gathered. What I'm saying is that I'd like this grand union to wait until the tourney is over. I don't care who wins the heart and mind of this young man, but I will tell you this. It may be amateur hour up here in some offices, but Spring Willows and the powers that be have a lot at stake in seeing that this tourney comes off well. That means happy patrons, a well-stocked merchandise tent, smiling staff and a club president with an obedient wife. Am I making myself clear?" he said, glaring at Cindy Cabiness.

"You don't have to worry about me, Billy. Denise and I are on board."

"Fair enough. Let's not have this conversation again anytime soon." With that, he was off to the parking lot.

"Now I'm really embarrassed," said Denise.

"Don't be. You have an ally in Mr. Sauers. You can't do any better than that."

CHAPTER SEVEN

Denise brooded through the remainder of the afternoon. Yes, the State Am needed to be her first and foremost item of business, but only after she confronted that cart girl. She purposely stayed late on a Thursday and approached her adversary in the parking lot. "Hey, you," she called out. "We need to talk."

"I'm going home," came the response. "I already accounted for snack and beverage inventory and turned in the cash before I left."

"It's not that."

"About what, then?"

"About how much time you're spending at the Pro Shop when you're supposed to be out peddling beer and crackers."

"I spend almost no time in the Pro Shop. Food and beverage revenues from the cart are through the roof, so I'm not sure what the issue is – and why it's a concern of yours. Seems to me your concerns have to do with merchandise and fashion, not Budweiser and Nabs."

"I'm saying you're bothering employees in the Pro Shop and disrupting workflow."

"And I'm saying that's pretty much bullshit. Look, I come to work at 9:45, restock the cart before I punch in at 10 and I'm out on the course by 10:05. Yes, I do consult with the starter to get a sense of where players are so I can plan my route most effectively, but that's to maximize sales. If going straight to the seventh hole is going to get me more revenue than starting on 18 and working backward, that's what I'm going to do."

"It would be less disruptive if you just consulted the tee sheet rather than interrupting the starter who is trying to do his job. He's trying to get the members off in an orderly fashion."

"Who am I disturbing at the Pro Shop other than the starter? Name them because I'm hard pressed to think of anyone up here I've spoken to in the last five days. You? This is the first time we've had a conversation in two weeks. McDevitt? Not hardly. He's too busy giving lessons and kissing up to well-heeled members who might sponsor him on a winter tour somewhere. Hell, he's even given up chasing skirts. The only other reason I'm in here is to give Binswanger a daily accounting of the take from my cart. So, where's the problem?" Cassie's temperature was rising.

"You spend more time with the starter than just checking the tee sheet," countered Denise.

"Look, I don't know what your problem is, but it seems to me you've got more pressing things to worry about than how I spend my day."

"I'm not the only one tired of watching you sashay around here with your sassy attitude and revealing clothes. It's not appropriate."

"It's not appropriate to leverage one's assets to help the club make money? Just how do you sell things in the Pro Shop, miss fashion plate?"

"I wear respectable clothes, advise customers and let the products sell themselves."

"That's what I do. I wear clothes appropriate for the job I'm asked to do in order to maximize revenue. And you know what? It works. And I've yet to hear a discouraging word from management."

"Well, you're hearing from me."

"You're not management," Cassie said, unlocking her car. "Anything else?"

"Members are complaining about your clothes and decorum. I'm telling you, this conversation is not over," said Denise, her ire rising.

"Look, miss college graduate. I don't know what your deal is, and frankly I don't much care, but I'm in this job to make money. I don't drive a late model vehicle like you. I drive this worn-out piece of crap because it's all I can afford, " she said, leaning against her faded, aging green Studebaker. "I'm saving every last cent to finish junior college and go somewhere respectable. I wasn't raised in the comfy confines of the North Shore. I don't wear fancy-label garments, but I know how to work my ass off and if it means offering an occasional slice of skin to get an appreciative smile and a few extra dollars then I'm all in. I've only got so many years with this body and while I'm here I will use it as a tool of the trade."

"Tramps like you get down and dirty."

"Look sister, I don't know who you've been talking to or where your mind wanders late at night, but you've got some misguided notions about me. My morals are way above board. I'm just leveraging what I have in a moral way, and so far it's working. The club is benefitting, I'm benefitting and the only objection I've heard to date is from you. So why don't you take your business elsewhere and leave me alone." Cassie turned to get in her car.

"If you keep acting that way during the State Am you're going to give the club a bad name."

"Puh-leese, there may not even be an on-course cart during the tournament, in which case I'll hardly be an issue now, will I?" said Cassie.

"I'm just saying."

"You know what? I think you're jealous. You think I'm trying to cozy up to Looper. He's a sweetheart, but he's not interested in me. He's sweet to everyone. He's sweet on Jessica Woolworth. If you're afraid of competition you need to set your sights on her."

"Excuse me?"

"Excuse you. He's giving her lessons. And she comes to the lessons dressed like some homecoming queen. And I've never heard of someone coming to lessons wearing Shalimar perfume. Nobody, but nobody comes to golf lessons fragranced up but Jessica Woolworth. And I think it's working. Two dates in ten days. Something's going on and it's not with me, sister. You want to take dead aim on someone, start with her. Now if you'll excuse me, I've got drive this piece-of-crap auto to the grocery store." Cassie opened the door and deposited her trim derriere on the Studebaker's ragged upholstery. Rolling down the window she said, "I'm not the problem." And drove off.

Dumbstruck in the gathering twilight, Denise wrestled with what had just transpired. Her frontal assault, designed to elicit a specific cease-and-desist action, seemed to fail on several fronts. If what she had heard was true, perhaps she'd eliminated a rival, but it appeared there might be an even more formidable one ahead. Jessica Woolworth was a step up in class. She found that distressing. Where to go from here? That would take some thinking.

* * *

Eighteen hours later, a waterlogged club member hustled into the Pro Shop. "That's some storm out there," said Cindy Cabiness. "I thought I was going to drown." She left her umbrella at the door.

"Mrs. Cabiness, how can I help you?" asked Denise.

"I am looking for one of those new State Am rain jackets. Mine is threadbare. Do you have one in pink?"

"We are not that fashion forward here, but we've got several in lapis, kind of a stunning blue. Would you like to see them? In, what size, a medium? They run a bit small, so a medium ought to fit you perfectly."

"This is pretty. It would go well with any number of my outfits. You know, I think your female merchandise line for the club ought to have some apparel in this color. Some sleeveless shirts and shorts in this color would sell really well."

A long pause ensued before Denise broached an issue she'd been contemplating for some time. "Mrs. Cabiness, may I ask you a question?"

"Certainly dear."

"It's about men."

"Again?"

"You don't have to answer if you don't want to."

"What is it, dear?"

"Hmm," said Denise, hesitating for a moment before pushing on. "What do your men do for birth control?" As she paused she lowered her voice. "You know like, like during…"

"Sex?"

Lowering her voice even further, Denise said, "Yes, sex."

"My dear, I don't know what to say."

"Oh please, Mrs. Cabiness I know you do… with all your experience and all."

Silence filled the back hall to the stockroom. "What occasions this thought? Surely you aren't contemplating… Do you even like this person?" Another pause. "Silly question. Obviously, you do, or you wouldn't be asking."

"Everything is premature, but I'm getting older and I want to be prepared."

"Prepared?"

"You know. In case it comes up. I'm curious about the prevention of… babies."

"Yes, I know… babies."

"Well…"

"Candidly, my dear, birth control is not my biggest concern. My tubes have been tied. But just to be sure, my men use Trojans. They are available behind the counter at most drugstores. All you have to do is ask. But if this young man, I'm assuming it's a young man, is upstanding and polite he will have his own protection."

"Oh, thank you, Mrs. Cabiness."

"My dear, take my hard-earned advice. Don't rush into things. And before you do anything make sure one of you has the magic band-aid before you go down this road."

"Band-aid?"

"A contraceptive." She paused. "A rubber."

"I feel so foolish even asking about this."

"Better safe than sorry, Denise. Good luck, dear girl."

That was only the second facts-of-life discussion Denise had had in her 21 years on the planet.

* * *

The following two days of incessant rain did nothing to tamp down the anxiety building on the hill. While still a month out, management was not happy about the prospect of putting tents and pavilions for the State Am up on boggy turf. Even Mr. O expressed concern to the green committee about his ability to keep the assigned spots dry. "Billy," he told Mr. Sauers, "there's only so much I can do if we get another spate of foul weather here. I can put down hay and straw and that will soak up some of the moisture, but I know you don't want a lot of that up there, especially around Eighteen green and the clubhouse."

"'Spate.' That's a new word for you isn't it? I'm glad to see education is making its way down to the maintenance shed."

"Agronomic administration building."

"Oh, now we're agronomists? You've come up in the world, Otto. Glad to see it. Now what about this damn water problem?"

"It's no problem if we get a spate of dry weather."

"There's that word again."

Mr. O soldiered on. "The ground up there is fine as long as we don't get torrential weather and the long-range forecasts don't call for that."

"But if we do, then what?"

"Hay and straw."

"Otto, I may not be the sharpest knife in the drawer, but what about boards and rubber mats around the pavilions like I've seen at some national USGA events? Looks like they've protected the turf pretty well. Using them would keep hay and straw from being dragged into the clubhouse by those with full grounds passes. Couldn't we get some rubber mats?"

"They're expensive to rent."

"Hang the expense. We're going to do this right. Besides, I think I can get the Illinois State Golf Association to foot part of the bill, and we can write off the rest as a cost of business. Why don't you check that out with Johnsy Wilkins, the superintendent at the Chicago Golf Club? You should know him with all those meetings you go to. I'm sure he has a supplier for all the regional tourneys they've hosted."

"He's a bit above my pay grade."

"Bullshit. He's a farmer and grovels in the dirt just like you. Find out who he uses as a supplier and get back to me on cost. Don't short-change coverage either. We don't want muddy feet in the clubhouse."

"Affirmative," said Mr. O.

Not long after Billy Sauers's visit to the maintenance shed, General Sweeney appeared on the hill, heading for Herr Hennessey's office. "He in?"

said the General to Teresa, Mr. Binswanger's secretary and the only office employee not at lunch.

"I'm afraid he's out right now. Can I help you with something?"

"He told me a month ago he could help me with some complimentary passes for the State Amateur."

"Mr. Hennessey is no longer in charge of complimentary pass distribution," said Teresa.

"Since when?"

"Since about a month ago."

"That can't be right. He assured me he was the source on this."

"Well, General, he's not."

"There must be a mistake."

"No mistake. You want a pass or two, you try and get them from Mr. Binswanger."

"One or two? I've got twenty guests coming."

"Good for you. Buy 'em."

"Buy 'em? At $10 a head? That's $200."

"Sounds about right."

"There must be some cut-rate for a local dignitary like me."

"Take it up with Mr. Binswanger. I don't see many freebies emanating from this office."

"This can't be right. I'll need a word with Mr. Binswanger as soon as he gets in."

"I'll leave him a note to call, but he'll just go to a higher source."

"I'll just go to a higher source myself, then."

"Feel free. I think you have Billy Sauers's number. I'm sure he'll be thrilled to take your call."

"This is not right. I was promised those tickets."

"Fork over $200. Or make your pleas to Mr. Sauers. And speaking from experience, good luck with that."

Sweeney was steaming. On his way out of the clubhouse he almost bowled over John Cabiness. "John, I want to exercise one of my board of director prerogatives for some complimentary tickets to the State Am for my visiting dignitaries."

"Complimentary? How many will you be needing?"

"They'll be twenty in my party, John."

"General, here's the deal: I'm the club president and I get four. As a board member you'll get two. More than that you'll have to dig into your own pockets. Twenty tickets? You've got to be kidding. Where's your military intelligence? If you've still got a problem, take it up with Billy Sauers." John Cabiness disappeared into the clubhouse.

"This is not right," muttered the General, slumping toward his car. "It's just not right."

* * *

Later that afternoon the D.O.G. himself returned to the hill, having attended to his latest member-relations activity. Just what those member relations actually entailed no one had yet been able to ascertain. The D.O.G. had been seen from time to time at lunch with various club members, but those occasions seemed to be liquid lunches, much more convivial in nature than ironing out green committee business or a way to enhance food and beverage revenues.

"Back again, Teresa," said the D.O.G. as he headed toward his office door. "Any calls while I was out?"

"You had two calls from an addled Mrs. Clancy, who was insistent you call her after you returned. She said you had her number. And you had a visit from General Sweeney about an hour ago."

"And what did the good general want?"

"Twenty complimentary tickets to the State Am."

"What did you tell him?"

"That he could buy them."

"And…"

"It didn't go over too well. I also told him that if he had a problem he could take it up with you. And that if he did you'd just refer him to a higher source."

"He probably wasn't anxious to hear that, was he?"

"Not when he realized that Billy Sauers was the higher source."

"What a pompous SOB. We'll just let him stew a while."

Later that afternoon, and acting to dispel a nagging feeling, Billy Sauers reappeared at the administration barn. "Otto, have you called Wilkins, the super at Chicago?"

"I was going to do that in the morning."

"I'll tell you what. Let me call the president of the club first. I've got a couple of other questions I want to ask him. Once I speak to him I'll get back to you and then you and Wilkins can transact some business."

"Sure thing, Billy. I guess I'll just stayed tuned."

Later that evening, Billy Sauers placed a call to the Chicago Golf Club president, Ellsworth Coggins.

"Ellsworth, Billy Sauers here. How's the IPO business? Got anything I'd be interested in?"

"Probably Billy, but it's a little early and I'm not permitted to disclose anything at the moment. However, and that's a big however, should things align as I hope, I will contact you and First Strike. I suspect you have some clients that would like a shot at what's in the works."

"I appreciate that, Ellsworth. As in finance, life and golf, we're all in this together."

"Indeed, we are. Now, since I suspect this is not a social call, what can I do for you?"

"You are correct. I'm calling regarding golf. As you know, we are hosting the State Am in a month or so, and while things are moving along, I have an uneasy suspicion that we are missing a few critical pieces."

"The kind that can bite you in the ass and bring embarrassment to the club? Those kinds of pieces?"

"You got it."

"Do you have pavilions, merchandise and food ordered?"

"Yes."

"Is staffing organized?"

"Yes."

"Where do you stand on ticket sales?"

"Not sure."

"That's a revenue component the Illinois State Am guys will be all over."

"We have a master plan that was put together by one of our staff members, but I have a sense it is incomplete. Do you have an old copy of yours that I might consult to check for holes in ours?"

"I'll do you one better. I've got a young college guy on my staff whose uncle is club manager at Inverness in Toledo. As you recall they hosted the 1957 U.S. Open. Anyway, this kid is a helluva golfer, but he helped his uncle a lot doing grunt work on other tournaments. How about I get him to call his uncle and get a copy of one of their master plans? Then I'll have him bring it out to you so you can review it. If you have questions we can convoke about anything you are missing."

"Review the plan like an audit?"

"Exactly like an audit. At the very least if you are behind on anything you'll know where to allocate resources."

"And for that you want…?"

"How about some comp clubhouse tickets for the duration of the tournament?"

"Done. How many?"

"Eight? I've got some clients who want to be reminded how special they are."

"Special treatment for special people. You want them mailed home, the office or will call?"

"Will call will be fine. Just put them in my name. We'll come as a group on the first day."

"In the meantime, any problem if I have our superintendent, Otto Olson, call yours? It's Johnsy Wilkins, if I remember correctly. I think my guy's got a few course prep questions."

"Not at all. Johnsy's one of the best. We are blessed to have him. Regarding the audit, my intern is named Alex Randolph. Who should he see and where? I'll get that plan sent Special Delivery. I can have him at Spring Willows in two days. I think we need to get rolling here."

"If we are going to do this right, he can meet me at the general manager's office. I'll have my documentation ready to go."

"Young Randolph's a bright kid. You'll like him."

And so it went. The conversation was but a prelude to Billy Sauers's scavenger hunt for all the loose ends of the master plan whose once semi-comprehensive binder had morphed into a haphazard paper trail. Billy Sauers put Binswanger, his secretary Teresa, and the D.O.G. on the hunt for missing pages which culminated in a ragged, semi-complete, master plan.

Before leaving the club office at 6:30, Billy Sauers called me. "Looper, day after tomorrow, you have a new responsibility. Wear a suit, tie, polished shoes and meet me at the clubhouse office at 7:30 a.m. I am going to introduce you to Alex Randolph. You and Randolph are going to his office in Chicago to dissect the Spring Willows' master plan for this tournament. Find out what we don't know. Then meet with Randolph's boss and learn what other holes we need to fill. Then report back to me. Once the audit is complete, we'll decide on a course of action. Oh, and plan to stay late."

"I was supposed to pull starter duty and give two lessons that day. What do I tell Starza and my lesson people?"

"I'll take care of it. This may be the most important thing you do all summer. Tee times and lessons can wait."

And that's how it went. No, please. No, thank you. No, are you available? Just be there.

Two days later at the appointed hour I appeared as ordered. As I walked into the director of golf's office Billy Sauers was rustling papers looking for a large envelope. "This work space could be better organized. Teresa does a good job, but I don't think her boss helps the process at all."

"What does the club need from me today, Mr. Sauers?"

"We need to find out what this master plan is missing and then run like hell to play catchup. Randolph's boss is Ellsworth Coggins, president of one of Chicago's biggest brokerage firms. He's also president of the Chicago Golf Club, which has put on a number of State Amateur events. He has offered to help us audit our master plan. Randolph will be coming to get the plan here," he said, motioning at the scattered documents. "Take them back to the office and examine each detail and see just what we are missing. I want you to digest what he finds and report back to me. Coggins will help in process, but you are my conduit. I'll probably meet with Coggins at some point, depending upon what you uncover."

"A minor point here, sir, but how am I supposed to get home tonight?"

"Take the El. Get off, call a cab. I'll pay the damn cab fare. Just get home ready to report."

Alex Randolph, a rising senior business major at Northwestern University, was a sharp looking fellow, clearly dressed for the Chicago Loop financial world. "Randolph?" asked Billy Sauers.

"Yessir, reporting for duty."

"Excellent. I'll have this plan for you as soon as I find an envelope. And meet Arlo Litton. We call him Looper around here. I'm sending him with you and the plan, so he can learn first-hand from some pros about how to run a tournament. He's going to report back to me. Tell your boss I really appreciate your club's willingness to help out."

"Yessir, I will. He values you and your support and sees you as an important ally when he becomes Illinois State Amateur Association president two years hence. 'Quid pro quo,' he said."

"He'll have my undying support if you can help us avert disaster."

With that we were off to the Loop in Randolph's late-model Chevrolet. "What seems to be the major concern here?" asked Randolph.

"Timeline mostly. There is a fear we are well behind. Secondarily, there is a lack of trust regarding some of the parties most responsible for execution. I'm supposed to digest what you tell me today and report back. Then we'll implement corrective measures."

"I see. Well, for starters, from the size of that envelope, the master plan appears a little thin. The ones my uncle produces at Inverness for state and Midwest championships are about twice the size of that. Secondly, I doubt we will get through this in a day. How were you going to get home from our office?"

"The El."

"Tell you what. We'll grind through this best we can. It will probably require a working lunch and dinner. If we aren't done by a suitable hour you can stay with me tonight. We have a company apartment close to the office. That way we can maximize our time together."

"I don't have a toothbrush or a change of clothes."

"We'll work it out."

The Normandy invasion has been called the longest day, but my time with Alex Randolph had to be a close second. He was astounded by the back-of-the-hand treatment and lack of detail given to some vital components of the master plan itself. "Holes, Looper. Lots of holes in this plan. My uncle promised to send an old master plan for an Ohio State Am. It should arrive Special Delivery sometime today. After we check it out you can take it back to your club and use it as a reference. Meanwhile we'll do an executive summary for your boss to get Spring Willows started on corrective action."

We quit for the night at 9:30. "There's a nice bar we pass on the way home. What you say we pop in for a brew or two?"

"Sounds like a winner," I said "but let me call Mr. Sauers. He is expecting a complete briefing from me tomorrow morning."

"Not happening, soldier."

Mr. Sauers's response to my news was matter of fact. "I figured," he said. "Just keep me apprised of your progress so we can get this show on the fast track."

Two brews were all we could manage before retiring to the corporate apartment, a well appointed two-bedroom abode more ostentatious than my family's house. "Nice digs," I said.

"Oh, yeah," echoed Randolph. "This actually gets used quite a bit. Mr. Coggins frequently puts up out-of-town clients here to save them lodging costs. Very much appreciated, I'm told."

The next morning Mr. Coggins himself checked in on us. "You boys been here all night?" he asked.

"No sir, we quit at 9:30, but the task at hand is a little incomplete for my taste. My uncle wouldn't give it high marks."

"How much more time do you need?"

"Early afternoon if we work through lunch," said Randolph.

"Then what?"

"We package up the executive summary and send Mr. Litton back to Spring Willows."

"Tell you what. I'm invested in this project coming off about as well as Mr. Sauers is, so here's what's going to happen. I'll call him this morning and tell him that I am reassigning you, Randolph, to Spring Willows until this thing come off."

"What about my internship?"

"This is it. One of the overlooked aspects of high-stakes finance is research. This may be golf, but it's on-the-job training of the highest order. You do whatever they tell you out there. When it's over I'll go over all the financial components of this operation with you. Didn't you tell me you have to produce a case study as a part of your graduation requirement?"

"That's affirmative, sir."

"Perfect. You've encountered an organization in a tenuous position and helped provide the solution for success. And trust me, you will provide a solution," he said sternly. "This is real world stuff. Plus, it's in a field you like and one with which you have some familiarity. Win-win.

"Good people out there, Randolph. The commute's a whole lot better, too. I'll bet you'll like it. Well, I'll leave you boys to your labors. Check in with me when you're done. I'll want to review what you've got. Also, if this next session looks like it is going through the noon hour, check with Dottie and have her order lunch for you. That way you can eat and whistle while you work."

"Yes sir. We're on it."

Our crash course did take us through lunch. The food sent in was enough for dinner. We finished the final bites just before winding up at 2:30. Our session with Mr. Coggins lasted until 4 when he rendered his opinion. "Good original thought and analysis here, boys. But, it looks like Spring Willows has some work to do. Work that needed to start yesterday. I'm impressed with the advance ordering of the merchandise and pavilion pieces. Someone had their act together on that. The rest is salvageable, as long as responsible parties can pull their weight. Randolph, I want some regular reports on their progress here. I think you and Mr. Litton will be a good team. Boots on the ground. You gentlemen better make tracks if you want to beat rush hour."

"May I make a call to Spring Willows before we go?" I asked.

"I already made it. I told Billy you'd be leaving by four. He wants you to meet him at the clubhouse at 5:30 to go over your report. Look sharp, be sharp, boys. And good luck. Mr. Litton, nice to meet you. Take care of my man here."

"Yes sir," I said. We headed out the door.

* * *

The meeting with Billy Sauers was all business. He had been on the phone with Ellsworth Coggins about the report before we arrived, so he was aware of the master plan's relative strengths and weaknesses. What he wanted was our thoughts regarding implementation strategy. "Boots on the ground, isn't that what your boss said?"

"Yes, sir."

"I like that concept. We've got enough potentates on the hill here to do the easy stuff, but the grunt work is going to fall to the hired help and some able-bodied supervisors. Are you boys up for it?" The room fell silent. "That's not a rhetorical question. I'm talking to you guys."

"I thought my job was to work the Pro Shop, pull starter duty and give lessons," I stammered.

"Nothing's changed except for any schedule modifications I dictate. The tourney comes first. We will not be embarrassed by a poorly run State Amateur, not as long as my name is connected to it. As of tonight, you men will be taking orders from me. I'll make that clear to Starza and anyone else. Randolph, you and Looper here will be partners in crime. We are going to get this right, starting right now. I will convene a meeting of the administrative help and all other affected parties for 2 p.m. tomorrow. At that gathering we will lay out a plan for moving forward. I will publicly, specifically, designate you two as reassigned assistants to the green committee whose main jobs will be to facilitate getting this tourney on track. I'll make it clear that you answer to me, doing my bidding. That's the good news. The bad is that you'll have to work with the D.O.G. some, but I'll make sure he's in line. You'll have the full support of Binswanger, Starza and Mr. O so there shouldn't be any trouble. Looper, first thing tomorrow take Mr. Randolph here to meet Mr. O and Starza. Then come see me and Binswanger in his office. At 10 we'll begin to activate the new New Deal."

"Yes sir," I responded. Then, like the Wise Men of old, we departed by another way.

"Tonight, why don't you stay with me," I said. "My sister is working a summer camp in Michigan and won't be home for a few more weeks. You can stay in her room unless you'd rather find lodging elsewhere."

"Let's do your place for now," he said. "I think we are in this pretty deep and it feels like 24/7 work. Propinquity might be the way to go in the short term."

I introduced Alex to my folks. Mom was kind enough to rustle up some grub and we gave her the short version of our two long days. "Sounds like a lot of responsibility," she said.

"That's probably not the half of it, mom," I responded.

I was right. The next morning the full magnitude of the job became clear when Billy Sauers revealed responsibility sheets that were to be passed out at the 2 p.m. meeting. "More than anything else, you guys are going to be first-line supervisors. Some older people may have a problem with that, but I intend to make it clear this afternoon that you two have my full authority to ensure plan execution as spelled out in these responsibility sheets."

And so it went. At 2 p.m. the assembled throng got chapter and verse of Billy Sauers's expectations. Questions were raised, answered and the anointed went their separate ways. "This exercise might actually have a silver lining," said Mr. Sauers. "This crisis may breathe new life and a sense of urgency into this club. Agents of change, that's what you men are."

"So, not yes men?"

"Better not be. I need strong-willed men of iron with spines to match and a take-no-prisoners mentality. Like me. You get the idea, yes?"

"Absolutely," I replied.

"While the troops are absorbing their responsibility sheets why don't you show Randolph around the course. He's going to need to know the lay of the land. Might as well do it now."

We cut through the Pro Shop on the way to the cart shed when we got waylaid by, "Hey there handsome. Haven't seen you around much lately."

"Denise, I'd like you to meet Alex Randolph. He works in finance in Chicago, but he's on loan to us to jumpstart tournament preparations. He's uniquely qualified since his uncle does this sort of thing at Inverness in Ohio."

"Really?" said Denise eyeing Randolph up and down. "So… you have a golf background then?"

"Yes ma'am."

"Don't yes ma'am me. We're practically the same age."

"I'm just trying to be polite, ma'am. That's what I was taught when meeting women I don't know."

"Manners. I like that. We don't always get that up here at the Pro Shop."

"Seems like a shame. At first glance this place looks top drawer, especially the apparel section. I'd think members would want to show respect in a shop like that."

"You'd think that, wouldn't you? But this can be a misogynistic environment. Respect can be hard to come by in some quarters."

"That's pretty stupid, considering a place like this could be a great revenue source if it were welcoming to women."

"So, Mr. Randolph," said Denise, casting a laser-like look on him, "Would you like to see what else we offer?"

"Sorry, Denise, we're about to tour the course. Maybe some other time," I interjected.

"Sure, I get it. You boys are important now. Mr. Randolph, make that return visit soon."

"Yes ma'am."

"And drop the ma'am."

"Yes ma'am," he said. We exited to the Pro Shop patio.

* * *

I decided the best tour would be One through Eighteen just as the players would have to challenge the course. Alex marveled at the lush landscape and course layout. He smiled when I pulled up to Six tee box hemmed in on both sides with tall trees and the extended chute out to the fairway. "From here this hole reminds me of Eight at Inverness. We used to have just as many trees in close to the tee box, but my uncle got smart when the turf got too thin from lack of sunlight. You have the makings of the same problem here. Need to thin out this tree-lined corridor sooner than later or the hole is in for trouble."

"We? I thought you were from Illinois?"

"I am, but I spent two summers working with my uncle at his course so I got to know golf pretty well from the ground up."

"You worked on the G crew?"

"Absolutely. That's all I did the first year. The next year I had some experience up around the Pro Shop. Mostly grunt work. Did some caddying too."

"Was that why Mr. Coggins loaned you to Spring Willows?"

"Probably. Plus he really wants a running start on his term as president of the state association. Remember, Chicago Golf Club hosts this thing in two years. So, yes, I think this transfer has an ulterior motive. Plus, he and Mr. Sauers are in the same business."

"Did you get to play Inverness at all?"

"Quite a bit. At 7,300 yards, it was a bit long for me until I got the hang of it."

"You play now?"

"When I can. This internship hasn't allowed much time for it."

"We'll have to get out and play some time," I said. "I'm sure we can sneak in some holes during twilight. This course doesn't get as much late day play as you'd think."

"I'm probably a bit rusty."

"Your muscle memory should take care of that. You carry a handicap?"

"I was a four my last summer at Inverness. My uncle called me sneaky long."

"You'd probably overpower this place then."

"I don't think so. My uncle always stressed strategic golf and course management rather than power. Suits me just fine."

As we tooled around Spring Willows, we made mental notes where the paying public was likely to wander. "I don't see people wanting to venture out on the first nine near as much as the back, do you?" he asked. "That's a far piece from the clubhouse if you want to walk to Three and Four. Looks like the holes closer to the clubhouse and the concession stand are going to be more inviting. Especially that hole you call Killer Ten. With that devilish pond, you'll have mobs of people there. Too bad there's no room to erect grandstands. Folks won't admit it, but they like to see golfers dump balls in the drink. Makes them see the players as human – like them."

I showed him Seventeen and regaled him with the saga of Mrs. Peck's heroic finish.

"Stories like that just reaffirm for me the need to grab opportunity while we can, Looper. I mean, just think how lucky we are to even have the opportunity to be in a place like this, even if it means doing the bidding of the well-heeled. Sure, some of them are jerks. There were a fair number at Inverness. You probably have some here too…"

"Oh, we got 'em, trust me."

"But when push comes to shove," he continued, "how lucky can we be working in a place like this? Warm afternoon fresh air, living among the elite, these legends in their own minds. We could be doing a lot worse."

"Amen to that." His words got me to thinking that maybe I wasn't appreciating my lot as much as I should. I mean I did consort with Billy Sauers and god knows he went out of his way to make sure I mingled with our club's movers and shakers. Food for thought.

"Question for you," said Alex as we moved up Eighteen. "That girl in the Pro Shop. What's her story?"

"Denise?"

"Yeah, Denise. I think I know her from somewhere."

"Really?"

"Can't quite place her."

"Let's see, Denise Long, recent college graduate. Been working here since January."

"She go to Northwestern?"

"Iowa State. Since January she's made some changes to the merchandising mix, has emphasized female fashion lines a bit more and got apparel sales at an all-time high. Women almost feel welcome in there now."

"I've seen her. And I'm pretty good with faces. Where'd she work before here?"

"I don't know every place, but I do know she spent at least one summer in the fashion department at Marshall Field in Chicago."

"Fashion department," a grin flashed across his face. "That's it, Marshall Field. My mother manages that fashion department. Looks like she's lost some weight since I last saw her."

"She's been on a diet and fitness kick. I think she thinks it is a way to better display the apparel."

"She got a steady?"

"Not that I'm aware of."

"You two aren't an item or anything?"

"No."

"So, if we ever had some time away from Priority One here there might be time for some social life?"

"Why not? I'm sure she'd entertain your presence."

"OK, I might have to think about this," he said with a wry smile.

Back at the clubhouse, Billy Sauers was wrapping up for the day. "How's the course look, Randolph?"

"I like it, though someday someone is going to have to make like Paul Bunyan and thin out the elms around Six tee box. Otherwise it looks like the course may be ready by opening day."

"Good to hear. Good to hear." He went on. "I will have in my possession by close of business tomorrow an expanded timeline of what I gave various responsible parties today. Your uncle's document will make that job much easier. The USGA could learn something from him.

"When I have it, I will share it with you, and we'll go over what I call the 'continuing review schedule.' I have already put the responsible parties on notice that you two will be checking in with them. Going forward they will be expected to hit thrice-weekly deadlines to ensure this event goes off as planned and in a first-class manner. Missed deadlines will not be tolerated and will be reported to me. Gird up your loins, boys. You may have to kick ass and take names. Don't be bashful about being forceful. The rubber hit the road today. Fortunately, I think the working stiffs got the message. Binswanger and I are in your corner. I'll be talking to the director of golf, who should be doing all of this but missed his chance. Between you and me I feel Herr Hennessey may be headed for an early departure. That information stays in this room. He will be doing what he does best, bullshitting members and performing ceremonial tasks. I'm just glad we didn't give him a long-term contract. Any questions?"

"No sir," I said.

"Looper, report tomorrow as normal to the Pro Shop, regular time. Do whatever you have scheduled until 3:30 then come see me and Binswanger in his office. Randolph, meet with Starza at 8 a.m. He knows you are coming. He'll fill you in on what I want out of the Pro Shop between now and tourney date. Come see me at 10. I want to know more about what you do for Coggins and about how your uncle works with his club in Ohio."

"Yes sir."

"Yes sir," I echoed. "We're on it."

Leaving Mr. Sauers I said, "Looks like we got our marching orders."

"Looper, I'm thinking this could be fun. We are essentially being given run of the club. This is a goldmine for my case study."

"Glad you feel that way."

"And Mr. Sauers seems like a buttoned-up guy."

"Not much goes on around here he doesn't know about. He can be a great mentor. Keep your ears open and you can learn a lot."

Supper at home turned out to be standard fare. Meat, potatoes, two vegetables and tapioca with raspberry preserves at the bottom for dessert. "Great spread, Mrs. Litton," said Alex.

"You flatter me, Alex. Since you'll be staying with us for a while let me warn you. We eat simple, healthy food in this house. We hit all the food groups in the course of a day, but we do not feast – and do not always have dessert. However, I do stock plenty of fresh fruit, so help yourself whenever."

"Thank you, ma'am. I will treasure every morsel."

We helped with the dishes. With the sun skimming the treetops we then repaired to our modest screen porch. "You ever play board games?" I asked.

"Monopoly."

"Ever play cribbage?"

"That a board game?"

"Old English game played with a deck of cards and a peg board. Fast paced, lots of strategy to it. The board is small enough to carry in a satchel, allowing you to play most anywhere."

"You got a board? Show me."

And that's how the two of us passed much of our spare time until our social lives took intriguing turns.

CHAPTER EIGIIT

The next day I spent the first hour squaring away the cart guys, the bag room boys and cataloguing sand wedges members had left next to greenside bunkers.

As I shuffled out to begin a 10-to-noon starter shift I noticed Alex at the far side of the Pro Shop in conversation with Denise.

"You used to work at Marshall Field, didn't you," began Alex.

"Do I know you from there?" Denise countered.

"We have an acquaintance in common."

"Whom might that be?"

"Do you remember a Wanda Randolph?"

"The department head. Great boss."

"That's my mother."

"Well, Mr. Big Shot, I hope you have her drive and intelligence because we'll need whatever brains you've got."

"You're kind, but I'm no big shot, but I think I'm smart enough to function around here. And just to be clear, I've come to you because I was told by Starza to learn how your area was going to function during the run up to, and through, the State Am."

"To be clear, I think my end is pretty well buttoned up. Thanks so much for your concern, Mr. Big Shot, but I'll take you through the drill." I think I saw her grin. "I placed all my clothing orders well in advance and I'm expecting two more shipments within the next week, so we'll have them displayed a minimum of two weeks before the tournament begins. Hats are supposed to be here in three days. My main concern regarding merchandise is umbrellas. They are attractive and pricy. The problem is shipment. When I ordered them I was told they were on back order, but should be here by July 15. If it doesn't rain it might not matter if they get here at all, but I'd like them in stock and on display a couple weeks before play starts."

"Sounds like you're on it."

"Did you expect otherwise? It's the other duties that vex me."

"Such as?"

"Such as whatever occurs to the brain trust up here. Right now it's scheduling volunteers. If you want to help out you can take a look at the assignment sheets for the various jobs."

"Oh-kay…"

"So, how long are you likely to be around here?"

"Until this event kicks off for sure. Don't know after that."

"So, I'll probably be seeing more of you, yeah?"

"Looks like it."

"Take a look at these sheets and see if they make sense, Big Shot. You ever work one of these tourneys before?"

"I have. In Ohio. Unless all the jobs aren't listed, I'll know fairly quickly if the numbers are right."

"So, I have a certified genius here?"

"Just someone a little more experienced in this task then you are, apparently."

"And for that I am so? Immensely grateful?"

"That'll do for a start," he said, grabbing the sheets and exiting to a patio table.

"Got a piece of work in there with the shop girl, Looper," he called to me.

"Oh, yeah," I said. "What's she got you working on?'

"Personnel allocation. Did you know at the Masters they call their paying guests 'patrons'?"

"We're not the Masters," I said, "though we'd probably like to think we are."

"Still, all in all, I'd say this is a very nice club." Alex delved into his assignment sheets while I attended to Mr. Detwiler's foursome as they tarried on the first tee trying to decide on the size of their afternoon wager.

"Any changes to the course overnight, son?" said his partner Charles Fleetwallace.

"No sir. Pin position is number three today. Tees have been moved up on the par 3s at Four, Ten and Seventeen and back on Thirteen to give a little variety. Other than that you should feel right at home. You gentlemen are up. I see the next group is assembling behind you. Tee off now and you won't have them driving into you."

"Tell them to wait," said a prickly Alistair Waits.

"Gentlemen, you paid for a noon tee time. In five minutes that will be gone and the next group will take the box. So, please, can we decide the final wager terms in the fairway?"

"Solid advice. Let's claim the box, men," said Detwiler. "Waits, you whale away first." The foursome mounted the tee box, took their first swings and descended down the fairway.

"Pretty smooth there, soldier. Don't know if I'd have been as diplomatic," observed Alex.

"It's been a learning process for me. Great education in human dynamics though. My shift is about over, you want to grab some lunch? I've got a lesson at one. If I don't eat now, it's not happening."

"No, you go on. I better scour these numbers first."

A visit to the kitchen unearthed a roast beef sandwich, two pickles, a bag of chips and a Coca-Cola. I snuck into Binswanger's office.

"Can I eat in here? I want to stay under the radar for a few minutes."

Teresa motioned me to an open desk. "Happy to have you. How you two managing with the big push?"

"The big push. Good term. OK, so far. We want to see this master plan from Toledo. With that as a guide I think we'll be more comfortable."

"As luck would have it, it just came in Special Delivery. Want to take a look? It's addressed to Billy Sauers, but I'm sure he'd be happy to let one of his agents look at it. Isn't that what you are now, an agent of change?"

"More like a facilitator."

"As you wish."

I opened the package, and it was indeed the mother lode. Chapter and verse spelled out for Inverness's last State Am. "You think I can share this with Mr. Randolph right now?"

"I don't see why not, given that we seem to be in an all-hands-on-deck mode."

I exited the clubhouse and retrieved Alex. "Master plan is here. Follow me."

As we began to pore over the document we could quickly see that it was in fact a very specific staging manual. Every contingency seemed addressed and each chapter concluded with a precise summary. "Goldmine," I said.

"I'm going to take this section on marshal assignments," said Alex. "Denise said she'd help me wade through some of this."

"Denise," commented Teresa, "how helpful."

"Just a working relationship," said Alex. "Nothing to get excited about."

"I've seen how she looks at you. Looks like she's working on her own master plan," said Teresa.

"Wouldn't know about that," said Alex. He helped himself to the loose-leaf pages he needed and disappeared out the door.

"How tall is that boy?" asked Teresa.

"Six-feet-four, I think. Long stride. At five-four, or whatever Denise is, she'll have to walk fast to keep up," I smirked.

"Don't underestimate women, Looper. They'll put wings on their feet when sufficiently motivated."

"Whatever you say. I have to give a lesson. If Mr. Sauers comes in, please tell him we took the liberty to jumpstart our assignments by looking at the master plan."

"I'm sure he'll applaud your initiative."

Outside Jessica Woolworth was waiting, dressed to the nines as usual, toting a Sunday bag and sporting just a dab of Shalimar. "Jessica, looking lovely as always. Since we are working bunker escapes today you won't need all those clubs."

"I'm taking them anyway because I'll want to putt out some of my shots."

"OK by me. Want to ride or walk?"

"Walk. I need the exercise." I took her statement as confirmation of her fitness compulsion. She was in great shape and walked everywhere.

* * *

Surprisingly, the sand in the trap on this day had yet to be disturbed. I took the first ten minutes to explain bunker basics: stance, positioning, grip, swing plane and how a lie in the trap affected each.

Suddenly she interrupted my rambling with, "Tell me about fried eggs. My father talks about them constantly."

"We're not ready for fried eggs yet. They are something we cover later, after you've mastered some basic escape strategies. Fried eggs are infrequent, and we don't have that many deep bunker faces on this course, so you won't face them very often. And even then you have to really plug the ball to be faced with that shot."

"But I want to learn how to hit it."

"We will."

"Today, I want to learn how today. You need to at least demonstrate by the end of the lesson."

The impetuous Jessica Woolworth was at it again. I knew if I didn't consent, I'd be badgered for the rest of the lesson. "OK, at the end," I said. "But for starters can we just try a simple escape from a fairway bunker? Greenside bunkers are another deal all together." I dropped three balls. "See that flag at the 150 marker on the driving range? I'm going to aim for that. Rather than reach it, my only goal here is to get out of the sand. I'm going to keep a level swing, shoulders parallel with my lie and just swing easy. We're looking for clean contact, nothing more." I swung three times, lifting the balls softly and crisply away from the beach. "No strain, no pain. You try it."

I dropped a ball in the sand. Jessica took a giant swing, dug the club in the sand and transported the ball two feet. "Let's try an easier swing this time," I counseled. Second swing, same result. "One more, this time with an EASY swing." Jessica sent up a sandstorm, creating a patina on her bronze-colored arms.

"Stop. You're better than this. Swing easy means just that. You don't need a huge back swing. Start at shoulder height. The other issue is that you're dropping your shoulders and digging into the sand. We're not building sandcastles here. The idea is to pluck the ball from the sand, not drive it in deeper." After fifteen minutes of tweaking the shoulders and positioning her feet, Jessica began to pluck the ball fairly consistently.

"Bunker play just takes practice. It's not like riding horses. You probably got on a horse and felt at home after the first lesson."

"I did," she said.

"Some people adapt to riding a bike and ice skating the same way. Bunker play, however, doesn't come as naturally."

"OK, I'll practice some before the next lesson. Right now we're almost done for the day, right?"

"Correct."

"You promised to show me the fried egg."

"I was hoping you'd forget."

"I don't forget promises," she said.

"OK, over to that greenside bunker to your left." She grabbed her Sunday bag and headed for the one steep face on the practice area.

"You know, I've got more time today. I know you do, too, because I asked Starza about your schedule. And since I am going to have to miss the next scheduled lesson for sailing I want to do the fried egg lesson now."

She had me and she knew it. I did have another hour before I had to meet Billy Sauers. I knew I could use the money and I enjoyed being in her stubborn company. "OK, fried eggs. Greenside bunker play is different from fairway bunkers. The one similarity is we are trying for escape, hopefully negotiating a satisfactory distance."

"How far?"

"Near the cup."

"How do I do that?"

"Give me a minute, Jessica. You're a smart girl; just listen to me for a minute. I read somewhere the top sand players get up and down from greenside bunkers about 65 percent of the time. Average is 48 percent. From a good lie in sand with average consistency like we have here—not too fluffy, not too firm—a decent professional expects to get the ball inside three feet."

"How do I stand?"

"Address the ball like you would for a fairway bunker shot. Shift additional weight to your front leg. Square the clubface. Make sure the ball is slightly forward of center. Ball position will vary based upon the trajectory and carry you want."

"What about the swing?" she said, almost annoyed.

"First thing's first. Once you have proper setup, take a steep backswing with extra wrist hinge and less arm action. Have the club enter the sand 1-2 inches behind the ball, driving all of your force into the sand and down behind the ball. The result will be a minimal, abbreviated, or nonexistent follow through. In normal greenside bunker shots you'll be using the bounce of the club to get out. The shape of the sole here," I said, showing her the bottom of the club, "dictates the amount of bounce."

"What about the egg? What you are showing me has nothing to do with the egg. At dinner tonight I want to explain to my father that I learned about the fried egg."

"May I finish?" I said. "The bounce of the club is very useful… except…" I paused "when the ball is fried-egged in the sand."

"Go on."

"A please would be nice."

"Sorry. Please."

"With the plugged – or fried egg – lie, you want to gouge the ball out using the leading edge of the clubface instead of sliding it through on its back edge, like you would normally. Make sense?"

"I think so."

I forcefully slung a ball into the bunker face. "Now you do it."

Jessica stared at the ball. "This looks harder than I thought."

"Once you understand the mechanics it will become easier. What's the first thing you need to do here?

"Put the ball in the middle of my stance."

"Then what?

"Take the club back."

"Not just yet. Square the clubface to your target."

"Oh yeah. Then take the club back."

"Yes… and…"

"Start the swing."

"As you take the club back, hinge the wrists more than normal and then come down on a steep angle. That manner of attack will allow the leading club edge to get under the ball and hopefully onto the green."

We spent the next twenty minutes honing mechanics, Jessica swinging and me raking the trap and dropping balls. The wind had picked up slightly, and she started to look like a sandman with each fried-egg explosion. When all was said and done, she ended the session displaying an aptitude for fairway bunker escapes. The fried eggs were still a work in progress.

"So, honestly, what's with the fried egg obsession? Most players couldn't care less about bunker play. And you have a fascination with buried lies."

"You really want to know? My father thinks he's an expert on every-thing. He's quite talented in a lot of areas, but he is especially competitive in athletics. Well, I inherited some of his genes. I can ride a horse really well. Better than he can, but he won't admit it. And soon, really soon, I'm going to be a better sailor than he is. We have a Flying Scot we keep at Sheridan Shore Yacht Club and I've been taking it out, unbeknownst to him, and getting to be a very good skipper. But the thing I really want to beat him at is golf because he thinks he's king of the links. He especially prides himself on his sand play. There is a standing bet in our family that if anyone -- me, my brother, or mother -- can beat him in a golf competition we get $100. I want that $100. Not for the money so much, just for the satisfaction of beating him."

She paused slightly, contorted her face a bit, contemplating something deep inside. Besides -- I don't know how to say this, so I'll just say it -- besides, I want to prove to him that I am the daughter he wants me to be."

"Perhaps you're better than that," I posited.

"I know I am, but I must… prove it to him."

At that moment I more fully understood the driving motivation for most things in Jessica Woolworth's pretty sweet life. I have to say I was impressed. Somehow, someway, someday, I thought, she just might be able to accomplish her goal, however difficult and demanding the process might be.

"My next lesson is in five days, right?"

"Correct. I'd like you to work on your short game some more. That's where you are going to pick up strokes on people. You need to be more accurate. Do not hit bunker shots to the exclusion of stuff off turf, understand? I know you want the $100, but if we polish the fundamentals, the shots from the trap will get much easier. I promise."

"All right, all right."

Returning to the Pro Shop, I noticed Denise and Alex viewing the line of State Am windbreakers that had arrived earlier in the day. "Hey Mr. Big Shot, we have a meeting in seven minutes," I said.

"I got it. I'm just getting a merch lesson here from Denise."

"Given that your mother is in the business I figured you wouldn't need much schooling in the latest fashions."

"New employee orientation, Looper. I'm just trying to learn a little more about my coworkers."

"How about we hustle over to meet Mr. Sauers as opposed to hustling the shop girl?"

"Looper, the shop girl has it all under control," said Denise. "Tall, dark and handsome here doesn't know everything about the merchandise -- or the shop girl – just yet."

On the way home Alex told me he had picked up a date for the evening. "Just going to the movies, maybe catch a bite afterwards. No big deal."

"More power to you, sport. Every dog has his day."

Little did I know he was about to forego our nightly cribbage games for evenings with the comely Denise Long.

CHAPTER NINE

Liftoff Minus 21 brought an "Oh Shit," from the general manager's office. As we were wrapping up our Friday status meeting, Mr. Binswanger asked the D.O.G. for an update on parking arrangements.

"Got it covered," he responded. "You asked me to commandeer fifty spots for VIP parking and they will be in the ancillary lot by the caddy shack, a mere seventy-five yards from the clubhouse."

"And what about other attendees?"

"Like whom?"

"Like the general public. No way in hell do we have enough parking on site for them. We were lucky to survive last year's international exhibition. Where are other people, the paying public, going to park? Didn't you start on that two months ago, after we first had this conversation?"

"Kind sir, I would remember if we had a conversation like that."

"So, you have done nothing about parking."

"Yes, I have. I have reserved the fifty spots by the caddy shack. I am having signs made up as we speak."

Binswanger was getting hot. "Jesus Christ, Harrison don't you have any sense? We are inviting the public. The majority will come by car. They have to have a place to park. In our case that means ancillary parking to transport them to our door. If buses get involved, we'll need a place for them to turn around. And the one piece of real estate on this property where they can do it is the lot by the caddy shack – unless you devise some kind of pass-through system so the buses do not have to turn around." Exasperated, he slammed his fist on the table. "Where's your brain, Harrison? You are excused from this meeting to secure parking for the ascending multitude. Don't come back until you have parking for at least a thousand guests and a way to transport them safely here and back to their cars. I suggest you begin calling schools and anyone else that has paved space to park vehicles. And charter bus services. Don't call any abandoned airports because there aren't any around here. And do not -- do not -- even think about trying to access the commuter parking at the train station down the street. Good day, Harrison."

Finding adequate parking around Spring Willows would have tried the soul of the brightest of men. Alas, for Harrison Hennessey, the assignment was probably the hardest thing he'd done in the last ten years. The truth is there was no, and I emphasize no, ample school parking anywhere remotely close to Spring Willows.

Normally, Billy Sauers would not have had time for Harrison Hennessey's dilemma. However, not wanting his hide on the line, Mr. Binswanger decided to update Mr. Sauers, knowing full well that if left unresolved the D.O.G.'s problem would become his problem -- and eventually Billy's -- with the resulting result reflecting poorly on the club and on Billy himself. "Goddammit, Bernard. Why did we hire that guy in the first place? Every day he reminds me of what a short timer he needs to be. The day we fire him can't come soon enough. What did you tell him to do?"

"I told him to start looking for parking space and contact bus lines for shuttle purposes. I suggested schools and said no way should he consider the commuter line down the street."

"I have no idea what use he serves this club. I'm outta here. I need to think about this. There has to be a better solution than school parking lots."

* * *

As I entered the Pro Shop from my starting post, Mr. Sauers hailed me from twenty yards away. "You done for the day, kid?" he asked.

"I think so, just got to…"

"No, you're not. Where's Randolph?"

"I think he's in the shop checking merchandise."

"Again? Grab your clubs and tell him to do the same. We're going twilight and we're going to resolve a transportation issue."

Club business and the run-up to the State Am had been taking its toll, and the chance to get out on the course provided some surprising psychic relief. Billy Sauers was no slouch with a club and the three of us traded blows for the first five holes with none of us more than 2-over. It wasn't until we got to Six tee that Mr. Sauers got to the business at hand. "Randolph, this is the hole you think needs to be thinned out, yes?"

"That's correct sir. Too much shade. You can tell that it has affected the turf by how thin it is."

"If we were to do that, what would be a good time of year?"

"My uncle did it at Inverness in February and early March. The trees were leafless and easier to handle. He got an arborist and timber professionals and cleaned out about 200 trees. Told me he probably should have taken out more but didn't want to aggravate the membership. 'Older members love trees' he said."

"Too many trees don't help the turf, do they?"

"No sir. Spring Willows could use some thinning. There weren't near this many trees when Donald Ross laid out the place."

"I dare say you are right. Switching subjects, I asked you gentlemen out here to help me resolve our latest State Am crisis. It seems the man in charge of parking has failed to do his job. In less than three weeks' time we need to find a thousand parking places and buses to transport our visiting guests. Any thoughts?"

"How much time we got to think about this?" I asked.

"Not much," said Mr. Sauers.

"How close to Spring Willows does the parking have to be?"

"Ideally, as close as possible."

"Isn't there an airport in Waukegan? There ought to be plenty of space out there. There's so much grass you wouldn't need the runways."

"Paved parking, Looper. And Waukegan is thirty miles away. I fly out of there occasionally. No. And forget O'Hare. Even if you could secure spots, traffic would be a nightmare. No thanks." He threw a ball on the teeing ground. "Boys, let's play. We can chew on this while I grind your butts into the ground. We're not getting eighteen in, but I want to have bested you both by the time it gets dark."

On Nine tee I said, "What about Baha'i Temple?"

"Looper, have you ever been there? Beautiful freestanding structure, nice gardens, but zero parking. Plus, they have services twice daily. That's a no go. But I like the way you think. Keep at it."

Mr. Sauers and Alex both birdied Nine while an aggressive first putt consigned me to a par. The sun was now casting its golden beams on the treetops. It was clear we were short on daylight. "Gents, we've got time for three more holes if we're lucky. I suggest we play Ten, mosey over to Sixteen and then play Eighteen back to the clubhouse. Following that I'd like to buy you dinner in the grille."

"Mr. Sauers, may I be excused from the meal? I have a prior engagement."

"Mr. Randolph, are you suggesting you have a date?"

"No sir, not suggesting. I do have a date."

"Anyone we might know?"

"Yes sir, I think you do."

"It wouldn't be that shop girl, would it?"

"That's correct, sir."

"And this isn't the first time you've seen her, is it?"

"Correct, again."

"You have good taste, Randolph. Have a good time tonight. Perhaps you and she can resolve the parking issue."

"Thank you, sir."

After that exchange, the three of us focused on golf, eager to complete our twelve holes before twilight disappeared. Pars all around on Ten and Sixteen set the stage for our shots into the gloaming.

"Shopping centers," said Randolph. "You got some shopping centers pretty close to this club. Old Orchard and Edens Plaza. They can't be more than three miles away. That's what? Ten minutes from Spring Willows?"

"Now we're talking," said Billy Sauers. "Big-ass parking lots, too. We just might be able to appropriate some of those spaces. We have members who own businesses at both places. That could be helpful in negotiations. Good thinking, Randolph. Much better than an airport or some godforsaken temple."

We finished the abbreviated round in virtual darkness. Billy Sauers and Alex shared medalist honors with me one back. "Enjoy your evening, Randolph. Tell Miss Long we are pleased the way she is orchestrating things at the Pro Shop. We have benefitted from her feminine touch."

"Thank you, sir. I will, sir." He hurried off.

We chewed on the parking conundrum over club sandwiches. "I can get the buses," said Billy Sauers. "Pierce Engel, one of our members, has a brother-in-law in the business, so that should be no problem, but there has to be a better solution than shopping malls. If we approached them I can see the stores bitching to the mall owners about lost business and parking spaces. And even if we did split the traffic between malls I envision it being too disruptive."

Mr. Sauers droned on, getting into club politics and then into investment decisions both good and bad. "You know, Looper, when I first got into finance, and especially the stock market, I thought I knew something. There was a period where market timing was all the rage. Jump into this, pull out of that, based on trends and history. I lost a lot of money early on. Then I became a student, a real student. I went to New York and met with some real pros. I talked to some high-profile individuals. Then I found a guy in Greenwich, Connecticut, who was making money hand over fist. "Screw market timing," he'd say. "Look for start-ups with sound plans and visionary people you trust. So I began going to New York for a week at a time four or five times a year. This guy put me in touch with like-minded souls and really helped me learn the business. I owe him a lot. When he died I paid his funeral expenses."

"Couldn't his estate have done that?"

"Of course, but I told his wife, paying for his plot and associated costs was the least I could do, given all he had done for me. Besides, this will leave a little more for you and the children I told her. She accepted and that was that. She's almost ninety now. I still get a Christmas card from her every year."

"Nice."

"You haven't said much in the last half-hour."

"I've been listening, trying to learn something. Oh, and thinking."

"Thinking about what?"

"Dyche Stadium."

"Dyche Stadium. Now that's a thought. Why the hell didn't we think of that before? Forty thousand-plus seats and empty parking spaces by the gazillions because..."

"Students aren't in school," I said.

"Not in school. Fucking A. Northwestern students and faculty are not in school in early August. And not more than ten minutes and three miles from Spring Willows. Brilliant. And better yet, I'm willing to bet we can swing a quid pro quo with the university and pay close to nothing."

"How's that?" I asked

"The provost is a good friend of mine. He once inquired about the possible use of Spring Willows for a function for his board of trustees."

"They could do that on campus. They've got some nice buildings of their own."

"No, he specifically wants that function off-campus and thinks Spring Willows would be perfect."

"He wants our clubhouse for a school function?"

"For a board function. There's a difference."

"Any other reasons he might give us Dyche stadium?"

"Remember son, we just want the parking lot."

"All right, the parking lot."

"Two big ones," he said. "His twin daughters are getting married the same day. Guess where they want to hold the reception?"

"Spring Willows."

"On Valentine's Day."

"I think we might have just gotten Dyche Stadium."

"I'll call him tomorrow and let you know what he says."

"You going to tell Hennessey?"

"Not yet. I want to see what he comes up with." Billy Sauers took a long drink from his tall glass of water. "I think you solved a big problem, Looper. Are you sure you don't want to work for me at First Strike when you graduate?"

"I have to graduate first."

"Keep it in mind." He gazed around the room. "You think we can handle this function, Looper? All the traffic could put some wear and tear on this place."

"The grass will grow back. You're limiting access to the clubhouse, right? I mean there are only so many clubhouse passes, so our staff and a little extra help from Iroquois Woods should handle it. We know the merchandise piece is in place. You've got a great food-and-beverage operation. What's not to like?"

"You think we should have mobile carts dispensing food and drink on the course during this event?"

"I would not. I think roaming beverage carts would be disruptive. If it were me, I'd set up some strategic food and beverage stations and let it go at that."

"Where?"

"Between Six green and Seven tee and between Twelve green and Thirteen tee. I'd keep everything else around the clubhouse."

"Nowhere else?"

"The goal isn't to feed the five thousand so much as it is to provide food and drink for those who want it. If I choose to follow players on the front and back nines the locations I mentioned will take care of their gustatory and liquid requirements. The rest you can service from a couple of stands around the clubhouse. Easier on staff."

"Who should run it?"

"We've got a good kitchen staff."

"I don't want them dealing with the public. How about that Cassie girl? Might need to lengthen her skirts a bit, but she seems made for a job like this."

"Honestly, she'd be great. Smart as a whip, too."

"I'll bet if we allowed her to work those two locations we'd do a land-office business. The men at this club like that girl."

"Not so popular with the women though," I offered.

"I've heard that, Looper. And I'll tell you how much it bothers me." He barely separated his thumb and forefinger. "On-course food and beverage business has never been better. Even Brewster at the Halfway House has quit bitching. Money talks, bullshit walks. Yes sir, I believe ol' Cassie needs to be in charge of those locations you mentioned."

"What about comfort stations?"

"Toilets?" said Billy Sauers.

"If we have a thousand people out here for an extended period, some are going to have to relieve themselves. I don't think we want the shrubs being watered or the woods fertilized with human waste."

"Hmm. In our current state our options would be what?"

"Clubhouse, to which you want to restrict access. Then there's the administration shed and the caddy shack. That's about it, except for member homes that line the course."

"Well, we know that's not happening. You're familiar with the super's shed and the caddy shack facilities. What do you think?"

"Doable, but only if the places are spruced up and the crowds aren't too big. Both Al and Mr. O have complained for a long time that there needs to be more toilets in those places. This might be a perfect time to upgrade."

"Good thought. I think I know the perfect supervisor for that job, too. This will be a an assignment for the director of golf, especially since we resolved the parking problem for him." Billy Sauers leaned back in his chair and looked thoughtfully. "Believe it or not, at one time the D.O.G. had a background in construction."

"I didn't know that."

"I'll pay him a visit in the morning and stress the importance of having those new toilets functioning within ten days. That will put an end to these liquid lunches and prolonged clubhouse absences he's been enjoying. Speaking of enjoyment, you've been enjoying Miss Woolworth's company a fair amount, have you not?"

"We've had a few dates, yes, but mostly I'm giving her golf lessons. Seems like she is on a mission to beat her father at something."

"He's a demanding guy. Very successful, but I imagine it's a tough house to live in, especially if you're his child. He gives them every advantage, but there is a lot of pressure to be the best at everything. I am surprised the kids are as well-adjusted as they are."

"Jessica seems driven," I said.

"Just like the old man. Settling for second isn't his style. He's not quite as good as he thinks he is at some things, but I'll give him this, he knows how to make money. He's done very well, and I mean very well, in investment banking and commercial real estate."

And with that the evening ended.

* * *

With the dawn came the first of several humid days. Billy Sauers had apparently scared the bejeezus out of the D.O.G. because by noon a contractor and several plumbers were surveying the possibilities for added restroom facilities. One o'clock brought me my only lesson for the day in the form of Jessica Woolworth. Khaki-colored shorts, navy blue halter top and Shalimar.

"Been practicing bunker escapes?" I asked.

"I can hit them cleanly now a good way down the fairway."

"I suppose you hit a few fried eggs as well."

"Of course. I want that $100."

"Is that all you want?" I ventured.

"I want you to teach me about the short game."

"The short game?"

"Pitching, chipping, things like that. Aren't you the one who told me that's where most strokes are won and lost?"

"Sounds like something I might say."

"We have an hour. Teach me."

Off we trundled to the practice area. I discussed the basics of each, stressing that, of the two, pitch shots required more loft whereas chip shots were taken closer to the green and spent most of the travel time running along the ground. We covered stance, ball positioning, length of swing, tempo, clubhead speed and hinging of wrists ad nauseam. Jessica's questions were nonstop. I'll give her this; she was curious. She wanted to know the why of everything. It was all I could do to keep the discussion practical without getting into the advanced physics of golf. Her hour-long lesson went quickly. She was engaged, focused and eager to learn, more so than any other pupil I had all summer.

As the lesson was ending she saved the biggest question for last. "Looper, I've been thinking – about us."

"Us?" I queried.

"Yes, us. We've been on a few dates now and we seem to enjoy one another's company, wouldn't you say?"

I hesitated, wondering where the conversation was going. Trying to sound neutral I responded, "I would say that's accurate."

"And so far, you've been doing most of the asking. Isn't that right?"

"That's true."

"So, let me ask you this. Will you go with me to Ravinia next week to the Kington Trio concert? My family has four season tickets, but my mother and father have other plans. I thought we could go and ask your buddy Alex and his date to go with us. We have pavilion seats but could have a picnic on the lawn before the concert. Something nice and informal. It would be a nice change from this State Am hullabaloo, wouldn't it?"

"A folk concert would be a welcome departure from staring at progress reports half the day."

"So, it's a date?"

"Absolutely."

"Check with Alex and let me know if it will be the four of us. If he doesn't want to go, I'll give two tickets to my brother."

* * *

At the end of my first sentence Alex was in. "I have no doubt Denise will want to go. But this won't get in the way of any tourney stuff, will it?"

"I seriously doubt it. Based on the progress reports I'd say things are coming together nicely. I even noticed the cement has been poured and the toilets are in place at both the administration barn and the caddy shack."

"Just in time, I might add," said Alex. "I have to ask, though. How was Hennessey able to get that job completed so fast when he screws up everything else he tries to do?"

"It seems in a prior life he had a background in construction. I think he called in some favors and treated the assignment as a commercial job rather than some simple residential exercise. I believe he led the contractors to believe that Spring Willows might be looking to renovate some other structures, and that they'd get extra consideration for the work if they executed this assignment pronto."

"What other renovation does this place need? The clubhouse? It's damn near perfect."

"He may have stretched the truth, though I have heard the tennis house is due for an upgrade."

"I've been down there. Nothing wrong with that whole complex. Maybe in ten years. Nothing needed before that."

"Alex, you're a genius. You know how sometimes great visionaries are so close to the forest that we miss the trees? We've all been stressing about comfort stations, right?"

"Yes."

"And we're adding a couple of toilets in the super's shed and the caddy shack, right?"

"Right."

"And in our hearts we know those still aren't enough seats to fill demand, right?"

"Right."

"But I have never heard a word mentioned about appropriating the restroom or the locker room at the tennis complex."

"It's perfectly situated in the middle of the course. And what's to keep the club from closing the swimming pool…"

"And letting spectators use the toilets in the bath house and changing areas?"

"Not a damn thing."

"So we're both geniuses. The pool area is perfect. It's close to the clubhouse with easy access to the course. Why didn't we think of that before?"

"Because we weren't thinking big picture."

"I will share our inspiration with Mr. Sauers. Maybe we'll get an 'attaboy' out of the deal."

As it turned out we did not get the 'attaboy.' Instead I received an 'we already thought of that.' In addition, to his credit, Hennessey had established traffic patterns, was getting signs made and agreed with Binswanger to open both tennis and the pool facilities to the public. "With those other toilets I think we'll have enough bun space to satisfy the masses," said Billy Sauers.

"Anything else I should know," I queried.

"You and Randolph should not plan to stray too far away from this place in the next two and a half weeks. There'll be a lot of activity and details that will require back-and-fill action by you boys."

"Isn't that what committees are for?"

"All committees are not created equal. Most are functioning, but invariably things fall through the cracks. I'll need you boys to catch them."

"And that requires a constant on-site presence?"

"This tournament is not going to run itself. The potentates are strutting around for sure, but they're not doing a whole lot, except for General Sweeney, who is still whining about comp tickets. I just want the working committees to have a fallback staff if loose ends get really loose."

"And this calls for morning, noon and night presence?"

"Yes."

"Are you sure?"

"That's what I'm saying."

"Well, let me ask this. Do we have permission to go to Ravinia next Tuesday?"

"The Kingston Trio concert? Looper, that night is nine days out from this tournament. We'll be in serious countdown mode at that time."

"It's just one night, Mr. Sauers."

"Who's 'we'?"

"Me, Randolph and our dates."

"Is his date Denise Long?"

"It is."

"And yours is Jessica Woolworth?"

I didn't deny it.

"So we're in the final phases of this club's highest profile event of the year and you want to abandon ship?"

"No, sir. I want to go out for the evening."

"We're nine days out, Looper. We could be in a crisis condition. I want you thinking about responsibility here, son."

"It's the evening, Mr. Sauers. Who will be onsite to screw things up here?"

"The possibilities are endless. The irrigation system could go haywire. Someone could vandalize the course. It would be a bad time for someone to do wheelies on the thirteenth green."

"When's the last time that happened?"

"The point is there's a first time for everything."

"Right," I said, resigned to cancelling a really fun evening. "What do you want me to do?"

"I want you to go to the concert."

"Really?"

"Go to the concert, have a good time."

"But you just said…"

"I know what I said and now I'm saying go to the concert. All four of you. Have a good time. I'm going to the concert, too. Elise and I love the Kingston Trio. Wouldn't miss them."

"So what was all this dereliction of duty talk then?"

"I was trying to make the point that you and those lovebirds Randolph and Long need to be on high alert as we hit these last nine days. Mark my words, things will fall through the cracks. All of us need to be ready. It's all coming together. My only concern is the unforeseen."

"Such as?"

"The weather."

*　*　*

The weather was perfect for Ravinia... for a brief while. And a harbinger of things to come. Jessica, pretty in pink and her broad brimmed hat with a trailing sky blue bow, and we other three made it through dinner – barely -- before the heavens opened up. With the first juicy raindrops Jessica uttered an "Uh oh. Boys and girls we need to grab this blanket and picnic basket and head for the pavilion." Looking around she added "FAST." A mere two hundred yards away we could see a wall of water headed straight for our picnic spot. Alex grabbed the blanket, I took the basket and Jessica said, "If we get separated we are in the fourth row. Everyone for themselves."

Jessica took off like a shot, sprinting past a middle-aged herd of well-heeled patrons. Alex grabbed Denise's hand as I trailed after Jessica. We didn't make it. The torrents caught us forty yards out and three of us arrived under cover soaked from head to toe. Jessica forgot to mention that we had to show tickets for entrance. As the backlog began to swamp the ticket takers, we searched frantically for our hostess. "Over here," came a familiar voice as we wormed our way toward the head of a growing line.

"You're dry and we're soaked. How did you manage that?" I asked.

"I ran faster than you slowpokes."

"You also knew where you were going."

"True, but we're all here now. Let's take our seats. You three can snuggle under the picnic blanket."

"I'm not sure I'd be all that welcome," I said.

"You're not," piped up Denise.

"Figures," I said.

Suddenly a loud thunder crack reverberated through the grounds. "That sounded like a military exercise," I noted. On cue the lights in the pavilion flickered and went out. Semi-darkness reigned.

"Do you suppose the Trio can perform without power?" Alex asked.

"Based on their first album, which is acoustic, I'd say yes," I offered.

They played without power well past the twenty-degree drop in temperature which left me with a persistent runny nose and reduced energy for the next six days.

CHAPTER TEN

"E njoy the evening, kid?" asked Billy Sauers.

"Loved the music."

"So did I. Reminded Elise and I of an old Pete Seeger concert we went to. He didn't need any power, either. How about your buddy, Randolph there? Did he hear any of the music, or were he and Miss Long just into some serious canoodling?"

"I wasn't under the blanket, so I don't know."

"You might tell him to be a little more discreet about that."

"You see everything."

"Not everything. Most things."

The day's progress meeting was perfunctory. The extended weather forecast called for four consecutive days of measurable precipitation. "I would prefer the club not put down those mats on damp turf," Billy Sauers told Mr. Olson. "They are already down under the erected merchandise tent. Luckily, we got the grandstand up by the eighteenth green just in time. Let's not put down any other mats until this monsoon abates."

"When's that going to be?" asked Binswanger.

"God knows," said Billy Sauers. "We need a Plan B in case this lousy weather persists past Monday. Emergency preparedness. Figure out how to manage with shortened timelines. This will undoubtedly mean overtime and conceivably extra staff. Randolph, you might call your uncle on this one. I don't remember any words in his plan for situations like this."

"I'll get right on it, sir."

His uncle wasn't much help, but he did suggest that bad weather could mean a lower turnout. "However, those guests who do show will very much appreciate a happy workforce," he counseled. "In shitty weather, if customer service personnel are upbeat and gracious your guests won't notice the inconvenience much at all. In fact, they'll feel like they are part of a special club if you handle them right. In case the weather is really bad and you have to postpone play, make sure you have a notification system so people don't trudge out to your course for no reason. If you can postpone far enough in advance you can get word to the newspapers, television and radio stations. Other than that you might want to call the telephone company and have them add some extra phone lines and get operators to man them so you can advise guests of weather updates. Call the phone company now so they can get the extra lines installed in advance. Last-minute stuff will not work with Ma Bell."

As it turned out, the phones were installed in near-record time only to have the weather do an about face. Brilliant sunshine graced the first tee Sunday morning. Still suffering from the sniffles, I was pulling an emergency starter shift. "Mr. Martin, your group is on the tee in ten minutes," I called.

"We'll be ready. Waiting for one more."

Three minutes later their fourth appeared, looking almost regal and immaculately dressed in grey slacks, an expensive polo shirt and spit-polished shoes.

He pointed at me. "That him?" he inquired of Mr. Martin.

"Yes, it is."

He covered the tee box in what seemed like three strides. "Son, I want to shake your hand and thank you for all you've done for me in the last four weeks."

"Thank you, sir, but I'm not sure what that is."

"Well, I think you do," he continued. "From what I'm told my daughter has been simply radiant the last month, and my wife ascribes the positive outlook to your presence in her life."

As I stood on the tee box the pins on the tumbler lock in my brain began to fall into place. "I normally play at one of my other clubs," he said, "but I took this match today to see firsthand what all the fuss was about. At first glance, I'd say my daughter has good taste."

"King, we're up," called Morgan Martin. "Let's go."

"Perhaps I'll see you later under less formal circumstances. Good luck to you, son," he said, returning to his foursome.

Good luck? What did that mean?

* * *

Thirty yards away, Cindy Cabiness wandered into the Pro Shop looking for a State Am polo for her husband. "Denise, you look happier these days. It appears your social life has improved."

"I think it's looking up," Denise said coyly. "I've had several dates recently – with the same person."

"How did you get Looper on your arm, dear?"

"Mrs. C, my dates have been with Alex Randolph."

"My, my. Do tell."

"It seems we have a little chemistry."

"So no need to invest in the Trojans."

"I don't think I'm ready for that quite yet," Denise said, blushing.

"Your rosy cheeks become you. Congratulations. See, there are other fish in the sea. Smooth sailing, my dear."

Denise blushed more profusely.

"Oh, don't wrap the polo; a bag will be fine. As for payment, just put it on my account."

* * *

In the clubhouse a less heartening discussion was unfolding. General Sweeney was unloading a salvo on the general manager regarding his comps.

"General, we've sent you your two complimentary tickets. There are no more for board members, plain and simple. You want twenty for your esteemed guests, pay for the damn things like everyone else. The Illinois State Golf Association is looking to make money on this deal. Spring Willows will not indulge you or anyone else with a free allotment. We are delighted to entertain your guests on the premises. They are welcome to enjoy our food and purchase some merchandise, but the operative word is 'purchase.' You want the tickets, buy them," Binswanger said emphatically.

"But I was promised tickets," the general insisted.

"And you shall have them," responded Binswanger, "as soon as you write a check."

"I have people coming from out of state."

"General, I don't care if they are coming from Timbuktu. They are not getting into the tourney without a ticket." With that the general manager turned to go, leaving the General humiliated and fuming.

"This is not right. Rank has its privileges. I'm a board member."

"For god's sake, General. Get it through your head. We all have rank – rank and file. You want to be useful? I understand Hennessey is to introduce players on the first tee. It's a seven-hour shift the first two days. He might be willing to share the spotlight. Get the list of names and memorize them. Practice pronouncing them, know where the players are from so you don't sound like a sniveling wretch in public. Stand tall, General. Enunciate so your guests will be proud of their host. You'll cut a sharp figure out there – if you stop whining. Now, please leave. I've got work to do. Teresa will be happy to take your money. Good day."

A reddening General Sweeney turned and exited the general manager's office. He ran headlong into Billy Sauers.

"Good afternoon, General."

"Billy, just the man I wanted to see. I was guaranteed complimentary tickets to the State Am and I'm having trouble accessing my allotment."

"Did you not get your two in the mail?"

"Yes, I did. It's just that I'm short the other eighteen."

"I'm shocked," said Mr. Sauers sarcastically.

"I was promised complimentary tickets," insisted the General.

"Quit being a cheap bastard and pay for the damn things," said Billy Sauers ducking into Binswanger's office.

"Some people," he said. "How'd that guy ever get to be a general, anyway?"

"Maybe it was a SNAFU or a FUBAR thing. Perhaps a momentary lapse of reason."

"All three sound right," said Billy Sauers, sitting down. "Now what about these revenues from last month?"

* * *

A little later, while passing the short game practice area, I ran into a lightly-perspiring Jessica Woolworth. "Been hitting fried eggs again?"

"Actually no, but I'm getting pretty good at them. Working mostly on those approach shots you've been talking about. But… I've been thinking about a playing lesson. I understand practicing real game scenarios can advance a player's golf education by leaps and bounds."

"You aren't quite ready for that. Most people never take them. They tend to be expensive."

"You think I don't have the money? Money is not a problem. You're saying I'm not ready."

"Yes, that's exactly what I'm saying. Plus, I don't think the club would allow me to give a playing lesson. That's for the staff professionals."

A quick pout turned to a beady look of determination. "OK, how about the next lesson we work on putting. We haven't done that in a while."

"Have we ever worked on putting?"

"No."

"Working on putting is an excellent idea. If we can get you rolling the ball well you might even have a chance in the women's club championship."

"Don't you have to have a handicap to play in that?"

"At some clubs, but not here. Players are flighted initially by handicaps and then it's match play head-to-head. You've played, what, like three 18-hole rounds in your life?"

"Four, if you count when I was nine."

"Then someone like you would qualify as a rank beginner. You'd be placed in the D flight."

"That's the lowest category, right?

"Correct."

"So, how do you think I'd do there?"

"Honestly, I think you might have a pretty unpleasant experience."

"You think I'd get blown out?"

"To the contrary. I think if you could putt, you would destroy the field. The blowback from the membership at your appearance in that flight would be cataclysmic."

"What do they have to complain about? They've never seen me play."

"That's part of the problem. Your long game is light years better than all the D-flighters, most of the C-flighters, and some of the weak A flighters. What you lack more than anything else right now is short-game experience."

"How am I supposed to get that if you won't give me a playing lesson?"

"How about I make an inquiry with a couple members? They might welcome you for a twilight round."

"Looper, I'd welcome your company."

"Likewise, but if you're entertaining even the slightest notion of playing in the club championship, let me suggest to a member that they take you out for a quick nine. That way they could assess your game and make suggestions in a real-game situation."

"You're sure you can't help me?"

"Look. Two years ago, I caught a lot of flak for caddying for Mrs. Peck when she won the D flight. Certain members thought the pairing was unfair. The club doesn't want to relive that and neither do I."

"Who are you going to ask?"

"I have two candidates in mind. I'll let you know what they say. In either case, you would enjoy their company and learn a lot. You in the D flight? I'd enjoy seeing that. You'd do very well."

"How well?"

"Let's just say you'd live up to your expectations."

"Looper, that's one of the things I like about you. You encourage me."

"Jessica, I'm just trying to get you to be the best you can be."

"Keep working on me. I'm a better person when I'm around you," she said, edging closer.

"This conversation would probably be more appropriately carried on in a less public place," I suggested.

"Just as long as it IS carried on," said Jessica. She grabbed her clubs and headed for the bag room.

* * *

Three more days of good weather left Spring Willows in an upbeat, anticipatory mood. Club business continued apace, barely inconveniencing members as the State Am countdown continued.

Sunday night, two days before the first rounds of the tourney, Carlisle Howard placed a call. "Billy, heads up. We might have a problem with the club championship this year," he said.

"Sweeney, again?"

"No, a potential flighting issue."

"What do you care? You should win the championship flight in a walk."

"It's not on the men's side. Women's tourney."

"Okay. What's the concern?"

"D flight."

"Again?"

"It's a little different this time."

"What's the problem?"

"Jessica Woolworth is thinking of entering the club championship."

"So?"

"Billy, she crushes it."

"She's a tennis player and a sailor. She hasn't played much golf, has she?"

"Five times."

"You've seen her play?"

"I went nine with her Sunday twilight. She's a player."

"Why were you playing with her? Why not Litton? He's the one whose been giving her lessons."

"He was concerned about the member reaction, like the blowback he got caddying for Lucy Peck."

"Still, why did you go and not Margaret Worth?"

"Looper asked Margaret and Margaret asked me. If any members saw us they might just think it was a father-daughter thing."

"You don't have a daughter."

"I did it as a favor."

"So you went and you saw what?"

"In a sentence if she could putt she could be an A-flighter. Shot a 43 with a triple on Five and a double on Two. She parred the first from 535 yards, absolutely refusing to play from the forward tees."

"Headstrong like her old man."

"A winner, I think."

"Here's the deal, the girl is really a sailor. She pilots the family Flying Scot like she owns the high seas."

"I'm not a sailor, but I know an athlete when I see one. She's a comer as a golfer. If she enters the club championship there will be some unhappy D-flighters."

"Can we make an executive decision and bump her up?"

"You're on the rules committee, you know we can't do that."

"Guess we'll have to contend with some disgruntled members," said Billy Sauers.

"You know what? Screw 'em. Young people are going to run the world someday. Might as well let 'em start now."

"First she has to enter. Maybe she won't learn how to putt and this conversation will be forgotten. Anyhow, first we've got to survive this other tourney. I've failed to ask. You playing?"

"No, my competitive am days are over. I still do member-guests with clients and all but grinding it out over four and five days is a thing of the past. It was fun and rewarding back when. Now I just enjoy golf for relaxation and trying to get Tinker interested. He shows some promise, but I'm not pushing it."

"You happy with how this tourney is coming together?"

"I should be asking you that."

"The big stuff is in place. We took care of transportation. The grandstand and the merchandise tents are up. Food is ordered, volunteers are ready and extra bathrooms are in place. Signage goes up tomorrow. We open for play Tuesday, the first two days of 18-hole stroke-play qualifying. Low 32 players will advance to two rounds of match play on Thursday. Quarter and semifinal matches on Friday with a 36-hole match play final on Saturday. The usual stuff. Sunday, we hand the club back to the membership."

"Hope the course doesn't get torn to pieces."

"Big dismantling won't start til Monday. We should be back to normal shortly after that. If the weather stays dry there should be minimal disturbance to the turf. Despite the crap I give Otto, he's done a great job getting the course ready."

* * *

On Monday, the course, the staff, the volunteers, the bus drivers and the food service personnel were ready. Even the director of golf was seen off to the side of the first tee rehearsing his greeting of the players. Committee heads finished up their final meetings as the merchandise staff began distributing apparel to volunteers, for which they'd paid a princely sum.

"I'll say this, I like the colors on the shirts for volunteers," noted Alex. "The hats are kind of nifty too."

"Denise has a good eye for color," I said.

"Agreed. She showed me the colors she was allowed to choose from. Some of them were downright ugly. But these should sell well," he said. "If they fly off the shelf we'll have a problem. She was told to be conservative in her order so as not to be stuck with dead inventory. But these shirts might go fast. Especially the ladies' lapis and pink. Too bad they wouldn't let her order rain jackets in pink as well."

"Bet the men's polos sell out by the second day. What's left will be towels, windbreakers, umbrellas, ponchos, divot tools and ball markers."

"There are a lot of windbreakers and even more umbrellas. Must have been wet the day those were ordered."

"It was and I understand Mr. Hennessey insisted on extra rain stuff given a long ago experience he had when his club hosted an event and the five-day tourney extended to more than a week."

"Brutal for a course and players when it gets like that."

CHAPTER ELEVEN

Day one of the Illinois State Amateur Championship arrived bright and chilly. Morning dew glistened off the white tee markers just a stone's throw from the gleaming clubhouse. By 7 a.m. the driving range and practice area was a bustle with the crack of persimmon meeting balata and crisp iron shots slicing the still air. The Pro Shop staff looked sharp in their Spring Willows apparel and club greeters welcomed the first parade of buses as they rolled up to the clubhouse entrance from Dyche Stadium.

On the tee box, Harrison Hennessey fiddled with a portable microphone and the volume control as he readied for his most public appearance in months. Three sharply dressed men advanced to the borders of the immaculate teeing area.

"Ladies and gentlemen, Spring Willows Country Club is pleased to welcome you to this 32nd annual Illinois State Amateur Championship. We hope you enjoy your day with us. We have hospitality volunteers who will be more than happy to assist with questions and your service needs.

"For the eight o'clock tee time will you please welcome our first contestant, two-time defending champion from the University of Illinois Golf Club in Savoy, Ed Moehling, Jr." Acknowledging the applause from the growing crowd, Ed Moehling Jr. stepped up smartly, put his peg in the ground and striped a 260-yard tee shot. More applause and several "holy smokes" ensued.

"And from the Butterfield Country Club in Oak Brook, please welcome Arthur C. Ellis." After twitching for what seemed an abnormally long time, Ellis deposited his opening salvo left in the first cut just short of Moehling's ball.

"Our third player, in his first Illinois State Amateur appearance, represents Danville Country Club. Please welcome Dornach Hinckley." A gangly, strapping young man in his early twenties mounted the tee. Dressed in a bright green polo shirt and pressed gabardine slacks, he appeared right at home in front of the gathering throng. He sent his first shot on a low, penetrating rope that settled ten yards past the defending champion's impressive drive.

Alex turned to me and smiled. "This tourney could be really interesting," he said. "I'm familiar with this guy, but I think he's unknown around here. He was a regular at Inverness. He played two years at Wake Forest but spent his junior year abroad and was injured his senior year. I saw him play. If he's recouped some of his earlier skills he could be a force. Now I've got a rooting interest."

We waited while the second group departed the tee. Harrison Hennessey had given the microphone over to General Sweeney, whose preening presence and authoritarian voice was up to the occasion. In a stentorian tone and with all the bravado he could muster he sent players Dave Huske, Tom Matey and Robert Zender down the greensward.

With no progress reports to review or lessons to give, the two of us had been ordered to remain on call to assume emergency duties. We were each given walkie talkies. "Patrol the property and check in on revenue-producing areas like food and merchandise venues. Randolph, I want you moving around. I don't want to see you in the merchandise area with Miss Long. That's an order," commanded Billy Sauers.

"Yes sir," said Alex, suitably chastened.

"Once an hour I want you checking the comfort stations. If there's an overflow issue I want you to resolve the mess. There is cleaning equipment close by. I know that because I placed it there myself. I do not want our guests to have a shitty experience. Understood?"

"We're on it," I said.

Play moved along relatively smoothly. Lower-handicapped players were gifted with earlier starting times. I anticipated players might have the toughest times with the fronting ponds at Killer Ten, the 163-yard par 3 with steep-faced bunkers and the 153-yard seventeenth. Both lived up to my expectations but the par-5 fifteenth, with its yawning traps, garnered the most griping from one Robert Ratchford, an eight handicapper from downstate Crab Orchard in Carterville. Regrettably, his tee shot trickled into the bunker, advanced but thirty yards only to settle under a lip that required two more hacks to get out. His snowman seriously dampened his chances to advance to match play, an opinion he was happy to share with one and all upon the completion of his round.

Per instructions, I made my rounds and toured the comfort stations. Alex and I had agreed to work on a rotation. I initiated my rounds on the half-hour, he on the hour. Happily, all stations were operating efficiently with the only foul-up occurring at one auxiliary john at the caddy shack, where a guest had clogged the facility with excess toilet tissue and then failed to push the plunger. Fortunately, I easily mopped up the overflow and rendered the area sanitary thanks to disinfectant and a heavy dose of gardenia air freshener.

Sales were speedy in the merchandise pavilion. There was a land-office business in polo shirts with only thirty-five gray smalls and mediums remaining by 3 p.m. Denise was doing a surprising trade in umbrellas, thanks to their vibrant outer edge rainbow pattern. "If it rains I won't have any to sell," she told Randolph.

The temperature remained in the low 70's for most of the day. Cassie roamed hither and yon, checking her food service sites. "People are buying," she said. "Our club sandwiches are selling out. We can hardly keep up, so we'll have to make plenty for tomorrow. As you'd expect burgers, dogs and chips are flying."

"Are fluids in demand?" I queried.

"Beer is moving well and Coke seems to be a staple. We've got that covered. Our beverage distributors are really good. Supply will not be an issue."

At the end of Day One, club management was thrilled with the club's performance. Binswanger was beaming. He even heaped praise upon Herr Hennessey and General Sweeney for the professional way they sent the players off the first tee. All but one player gave the course a thumbs-up for its conditioning and fairness. The single registered complaint came from Ratchford, who took umbrage with the positioning and consistency of the sand on Fifteen.

Clubhouse leaders at the end of the day were Moehling, Huske and Ellis, who posted opening 69's. One back was Prestwick's Country Club's Earl Ziff. Six players posted 71's, including the relatively unknown Dornach Hinckley.

Wednesday's brilliant sunshine once again greeted the 132 competitors, the flock of volunteers, our gaggle of guests and club staff. Starting positions were reversed, giving Monday's late finishers little more than sixteen hours before mounting the first tee. The initial introductions proved an embarrassment as General Sweeney failed to pick up the proper starting schedule. The first group was to be the threesome of Edward Mullins, Sergeant Bostwick and Ellwood Wilson. Unfortunately, the good soldier introduced Mullins as Moehling, Jr. Being a good sport, Mullins teed off, but liftoff came to a halt when Bostwick was announced as Arthur C. Ellis. After a brief pause Herr Hennessey handed the General the proper list and all was forgiven.

By midday, State Am polos were essentially gone, leaving Denise Long miffed at the club's insistence to be conservative in ordering. "We could have made some serious money with those polos," she told Alex. "All I've got left are Spring Willows shirts."

"All? Put 'em out, girl," said Alex. "That's money you don't have to share with the state association. Pure gravy. You're in merchandising. At a shindig like this people want a piece of memorabilia. I'll bet you a good percentage of the people visiting this event haven't been to this club much, if ever. Sell them Spring Willows gear. Surely they want a momento."

"I knew I liked you for some reason," she said, heading for the stock room.

Cassie had gotten the kitchen crew to come in early and make a significant supply of club sandwiches. The club's Coca-Cola distributor brought in and set up two other beverage stations and resupplied others with cases of ice-cold Coke. Burgers, dogs and chip sales topped Tuesday's take. One surprise was the amount of business produced at the refreshment stand by Thirteen. The original plan assumed the stand wouldn't do much at all. Late in the day Tuesday, savvy visitors realized that they could use an extreme western entrance to the property and leave their vehicles in the administration barn lot, thus avoiding a bus ride and congestion at the main clubhouse. Above-average food and beverage sales were a happy result.

A first aid station situated just behind the swimming pool complex had only a few visitors, Dr. Roland Winter reported. "Three bee stings, five cases of sunburn, six blistered heels," he said. "Of course, I did have a badly sprained wrist from one player. Seems like he tried to advance his ball from the woods on Fourteen and struck a hidden root. He told me he finished 10 over on the last five holes but he'd be damned if he would withdraw."

The other casualties on the day were those who failed to qualify for match play. Tuesday's unhappy camper, Robert Ratchford, remained so when his second-day 75 left him one stroke off the cut. Starza said he was glad to see him go because it had been a long time since he'd heard so much bitching about the Spring Willows layout.

Six over was the cutline. Moehling was the medalist for the third year in a row. Huske, Matey, and Zender advanced as expected, along with a host of annual contenders. "Who the hell is this Dornach Hinckley?" asked former champion John Morrell. "I thought I knew all the top players in this state."

"Don't know him," said Starza, "but we've got a kid here working for us who's seen him play. He says Hinckley played at Wake Forest and was injured one year in college. Just returning to the game, apparently."

"Moehling says he hits it a ton. Sharp short game, too. He thinks he'll be playing Friday."

"That's high praise coming from Ed, Jr."

"It is. Well, I'm not going to worry. I've got two matches tomorrow."

"So you're just going to roll through the morning round?"

"If I can't beat Peter Mahoney by the thirteenth hole I better give this game up."

"Best of luck to you."

Wednesday's sunshine gave way to Thursday's humid, blustery thunderstorms. Intermittent squalls punctuated by high winds made for slow play and a delayed afternoon round. All but three of the usual suspects advanced. John Morrell's walk in the park ended with him 1-up after 22 holes and thoroughly disgusted with his game, the course conditions and the weather. Ellis triumphed, 3-and-2 while Dornach Hinckley dispatched Zender, 6-and-5.

At lunch, multi-time quarterfinalist Davis Antrim cornered Robert Zender. "Dave, A, what happened out there and B, what did you see?"

"I played like shit and the weather didn't help," Zender said. "My feet slipped on Six tee and I hit a cannon OB. I found the sand on Ten and took two to get out and the damn clubs slipped out of my hands at least three times."

"OK. I get it. You're unhappy with your play. But at 6-and-5, it wasn't all you. This kid must have game."

"He doesn't hit it for shit. He's lucky as hell. The bounces he got. It's like some heavenly force was guiding his ball."

"What else?"

"He's a slow player. Takes ninety minutes to line up every putt. He never said a word the whole round. Very antisocial."

"Like you, that's very helpful." Antrim turned to go. "Bob, put on a happy face; cheer up and go home. Drive carefully, it's wet out there."

"Yeah, yeah. Now I've got to cancel my hotel. I bet I'll lose a night's deposit too," said the disgruntled loser.

In the Pro Shop, Davis Antrim cornered the resident pro. "Stan, what do you know about this Hinckley kid?"

"Hits it a mile, doesn't he?"

"So I've heard. But he must have something else going for him. What did he shoot this morning?"

"Two over through thirteen, thanks to a double on Three," said Starza.

"Respectable for only third time around the course."

"I'll say."

"What else do you know about his game?"

"Nothing. Did you ask Zender?"

"He was no help. Too busy moping."

"With a different attitude he could be a contender. What time you off?"

"Two twenty against Dowd. Probably will be a long match. We've split previous matches, and they've always gone the distance. Wish me luck."

"Good luck."

CHAPTER TWELVE

As it turned out, Davis Antrim needed luck to survive. After jockeying back and forth, he and Dowd found themselves all-square at Seventeen when Dowd's errant 7-iron landed long left in the greenside bunker. A bladed sand wedge landed his ball in the drink, resulting in a double-bogey five. When the two parred Eighteen, Antrim emerged with the win, 1-up. Four rounds down, three to go for the finalists, whomever they were to be.

Friday's play opened on a misty, sodden course. Mr. O had the greens properly cut and rolled before the first twosome teed off. Balls in the second cut of rough were harder than normal to get back into play, loss of distance being the main casualty. Wet weather and fewer players led to fewer spectators, but those who did choose to traipse around were readily identifiable by their State Am and Spring Willows umbrellas.

Of the morning rounds, one ended on Sixteen when Ed Moehling, Jr. closed out Edwin Spence. Two others concluded 1-up while dark horse Dornach Hinkley spread-eagled an outgunned Arthur C. Ellis, 7-and-6.

"Worst beating of my life, Stan," said Ellis. "I played well, four over through 12. I can't play much better than that. I'd love to blame the weather, but wet conditions had nothing to do with it. He flat outplayed me. He made a downhiller on Ten from the top edge of the green that Arnold Palmer would have loved. That boy's a player. Whoever gets him next will have their hands full."

The lucky contestant was Ed Moehling, Jr. Neither man had any preconceptions about his opponent. The first-round match had given each up-close-and-personal views of his opponent's personality, strengths and weaknesses. "Good luck, son," said Moehling on the first tee. "May the best man win."

"Same to you, sir." Off they went with a growing gallery in tow. The pair played quickly with a singular focus, addressing the ball, swinging with precision and parading forward. Conversation was infrequent, with an emphasis on sending the ball into the cup. The gallery found itself hard-pressed to keep up. Those who chose to watch approach shots rather than stake out spots beside the green often found the players holing out as they arrived.

The second twosome of Antrim and Edwin Pierce, with their small but loyal following, soon found themselves all but left behind. By the eighth hole Moehling and Hinckley were three holes ahead and tied at two under. As they mounted the tenth tee, Moehling asked his opponent, "Want a drink or a snack from the Halfway House?"

"Thanks, I'll take a cup of water if they have it."

"You know," said Moehling, "this might be a three-hour round if we keep going like this."

"Not if we're still tied after 18," his lanky opponent replied. A receptive, moist green led to two more birdies. The pair then ambled off to Eleven.

"Must be some match," Starza said to no one in particular. "If it wasn't so wet I'd tromp around out there myself and watch the slugfest."

"If it goes eighteen you can angle over to the green and watch the finale," said John Cabiness. "Or, if it's not over, you can join the cavalcade going extra holes."

Which is exactly what the old pro did. Both players were all-square, a combined eight under, after eighteen holes. Starza greeted them as they walked off the green. "Gents, you can proceed straight to the first tee or take twenty minutes to regroup, wash up, whatever. Resume play when you're ready."

"We'll take a break," said Moehling. "Want to grab a bite, Dorn?"

"Sounds good."

"What do you guys want to eat?" interjected Starza. "I'll get it for you."

"One of those club sandwiches and water would be great," said Hinckley.

"Make it two," responded the two-time champ.

"These guys almost seem like buddies," Starza said to Cabiness.

"If that were me, I'd want to be as far away from my opponent as possible," said the club president.

"Maybe he's trying to psyche him out."

"I don't know. They look pretty friendly out there."

As the warriors were finishing their sandwiches, the bedraggled duo of Antrim and Pierce were seen trudging up the eighteenth fairway. "Looks like old Davis might have prevailed there," said Starza.

Heads down, the tired soldiers dropped their bags and headed to the Pro Shop. "And the winner is…?" asked Starza.

"I won 3-and-2," said Antrim, "but we're both worn out, aren't we Ed?"

"Damn right. I need food and a shower."

"What was the decisive moment?" pressed the pro.

"Believe it or not, I airmailed my hooked drive on Sixteen behind one of only two trees on the entire hole. Like the brilliant tactician I am, I played my second down Fifteen, caught that monster trap and lost the hole and the match. I'm pissed at the way it ended, but my opponent played better than I did, so that's the story."

"Weather wasn't a factor?"

"Not in the slightest, but I notice the wind's picking up pretty good. That will dry things out for tomorrow's final. By the way, where did those guys go and who won? They were long gone by the third hole."

"All even after eighteen. They're getting ready to resume as we speak."

"How'd they look? You think Moehling's got a chance for a three-peat?"

"Honestly, they looked refreshed and chummy – almost like a friendly Saturday round. Must be playing some hellacious golf though. They're both four under."

"If I weren't so beat I might follow them for a bit," said Pierce. "Maybe I'll just watch them tee off and rest my bones right here."

"I'll go with you to the tee. Then I'm going home. Stan, will you call me and tell me who wins? Title match tee time at 10?"

"Yup."

"I'll be here at 9:30, then. Thanks."

Clearing skies and a strengthening breeze greeted those on the first tee for the nineteenth hole tee shots. Hinckley lasered his drive right center while Moehling countered with a bullet shorter and left. Both grabbed their bags with less enthusiasm than previously and proceeded down the fairway. Walking together like old buddies, the two ambled after their respective balls.

"Those guys are acting like they've known each other all their lives," said the general manager. "I don't think they've ever met before this tournament."

"We'll, they sure as hell can play," noted Starza.

In the gathering twilight, only a score of interested spectators followed the players for what was essentially their third round of the day. Each player registered birdie, par, par before the match ended on the 213-yard par-3 fourth, fittingly on the farthest green from the clubhouse. Still first off the tee, Hinckley put his tee ball pin high -- exactly 17 and one-half inches from the cup. "Now that's a shot. What's that, the length of the leather grip on my 4-iron," said Moehling, who barely made the green and left his woeful birdie attempt twelve inches below the hole.

Amidst scattered applause Hinckley tapped in for a two, turned, shook Ed Moehling, Jr's hand and said, "Some round."

"Got that right," said Mochling.

"You know, Dorn, people are going to say I lost this match, but you and I know better. You outplayed me. Maybe just barely, but I feel like I'm the biggest winner. I thoroughly enjoyed this."

"Me, too."

Starza had been monitoring the match's progress from the Pro Shop and after the two teed off for the second time he dispatched Randolph via an extra-large golf cart to follow the match. After the semi-finalists exited the green on Four, Randolph presented himself. "Gentlemen, I've been ordered to escort you and your clubs back to the clubhouse. You've had enough exercise for the day."

"I'll buy that. Time to turn in the scorecard and take a hot bath. How about you, Ed?"

"Absolutely. In a way, I'm glad I'm not the one who has to go 36 tomorrow."

Randolph sped along in the gathering darkness, listening to the idle chatter of warriors recounting their round. "You want me to drop the clubs in the bag room?" he asked.

"I'm taking mine with me," said Ed Moehling, Jr.

"Me, too," added Hinckley.

"How about I at least let the staff clean the clubs? In fact, if you leave the shoes, I can have them polished."

"No, I'll just take mine with me," said the loser. "I need to get back to Savoy tonight. It's about a three-hour drive."

"How about you Mr. Hinckley? I can have those shoes polished while you turn in the scorecard."

"Really? Have at it then. I'll just pad around the Pro Shop in my socks for a while."

In ten minutes Randolph had the shoes polished and the clubs cleaned. "All squared away?" he asked.

"Yup, I am now officially in the final. What's the weather supposed to be tomorrow?"

"Sunshine and seventy-five degrees. Should be a great day for golf, spectators and the club. Where's your car? I'll lug these to your vehicle."

"Just down the lot. Nice touch by the club to have reserved parking spaces for the quarterfinalists. I'll say this, Spring Willows has done a great job putting this event on. Terrific course, impressive clubhouse, pleasant volunteers. Fine weather three out of five days. What's not to like?"

"Glad you enjoyed your stay."

"See you tomorrow."

It was closing in on 9 p.m. as Randolph readied to depart the Pro Shop. "The only thing I don't get," began Starza, "was how friendly those guys were at the end of the match. I mean, there must have been at least fifteen years difference in age, and they waged war for more than five hours. In my day I was taught to hate my opponent and not say much during a match. At the end there they looked like long-lost brothers. What's with that?"

"I did glean one tidbit on the ride back to the clubhouse from Four that might explain the chemistry," said Randolph.

"What's that?"

"If I heard it correctly, Hinckley has agreed to pair up with Mr. Moehling for his member-guest three weeks from now."

Starza's loud guffaw punctuated the empty Pro Shop. "Well, that explains a lot. Do you know about that member-guest?"

"No sir."

"I do. We've had several Spring Willows members play in their soiree down there. Moehling's club does a terrific weekend. Wives are invited, great gifts, superb Friday night couples' dinner, expensive prizes. But the really big thing is the Calcutta they run. Seventy percent to the winning team, often in excess of $10,000. I'm betting old Ed has his eyes squarely on the top prize. If that's the case, I'd say he did just fine at this year's State Amateur, even if he didn't defend his title."

A brilliant cobalt sky reigned over the evaporating dew as the contestants emerged from the driving range and practice area. A multi-hued crowd surrounded the tee box as Davis Antrim and Dornach Hinckley mounted the tee. "Ladies and gentlemen," intoned Harrison Hennessey, "the Illinois State Golf Association and Spring Willows Country Club are proud to present today's championship match. First up for the 10 o'clock tee time, from Westmoreland Country Club in neighboring Wilmette, please welcome Davis Antrim." Enthusiastic applause preceded Antrim's well-struck missile that sailed 240 yards dead center. "And now, from Danville Country Club, first-time contestant Dornach Hinckley." Placing his ball squarely between the markers, Dornach Hinckley, in a pale blue polo and white slacks, uncoiled a rocket that sailed 25 yards further.

For cognoscenti that was a harbinger of the rest of Davis Antrim's day. He played well, but was no match for the newcomer. Hinckley had him by three at the turn, five after eighteen before closing him out, 8-and-7.

"That was a thrashing," I said after the awards ceremony.

"The club returns to semi-normal tomorrow," said Starza. "Things will ease up a lot then. People will start to go on vacations. The only thing on the horizon will be the club championships."

"Club championships. I almost forgot about them."

"Well, the members will remind you. As I think you recall, things can get a little testy around then."

I tried to ignore that last D-flight memory. "Man, I am tired," I said. "Can I go home now?"

"Be my guest."

CHAPTER THIRTEEN

The following week brought two invitations, both of which felt more like command performances. The first was extended by Billy Sauers in yet another evening phone call. He wanted me and Alex to meet with him the following day for our take on the tournament. After ninety seconds of banal chitchat he asked how I was holding up.

"Honestly, Mr. Sauers, it's been a long month. I'm glad this event is over so life can get back to normal."

"It seems to me that normal went out the window when you started taking up with Jessica Woolworth. I hear tell you've been seeing quite a bit of her lately."

"She's good company and we get on well together."

"Yeah, yeah. I'm not going to interrupt your social life. Anything about your work life I need to know?"

"There is one thing. Remember a while back you said I should keep my eyes open for any more possibilities like that small golf company in California we talked about?"

"I do. That worked out pretty well. What do you have in mind?"

"Have you been out to Des Plaines lately?"

"Not really. Too busy here and downtown."

"There is an eating establishment there that's very popular with teenagers and young adults. The place sells hamburgers, French fries and milkshakes mostly. But it is overrun in the evenings and I hear it does brisk business during the lunch hour. The food is quite good, served quickly and cheap.

I first visited about three months ago and noticed the customer turnover. Jessica and I have been going over after the movies. The place is a drive-in and the parking lot is wall-to-wall with traffic. Really popular. I just have the feeling the concept has staying power."

"Why would I be interested in a hamburger joint?"

"This one is different. I don't know exactly what the business model is, but it's different and, best I can tell, it's working. They even have a sign outside advertising how many hamburgers they've sold nationwide."

"Why are you telling me all this?"

"I think there are franchising opportunities."

Suddenly the tone on the other end of the phone changed. "What did you say the name of this place was?"

"McDonald's."

"Like the farmer?"

"Close enough."

"And it's where?"

"Lee Street in Des Plaines."

"A lot of growth out that way." Another silence and then, "See you tomorrow at 10."

* * *

The following day Mr. Sauers met us in Binswanger's office. "You boys get an A for your work on this tourney," he said. "You helped get the master plan and staff back on track and kept everyone focused. I liked, and the tournament committee liked, the response you got. You engendered a kind of 'we're all in this together' mentality that seemed to resonate with everyone, especially the working class. What I need now is that executive summary we talked about for the September board meeting. I'd like it sooner rather than later so I can review it before I present it. I have no doubt the summary will be thorough and a true reflection of actual events. I do not need chapter and verse of every action taken by every department. You can reference the master plan, but just highlight key actions and events. Feel free to name names where appropriate. Document major shortcomings, and place blame as appropriate. Between the two of you I expect a treatise that will serve as a literary culmination of this memorable event for our club."

"Treatise, sir? That would seem to connote a lengthy document."

"Perhaps I have succumbed to hyperbole here, Looper. I do not want *War and Peace*. Write something clear and concise. Break it down into manageable sections. Keep it to ten pages or less. Four would be better."

Turning to Randolph he said, "There is no reason this can't serve as an outline and base document for that case study you have to write. I know your official time with us has expired, but stay here and take whatever time you need to write that case study. You have all the research and facts. Write and polish the draft. That way you'll be done before school starts and your boss can review what you've written. I'll call Mr. Coggins and tell him you are finishing up some tourney work for me. He won't mind. I'll bet the shop girl won't mind, either."

* * *

The second invitation came Tuesday afternoon from Jessica Woolworth following her putting lesson. "You are getting pretty good at this," I said. "If we can dial in the speed a little more, you'll be on your way."

"Maybe."

"Not maybe. The best putters in the world will tell you putting is all about speed -- not direction. You need to worry less about direction and find an easy tempo. We want more body and arm movement and connectivity and less wrist and hand action. Holding arms and wrists firm as opposed to jabbing and being handsy will make you a serious competitor."

"I'm thinking about entering the club championship."

"Do you think that's a good idea?"

"Yup. You do too, but you're not saying much."

I turned away and rolled my eyes.

"I want to enter because I want to show my father I can be a player at something he's also good at."

"How about just doing something for yourself?"

A serious look came over her countenance. "We're still going out Thursday, right?"

"Yes."

"Change of plans then. Come over at 6:30."

"Not 7?"

"6:30, for dinner with me and my parents."

"Anything else I need to know?"

"Nope, just come for dinner. Just the four of us. You'll like my mom a lot. You two have a similar manner. See you then," she said disappearing.

* * *

Wednesday and Thursday Alex and I labored over the executive summary. We divided the duties topically and found ourselves prone to including too much detail. "We have to remember this is supposed to be a summary," I said.

"I wish we had all the revenue and expense figures," he said. "We have some really rough numbers, but Mr. Sauers is going to want firm figures when he presents this thing."

"How about we get all we can, best guesses and all, and then note final numbers to follow and he can plug them in. Surely he doesn't expect a complete financial statement two days after this thing is over."

"Let's do as complete a revenue and expense report as we can using what we can get from Denise. Most of her expenses were incurred before the tournament started. I'll bet she's got a solid approximate figure on revenues. She stayed late every night counting cash and receipts. The merchandise operation can be our model."

"Sounds like a plan."

"You know what? I bet Cassie has a good handle on concessions money, too. I'll contact her."

I left Alex so he could have some quality time with the shop girl and grind through the merchandise numbers while I went to give two lessons. The first was to a Mr. Cuthbert, who needed basics on long-iron play. The second was my third lesson with ten-year-old Timothy Albright, who clearly wanted to be anywhere but on the practice range.

"It's too hot here. I want to go to the pool – now!" he yelled at his mother.

"Timmy, after your lesson." The byplay went on for several moments when his mother quelled his petulance with, "If you don't take the lesson, there will be no pool and James cannot come over and spend the night."

A pout, a frown and an ugly face thrown at his mother's retreating exit ended the debate.

Looking for a way to make the lesson bearable for both of us I said, "Timmy, what golf thing would you like to do for the next 40 minutes?"

"I want to swing at the ball with the driver. And then I want to hit the ball out of the sand trap."

"OK, grab your bag and let's go down to the end here." We deposited his bag. "Get your driver. Here's how this is going to work. I'll put the ball on the tee and you swing. Do you remember how I told you to stand and set up?"

"Sort of." For the next two minutes I reviewed stance and swing. After that I took ball after ball out of the ball bucket while he whaled away. "Stand a little farther away when you swing," I counseled.

After twenty-five minutes we were both pretty sweaty. To his credit, Timmy had gone from cold topping to worm burner to slightly elevated eighty-yard drives. "Much better than last week, don't you think?"

"Yeah, but can we hit some sand shots now?"

For the next twelve minutes, Timmy moved mounds of sand around the bunker. If he made proper contact with thirty-three percent of his swings I'd be surprised. At the end of the lesson he was in a happier mood and ready for the pool. He had also succeeded in giving us both a heavy coating of sand that clung to every pore on our perspiring bodies.

I escorted him back to Pro Shop where we met Mrs. Albright. "How did it go, boys?"

"It was pretty cool, mom. I hit some drives and sand shots today. Now I want to go to the pool."

"Here's your suit. Go into the changing room, put the suit on, and shower before you go in the pool," she said. With a shuffling gait, Timmy took off.

"Well, he's certainly in a better mood."

"We just tried to make it fun today. He actually learned some things and hit some pretty good shots."

"Shall we set up another lesson?"

"Honestly, I'd ask him. I'm happy to give it if he wants, but if he's out here because you and your husband want that for him, I'd wait a bit. He won't miss a thing by going a week or a month or longer without a lesson. The important thing is for it to be fun for him. Does he have another sport he likes?"

"He likes tennis, but neither my husband nor I play."

"That could be why he likes tennis. Might be something to think about. As I said, I'll be happy to give a lesson if he wants it. Anything else I can help you with?"

"No, thank you. I'm glad he had a good time. I'll think about what you said."

I turned and headed for the Pro Shop. By this time it was past 5:30 and Starza was getting ready to leave for the day. "What happened to you? You look like the sandman."

"The last lesson involved bunker play and I got the worst of it."

"You got a change of clothes?"

"In the car, but I didn't figure to be hot and sweaty at the end of the day."

"So take a shower."

"I don't have time to go home."

"Looper, just take your damn shower at the club. Go into the men's locker room like you own the place, take your shower and go on about your evening. There's not one person in this place who would think the first thing about it. And if they do, tell them I told you to do it because you were meeting some important club people. That last part is true, right?"

"Actually, yes."

"Well, dismissed. Go to it."

CHAPTER FOURTEEN

Allgussied up, I presented myself at the Woolworth home.

"Nice blazer, young man. Welcome to the Woolworth hostel," said Jessica's father as he answered the door. "Not the Waldorf, but it will do, I suppose."

"Thank you, sir." Suppose nothing. It was a nine-bedroom expansive stone manse, equal to any mansion I'd ever seen.

"Since this isn't a business meeting, take off your jacket and stay a while. We'll be moving to the patio for grilled steak or chicken in a bit. You won't need your jacket out there. Which entrée do you prefer?"

"The red meat, if you please, sir."

"Done how? I'll be grilling."

"On the rare side, please."

I turned down the offer of hard liquor and accepted a lemonade.

"Many college boys would jump at the chance for the hard stuff. We stock good libations in this house."

"I don't doubt that, sir, but I've seen what it can do to some members at the club."

"I like the way this young man thinks, Jessica."

"I told you he's well-grounded, father."

Turning to me the man of the house began probing. "What are your plans for the rest of the summer now that the State Am is over?"

"I've got duties at the Pro Shop, and I've been assigned to do an executive summary on the tourney for the club's September board meeting. But I hope to have it done by the end of the month before I go back to school."

"What's your major?"

"I intended to study history, but I seem to have an aptitude for finance, macro-economics and marketing. Guess that makes me a business major."

"Have you thought about graduate school?"

"Not really."

"You might want to look into that. There are some good MBA programs out there. Me, I went to Wharton in Philadelphia. Harvard's got a great program, too. Places like that can get you a good job on Wall Street."

"Not sure I'm ready for anything that big time, sir."

"Maybe not, but a diploma from one of those schools could open a lot of doors for you. Just a word of advice, look to the private sector. Better chance of advancement – and this is a big one -- a larger salary."

"Yes sir."

"Son, you can stop the 'sir' stuff, OK? We're all friends here. My name is Kingston Woolworth. My friends call me King. At the very least, call me Mr. Woolworth."

"Yes sir," I said.

"Let's mosey to the patio. I've got to start the entrée. Hope you have a big stomach. We eat large portions in this house."

"I only had a sandwich at lunch, so I think I'll be ready." I was not ready for the 20-ounce porterhouse he dropped on the large grill built into the patio terrace.

"Keep an eye on this one here. It's yours. Advise me when it looks prepared to your taste." King Woolworth slathered on a butter patty, followed by ground pepper and a pinch of salt. In the left corner of the grill went two much smaller chicken breasts. "Our ladies like more modest portions," he continued. "Something about keeping trim figures."

"Looks like that approach has been working," I said.

About the time the meat landed on the table Mrs. Woolworth deposited the ears of corn, a basket of rolls, Caesar salad and a bowl of cold blueberries. After a quick saying of grace Mr. Woolworth grabbed the rolls and passed them to me on his left. Without stopping I offered one to Mrs. Woolworth.

"Don't you want a roll?" queried Jessica's mother.

"Yes ma'am, but I was taught to offer them to the hostess first."

"Very thoughtful, but I insist."

I plucked one from the ornate basket and passed it back.

Dinner progressed quickly, with conversation ranging from current affairs to country-club politics. The latter was a subject in which I was well-versed. "Just a question, Mr. Woolworth. In your opinion, did Spring Willows acquit itself well with last week's tournament?"

"I only made it opening day, but from what I saw the operation was running smoothly, and the guests were having a good time. Member feedback seemed positive. Any issues from your end?"

"Not that I observed. Aside from the wet weather I think we fared quite well."

"Dessert tonight is sorbet. The choices are lemon, lime, orange and raspberry. What'll it be?" said Mrs. Woolworth. "Before you answer, tell me what we are to call you. My husband keeps saying 'son.' Jessica has yet to speak your name, and I am not about to stoop to 'hey you.'"

"My given name is Arlo Litton, but in the last three years because of the golf connection most everyone calls me Looper."

"What would you like us to call you."

"Looper is a lot less formal. How about we go with that?"

"OK, Looper it is. Please call me Erica if you're comfortable with that."

"Thank you. May I use Mrs. Woolworth for now?"

"Of course."

No one wanted lime. Jessica opted for the orange while Mrs. Woolworth and I went for the raspberry. Jessica was just putting the second spoon to her lips when King asked what seemed like an odd question. "I've been wondering, on these evenings you two go to the movies, where do you go to eat afterwards? Dairy Queen? Tastee-Freez?"

"We found this really neat burger stand with milkshakes in Des Plaines," said Jessica. "It has become really popular. Sometimes cars can't get into the parking lot it's so crowded. They cook the food quickly, serve it fast and it is sooo good. Burgers cost fifteen cents. Kids from all over go there. And they're open until 11. You and mom might even like it. Business is crazy there. I bet they are making a lot of money. You're in commercial real estate, you ought to check it out."

"Young lady, I'm into big office buildings in downtown locations, not hamburger stands."

"Yes, but you are doing shopping centers in the suburbs, too, right? When Old Orchard and Edens Plaza close up at night where do you think kids go? They go out for food -- and right now they are going McDonald's in Des Plaines. If you don't believe me, see for yourself. That place is doing something right."

As I had been taught at home, I helped Mrs. Woolworth clear the table. "Very thoughtful of you. I don't get a lot of male assistance at mealtime around here," said Mrs. Woolworth.

"Just ingrained. My father travels a bit so we see him mostly at weekend meals, and my mother makes an effort to make her best meals of the week when he's home. In return, he does the dishes, a task into which I was dragooned at age eight. It's the least I can do."

"What does your father do then, dear?"

"He works for Radio Corporation of America as a field engineer. He has a nine-state territory here in the Midwest. He leaves on Sunday nights and gets home on Fridays. Best I can determine he's a problem solver for RCA distributors and high-profile residential clients."

"That sounds like technical work," said Mrs. Woolworth.

"It is, but he's good at it, thanks to the Coast Guard training he got during World War II. He was stationed at radar installations all over the Pacific, from New Caledonia to the Aleutian Islands. He was even in the Philippines for a while. Well-traveled. Doesn't talk about it much, though."

"Most soldiers don't. My father was a rear admiral during the Solomon Island skirmishes. He'd just as soon forget all about it. Can't blame him, can we?"

"No ma'am. I think not. Brutal business all the way around."

In the other room I could hear Kingston Woolworth engaging in family business, a conversation he redirected upon my return. The evening ended with a cordial display of pleasantries and the usual "I hope we'll see you again," after which I bought my leave, surprised that in the entire evening the words "golf" and "sailing" were only mentioned in passing.

CHAPTER FIFTEEN

My next encounter with King Woolworth came sooner than expected. Standing alertly outside the Pro Shop for yet one more Sunday shift as starter I checked the tee sheet for the day's first pairings. The 8:00 a.m. tee time was held by none other than Billy Sauers and Margaret Worth. "Looper, I thought they'd give you the weekend off, given all the extra hours you logged recently," she said.

"We're short one man today. I live close by and got the call so here I am… at your service."

"And why not," said her partner. "Our other players will be here presently. I saw them pulling in ten minutes ago."

"Why are you out here so early? You could've had a 1 o'clock tee time."

"Why not? Tee off at 8:00, home by 12:30, beat the midday sun and move on to other things. Early to bed, early to rise, Looper. That's the key to success. Speaking of which, here comes the rest of our foursome."

Out onto the Pro Shop patio who should emerge but Mr. and Mrs. Kingston Woolworth. My heart sank. What the hell. Was this old home week or what? "Looper, good to see you," boomed the King himself.

"So nice of you to join us the other night," said his wife, extending her hand. "I hope you enjoyed the warm corn, cold blueberry combo," she said.

"Delightful blend and part of a wonderful evening," I stammered before announcing, "You're up."

As I was to learn much later from Billy Sauers, what started out as a purely social round evolved into a fairly intense business discussion. "How's the commercial real estate business these days, King?" began Billy, as both men traipsed after tee shots sprayed slightly left of the sixth fairway.

"Office occupancy is about eighty-nine percent in my Loop properties. I still do a little residential work for several high-net-worth individuals. That's about it. The good news is that the revenue is flowing at a pretty steady clip."

"Looking to get into anything else?"

"You know me, Billy, I'm always looking. You have anything in mind?"

"I've been doing some thinking. The war's been over a while now."

"Which war?"

"Come on, the big war, the one that really counted."

"And…"

"And you and I have done pretty well, but the world is changing. Everything is expanding. Habits are changing, and unlike when we were growing up, people have money – and they are spending it. No longer on just necessities. But with changing habits come lifestyle changes, wouldn't you agree?"

"Of course," said King as he slashed a 5-iron just short of the sixth green.

"I took a little ride out west of town the other night to look around. Lots of new businesses going up. Not everything's downtown anymore. Look at the suburbs west of here. Shopping centers like Edens Plaza and Old Orchard are sucking up discretionary income like you and I never had." Billy Sauers eyed his Titleist and hit a flyer twenty yards right and short of the putting surface.

"My wandering took me to Des Plaines and this hamburger stand I heard about. I couldn't believe the traffic there at 8:30 at night. I would have thought people were done eating for the night, but no, they were driving in and out of there nonstop. I parked across the street and just watched for thirty minutes. An unending stream of cars, driven mostly by young people. Lots of teenagers."

"That's it? You watched kids driving and eating?"

"No, I decided to go for a closer look. Turns out there are about only nine items on the menu, with the big movers being hamburgers, French fries and milkshakes. Someone takes your order and in minutes it's delivered to your car. Burgers for 15 cents. It appears to me that the whole concept is based upon speed, lower prices and volume."

"Better go hit your ball," said King, "the women are on the green."

Billy Sauers's enthusiasm continued up the seventh fairway. "So, I've been watching this operation for a while now, right? When the girl comes to my car with the food I say, 'Who's the owner here?'"

"I get the 'I'm not sure' answer, but I know he comes in at 10 o'clock every morning."

"So what did you do?"

"What do you think?"

"You went back the next morning."

"Right, I think I annoyed the hell out of him. Turns out it's a franchising deal and I got the name of the guy who sold him the franchise. You know a guy by the name of Ray Kroc?"

"Sounds vaguely familiar. I've seen him connected with some land sales in the northwestern suburbs here. So how'd you hear about this place?"

"Looper mentioned it to me."

"You know, he was over the other night. He and Jessica mentioned the place as somewhere they go after the movies."

"I tell you, King, they're not the only ones. I have to believe there's real potential."

"You know what that reminds me of?"

"Motels and the deal we did with Kemmons Wilson, from Memphis."

"I'm thinking this Kroc guy is on to something. Look at Holiday Inns; they are going gangbusters right now. He's opening like two a week. You can't tell me this instant food service thing won't get huge. Everybody's on the move these days."

A loud "hey" floated across the seventh green. "Margaret and I want to play golf, so we are going to move on ahead. You titans of industry can go at your own pace. We're going to eat in the clubhouse when we're done. If you get really far behind and can't join us for lunch then one of you can drive the other home."

And off the women went. "King, think of the commercial opportunities with this hamburger thing. Watching outward expansion, you could pick up property on street corners in growing areas, sit on it a while, and then sell it to Kroc or franchisees and make a killing. You've got the resources yourself, or you could find investors to partner with."

"Investors like you?"

"Sure, why not? Something else I'm thinking. Talking about this land grab approach, someday, someone with a lot of money is going to study these new interstate routes and start buying up land around the interchanges. You don't think Kemmons Wilson isn't thinking about that?"

"No doubt. Interchanges, lodging and food. Sounds like a recipe for success," said Kingston Woolworth.

By now the men were two holes behind their former playing partners. "We better start moving. That group behind us looks like they're getting antsy."

On Sixteen Kingston Woolworth asked "Billy, what do you think about this Litton lad? Seems like a bright boy to me."

"I've known him for three years now. Intelligent, well-mannered, highly motivated. I think he's got a future. Kind of reserved sometimes. Doesn't give himself enough credit."

"He seems to be a good influence on my daughter. She's been hanging around him a lot. And frankly seems the better for the association."

"What do you really want to know?"

"One of the reasons we joined the club long ago was to associate with the right people. I've enjoyed a good station in life. I guess deep down I wanted to give that opportunity to my kids… to associate with well-bred, intelligent people as we do."

"You mean monied people?"

"Well, hopefully she'd associate with people of means. In the past she's dated a number of the young men at the club, but she's been singularly unimpressed. She likes Looper's down-to-earth approach. Keeps her grounded, unlike a number of these trust fund babies."

"King, Looper does not come from money. His family is a well-grounded, upstanding middle-class unit. His father works hard. His parents have taught him impeccable manners, which is one reason he's succeeded at the club these last three years. I can tell you he is very well-liked and respected by the membership. I've used him as a terrific source of information, especially at the ground level. My company has already invested in a golf equipment company because of him – and all they make is putters. Damn good ones, too. I don't know what he plans to do after graduation, but I've suggested he come work for me. He's a finance/marketing major and has a business savvy that I don't see in many other young bucks. Jessica and your family will have to go a long way to find a better citizen and prospective son-in-law."

"And he told you about that hamburger place?"

"He did."

"Might be something to look into."

"If I had a daughter I'd be calling him to ask her out. He's smart, has an eye for business, and understands human nature better than most."

The men finished their round thirty minutes behind their original partners and caught them finishing their vichyssoise and fruit salads. "We're going home," said Erica Woolworth. "You boys do what you like."

"Thank you, ladies. We enjoyed the round."

"We enjoyed your company for the first six holes. King, you'll have to go home with Billy."

Over Kobe steak salads and several cold lagers, Billy Sauers and Kingston Woolworth discussed the eventual fate of Harrison Hennessey. "The guy's got to go," said Billy Sauers. "He hasn't pulled his weight. Big disappointment. I should have been more involved in the interview process," he said.

"Fire him."

"He's got a two-year contract."

"That's never stopped you before."

* * *

The telling conversation took place two days later. As a prelude to a full employment committee meeting, Billy Sauers and John Cabiness summoned Harrison Hennessey to the general manager's office.

"Harrison, thanks for coming on such short notice. Binswanger was called away and asked me to fill in for him."

"Billy, I think I know why you two are here, so before you go any farther, let me state my case."

"Harrison..." began Billy.

"Please. Time was when I was a hell of a pro. On the tour level and as a club professional I was proud of the golf I played and the work I did. The membership, wherever I served, was pleased, too. I'll be the first to admit I'm not the man for this job anymore, at this club or probably any club. I am embarrassed to say I took this director of golf position as a sinecure. My work ethic has been poor. I have had way too many lunches off-premise. In the last six months I've realized I don't want to be in charge anymore. I'm 65-years-old. Your club needs a younger man in this role."

Billy Sauers and John Cabiness sat in silence as it became clearer that a mutual parting of the ways might be in the offing. "Aside from the generous salary my time here has afforded me, I've also received another blessing I would never have imagined. In March I met Barbara Clancy, a club member and divorcee, and we have formed a strong bond. She and I are pondering matrimony... within the next three months."

Billy and John Cabiness let him continue. "I suspect today's meeting might contain the suggestion of resignation or possibility of termination, pending an employment committee review. I understand the need to address my performance now that the State Am is over. I also know I have a two-year contract."

John Cabiness was about to act presidential when the D.O.G. waved his hand. "Please let me finish. I don't think it's fair for me to hold the club to that agreement. I haven't kept up my end of the bargain. I suggest that I act like a director of golf for the time being, arrange the seeding for the club championships, and then quietly depart on a date to be determined by the committee. I'd prefer that my leaving be seen as a retirement and then the club can get on with finding my replacement. I'm well-connected in golf circles and can even suggest some worthy candidates who would meet Spring Willows' expectations."

Billy Sauers and the club president weren't speechless, but may as well have been. They looked at one another. "We'll take your suggestion to the committee, Harrison. I think it will be greeted favorably," said Billy. "In the meantime, why don't you start working on the tournament flighting?"

"Sounds like a plan. Anything else?"

"No, I think that will do for now," said John Cabiness. With that, the three exited the clubhouse. Under the front portico Billy Sauers turned and said, "That was easier than I expected. Why can't all terminations be that easy?"

"Beats me. Barbara Clancy. Didn't she get a handsome divorce settlement a while back?"

"That she did," said Billy Sauers.

CHAPTER SIXTEEN

Seedings for the club championships were fairly cut and dry. Information regarding intent to play and the application deadline of August 2 had been posted in the Pro Shop since June. The D.O.G. went about his assignment diligently, using handicaps to set the brackets, breezing through all flights before encountering several players in the D flight with no handicap.

"Stan, I haven't seen this for a while. Got a couple of entrants in the D flight with no listed handicaps."

"Really? I was sure every man who played in this club championship had a USGA handicap."

"Talking about the women's brackets."

"How many players do you have like that?"

"Three."

"How many players in the bracket?"

"Twenty-seven."

"OK, just give the top three seeds byes and then place the non-handicap people against seeds four through six. Since you're almost done with the pairings, we'll announce that first-round matches must be done in six days. That should give everyone enough time to get on the course."

And that, boys and girls, is how Jessica Woolworth got paired against Kelly Blanchard. Three hours later, as I was headed for the first tee, Starza stopped me at the Pro Shop door. "Looper, a word, if I may."

"Sure, Mr. Starza."

"Club championships start in two days, so traffic on the first tee will be ramping up. In many cases anticipation will be high. Feathers may get a little more ruffled than usual. I would appreciate it if you would use your best cool, calm and collected demeanor and instill some manners in those who require it. Civility on the tee is a must. I don't care what they do on the course…well, actually I do, but around the epicenter here I'd like to maintain an aura of professionalism as best as the competing members will allow."

"Pairings are set then, yes?"

"No set days for the flights, so they'll be a mixed bag of players out there. Pace of play could be an issue, so let's make sure you send the players off promptly. The onus is on members to set their matches. If they can't make it work then someone forfeits. When the matches are over, players are to report scores immediately inside the shop."

"Any surprises in the seedings?"

"I didn't study the brackets. Howard and Worth look like the top seeds again: no surprise there. We'll be busy for the next two weeks as players move through the brackets. Might want to watch your lesson load with that in mind."

"Will do."

Ten seconds later I was stopped at the door, "I want one of those lessons." I turned to find the familiar figure of Jessica Woolworth sauntering toward the Pro Shop door.

"Your hair looks wet."

"Been sailing. Something else I'm getting good at."

"Brimming with confidence as usual. I like that in an athlete."

"Well, yeah, this athlete needs one of the putting lessons you've been pestering me about."

"When, two or three days?"

"Tomorrow."

"What's the rush? You've got a lifetime to learn this game."

"I've got six days to win my first match. I entered the club tournament. I'm seeded, like last, in the D flight. My first match is against Kelly Blanchard."

"First match? You entered the club championship?"

"When I played with Mr. Howard, even he said I had some talent."

"What else did he say?"

"That I needed to learn how to putt."

"How about 4:30 tomorrow?"

"Fine. We still going out later?"

"Absolutely."

"One other thing. What do I need to know about Mrs. Blanchard?"

"Mrs. Blanchard? Let's see, fairly new to the game. Took it up three years ago as a social activity but found she liked it. Doesn't play as much as she wants because of two young children at home. Medium-length hitter, occasionally wild with her driver, decent putter according to McDevitt. Her future is probably ahead of her. Played some recently and has started keeping a handicap. Nice lady. You'll enjoy her. Should be a good match."

"That's helpful."

"One other thing. One advantage you have is that no one knows anything about you. They may know you as a tennis player and sailor, but you'll probably be a surprise to some folks in D flight."

* * *

An even bigger surprise was the tenor of the match played two days later. Cindy Cabiness, playing in the following twosome, reported back. I was passing through the Pro Shop when I heard, "Mr. Starza, I saw the oddest thing today. Kelly Blanchard was playing this tall girl in a D-flight match. I swear they carried on the whole match like they were best friends. I thought these club matches were supposed to be duels to the death. These two looked like golf was the least important thing they were doing out there. I don't even know who won."

"Mrs. Cabiness, the Scots who invented this activity considered the social component one of the defining virtues of this Grand Game. I think we should celebrate the fact that these two women enjoyed the exercise, fresh air and one another's company."

"I wish everybody in the C flight felt that way. It would make playing a more comfortable experience if you ask me."

"I couldn't agree more."

Later that evening, I picked up Jessica and headed to the Northwestern campus to see a summer-stock performance of *Pygmalion*. "So, Alex has gone back to Chicago for the rest of the summer," she said.

"Well, during the week. He's with Denise on the North Shore most weekends."

"They look like a good match," said Jessica.

"She's been hanging out with his mother. Looks like the connection they established at Marshall Field had some legs."

"You think that relationship will go anywhere?"

"I don't know. She's out of school; he's got a year left at Northwestern, so they'll still be in the same neighborhood. It's a possibility."

"He had some big project to do, right? For school? Something to do with the tournament?"

"A case study regarding preparation, execution and analysis of the State Am. Pretty thorough. I helped him with his draft some. Billy Sauers read it and made some suggestions. I think he's hoping for a seal of approval from his boss. If he gets a thumbs up, he'll polish it up and use it as a senior thesis. Should be a pretty impressive body of work."

"Speaking of an impressive body of work, I won my match this afternoon."

"I overheard Mr. Cabiness describing the match. Sounds like you guys hit it off."

"I was expecting this tooth-and-nail battle, but it was really pleasant. I had a great time. Mrs. Blanchard was nicer than a lot of women I've played tennis against. She was really pleasant," she said emphasizing the really. "She told me to call her Kelly. I came away with a new friend and a babysitting job for next Tuesday."

"And you won."

"And I won."

"Tell me about it."

"Well, I hit it farther than she does, but she putts better, so it kind of evened out."

"OK, let me try again. How did you win and what was the score?"

"I won on the last hole. We were tied and I remembered we had a date and I had to get home to clean up, so I went after the drive. I probably hit it 50 yards past her. And I got to the green in three strokes and took two putts. She took four to get there and two-putted, so I won."

"That's it? That's all the detail you have for me?"

"That's all I remember – except I had the best time."

"Sounds like you may be playing for all the right reasons."

"If all the other matches are like this, I certainly think so."

In a perfect world they would have been, but as we all know it's not a perfect world. Before proceeding to her second round opponent we devoted Wednesday's lesson entirely to putting. Try as I might, Jessica couldn't master pace to save her life. Her direction was good. She seemed to read line and even picked up nuance regarding grain, but pace seemed beyond her.

"Jessica, putting is all about one thing and one thing only. You want to guess what that is?"

"No," she said petulantly.

"Speed. All putts are speed putts. Direction is no good if you don't have pace right. Right now, you are either blowing the ball by the hole or leaving it woefully short. Let's try this. I'm going to put this 5-iron twelve inches beyond the hole. I want you to see if can stroke the ball just to the 5-iron."

"If you say so."

That approach seemed to bring some consistency to her efforts. Sixteen of her next thirty putts almost reached the 5-iron, nine rolled right over the shaft, three fell short of the hole and two found the bottom of the cup.

"Why do I want to roll the ball to the 5-iron when the hole is in front of it?

I'm already hitting it past the hole."

"Correct. You are hitting it past the hole," I said. "But there's a difference between twelve inches past the hole and five miles. We want you to roll it as if you are going slightly behind the hole so that it will always have enough PACE to get to the hole, especially on uphill putts."

"OK, that makes sense."

"Proper pace, combined with your awareness of direction – and plenty of practice -- could make you a deadly putter. And I promise you will win more holes with putting than driving. In match play, putting almost always determines the winner."

"I play Mrs. Loos in my next match. I've seen her on the tennis courts, but I've never met her. She looks kind of athletic."

"Mrs. Loos? I haven't seen her play a lot."

The two never did play. Several days before the scheduled match, Mrs. Loos received a call from her sister in Cologne. Their mother had died of a stroke. Mrs. Loos left within twenty-four hours for Germany. She told Starza that after the funeral she and her husband would be taking two weeks urlaub and would be defaulting her match.

CHAPTER SEVENTEEN

"Who the hell is Jessica Woolworth?" demanded perennial D-flighter Jocelyn Price.

"I believe she's in the D flight, Mrs. Price," McDevitt said.

"I know that, squarehead. Where did she come from? Is she a new member? I don't recall seeing her on the course."

"I understand she's new to the game."

"Does she have a handicap?"

"Mrs. Price, you don't need a handicap to enter. It is just preferred that you do. She was seeded at the bottom of the flight. She's won her two matches and now she's in the quarters."

"And she only played one match."

"That's correct. Mrs. Loos had a death in the family."

"Jocelyn," said her companion Emily Newby, "why are you upset? You don't have to play her next."

"Still it seems unfair. The rest of us have to grind through two rounds and she gets a free pass into the quarters."

"Jocelyn, don't be such a poor sport. Golf is supposed to be fun, and not just when you win."

Mrs. Price shot an evil look at McDevitt. "When's my next match?"

"Tuesday at 10:00 against Mrs. Cartwright."

"When's that Woolworth cheat play next?"

"Jesus, Jocelyn. Don't be such a witch," said Newby. "She plays at 10:30 against Susan Whippet."

"You knew that and you didn't tell me?"

"What's there to tell you? I haven't seen her play."

"I expect you tell me everything after your match. I'm going to beat that… that… girl."

Jocelyn Price left the Pro Shop. "You coming?" she called to Emily Newby.

"Some people," said Emily Newby to McDevitt.

* * *

Tuesday dawned with a heavy mist that gave way to a humid mid-morning. The draw against Susan Whippet was going to be a test of fortitude for Jessica. I first met Mrs. Whippet (known in some quarters around the club as Snidely Whiplash) two years before. She had been Mrs. Peck's D-flight semifinal opponent. As Mrs. Peck's caddie I witnessed her mean-spirited demeanor and gamesmanship firsthand. I figured Whippet hadn't mellowed much, and I suspected once again she'd be a handful.

The day before, I approached Jessica on the putting green. She had placed a 5-iron twelve inches behind a hole. "I've been practicing at home on that Persian rug we have in the hall," she said. "This 5-iron behind the pin is actually a pretty neat idea. I'm finding that I'm starting to get dialed in on some of the faster greens."

"Technically, all the greens are supposed to be the same speed. Where they might seem to change are on uphill and downhill putts," I said.

"The rug is pretty threadbare and kind of fast. I'm gauging the fast, flat putts better than the ones with elevation. I don't have the hang of the slow ones yet."

"Tomorrow is supposed to be humid and the turf's a bit wet, so the greens won't be as fast as the Persian rug at home."

"I'll see if I can remember that." As we spoke she stroked three very smooth and properly modulated putts. "My next opponent is a Mrs. Whippet. She's been around a while, yes?"

"Correct. Mrs. Whippet is a competitor. The match will not be the sweetness and light you had with Kelly Blanchard. She's a hard-nosed 53-year-old. Not terribly friendly. She's fairly consistent except for occasional wild hooks. She's not above doing little things to annoy her opponents."

"Like what?"

"Like making noise on your back swing, making you put the flag back in the hole when she could just as well do it herself."

"So… gamesmanship."

"Exactly."

"No big deal then. I encounter that all the time in tennis tournaments. It actually hones my concentration because it tees me off."

"You'll be right at home then."

With twenty minutes to go before the Whippet-Woolworth match, both players attended to their final preparations. With a look of confusion Jessica accosted me in the Pro Shop. "You don't look ready to go," she said.

"Go where?"

"Go eighteen."

"I'm not playing," I said.

"You're my caddie."

"That's news to me."

"I requested you as a caddie for today's match and Mr. Starza confirmed it. So, buddy, get ready," she insisted.

I turned to the pro. "Stan, what's the deal here?"

"She made the request last night and I said she could have you for the round."

The Pro Shop door closed with an emphatic thud. "I just caught the tail end of this conversation," said Susan Whippet. "Is she getting him as a caddie?" pointing at me.

"Yes, she is," said the pro.

"Then I want to request one, too."

"This is kind of short notice, Susan," said Stan.

"No problem. Pointing at me, she said, "If she gets him, I want him," motioning toward the assistant pro behind the counter. "If he's going to be reading greens and clubbing my opponent, I want Mr. Timmons doing the same for me."

"That's going to leave us a bit short staffed in the shop, I'm afraid."

"That's your problem, Stan. I saw the director of golf's car in the parking lot. He's got, what, three more days here? Give the short-timer something to do. He knows how to read tee sheets and check players in. Meanwhile, I want Mr. Timmons as my caddie."

And so the four of us exited the Pro Shop, gathered some clubs and headed to the first tee. "What the hell," said Peter Timmons. "I haven't caddied in seven years."

"It's not like you don't know how to do it," I said. "Look at it this way. You'll get to know some members a little better this way."

Rather than proceeding to the teeing markers, Whippet motioned the assistant pro to the rear and left of the tee box. As I went to grab some pencils and scorecards she was making clear his duties for the day. "Look, I want to win this damn match. I lost to him and his pathetic old golfer two years ago, and I don't want a repeat of that embarrassment. Your job, and what I'm paying you for today, is to find and leverage every fair advantage for me that you can. That means suggesting lines of attack and especially, I repeat especially, helping me read putts." Peter appeared a bit stunned but got reoriented with the D.O.G.'s pronouncement. "Whippet-Woolworth, you're up. To the tee box, please."

Whippet assumed the box. She smacked a good one straight down the middle. Jessica followed suit and we were off. In the early going, though the players' shots ended relatively close to each other, our opponents chose to march on the opposite sides of the fairway, only venturing midway to address their balls. True to the earlier mandate, Peter stood behind Whippet on each green, helping her with her line.

As we exited the fourth green, the new assistant pro sidled up to me and remarked, "that Whippet women is pretty intense. If she'd just stroke it where I'm suggesting she might be ahead instead of all-square."

"Intense is a kind word," I suggested. "You probably never had a loop quite like this one."

"Never," he said, peeling off to join his player.

The hijinks Whippet employed two years ago in her match with Mrs. Peck were kept under wraps with one exception. On the tee at the par-3 thirteenth Peter went to get some water for his player. Jessica was in mid-swing when Whippet toppled her bag. The noisy jostling of her clubs caused Jessica's tee shot to go offline short and right.

"Sorry about that," came the weak apology. Peter looked embarrassed. I was enraged. Jessica was merely annoyed.

As we went to retrieve her ball Jessica said, "Really. How necessary was that? I was getting used to her cold-shoulder routine, but that was just rude."

"You want my take on this whole thing? I'm proud of you. You're playing well. No one has been more than 1-up the whole way. Your putting pace has improved leaps and bounds from two weeks ago and you seem impervious to Whippet's bad manners. Hang in there. I don't know exactly how, but I think youth will prevail here."

"I may lose in the tourney, but I sure as hell don't want to lose to her."

We did lose Thirteen to go down one, but Jessica got it back on Fifteen with a healthy drive and some superb short-game play. All even on the seventeenth tee, Jessica deposited her first shot in the left-hand trap. "That looks embedded," offered Mrs. Whippet.

"Quite possibly," muttered Jessica. Whippet then hooked her 4-wood further left, leaving her with a dicey twenty-yard shot to the pin over a bunker. "That looks like trouble," Jessica said, departing the elevated tee.

Peter and I picked up our bags. "Getting a little testy," he said.

"I think my player's had enough. That falling bag stunt on Thirteen pissed her off."

"I haven't enjoyed this round much," said the assistant pro. "All Whippet's been doing is bitching about everything under the sun. She complains you shouldn't be carrying her bag because you've been giving her lessons. Your player shouldn't even be in the flight because she doesn't have a handicap, et cetera, et cetera. And then you should hear her start on the membership. I've heard enough dirt on the female players around here to last me a lifetime. Please, someone, preferably your player, end this soon."

"Timmons, I need you."

"Mrs. Whippet," said her caddie, "that pin position close to the bunker doesn't give you a lot to work with. The safe play is just get on the green at all costs. Don't get fancy and go for the pin. Ending twenty-five feet away will be a great shot." Readying her stance, Whippet swung and put her ball fifteen feet short of the flag – in the trap. Still away, she took her stance in the sand, swung, and then sent her ball to the far side of the green. With one giant display of sportsmanship she took her club and delivered a tomahawk chop into the trap. "Shit," she uttered.

I handed Jessica her sand wedge. "You can do better than that," I said softly.

"Damn right." She surveyed her fried egg and delivered the shot of the round, depositing the ball five inches from the hole. Whippet dropped her putter, picked up her ball and said to Peter. "Get my clubs. I'll meet you on the tee."

Play on the home hole was anticlimactic. After Jessica's sand shot her opponent was done. Jessica powered her drive up the fairway while Whippet sprayed her tee shot into the left rough and limped home with a seven. Jessica's misplayed approach led to a two-putt six and a 2-up win.

Picking up his player's clubs, Peter asked, "Would you like these in your car or the bag room, Mrs. Whippet?"

"You know, Timmons. I could have beaten that girl if her caddie hadn't read her line all afternoon."

"If I may say so, Mrs. Whippet, he barely read her line at all. She has a real ability to gauge line. She just needs to be a little better at pace. Here's the other thing: that match today was really competitive. If you want to know the truth, you both belong in a higher flight."

"I knew she was in the wrong flight. I knew it."

In the parking lot I lowered Jessica's bag into the trunk of her car. "When do you get off this afternoon?"

"Four."

"How about I pick you up and we do something different?"

"Like what?"

"Like, I take you sailing? You ever been?"

"Once, maybe. A long time ago."

"I think you'd like it."

"Don't I need special clothes and a sailor's hat or something?"

"You'll be fine. I'll be back at four."

"Sounds good to me."

* * *

Jessica reappeared promptly at four, driving a late model Buick.

"Doesn't your father have any old cars?" I asked.

"Not really. Lately it's been a new car annually. He's gotten a taste for British cars recently. That's why he drives that E-Type."

"Must be nice," I said.

"Nice for him. I don't worry about it as long as I can get from here to there," she said, wheeling the Buick out of the lot and heading for Lake Michigan. "Have you ever been in a regatta?"

"A sailboat race?"

"Yes."

"Have you?"

"Sure. They have them about twice a month at Sheridan Shore. I intend to compete in another one very soon."

"Doesn't your father race in those things?"

"All the time."

"How many boats does your family have?"

"Just one."

"If he's in every race, what are you going to do for a boat?"

"In exchange for some French tutoring, I've been using Mr. Chambers's boat a lot. It's actually been a sweet deal. My dad has no idea I've been practicing. Mr. Chambers rigs the boat the same way my dad does, so there's not that much difference in the handling."

"What's all this leading to?"

"The Labor Day weekend regatta at the club. I intend to enter and beat my father."

"Won't Mr. Chambers be needing his boat?"

"He's going fishing in Canada and will be gone for ten days. He's given me permission to use his boat."

"Does your father know about this?"

"Of course not. That's part of the plan."

"The plan?"

"To win that $100. I intend to register at the last moment and take him by surprise. I figure if I distract him it may work to my advantage."

"So, if you beat him in the regatta you win $100?"

"That's the standing bet. Beat him in something athletic."

"Why is this so important – beating him?"

"Looper, believe it or not, I've thought about this quite a lot. Even when I was five I felt like I had to prove myself to him. My brother doesn't have to do anything except exist. He's a male so his ability, in my father's eyes, is a given. Me, I've got to overcome this gender thing."

"Jessica. What's not to like? You're smart, great looking and athletic as can be. Isn't that enough?"

"Well, if it is, he hasn't given me much indication."

"He ought to open his eyes then," I said "and start checking the inventory of his peers. They'd kill to have a daughter like you."

"That's sweet of you to say."

"It's the truth. I like to think the truth wins out."

We parked the car at Sheridan Shore Yacht Club and made our way through the slips until we got to Mr. Chambers's *Spindletop*. Painted white and aquamarine, his 19-footer was befittingly named for the 1901 gusher that led to a turn-of-the-century oil boom. Mr. Chambers himself had been a one-time oil field wildcatter who made his money finding black gold in the arid Texas Permian Basin.

As we began to unfurl the sails, I asked "When did you get into sailing?"

"I might have been ten. No, I *was* ten because my first time out was with my dad as a birthday present."

"When did you start to get serious about it?"

"At fifteen I started playing around with it, but even then, I didn't do much because of tennis. Then, two years ago I started to get serious. I'd take the boat out when my dad was away on trips, and I made a deal with the harbor master not to say anything. That's worked so far because I haven't damaged the boat. Last year it occurred to me that I might be able to beat him. I've noticed in light winds I'm a better skipper than he is. For one thing, I have more patience than he does. He likes heavier weather when the winds are up and he can haul ass. Kind of a macho thing. Trouble is when he moves fast he can be reckless. That does him in sometimes."

"When the Labor Day weekend showdown arrives, how is that going to work?"

"It's a five-race competition, two races Saturday, two Sunday and one Monday. Lowest aggregate placing wins."

"And you're going to win?"

"Oh no. There are a lot of first-class sailors in the club. I am nowhere near as good as they are, but I'm going to beat my dad."

"And win the $100?"

"And some respect and approval."

"Don't you already have his respect?"

"Probably, but I want the approval -- and I aim to get it."

Winds late that afternoon stayed at a steady eight-to-ten knots. Jessica displayed a deft hand at the tiller and gave me the distinct impression that she might well accomplish her objective. In the cockpit I felt like a fifth wheel as she handled the sails with aplomb. I pulled lines when told to, switched sides of the craft upon orders and admired her role as master of the ship.

CHAPTER EIGHTEEN

Back at Spring Willows, Jessica's semifinal match brought several surprises. The first was her opponent, a Mrs. Brian Bidwell. Her given name was Ophelia but was known by the few friends she had as Ophie. Ophie was a portly, bitchy, come lately sort, barely tolerated by the club's blue bloods. Born and bred in Branford, Connecticut, she acted as if she had come over on the Mayflower. Such lineage held no sway with our Midwestern elite. In truth, Spring Willows members -- at least the pleasant ones -- if not salt of the earth, were at least down-to-earth folk. Ophie's problem, at least one of them, was that she felt above these well-grounded folks. Brian Bidwell was the well-to-do owner of a confectionary company specializing in caramel candy bars. He wisely kept out of the way of the person who wore the pants in the family.

At 9:30 a.m. I met Jessica on the putting green. "How do we feel today?" I queried.

"We're loose," she said, indicating we were in the match together. "I've already been to the range and the short-game area. A little time here and I should be ready to go."

"You seem to be taking this seriously."

"Damn right. I've decided I just might win this thing for me. So here I am. I know nothing about my opponent. What do you know about her?"

"Let's worry about the putting. You'll find out about her soon enough."

I didn't have to say much on the green. Jessica had found a practice regimen that seemed to work for her. Strangely enough, she still put her 5-iron behind the hole, but her putting pace had become much more measured.

Combined with her sense of direction, she was becoming almost deadly with the flatstick.

Just outside the Pro Shop we were interrupted on our way to the first tee by Margaret Worth. "Jessica, I want to compliment you on your game. Good luck today. The women at the club are rooting for you. Here, take this ball marker. It's been a lucky talisman for me over the years. I had it in my bag when I won my first club championship."

I was positively dumbstruck. "Holy smokes. That was huge," I said.

"She's such a nice lady," Jessica said, oblivious to the magnitude of the gesture. "I think I'll use this today."

"Do you know who that was?"

"Oh sure, it was Mrs. Worth."

"And?"

"She's the women's club champion."

"Right." I let it go at that. To me, Mrs. Worth had effectively said all of the women -- women who counted anyway -- were rooting for Jessica. What an endorsement.

Ophie presented herself on the tee in dark blue shorts, white top and a blue, long-billed visor, something like a Caribbean bone fisherman might wear.

"So, you're the hotshot tearing up the D flight," began Mrs. Bidwell.

Jessica hesitated. "I don't know about that. I'm just a player."

"Well, we'll see about that," her opponent said brusquely.

Peter Timmons summoned the players to the tee. "Ladies, good morning. You're playing in the D-flight semifinal."

"We know that Junior," fired Mrs. Bidwell. "Say what you've got to say and let's get on with it."

"If you let me finish, Mrs. Bidwell, I'd like review the rules of engagement."

"We know the rules of play. Now will you please just let us hit our damn balls."

The assistant pro persisted with a review of match-play protocols, ending with the plucking of numbers out of a hat. Mrs. Bidwell drew the number one and took the box, hit a slightly off-center drive that traveled 180 yards into the fairway. Jessica followed suit, 180 yards out, five yards to the right of Mrs. Bidwell's ball.

"What is her problem?" said Jessica, as we trailed her opponent down the fairway. "Do you have to be rude to play this game?"

"Apparently it helps some players. And what's with your drive? You could have hit it 220 easy."

"Looper, I'm starting to think I don't like this lady. I want to see what she's got, so I want to go stroke for stroke with her for a while."

"That may mean losing a chance to go up several holes."

"Let me play it my way for a while. I want to see if I can make her uncomfortable going head to head."

Jessica's way meant matching Ophie's poor and occasionally brilliant play shot for shot. By the seventh hole we learned Mrs. Bidwell's approach shots from 75 yards and in could be awfully good. Jessica's eye for putting lines served her well -- except when she failed to control her tempo.

My player was unusually silent for the first nine. Trudging to the Halfway House and the tenth tee we got our second surprise. Talking to Brewster was none other than Kingston Woolworth himself.

"Dad, what are you doing here?"

"Just thought I'd come out here and see how my little girl was doing."

"Your little girl is pissed," she said. "My opponent is a bitch. The match is all even but I'm about to fix that."

"That's my girl," he said.

"By the way, I'm not your little girl anymore."

Kingston Woolworth just smiled. "And how's your day going, Looper?"

"Just babysitting, Mr. Woolworth."

"Keep it up." With that he left the tee box.

The destruction of Mrs. Brian Bidwell did not go as planned. Ophie damn near aced Killer Ten to go one up. She parred the eleventh hole when Jessica's drive uncharacteristically found the ditch that traverses the fairway. Two down after 11.

"Time to fire up here, princess. You gave up some opportunities on the front nine."

"Carry my clubs and shut up. I know what I'm doing."

"We've got two more par 3s and if she plays them like she did Ten you're down four with only five holes left."

"I know how to count, Looper. Be my caddie, not my therapist."

On Twelve, Jessica unleashed the beast. She hit her drive 230 yards and won the hole. Ophie countered by winning Thirteen with a well-struck pitch-and-run to two feet while Jessica pulled her 3-wood into the road. Down two with five left.

"You know Jessica, I'm liking this match," said Ophie. "Most players, especially beginners like you, can't keep up with me. But you show signs of staying power. Still, my guess is you don't have what it takes."

We approached the fourteenth tee. Why would someone say that? And stir the bee's nest? It made no sense to me.

Unfazed, Jessica responded, "You may be the better player, Mrs. Bidwell, but the better players don't always win."

"We'll see about that," said Ophie whose ill-struck slice landed within a foot of the fairway ditch on the right.

"Hazardous territory over there," said Jessica, who then uncorked her longest, straightest drive of the day on the way to winning the hole. A similar performance on Fifteen squared the match.

"You were lucky to have me threaten the hazard there at Fourteen. Without that I'd have this thing won."

"Maybe. But you did and I didn't. And we're all even. Game on, sister."

Me? I'm saying nothing. My player was in command, sailing. I was just a caddie, humping the bag for a pretty girl against an ugly woman.

Jessica absolutely blistered her drive on Sixteen. She put it miles past the midway pond, which Ophie visited with her tee shot. Jessica's long approach iron found the green and two putts later we were 1-up. We remained so after both players parred the penultimate hole.

Forehead pressed against the clubhouse glass; Kingston Woolworth gazed down the eighteenth fairway. "King, I'm surprised to see you here on a weekday afternoon. No real estate deals today?" asked Starza.

"Oh, plenty of those. I have lawyers looking at several franchise opportunities. I just thought that I'd come out and see how my daughter was doing. Elise Sauers, among others, mentioned that I ought to get off my duff or I'd miss a seminal moment in her development."

"I'm surprised you haven't been here sooner. She's lighting up the D flight with her A-flight talent."

"Really?"

"Really. She's athletic as hell and takes instruction very well. Looper has been schooling her on the game. She's responding with a march through the D flight. Early on there was some bitching from the female members, but it has kind of subsided," said the pro.

"Bitching? About what?"

"No handicap, for starters. Plus, she has Looper, the best caddie in the club."

"Looper's the best caddie in the club?"

"King, surely you're not deaf and blind. He's respected by the entire membership and most of the staff. His rep has been growing for three years now."

"Stan, I'm wondering if I've been underestimating my daughter. We've never been very close, and honestly that's my fault. Somehow, I'd like to establish a connection."

"Being out here today is a good start."

"I wonder what the status of the match is," King said.

"Judging from the postures I'd say your daughter is ahead. I never saw a winner slouching the way Ophie Bidwell is right now."

In what looked like a formality, Jessica Woolworth lagged a thirty-footer to two feet and tapped in for a winning par. Handing her putter to me, she turned to shake her opponent's hand. "Don't bother," said Mrs. Bidwell, dismissing the outstretched palm. "You're in the wrong flight, sister," she said, almost throwing her club at her caddie.

"So much for sportsmanship," I said. "I'll clean your clubs. Where do you want them after that?"

"The car."

"Go to the Pro Shop and post your score. Here's the card."

Ten seconds later Kingston Woolworth left the Pro Shop by the back way. Jessica crossed the threshold and approached the head pro. "How'd it go, Jessica?"

"Not the most pleasant round I've played in my brief career."

"Thought your opponent looked unhappy there at the end."

"I won, 2-up."

"Congratulations."

"I hope my next opponent isn't such a harpy. Do you know who I'm playing next?"

"It will be either Jocelyn Price or Rhoda Charles."

Charles stomped all over Price, 6-and-5. "Well, that wasn't pretty," said Mrs. Price, as she handed Starza her scorecard. "I won the first hole and that was it. I'd like to complain, but I got beat by a better player. Even at my best today I'd have come out on the short end."

"Not everyone is that gracious," said the head pro. "You've seen both players, who will win this remaining match?"

"I have no idea, but it won't be me."

"C'mon, give the old pro something for clubhouse conversation."

"I don't know. Today Rhoda just pounded the ball and kept it straight. But the Woolworth girl does that, too. Short game and putting is about even. Whoever wins will be the person who makes the fewest mistakes."

"That's true in any game. What else? Course management, intangibles, comfort on the course? Give me something."

"Stan, are you going to make a wager on this?

"No, but the club pro is supposed to be all-knowing about things like this. I can recite chapter and verse about flights championship through C. I'm a little weak on the D flight."

"Even with Looper schlepping bags for D-flighters?"

"He doesn't talk about his rounds with members."

"Smart boy. OK, here's something. The chemistry he has with the Woolworth girl on the course is really good. He makes her comfortable out there. Push comes to shove, I'd pick Woolworth."

"That's your choice?"

"That's my choice. I expect a cut from your winnings."

"Nobody is going to be placing bets. At least not me."

"Yeah, yeah," said Jocelyn Price, exiting the Pro Shop. "Don't forget my cut."

CHAPTER NINETEEN

The D-flight final occurred two days later as the third morning match behind the B flight of Patterson and Swanson and the C flight tilt of Broderick and Effingham. An hour before the match I met Jessica on the driving range to warm up and review fundamentals. "I want to keep it simple today," she said. "I feel like I've got a routine that's working pretty well. When I want advice I'll ask, OK? Otherwise just club me and stay out of the way."

"Did I say something wrong? I thought we were a team here," I said.

"We are, but today I want to do this on my own. I don't want anyone saying I won this, *if* I win this, because of my caddie."

Jessica went through her bag from short through longest clubs, hitting some disastrous seven irons, but crisply striking long irons and smoking her woods. Ten minutes in the short game area led to the putting green. She chose the left quadrant, walked to the first hole location and placed her 5-iron behind the cup.

"Is that really necessary?" came a voice from the far edge of the green.

"It's how I practice," she responded.

"Not very considerate of other players."

"I don't see how that bothers you from the far end of the green over there."

"Just saying, not very considerate," came the distant voice.

"Since there is no one else out here, I believe that's your problem," said Jessica.

After six straight five-foot practice putts blasted two feet past the hole and over the 5-iron Jessica stopped, looked at me and said, "Who was that?"

"Ah, you just met today's opponent."

"Not very pleasant, that's all I can say. Tell you what. I feel out of sorts. Do me a favor and leave me alone for a bit. Go to the Pro Shop. I'll meet you on the tee. Take everything but the putter, the 5-iron and these three balls."

"You sure?"

"I'm sure. I need to get centered."

I departed the green, toting her bag before depositing it just short of the first tee. Inside the Pro Shop Denise was laying out fall tangerine sweaters and umber slacks. "Looks like Halloween in here," I said.

"Hey, handsome. Feast your eyes on the colors that the fashion industry has decreed will be must wear apparel for the fall season."

"Where are the black masks?"

"No masks, but there are some black hats and standard black slickers. You need some for today's bright, 80-degree weather?"

"I'll do just fine with my polo and khaki shorts, thank you."

"Don't you have a match today?"

"My player has banished me to the Pro Shop while she collects herself."

"Her opponent has been in here running her mouth. If she were polite I'd say she was brimming with confidence, but given her attitude I'd say she's just arrogant."

"We've encountered that before. Guess we'll just have to go with the flow," I said, studying the slacks. "How are you and Alex doing?"

"Better than ever. He's wrapping up his job this week. I'm off this weekend and he's coming with me and my folks to our place on Lake Geneva over Labor Day."

"Nice."

"All the way nice. We seem to have a symbiosis."

"A match made in heaven, no doubt."

"Maybe, maybe," Denise said dreamily.

"Well, good luck with your love life. I've got a match to play."

"Oh right. You and Cinderella. Good luck to you both, Prince Charming."

"Yeah, good luck, Prince Charming," echoed assistant pro Peter Timmons.

"I don't need that right now," I called to him.

"We all need a little love in our lives, Looper."

I let the door slam and heard Denise holler. "Looper, don't slam the door."

* * *

Jessica had yet to make it to the first tee, so I wet a few club towels, retrieved her bag and placed it near the teeing ground. Upon hearing hard approaching footsteps I turned smack into the imposing frame of Rhoda Charles.

"You again."

"Hello, Mrs. Charles."

"I figured with the way that girl was playing you'd be on the bag."

"I'm just a caddie today, Mrs. Charles."

"Just like two years ago with Mrs. Peck."

"It's a little different this time."

"I hope so," said Mrs. Peck's former D-flight opponent. "I plan to win this time. I figure your girl isn't really match-tested and if I hang around long enough, she'll wilt under the pressure."

"Should be a good match," I said, trying to keep things civil.

"Looper, we meet again," piped up Kelly Wright, Mrs. Charles former and present caddie.

"Kelly," I acknowledged. "You guys ready to go?"

"Oh, we're more than ready," said Mrs. Charles. "Soon as your player decides to show up."

"Oh, she'll show up," I responded. "Rest assured."

When *would* Jessica Woolworth show up? After the first four holes we were down four.

"Not the way I wanted to start the match," I said. "Is something wrong?"

"I'm having trouble concentrating."

"I can see that."

"I'm thinking about sailing and a conversation I had with my father last night. I'm still trying to sort it all out."

"Can you think about sailing after the match?"

"I don't know. The conversation was really interesting. I'm still processing it. It was actually kind of freeing," she said, as we strode along the fifth fairway approaching her drive. "Want to hear about it?"

"Will it help your golf game?"

"It might," she said, sidling up to her ball. Grabbing a 4-wood, she took a stance, measured a practice swing and smote the ball.

"Whoa, that's your best shot of the day," I said.

"Yeah, yeah, I bet talking about it will help." Picking up her pace, Jessica turned to me and said, "Looper, keep up here. I can't talk to you when you're lagging behind like that."

"Yes ma'am."

"Last night, I felt like, for the first time in a long time -- no, make that forever -- my father was trying to understand me. Like I was a person and not just this child to be molded into some image of perfection. I felt there was an attempt at a human connection, like maybe I was valued for something other than being this really good athlete or good-looking girl." She reached her ball ten yards from the green. "Give me that 8-iron," she said. "I'm going to run this sucker up to the hole."

"Jessica, let's not be rude. Mrs. Charles is still thirty yards behind you. Let's play nice and let her hit first."

"Oh, right, then I can run it up to the cup."

And run it up she did, a scant six inches from the hole. Down three heading to the tee-lined chute at Six. "I'm still trying to figure out what occasioned this conversation with my dad. Neither sports nor school came up once. Did you know that?"

"I did not know that" I said, "but I know you're first up on the tee here."

"Oh, right." Placing the peg in the ground, she took one practice swing before lacing her driver straight and long. "I mean, he asked my opinion on things. The last time I got questions like this from him was when I was five and he was trying to convince me I could ride a bike. It was as if he was trying to get to know me all over again."

As a therapist, I was in uncharted territory. My player was off and running, mostly running her mouth about her father. And almost running to the ball. Her gait had stretched immeasurably and while her focus seemed miles away from the golf course her play couldn't have been better. We found ourselves outpacing our opponent in marching to every shot which at first seemed a bit impolite, but it dawned on me that this was an effective way to distance ourselves from the acidic barbs that Mrs. Charles might toss our way.

An approach to five feet and a well-struck putt on Six put us down only two. As we strode to the seventh tee, Jessica was starting to switch into high gear. "Looper, you've met my dad. What do you think? Where is this all coming from?'"

"Jessica, I have no idea what goes on behind closed doors at your house. Your folks seem like really nice people who have produced a charming and talented daughter, but what's come before or gone into that production, I'm pretty clueless."

"Something different is going on, I can sense it," she said, powering yet another drive right-center, 230 yards out. "I need to figure this out, and you can help me."

"How about I help you win this match?"

"The match, the match. Golf, Jesus, is that all you think about? This conversation with my father last night was really important, like a seminal moment in our relationship. Seminal, Looper. Can't you get that? It feels like a seismic event."

I can be slow on the uptake sometimes, but it began to dawn on me that my job was no longer as a caddie but as a listener. As we strolled down Seven at an accelerated pace I decided my goal for the remaining holes was to live the caddie maxim: 'Show up, keep up and shut up.'

"We're outpacing our opponent," I said.

"Tough noogies. That's her problem."

"No one is saying you have to talk to her, but let's just play in turn, et cetera."

"You're saying be civil even if she isn't."

"That's what I'm saying. Look, with your pace and current level of play you are creating distance from her."

"Looper, I'm one down with ten holes left right now. To be honest, I don't want anything to do with her. But I do want to figure this thing out with my father, so let's just keep on working on that. That's the most important thing right now. There's always another day for golf."

I almost wanted to say something about the here and now but I decided we were in full therapy mode.

We traipsed to the Halfway House where Starza and Brewster were inventorying packs of Nabs. "Kelly, Mrs. Charles, you want anything from here?" I asked.

"I'm going to the ladies' room," said Mrs. Charles. "Wright, get what you want and put it on my account."

"A bag of chips and a Coke, please," said Kelly.

"Jessica, how about you?"

"A cup of water."

Starza sauntered over. "What's the deal here, Looper?"

"Sunday stroll, Mr. Starza. Just a friendly match between members…"

"Don't give me that bullshit. What's the score?"

"Who's asking?"

"Don't get cute. I'm asking. I'm your boss and I'm curious. Some members in the lunchroom are curious, too."

"What do male members in the grill care about a women's D-flight match?"

"You know how things work around here."

"So there's money on this match."

"Correct."

"Is Billy Sauers in there?"

"No, but his presence is…"

"Lurking?"

"That's a good way of putting it. Tell me this," said Starza. "How does the match stand? Any momentum?"

"We lost the first four holes…"

"Holy shit," the pro muttered under his breath.

"But we're only down one. This thing is going to go for a while."

"Charles won the first four holes and now she's up one."

"Yes."

"So momentum is on your side?"

"That's the way I see it."

"For anyone in the grill with a rooting interest, your best guess is…?"

"Really? We're playing this game again?"

"Looper, you've been here long enough to know that fortunes are won and lost…"

"Fortunes?"

"I'm overstating for effect. Wagers of modest size occasionally transpire between members on a match like this."

"And you are looking for some insider trading info?"

"Not insider exactly, just an opinion."

"So, what do you want, insider or an opinion?"

"I want whatever you got."

"The players stopped talking to each other on the fifth hole. They are in their own worlds right now. If I can keep my player on task I think we'll win."

"Win how?"

"You are asking for a number. I can't give it to you. If Sigmund Freud were on the bag he might, but I can't."

"Freud?"

"Stan, you'd have to be here to understand. My opinion is we'll win. I don't have a number. Hope that helps. I've got some holes to play," I said, moving the clubs to tee markers.

"May the best player win," he said, heading for the clubhouse.

"What was that all about?" said Jessica.

"The usual. Match status stuff. How's the course look, do we need to syringe any greens? He wants to advise Mr. O of any anomalies we've seen on the front nine."

"I didn't see any, did you?"

"More importantly, what do you need from me?"

She turned and smiled, longer than normal. "Keep listening and carry my bag."

* * *

Back at the grill, Starza met a grilling of a different kind. "What's the deal out there, Stan?" said Everett Pace.

"Hansel and Gretel are down one but making a move after being down four early in the match."

"Jesus, I didn't expect to hear that," said Eldridge Wankum.

"Judge, you're the bookmaker here. How's our fund doing?"

"Let's just say the wagering has been strong, especially since some of the contestants in play haven't been very likeable people."

"Just to be clear," said Charles Fleetwallace, "these transactions aren't exactly legal, are they?"

"Technically speaking, no," said Judge Gleason. "I like to think of it as a home poker game. What the authorities don't know won't hurt them."

"And this coming from a judge."

"Correct. But I am not a member of the local constabulary. I'm not even an extension of the judiciary."

"No Judge, that's because you are the judiciary."

"Not here, gentlemen. I'm just custodian of the funds."

"Out of curiosity, and you don't have to mention any names here, but is there any really big money down on this match?"

"Gentlemen, we businessmen have our confidences. Think of me as a Swiss bank."

"We know you better than that, Judge," said Eldridge Wankum. "Any big bets?"

"One sizable, another of the more modest variety, and then the usual amounts."

"I bet Billy Sauers laid the big one, didn't he?"

"I'm not at liberty to divulge that."

"Judge, give us something here."

"OK. Yes, Billy placed a bet, but not the big one. Big bet was for, are you ready for this? $5,000."

"Whoa. Serious money."

"Yes, it is."

"On?"

"The filly."

"Interesting," said Eldridge. "Last question, if not Billy Sauers, then who?"

"Can't tell you."

"It won't leave this room. We're a secret society."

"Eldridge, you and I have been members of this club for a long, long time. Secrets have never been alive and well here. You know that. All I can say is that I was surprised with the amount of the bet and its source. And it wasn't Billy."

"Did I hear bet?" came a question from a late arrival.

Heads turned. Judge Gleason was the first to speak. "King Woolworth, for a guy who hones his game at Westmoreland you've been spending a fair amount of time at Spring Willows."

"What can I say? I have a rooting interest these days."

"I bet you do," said Eldridge Wankum.

"Anybody know how my daughter's match is going? I just pulled in. Thought I'd get some lunch and an update."

A strange silence permeated the room as if no one knew where to take the conversation. Finally Starza spoke up. "Last we heard players were headed to Ten. Rhoda Charles was 1-up. That's about all we know."

A waiter appeared and brought Kingston Woolworth a toasted club sandwich. "Will that be all, sir?"

"A lemonade too, Curtis, if you will."

"Yes sir, coming right up."

"All I know," said King Woolworth, addressing the group, "is my daughter has the best caddie. For that reason alone, if there was any betting to be done I'd place a wager on her."

More silence. "Did I say something wrong?" King Woolworth asked, munching his sandwich.

"Don't think so," said the Judge. "I think we were just contemplating the match."

Back on the course the next three holes continued nip and tuck. Both bogeyed Killer Ten. Rhoda Charles found some magic in the ladies' room and won the eleventh hole but then gave it back after taking a double on Thirteen. On Fourteen tee we were still down one.

"Time to let the big dog eat, Looper," Jessica said, reaching for her driver. The sound of ball on persimmon reverberated as the sphere rocketed down the fairway.

"Jesus," said Kelly. "Where did that come from?"

"Shut up, Wright. Give me my club," instructed Mrs. Charles.

"Yes ma'am." He handed over the weapon of choice.

In a brazen attempt to mimic Jessica's mammoth drive, Rhoda Charles swung out of her shoes. At impact, her back foot shifted, with her right heel elevating ever so slightly. Instead of contacting the ball squarely she short-armed her swing and toed the ball 150 yards into the right-hand ditch. Kelly began to trot to the disaster zone.

"Need help?" I called.

"Might," he declared, and I followed him to the entry point. We didn't have to look long. The ball had settled in seven inches of water in the middle of the ditch. Mrs. Charles could get a club on it, but it would have been a foolish, futile effort.

"Retrieve the ball, Mr. Wright. I'll take a penalty and hope my opponent butchers the approach."

Mrs. Charles hit a fine recovery thirty yards short of the green, but when my player's third shot settled pin high twenty feet from the cup her ensuing two putts tied the match with four holes left.

"What I can't figure out," said Jessica as we left the fifteenth tee, "was what inspired the conversation in the first place."

"With your father?"

"Of course with my father. What do you think we're doing out here?"

"I thought we were trying to win a golf match." I paused for a moment thinking I might have overstepped my role.

My instinct was confirmed. "Stop," she commanded, as she stood in the middle of the fairway.

"At least that's what I thought we were trying to do," I said meekly.

"Right now, I don't give two hoots about this tournament. Your job, until we get to the clubhouse, is to help me figure out this thing with my father. We were doing fine when you were just listening. Right now, you aren't listening," she said, her voice rising. I could see our opponents casting curious glances as our volume increased.

"Looks like caddie and player are having a disagreement," said a smiling Mrs. Charles.

"Who knows?" said Kelly. "You're away."

"Not for long," said Mrs. Charles, as she bludgeoned a 3-wood.

Jessica's response was a lightly struck 4-wood that negated her advantage off the tee. I tried another tack. "Maybe your dad is starting to feel some separation anxiety. You've got what, another year at school? I'll bet he's beginning to understand that his talented daughter, with whom he probably wished he had a closer relationship, may be leaving him soon. Maybe that's the reason for his attempt at connecting."

"Hmm. I hadn't thought of it that way. Keep talking."

We strode up the fairway after her ball. "He's probably proud as hell of you, but doesn't know how to show it -- or how to say it. Let's face it, how does anyone with the name King establish a warm and fuzzy relationship?"

"Great for business, though, if you're the boss. And my father always liked being the boss."

"He and your mom seem to get on well."

"That's different. She's got his number. With everyone else he's the boss."

"Well, maybe last night was an attempt to change that."

"Maybe so. Give me my 8-iron," she demanded. With that Jessica hit her best shot of the day, a parabolic arc that clanged off the flag and trickled five feet away.

"There will be more of those if you quit talking about golf and keep listening," said Jessica.

I handed her the putter thinking once again that I was pretty sure I didn't understand women. The adversaries tied the hole, marched to Sixteen and halved that hole thanks to some weak first putts.

Seventeen was playing its usual 153 yards. There was zero wind and the flag hung limply like a wrinkled dish rag. Both players deposited their balls in the left-hand greenside bunker. Mrs. Charles was thirty feet from the flag with a slight uphill lie. "I like my chances here, Wright," said Mrs. Charles. With that she blasted a respectable sand shot five feet from the hole.

And then for the first time in about five holes Mrs. Charles spoke to us. "That looks like a mean fried egg, Jessica. Tough break, embedded like that."

I had to smile. Rhoda Charles had no idea what she was walking into. Why would anyone wave a red flag in front of a bull?

"You're right, Mrs. Charles." Jessica grabbed her sand wedge, stepped into the bunker, squiggled her feet and viciously, but deftly, deposited the ball eighteen inches from the pin. "Fried eggs go well with toast," she said, casting a steely smile at her opponent. "And you're toast."

"Son of a bitch," muttered Mrs. Charles to Kelly Wright. "She couldn't do that again in a million years."

To her credit, Mrs. Charles made her nicest stroke of the day and holed her putt. Jessica did the same and we all walked to the eighteenth tee. On the box Mrs. Charles said to Kelly, "Go wash my ball." Properly chastened, he performed ablutions and handed it back. "I said wash it. This doesn't look clean. Forget it," she said, getting more agitated. "Give it to me, I'll wash it myself."

At the ball washer she placed the ball in the holder and maliciously maneuvered the handle in violent fashion, practically scrubbing the cover off the ball. Just then Peter Timmons rolled up in a Club Car. "Stan asked me to come out and see if any of you needed anything to eat or drink. I've got some Nabs here and some Cokes."

Eight eyes glared at him and nobody said a word. "So, how's it going? I see you're still playing. Must be a close match," he said, belaboring the obvious. More silence. "OK, anybody want anything to eat?" Four heads swayed back and forth.

"OK, I'll see you then." Casting a furtive glance at me, he said, "Looper, may I have a word?"

"Peter, I'm busy with my player here, I can't talk right now," I said while subtly moving my right hand twice parallel to my beltline.

Later I confirmed that Peter was dispatched to the eighteenth tee to specifically learn the disposition of the match. He correctly deduced the match was all square but could not conclude match momentum based on the icy stares he received from the participants.

"You must have learned something," said Starza.

"I didn't learn squat. It was like staring at totem poles. No one looked happy to see me."

"Guess we'll just see how this plays out."

"For grins, let's go out to the eighteenth green."

What the small throng from the grill saw was two striding females and their bagmen soldiering up the fairway. Two well-struck drives left both players 180 yards from the green.

"So you're suggesting my father was making an effort to get to know me as a person last night?"

"Yes. And I think he is very inexperienced at doing that with you. Like you say, he's never been exactly touchy-feely with you so he's probably at a loss as to how to start this new stage in your relationship. Truth is, you might have to help him because I bet he doesn't know how. He's used to being large and in charge and perhaps he's learning, maybe for the first time, that it doesn't work with you. And least not like it used to."

"You're right. He's always been the boss."

"Maybe he's just starting to realize he doesn't want to be the boss with you all the time. That he just wants to be your dad."

"Hmm," came the reply.

"So, you see how that might change the dynamic?"

"Absolutely," she said, grabbing a 4-wood and crushing it seventeen feet past the flag.

Up by the green Eldridge Wankum said, "Where the hell did that come from? That looks like something Margaret Worth would hit."

"I was in the men's room. What did I miss?"

"Your daughter just hit the shot of the day to less than twenty feet."

"Do we know how the match stands.?"

"No idea. We sent Timmons out to get a read and the players wouldn't talk to him."

"Did you try the caddies?"

"They were mute too, though we think Looper indicated the match was all square."

In that moment Rhoda Charles's approach was twenty yards short of the green. Her stubbed 8-iron chip attempt left her fifteen feet below the hole.

Jessica's putt for birdie appeared to be a matter of pace. "This is a speed putt," said Jackson Walsh, acting like a know-it-all.

"Mr. Walsh, they're all speed putts," said Peter Timmons. "But this will be a runaway freight train if she strokes it too hard."

"Here's the putter," I said to Jessica. "Think 5-iron behind the hole."

"Looper, be quiet."

Jessica's putt required nothing more than a straightforward lag. Steadying her feet, she calmly addressed the ball, looked twice at the cup, and lagged the ball to five inches left of the hole.

"Balls of steel," said Walsh. "Let's see what Charles has." Needing a fifteen-foot uphill putt to tie the match, Rhoda Charles strong-armed her ball directly online so that it hopped directly over and past the hole by three feet. Her comebacker was good for a bogey but when Jessica dropped the five-incher the match was over.

"King, congratulations. Looks like you've got another winner in the family."

"Thank you, Eldridge. Family, that's got a nice ring to it. Thank you very much."

"I haven't seen you smile that much in five years, King," said the Judge.

"More than you know, Judge. More than you know."

Back on the green, the post-match pleasantries, if you could call them that, were winding down. I collected the putter as Jessica extended her hand to Rhoda Charles. "Well played, Mrs. Charles."

"You don't belong in D flight," Rhoda said icily, ignoring Jessica's extended phalanges. "You should never have been in this flight to begin with. Just so you know, I'm going to lodge a complaint. You being in the D was tantamount to cheating and cheaters never prosper." Rhoda Charles turned to

Kelly. "Get my bag, take it to the storage room and make sure they clean my clubs real good. I don't want the stain of this match anywhere near my clubs."

"Yes ma'am. I'm on it." Kelly picked up the bag, paused as I was cleaning Jessica's putter, and said, "You guys were smart walking ahead and staying away from us. She didn't have a nice thing to say about anyone or anything the whole round. I'd have gotten a nice tip if she'd won. I'm glad she didn't." He hoisted the bag to his shoulder. "See you around."

As the elder statesmen headed back to the grill, Peter Timmons returned to the Pro Shop.

"Who won?" asked Starza. "I got a call from the Illinois State Golf Association as that group was heading up the fairway."

"Gretel lagged a fifteen-footer to within five inches for a winning par."

"Gretel? As in Hansel and Gretel?"

"Stan, wake up," chimed in Denise. "Cinderella and Prince Charming took down Rhoda Charles and the vanquished did not look happy about it. She even refused to shake Jessica Woolworth's hand."

"Oh boy, I hope that's the end of it."

"Based on the post-match posturing, I don't think it is," continued Denise.

A banging Pro Shop door interrupted the procedure. "I thought we fixed that door," said Denise.

"We did but the spring is a bit tight and if you don't hold the door . . ."

"I know how the door works, Peter," sputtered Denise. "People need to close it gently, that's all."

"Maybe you should put up a sign," said the assistant pro.

"Maybe people should hold the door and close it gently."

"Where's Stan?" Rhoda Charles demanded.

"Right here, Rhoda. What can I do for you?"

"I want to lodge a protest regarding the D-flight championship match."

"On what grounds?"

"A player playing out of category."

"Are you referring to yourself, a one-time B flighter?"

"That was years ago, before my shoulder surgery."

"Fair enough. State your case."

"I don't want to just talk about it right now. I want a formal hearing, and I want this to go before the competition committee. I have a right to do that."

"You certainly do. But briefly outline the basis of your complaint."

"Basically, she had no handicap, but she was clearly better than almost everyone in the flight."

"Even you?" asked Starza.

"Not me, but others. The committee should have recognized that with the original flighting and slotted her accordingly."

"Rhoda, you know, as a former member of the competition committee, that players with no handicap history are placed in the lowest flight. That's what was done with Miss Woolworth."

"Putting her in the D flight gave her an unfair advantage. She's terribly athletic. She's practically the best tennis player in the club. I'm telling you her placement wasn't fair. And here's what else wasn't fair, letting the club starter caddy for her. Clubbing her every shot, reading putting lines. My caddie couldn't do that."

"Mrs. Charles, if I may say so, when I observed your match from afar I didn't see any caddie giving assistance reading greens or giving distances," offered Peter Timmons.

"You weren't out there long enough, Junior," she shot back. "Patently unfair, Stan. I have a case here and you know it."

"Rhoda, with all due respect, I'm not sure you do. But you are entitled to lodge a complaint. You have three days to file a written one. Submit it to me. State your case and I will take it up with the committee. You will also have the opportunity to state it in person if you so desire. Once you have your hearing and the committee renders a decision, that's the end of it. No appeals. Understood?"

"I will have my written statement to you within twenty-four hours and expect a speedy hearing."

"Due process in due time, Rhoda. The committee plans to meet once all club championship flights are completed. That will be within six days, weather permitting."

"All I want is a fair hearing."

"You shall have it," said Starza.

"Thank you," said Rhoda Charles, exiting stage right, being sure to let the door slam one last time.

The tall, muscular presence of Kingston Woolworth reopened the door. "She could have at least held the damn door," he said. "What was that all about?"

"Sour grapes," offered Peter Timmons. "Seems your daughter's opponent wants to protest the match."

Kingston Woolworth furrowed his brow. "On what grounds?"

"That your daughter's too good," laughed Starza.

"I don't know about that," said the father of the winner.

Just then the Pro Shop door reopened and closed noisily, followed by a "Can we just fix the damn door?" from an exasperated and by-standing Denise Long.

"How can I help you, young lady?" said the old pro to the newly-arrived Jessica Woolworth.

"Mr. Starza, I'm here to report the score of my match."

"Please do. How did it go?"

Jessica noticed a familial presence at the far end of the counter. "Father? What are you doing here? Aren't you supposed to be at work?"

"Probably, but this seemed like it might be a special day. And after our conversation last night I thought I'd slip on over here and support my daughter." King Woolworth cleared his throat. "How'd it go?"

A broad smile creased her cheeks. "I had a really good time and – I won. I think our talk last night was pretty special. And Looper helped me understand some things about it."

Starza rejoined the conversation. "Jessica, if I may ask, what was the score?"

"1-up."

"1-up. Close all the way?"

"No. I was down four after the first four holes before getting down to business."

"I'd say that's one of the bigger comebacks we've ever had in a women's championship final. Not to put a damper on your victory, but Mrs. Charles was in here several minutes ago and said she plans to protest the match."

Jessica pursed her lips and raised her voice. "What?"

"That's what I said," said her father.

"She's entitled to protest," said Starza. "There's a formal procedure and as tournament director I am obligated to follow it, but between you and me I don't think her protest stands a chance. In any case, there will be a decision in less than a week. Historically, baseless protests fueled by jealousy usually don't get very far. You didn't hear it from me, but I'd sleep well tonight. Your reward will be a golf trophy to go with those you've earned for tennis and some 'well dones' from the members. Your win will be a popular one with the membership."

"You're sure?"

"I may not know much, but I'm sure about that. Congratulations."

CHAPTER TWENTY

Fifty-four hours later, Carlisle Howard, the men's club champion, received a late-night call. "Lisle, it's Billy. Sorry for the lateness of the hour. I heard you made a killing on the D flight."

"You hear that from the Judge?"

"I profited, too," said the caller, "but not to the extent you did. I was just a little uncertain given the filly's inexperience."

"Not me. After that Sunday round I had with her I could tell she was a comer. And I really, really liked the pairing with Looper. I figured that duo could take out anybody in the D flight. Billy, we need to find a way to get that young man involved with us. You've made some good money based on observations he's had. That golf thing, this hamburger deal we're working on. He's got a future. Might as well be with us."

"You're right about that."

* * *

The Woolworth-Howard-Worth luncheon at Spring Willows following Jessica's D-flight triumph was notable for several reasons. The first was that this grouping was together at all. One snide women's B-flight disappointee referred to it as the convening of champions. "Look at Ms. Pretty in Pink cavorting with Carlisle Howard and Margaret Worth over there. If I didn't know better I'd say they were fawning over the Queen of the Ball."

"Now, now Leslie. Let's not be jealous. You had your chance with Carlisle twenty years ago. Let the young lady enjoy her moment in the sun."

"She needs to go back to tennis where she belongs."

"Why is that?" said her companion. "Because she'll be in B flight next year?"

"She's been pampered. She's gotten lots of lessons and a lot of attention from the Pro Shop this year. More than other female members get, I'll tell you that."

"Leslie, she paid for those lessons. Give her some credit. The girl has talent. Just because she's young and good looking doesn't mean she's a bad person. I kind of like how she took down Susan Whippet and Rhoda Charles. I'd much rather have a pleasant personality win the D flight than those dour dowagers. This place could use a breath of fresh air if you ask me."

"She hasn't paid her dues."

"Where have you been for the last six weeks? She's practically abandoned the tennis courts. She's been up here working on her game almost every day. She's paid some dues and worked her butt off. Eat your Caprese."

Meanwhile, at the other table, the aforementioned threesome was engrossed in the finer points of putting. "Looper tells me you have a real sense of direction on the green. That's unusual for a new player," said Margaret Worth.

"I think I've been lucky that way. I've got really good eyesight and been able to… to … judge how the ball will move. What I still struggle with is speed control. My tendency is to blast the ball by the hole," Jessica said. "In fact, when I started, Looper made me put a 5-iron twelve inches past the cup to help me develop a sense of pace. 'Never up, never in,' he said. Something like that.'"

"He's right," said Carlisle Howard.

"When I go back to school I'm going to miss this place. This has been a special summer for me," said Jessica. "The golf has been important, and the D-flight thing has just been the icing on the cake. Mr. Howard, our round together meant a lot. You gave me some tips, but the fact that you even asked me to play with you was really special. And Mrs. Worth, that ball marker. I used it every remaining hole of the D flight. Every time I put it down I thought, 'I wonder how Mrs. Worth would stroke this putt?' You've got your championship match in a couple of days. Do you want it back?"

"No, Jessica. That ball marker has a new home with a new champion."

"I'm just a D-flight winner, not a champion, Mrs. Worth."

"Jessica, the ball marker is where it needs to be. Keep it, use it; it's yours now."

"Thank you. It's very special."

"That's not the only special thing you've had this summer, is it Jessica?" queried Mrs. Worth.

A red glow crossed Jessica's countenance. She looked up, almost embarrassed, and red as her raspberry sorbet. "No, no, it's not."

"You know, Jessica, a lot of people around here think very highly of that young man," interjected Carlisle Howard.

"I've noticed that."

"That young man is going places," he said.

"Lisle, we're not in the matchmaking business. I think we older folks need not trespass into such tangled webs. Affairs of the heart transpire of their own accord and are not to be trifled with by we bystanders."

"I'm not meddling, Margaret. As a businessman, I'm just offering an observation that the boy has promise, the kind of prospects that any girl in her right mind, especially one who goes to Radcliffe, ought to be cognizant of..."

"Lisle, not here!"

"And act upon. There, I've said it. And I'm not the only one who thinks that."

"Lisle, the Spring Willows membership doesn't get a vote in the affairs of the heart," said Margaret Worth.

"Well," said a worked-up Carlisle Howard, "they ought to. Some opportunities are just too good to pass up."

Flush-faced, Jessica Woolworth interceded. "It's OK, I know what you're intimating. I've had thoughts like that myself. Looper has made me feel good about myself. My parents seem to like him, so... I'm just enjoying the here and now."

"And that's how it should be – with no help from outsiders," said Margaret Worth, glaring across the table.

CHAPTER TWENTY-ONE

What the lingering days of summer brought were blossoming love, a Labor Day weekend regatta and some training not normally given to temporary help. On Tuesday afternoon, Mr. Binswanger summoned me to his office. "Looper, just want to share with you some numbers, a final financial accounting from the State Am."

"That seems a long time ago, Mr. Binswanger."

"Agreed. But your actions helped keep Spring Willows in the black. I want to show you the spreadsheet I'm sharing with the board tonight. That figure there, $20,016, represents pure profit to the club. That's over and above expenses. Kudos to Miss Long for managing the merchandise flow, which accounts for a nice chunk of this. Food and beverage and ticket sales account for most of the rest of the remainder. And Cassie Saunders, I can't say enough about her. She found a way to streamline the serving lines and we moved some real traffic through them. Might have to send her a bonus check."

"I know whatever you could spare, she'd really appreciate. She'd put it right to school expenses."

"Really? I might do that then. Wouldn't be much, but…"

"Anything would be appreciated, Mr. Binswanger."

"Hats off to you and Randolph for your role in this bottom line. If I do say so myself, Looper, you seem to have an aptitude for country club life. If you ever need ideas for a career, you might consider a job like mine. You'd be good at it, and I'll be glad to tell anyone who asks about your talents. You have the kind of personality that works well with a variety of clientele. And at a place like this, that's not easy. Keep doing what you're doing. Your folks have done a good job with you."

"Thank you, sir. I don't know what to say."

"Say nothing. The club appreciates the job you do. Well done."

About the time I got my attaboy from Mr. Binswanger, Jessica got a call from Oliver Chambers. "Jessica, I see from the yacht club logs you've been out on *Spindletop* quite a bit."

"I hope I haven't been abusing the privilege, Mr. Chambers."

"Quite the contrary. How's it been going?"

"I think I'm mastering this sailing thing. I'm not as good as you are, but I'm making progress anticipating change of wind direction. I'm even moving from starboard to port in the cockpit without the sails flapping. I'm understanding luffing better, too. I think I run a pretty tight ship these days. I hope I've been leaving the boat in clean condition when I come in."

"You've been doing just fine. By the way, is that deal with your father still on?"

"The $100 deal?"

"Yes."

"Still on."

"The reason I ask is that I've had a change in my Labor Day plans. I'm going to be staying in town. I'm not going fishing in Canada."

There was a pause. "I guess you'll be needing your boat then."

"To the contrary. I broke my leg. I'm in a cast and not very nimble, but I do want to sail Labor Day weekend."

"I see. You need your boat."

"I'm only semi-mobile at the moment, but I do want to race. I thought you might need a crew member. If it's all right with you, I'd like to formally enter the regatta with you as captain and me as crew."

"But you own the boat. Won't you be captain of record?"

"I'll enter the boat name and just leave captain and crew names out. People will assume I'm captain because I own the boat. Before the first race I'll be called by the commodore and reminded I need to complete the application. Then I'll put you in as skipper and me in as crew."

"Is that legitimate?"

"Jessica, lest you forget, I was once commodore here. It will work. That way, no one will know, especially your father, who the skipper of record is. With luck if you finish ahead of him in the standings you should get the $100."

"Shouldn't we practice together?"

"We should. Are you free Thursday and Friday afternoons?"

"I'll make myself free."

"Excellent. Why don't you meet me at Sheridan Shore at 2:30 and we can have a practice run. There shouldn't be many regatta skippers out during the weekday afternoons, so we can pull out of the harbor incognito, as it were."

"Thank you so much. I look forward to it."

* * *

Thursday at noon, eight days before the regatta was to begin, Jessica stopped at the Pro Shop looking for her boyfriend. "Not here, Jessica," said Denise Long. "Try the clubhouse. I think he's in Binswanger's office."

"I'm not going to interrupt that. Will you just tell him I'll be home by 7 tonight, but not to pick me up before 7:30. I don't want to keep him waiting."

"Sure thing."

"You and Alex are still an item, right?"

"Absolutely."

"Are you doing anything tomorrow night? If not, I thought you two could come over and we could have a light supper and just hang out on the patio."

"We have plans, but nothing firm. That sounds like a lot of fun. I'll let him know we now have plans. What time should we arrive?"

"Seven should be fine. Come casual."

"Can I bring anything?"

"Just yourselves."

"Good afternoon, ladies," I said, quietly closing the Pro Shop door.

"Thank you," said Denise.

"Any time. So, what's up," I said, turning to Jessica.

"I'm headed to the lake. Please don't come tonight before 7:30. I'm not sure what time I'll get back to dry land and be presentable."

"Right. OK, 7:30 then," I said as she bought her leave.

"Binswanger again? You guys are getting pretty buddy-buddy these days."

"A little more than I'd like. This time it was about an advanced degree in hospitality management. Apparently, Mr. Binswanger thinks I'd be a good country club manager. He says Cornell and Michigan State have the best hospitality programs in the U.S."

"Do you want to be a country club manager?"

"I don't think so, but someone wants me to. And they've been talking, so he's being proactive."

"Who has he been talking to?"

"No idea. But I suspect the list is small. I get on with all sorts of people apparently, so that's part of his pitch. You know, Denise, you'd be a better candidate for that sort of thing than me. I'll bet you'd be one of the few female country club general managers in the U.S."

"No, thank you. I'll stick to fashion merchandising."

"Just saying. If you told Binswanger you were interested, you could get him off my back."

"If I did that, you'd owe me big time."

"No doubt about it."

"But I'm not going to do you that favor. I am, however, going to do you a different favor and drag Alex over to the Woolworths' tomorrow night so the four of us can have a casual supper. Jessica said we are to come at seven."

"Sounds like my Friday evening plans have been made. Thanks for telling me."

"Any time."

* * *

Down at the yacht club, Jessica unfurled the sails on *Spindletop* and headed out of the harbor on a freshening breeze. For the next hour she practiced tacking to starboard then to port, sighting imaginary buoys and exploring the fastest ways to reposition herself in the cockpit. A mile from land the wind increased measurably. As she sat farther aft, she found enough velocity to get the nineteen-footer to plane, sending a cascade of spray past the speeding hull.

Returning to shore, Jessica hove to, found her mooring, and tied up *Spindletop*. As she was embarking, she heard a familiar voice. "Jessica, just the person I wanted to see. Looks like you've been out on the water again."

"Father, what are you doing here? I thought you were in the Loop all day today."

"I was, I was, but with the regatta coming up I figured I needed to get some time at the tiller. I see you used Oliver Chambers' boat. You know you can use the *Outcast* any time you want."

"I know. Mr. Chambers has urged me to sail *Spindletop* to see if I notice any differences between the two boats."

"Are there any differences?"

"Only slight ones. I mean, they're both Flying Scots. How much difference can there be? The rigging is essentially the same. So, not much difference at all." She paused, a bit embarrassed at having been found at the yacht club on a neighbor's boat. "Dad, I've got to run. Looper is coming to get me and I need to get home and clean up."

"I understand. Please tell your mother I'll be late for dinner. I forgot to call her before I headed here."

"Sure thing. Great evening for a sail. The wind is up. You'll have fun out there." Grabbing her windbreaker Jessica called, "Stay the course, father."

"You know I will," he said, stowing his gear.

CHAPTER TWENTY-TWO

Twenty-seven hours later, two young couples convened at the home of the Woolworth family. As Jessica rolled out a plate of appetizers, she gave instructions to me and Alex on how to start the patio grill. "Look, there's hamburgers for the gentlemen and chicken for the weaker sex. And I want the poultry cooked to perfection. Denise, do you like your chicken moist, dry, or in between?"

"First of all, I'm not buying this weaker sex stuff, and I know you aren't either."

"Of course not, it's just a feeble attempt to make their bloated egos feel good about cooking us dinner."

"Now we're getting somewhere," said Denise.

"I'm going to the kitchen to get the meat. Be back in a moment."

The moment was to be a long one. By the sink was Kingston Woolworth himself. As she opened the refrigerator door she heard, "Jessica, I meant to ask you a question yesterday, and in the heat of the moment failed to do so."

"What was that?"

"Well, with all the sailing you've been doing, I was hoping you might crew for me next weekend in the Labor Day regatta."

You could have heard a pin drop. Jessica stared at the refrigerator's third shelf, where the chicken breasts and plump hamburgers returned her stunned gaze. As she held the door, the frigid air passed imperceptibly into the massive room. Seconds slowed. Fowl and burgers remained motionless.

Jessica strangled the appliance door handle. Her jaw dropped. Her eyes fixated upon the refrigerator's innards.

"Jessica? Is something wrong? I asked if you'd like to crew for me next weekend. On the *Outcast*."

Slowly, very slowly, she turned toward her father. With a look that can only be described as pale and wan she opened her mouth and uttered nary a sound.

"Jessica?" King Woolworth took two steps toward his daughter, her hand still firmly placed on the refrigerator door handle. "You're letting the cold air out."

"I, I know," she said finally.

"Well, would you like to do it? You and me, the Woolworth team on the high seas? We're athletic. We can handle boats. We'd be great together. Heck, we could even make a run at the trophy."

Still nothing but confused looks.

It was at that moment that I stumbled into the kitchen. "Jess, the grill is fired up, just waiting on the main course out here." Father and daughter stood five feet apart, in the midst of what appeared to be a very uncomfortable situation. Unsure of what to do, I did an about-face and tiptoed away.

"Hey champ, where are the burgers?" Alex asked me.

"And the chicken?" added Denise.

"I don't know. In the refrigerator, I think. But there is something going on in there that I don't understand. Jessica and her dad are in some kind of standoff. The refrigerator door is open and only her dad is talking. I think we move to Plan B, which is wait here and watch the grill burn some more."

"Can I be of some help?" asked Denise.

"I doubt it. Must be a family matter. Just take another sip of your lemonade."

Back in the kitchen, Jessica managed to shut the fridge door. She turned to her father with the saddest eyes he'd ever seen. She wanted to cry but wasn't quite ready. After twenty years of waiting for a sign of approval here it was, coming, in of all places, the family kitchen. She contorted her lips, dropped her shoulders, and let her chin fall to her chest. And she uttered the words, "I can't."

"Can't—or don't want to?"

The tears began to flow and then gush. Sobs that began as a whimper escalated. As the decibels increased, King Woolworth was clueless as to what to do. His daughter eased his uncertainty as she ever so slowly approached his tall frame, wrapped her long arms around his muscular torso and placed her head on his chest, saying nothing, only sobbing uncontrollably.

Kingston Woolworth was in new territory. For a guy long on business savvy and the art of the deal he had no idea how to handle this form of inter-personal interaction. To his credit, he failed to act on his first instinct, to say something in an attempt to make it right. Somewhere in the recess of his brain he realized that the best course of action would be to let it go, whatever it was. So he stood there, slowly closing his massive arms around his crying daughter. One minute became two, then three.

Erica Woolworth took a step into her kitchen and quickly left. Detouring through the living room, she stepped lightly through the large French doors and entered the patio. "What's going on in there?" she asked.

"We don't know," I said. "But there's been some real emotion, and it's been going on for a while now."

"I'm stunned," she said. "I've seen my husband hold his daughter maybe twice in twenty years. He last did it on her first birthday. It appears the refrigerator, which was open when I trespassed, is witness to a tectonic event. No, more than that, witness to history."

"As your invited guests we are just staying out of the way," I said.

"And waiting for your dinner, I suspect," said Erica Woolworth.

"That, too, but we have plenty of time for that. We can always eat later."

Back inside, as the sobbing ceased, King Woolworth tried to continue the conversation.

"Why not? Why can't you sail with me?"

Taking one step back Jessica said, "because I'm committed to Mr. Chambers and *Spindletop*. He's let me practice on his boat all summer long and wants me to skip his boat in the regatta."

"Why didn't you tell me that?"

"Because… I wanted it to be a surprise… and because I wanted to beat you at something."

More strange territory. "You don't have to beat me to be my daughter."

"Yes, I do. It's been that way for twenty years. I could never be your little girl. I had to be better than everyone. And the challenge you always put out was I had to beat you to prove I was worthy of your name."

"I never said that" he said, squirming.

"Maybe not, but your actions said otherwise."

Later, in the far recesses of the stately house, Kingston Woolworth poured a glass of Johnny Walker Black. He lounged back in a large rouge leather chair, drink in hand.

His wife took a seat across from him, smiled and said, "Do you want to talk about it?"

"I don't know what to say. I don't even know what to think. I'm confounded. I'm at a total loss."

"Human emotions haven't always been your strong suit, King, especially when it comes to family matters."

"I know, but I feel like I've been punched in the gut. For the first time in forever, I don't know what to do. Hell, Erica, I don't even know where to start."

"Maybe you need to start by doing nothing. This isn't a business problem that needs to be solved in a heartbeat. It's been two decades in the making. There's no deadline, no closing bell. How about you just cogitate, talk to her -- and process. Don't you think this might all be new for her, too? King, over the years you've shut yourself off emotionally from your family. You're a wonderful provider. We want for nothing in this house. She's wanted for nothing; she'll tell you that. Wanted for nothing -- except her father's love and acceptance -- for who she is. Don't you think that maybe she was trying to tell you that tonight?"

"All I did was go into the kitchen and ask if she'd like to crew for me in the Labor Day races and she burst into tears. Not just tears, she was bawling… forever. I didn't know what to do."

"You did the right thing, King."

"What do you mean?"

"You held her."

"You saw that?"

"Briefly, I started into the kitchen and quickly turned around. I think you gave her what she needed in that moment. An emotional, human, personal, fatherly touch. That's pretty powerful if you've been waiting for it for twenty years."

"I don't know."

"I know you don't. And I can tell you if you truly want a relationship with her it is only the beginning. She's going to want more of that. And I suspect you want more of that. She's a wonderful girl, wonderfully gifted in so many ways. If you continue to give her that validation, for who she is, not what she does, both of your lives will be fuller and more rewarding. Trust me. You made a good start tonight. Keep it up. All Woolworths will be better for your efforts."

* * *

Twenty-four hours later the scheduled Woolworth-Litton movie date got redirected by Jessica. I showed up at the appointed hour when Jessica told me, "No movies. We're going to Indian Trail in Hubbard Woods. I've made reservations for us at 7:30."

"I'm not dressed for it."

"You look fine. Maybe even handsome. No questions, no objections, I'm buying, let's go." And with that we headed out.

From the living room window Kingston Woolworth turned to his wife. "I like that boy. I really do. I like how he is with my daughter. And I like how she is with him."

"What are you saying, King?"

"That I like them as a couple. The boy has smarts – and people skills through the roof. Jessica will have to go a long way before she finds a better prospect."

"Our relationship aside," she smiled, "all marriage isn't about prospects you know."

King shook his head. "No, it's not. But it's a big plus, wouldn't you agree?" He stared past the sweeping, manicured terrace.

"I agree."

"How long have they been seeing each other now? Six, eight weeks? What's she think of him?"

"We haven't talked a great deal about that. No mother-daughter stuff. But from the way she acts, I think she's sold."

"Long term?"

"It's probably too early to tell. Clearly, she likes what she sees. She did disclose one telling thing about three weeks ago. She said, 'He gives me confidence and makes me feel good about myself. "

"That's a helluva start."

"Oh, and I'll bet she didn't tell you about her power lunch, did she?"

"What lunch?"

"It was an impromptu affair with Carlisle Howard and Margaret Worth. Seems they wanted to congratulate her on her D-flight championship. Very pleasant, she said. It got a bit sticky toward the end when Margaret asked about her summer social life and indicated she thought Jessica and Looper hit it off pretty well. According to Jessica, Lisle went in with both feet, spontaneously pitching Jessica on Looper's finer qualities as a young man with prospects. Margaret tried to shut him up, and she finally prevailed. I think Jessica found the conversation a tad unusual, but in some way it validated her choice."

"You got married right out of college."

"I did. And I did very well for myself. But Jessica is not me. She has the whole world in front of her. I did too, but you were a lot of my world, and I still feel I made the right choice."

"That is reassuring."

"But until I'm asked, I'm staying out of any relationship she has with that young man. I suggest you do, too."

"Lisle Howard is not the only person high on that boy. Billy Sauers is right up there, too.

He likes Looper's business instincts."

King…"

"Just saying."

CHAPTER TWENTY-THREE

"Why the change in plans? I was kind of looking forward to the movie."

"We can do the movie another time," said Jessica. "I've been confused since the other night, and I just wanted a chance to talk to you alone. Not at the house, not over a Coke after a movie. Some place nice and civil, where we could have a conversation without any interruption. I like this place. It's pretty quiet and the food's good."

A waitress advanced to our corner table, left two menus and departed in search of two glasses of water.

"What do you want to talk about?"

"A lot of things. I want to talk about my dad, about the regattas, about school and… about us."

"About us?" I looked at the ceiling and then around the room, waiting for the rest of the sentence. "Us?" I stared again, this time avoiding her beatific countenance. "Wait, is this the talk?"

"What are you talking about?"

"My mother once explained that when couples start getting serious there is a conversation of substance… about the relationship."

"The relationship?"

"Yes."

"That's part of what this dinner is about, yes, but not all. As you well know, two nights ago I experienced a seismic shift in my relationship with my father. To put a word on it, the encounter was tender. It was also awkward. I cried. I don't cry a lot."

"I know."

"But it got me thinking about other aspects of my life. Things like the here and now, what I want from life, my future. Things like that."

I seized my napkin, unfolded it, placed it in my lap and leaned forward as Jessica continued. "One thing I learned from my father at an early age was to stand up for myself and ask for what I want. What I want is a relationship with you."

"You already have one."

"Yes, and I want to discuss the one we have."

I squirmed atop the padded seat cushion.

"What are you going to do after graduation next year?"

I was caught off guard. "You're a senior, what are you going to do?"

"I'll tell you about my plans in a minute. I want to hear, as of this minute, what your plans are."

"I'm not dead certain."

Sensing vacillation, Jessica pushed further. "Fine, best guess right now."

"I'm giving thought to graduate school."

"Specifically."

"Specifically business school. It's been suggested by people we both know that I should consider getting a master's in business. And in exploring that possibility it's become pretty clear that an MBA from the right school can be a ticket to some well-paying jobs. I'd like to have a standard of living a little higher than my dad's, so that's a good motivator. What about you?"

"I'm an art history major. People think all we do is look at paintings twenty-four hours a day, but there are some intriguing niches in the field.

There is curator work, collections, acquisitions for museums and galleries, sales and art-dealer stuff that extend far beyond the academic side. This fall I'm going to be interning at the Boston Museum of Fine Arts and second semester I'm going to Italy and I'm going to take courses at the Accademia d'Arte in Florence, one of the best art-learning environments in the world."

"What about graduation?"

"What about it? I graduate in December. I have almost enough credits to graduate now. I'll get my degree, go to Florence, immerse myself and then come back to get an advanced degree in some form of art history."

"And go where?"

"I don't know. I figure between my seventh semester and time in Florence I'll get a better idea. Right now, I feel like I don't know what I don't know. But enough about me. Have you decided on a specific graduate school?"

"Harvard and Wharton keep popping up, but there are a bunch of places with excellent schools. Michigan and Northwestern, for example."

"So, you've done some thinking?" Jessica offered.

"Some," I said, taking a sip of water. "Do you mind if we order? I haven't eaten since a club sandwich at noon."

With the meal order in, Jessica pressed on. "OK, so we both have plans for next year. In the meantime, what about us?" she said, her piercing eyes flashing over the glassware and cutlery, penetrating and disrupting my thought processes.

Continuing the grand inquisition, I said, "You're sure this isn't the talk?"

"Looper, this is not the talk. This is two good friends having a frank conversation about futures."

"Whew, for a moment…"

"About our future."

I waited for the rest of the sentence, expecting the word 'together' to fall from her lips.

It never came, but it didn't matter. The train was rolling. "I'll start," she said, letting me temporarily off the hook. "My summer improved immeasurably, no, dramatically, since I went for golf lessons. And the reason, plain and simple, is you and the bond we've formed. You've helped me find – and hone – a new skill. As I've said before, you've given me untold confidence. I feel better about myself and every facet of my life since I met you. You've helped me understand my father better and, in some way, maybe paved a way for me to accept the affection he showed me the other night."

I followed her words closely, nodding in tacit agreement. Then she uttered, "This, our relationship, means so much to me. It's been transformative, and…" reaching across the table and grabbing my wrist, she said, "I want to be with you."

Her words arrived simultaneously with the salad. Staring at me, the waitress said, "Say something to her."

With no ready response and a dry throat, I again reached for a glass of water. Her rapturous smile and the deafening silence only compounded my discomfort. I fumbled the sourdough bread, my right hand clumsily fishing for the butter. It wasn't checkmate, but I was experiencing a moment of truth.

I said, "Jessica, this has been without a doubt the best summer of my life. Two years ago I got introduced to Spring Willows and the woman in my life was a 67-year-old grandmother. Last summer I groveled in the dirt for Mr. O, got further educated in the Spring Willows' way and met some pleasant young ladies. This summer has been different. I've gotten more respect, often unexpected and, best of all, I met you. We have a very warm and, at times, intimate friendship. In many ways we are kindred souls. I love your wit, charm, beauty, forthrightness, athleticism and how you care about me. Sometimes I wonder if I am worthy of that affection, but I treasure it. And to be brutally honest, I want it to continue."

I squirmed a little more but warmed to the task. "I don't know what the future will hold, for you, or for me. Maybe I'll end up at Harvard Business School and you'll come back and work at the Boston Museum of Fine Arts. Maybe I'll be in Philadelphia at Wharton and you'll be in Paris. All I know is that when I can—and while I can – I want to be with you."

"We're good for each other, aren't we?"

"Yes. We are."

Much later, after the red snapper and sirloin had been consumed, I queried, "You staying with Mr. Chambers and his boat?"

"Yes. Tough, emotional decision, but I wanted to keep my promise. And I still want to beat my dad."

"And win 100 bucks."

"You know, after the other night it's not about the $100 at all. In fact, it was probably never about the $100. I've decided it was about the respect of accomplishment and especially about recognition as his flesh and blood – as cherished flesh and blood. I've come to realize my dad loves me. He's always loved me. He just hasn't known how to show it."

"That's kind of sad. He's lost twenty precious years."

"I also told him I was not going to renege on my commitment to Mr. Chambers. And that no matter what came from the regatta, win, lose or draw, I still wanted to be the daughter to him that I was in the kitchen Thursday night. You know what he said then? He said, 'How about you start calling me Dad?' And I said 'Really? After twenty years?' Then his shoulders kind of sagged and he said, 'After twenty years -- because I think there's another forty to come. At least I hope so. The two of us will just have to make up for lost time, starting now.' And that's how we left it."

CHAPTER TWENTY-FOUR

Jessica spent Monday and Wednesday afternoon fine-tuning her partnership with Oliver Chambers and discussing seafaring duties aboard *Spindletop.* By twilight's end the boat's owner had gotten fairly adept at navigating the cockpit, full length leg cast and all. "Jessica, I think we've got this captain/mate thing worked out pretty well. The way I see it, the only intangible is going to be the weather."

"Is it going to be an issue?"

"The five-day forecast is calling for fairly calm conditions on Saturday, stormy weather Sunday and high winds Monday. If the forecast holds, we're going to get a bit of everything. It's going to test our sailing skills, that's for sure."

"Sounds like an adventure."

"An adventure indeed. Saturday, you'll need to go to the skipper's meeting. I've briefed you on the things you need to know, but there may be some last-minute changes, rules of engagement, et cetera, the commodore wants to dispense. As the boat's owner, I'll go with you. It will also give you a chance to eyeball the competition."

"How many boats are in this thing?"

"Twenty-four or twenty-five. I saw the preliminary start list on Tuesday. I doubt there will be any late additions. When's the last time you raced?"

"In June, my dad and I went out and competed in a Sunday race on Father's Day. I think we finished sixth. He was kind of hot. He thought he got cut off rounding the third mark. He said some unpleasant things about Mr. Osborne and the *Liquidator.*"

"Ah yes, Jerry Osborne and the *Liquidator*. Intense man. I'll give him this, he's good with that boat."

* * *

At Spring Willows I was getting my marching orders for the weekend. "Looper, this will be a busy weekend at the club. I need you here all weekend, behind the counter Friday and Saturday and as starter Sunday. I'm not sure about Monday yet."

"Mr. Starza, I have a favor. I've accrued considerable comp time because of the State Am. If at all possible, I'd like Monday off."

"Big plans?"

"Just something important I'm trying to work out. I'll work late Friday, Saturday and Sunday if necessary."

"Just important, or really important?"

"Really important."

"All right then. Timmons owes me a day for the wedding he went to in late June. You're off the hook." He paused. "And Tuesday is your last day, right?"

"Yes sir."

"Come to the Pro Shop at 9 a.m. and be prepared to caddy in the afternoon."

"I thought the course was going to be closed the day after Labor Day."

"It is, but I've had a request for your services. Tee time is noon."

"Whose bag am I lugging?"

"It's a single. Billy Sauers."

"Who else?"

"Just be ready to go."

"Will do."

At Sheridan Shore the newly assembled crew of *Spindletop* was ready to go when they showed for the skipper's meeting at 8:30 Saturday morning. The commodore reported there were twenty-five craft entered in the weekend series with the low-scoring winner getting his (or her) name on the treasured Commodore's Cup, a magnificent twenty-five inch sterling silver trophy dating to 1909. Second and third place winners were to receive engraved sterling silver plates. Fourth through sixth were to get fancy ribbons that reminded Jessica of the overblown silk ribbons awarded at horse shows.

"I'm not concerned about prizes, Jessica," Chambers said. "I just want us to compete well. I am confident we have a fast boat and a competent crew. As a team I think we'll surprise some people."

"I'm looking forward to this. I'd like to beat my dad, so if I have a goal this weekend, that's it."

"Who does he have on his boat?"

"He's going it alone on Saturday and Monday. My brother is crewing Sunday."

"If the weather is inclement Sunday, he'll want him on board. Let's get *Spindletop* rigged and out on the lake. I make the winds to be about eight knots. Brilliant sunshine, no clouds. Got your sunglasses?"

"Yup. Sunscreen too."

The morning race, two times around three buoys, produced little drama and some fine sailing. Jessica, at the helm for her first race in *Spindletop*, acquitted herself well, finishing twelfth. "Jessica, nice piece of sailing out there. You even took us past some former winners. Did you feel comfortable?"

"Actually, I did. I've been using tips you gave me, especially looking for dark patches that signal more wind. Wearing these polarized sunglasses really helps to distinguish between puffs and lulls on the water. I guess it might be different if we didn't have sun though, wouldn't it?"

"Not as much as you think. Dark patches and ripples are what we are looking for. The goal is to sail to the wind. Let's go get some lunch. I'm sure the old salts there will be digesting every tack and jibe. I'm just happy to be on the water."

"You moved pretty well port to starboard without your crutches."

"Thank you. I hope I didn't obstruct your movements."

"Not at all."

"Well, we're good then, but I do need my crutches on land." With that the two mariners began the walk from the dock to the Sheridan Shore clubhouse.

* * *

Over large tuna salads and cantaloupe, the two replayed the morning's sail. "Mr. Chambers, what would you have done differently this morning? I felt we, I felt I," she said, correcting herself, "could have been a little more competitive."

"To be honest, not much. You were great on the course. I really liked how you seemed to anticipate wind shifts. Lots of sailors never master that nuance. They spend all day looking at the tail thinking it's going to tell them what to do. All it is is an indicator. You seem to sense the wind's subtleties. That's a gift. We can tighten the sails a bit on the course now that you've got your bearings and you're feeling comfortable in crowded quarters.

"As we go on, and your comfort level increases, I think we can get a little more aggressive at the start. Did you notice how congested it got at the run to the line? Especially how *Liquidator* and *Fast and Loose* seemed to bully half the fleet to hit the line at the precise second the race started? That's just experience and a function of two pushy personalities. There are times when races are won and lost at the start, all else being equal. Of course, the downside," he continued, "is if you overshoot the line then you have to start over and you've essentially lost the race right there."

The scraping of a heavy chair on the oaken floor interrupted their dialogue. "Oliver, how did my girl do out there this morning?"

"King, you'd have been pleased. Your daughter sailed like a champ."

"I trust you were in command, seeing as it's your boat."

"My hand never touched the tiller. All I did was pull some lines and get in the way."

"You sailors must have done something right to finish twelfth."

"We did well, given it was our first time together. I couldn't have asked for a better captain. How'd you fare?"

"Finished eighth. The only troubles I encountered were self-inflicted. On the second reach I tried to tack against *Boom or Bust* and he luffed the hell out of me, and I lost five boat lengths in a heartbeat. Other than that it was a good morning."

"Glad to hear it."

"Winds are supposed to be light and variable this afternoon. Do you believe that?"

"I'm not going to believe anything until I get out of the harbor," said Oliver Chambers.

"Smart man. You doing alright, young lady?"

"Dad, I'm doing fine. I'm in good hands here. In fact, I'm in good hands everywhere these days."

"And in good arms, too," he said with a smile.

"That too," Jessica said.

"See you two soon," he said, replacing the chair.

* * *

As *Spindletop's* crew readied their craft under cerulean skies and building cumulus clouds, Oliver Chambers said, "I think the wind may be a little trickier than this morning."

"Like how?"

"Maybe more unpredictable. Just a feeling."

"Does that help or hurt us?"

"It will come down to anticipation. That may play to your strengths."

With ten minutes to go, prerace jostling for the run to line seemed testier than in the morning. "Am I imagining things or is this prestart more congested than last time?"

"Correct. In fact, I see people doing some pretty dumb things out here. Right of way seems going out the window. You don't want any part of this. Come about and let's stay out of the traffic for the next six or seven minutes. We'll let the field play bumper cars for a while."

Six minutes passed. Jessica scanned the horizon. "Mr. Chambers, there's some heavier wind offshore headed this way. What if we hit the line with the spinnaker flying? Couldn't we catch the field unawares? I mean, from back here we could get a running start at the line. Didn't you say there was always more room closer to the buoy than people think? Maybe we could squeeze through there on the inside."

A broad smile creased Oliver Chamber wizened brow. "I knew I chose you for a reason. Have you handled a spinnaker enough to feel comfortable pulling it off?"

"I'm pretty confident."

He scanned the horizon for himself. "If we pull it off, you know we'll piss off some people."

"Get the spinnaker out of the bag there. Then ask me if I care."

"That's my girl."

Jessica smiled even more broadly than before. "That's the second time I've heard that this week." She hummed to herself. "Feels pretty good."

With ninety seconds left, *Spindletop* hoisted its spinnaker and started its run for the line. Concomitantly, a steady puff of wind filled the huge sail as *Spindletop* surged past the flatfooted fleet.

"Shit," came the anguished cry from the owner of *Zephyr*.

"Son of a bitch, she's getting away," said Jerry Osborne on *Liquidator*, as *Spindletop* took off for the first mark, well in front.

As his Flying Scot pulled away, Oliver Chambers just smiled. "If we don't do another thing this weekend this will be a helluva highlight. Great call, young lady. Let's trim the sails and see what happens."

What happened was *Spindletop* stayed the course and finished third, getting passed only on the fourth and fifth legs by eventual winner *Electra* and second place *Running Tide*. As they stowed their gear, Jerry Osborne, not the most pleasant skipper in the fleet, stopped by *Spindletop*. "Helluva move out there, Oliver. I thought about it, but too late. Great call. That ought to put you in pretty good shape for Sunday."

"Wasn't my call, Jerry. The captain suggested it and I agreed. It was kind of fun blowing by *Zephyr* that way."

"*Zephyr* and a lot of others. I just wanted to say nice piece of sailing by you and the girl," as he reached over to shake her hand.

"Thank you, I'm Jessica."

"Me and the fleet will be watching you," he said, before moving up the pier.

"What's the game plan for tomorrow?" Jessica asked.

"Skipper's meeting at nine. Should be much shorter than today. I suspect the commodore's big topic will be weather-related. Do you have a rain slicker? You might need one. It's supposed to be wet and windy in the morning."

"I have a raincoat and rain gear for golf."

"That won't do. I've got an extra sailing slicker, tops and bottoms. You can wear those. You'll want to stay dry as possible, especially since we've got two races."

"You know, Mr. Chambers, this sailing stuff is tiring work. There's more mental stress to this competition than I first thought."

"Kind of fun, isn't it?"

"Absolutely, but kind of exhausting too." She began to gather her things. "Do you need any help getting to your car?"

"Only getting out of the boat. If you'll get my crutches, I think I can make it."

"Here they are. See you in the morning."

* * *

Back at the Woolworth manse, three family members gathered for dinner. "Where's Eric tonight?" Jessica asked.

"Out with Cynthia, I believe," said her mother.

"Again," said Kingston Woolworth.

"Is that a growing concern?" asked his wife.

"No, it's just they've been going together for three years now."

"And that's a problem?"

"No. I mean, I would have expected some kind of movement in all that time, that's all."

"All in good time, dear. All in good time." Erica Woolworth then turned to the as-of-yet unspoken topic of the day. "How did you sailors do today?"

Jessica kept mining her food as King said, "All in all, quite well. We were the only family in two different boats. I finished eighth and seventh and Jessica placed twelfth and third."

"You two are tied after day one?"

"It appears so. Jessica made the move of the day, though; one they're still talking about at the club."

"What was that?

"In the second race in the run for the line she raised a spinnaker and blew away the field. It wasn't even close. She and Oliver Chambers shot off to a huge lead and held it until when, girl?"

"Fourth and fifth legs," she smiled.

"Great piece of sailing," quipped King. "I'm sorry you didn't come to the clubhouse after the race, Jessica. All the captains were talking about it. You definitely got their attention. I was proud to be your dad."

"I'm proud to have you as my dad, so we're even," she grinned.

* * *

Sunday morning dawned warm and blustery. "Jessica, here are the slickers. Put them on before we go down to the boat. I'm betting the rain will start before race time and you won't be able to put the pants on once we are under sail. And, you'll probably get hot and sweaty before all is said and done. I hope that won't bother you."

"I get hot and sweaty playing tennis."

As the two rigged the boat, the grey clouds turned greyer and a fine mist began to permeate the yacht basin. "Foul weather ahead," said the boat's owner.

"That's a problem?"

"Only for the guy trying to keep his cast dry. That's why I brought this plastic sheeting. We'll manage."

Easing out of the harbor, Oliver Chambers noted the variability of the wind. "Probably have to do a lot of changing course today. The competition committee set things up to help us out, but we're still going to have to do a lot of tacking and jibing. Just so you know. Keeping the sails tight will be an effort."

"You and me, we can do it," she said. "Too bad we can't do another early spinnaker trick and blitz the field again."

"I'm afraid that's a once-a-season opportunity, but it sure works great when you can pull it off. I think this morning is going to be one of those 'slow and steady wins the race' things." Sailing off to the east Oliver Chambers said, "In about thirty seconds come about and let's go join those crazies jockeying for position."

Spindletop crossed the starting line fourteenth and settled in under moderate winds and unsettled weather. The mist had turned to drizzle, and the race unfolded amid drab and dreary skies. Sixteenth at the first mark, *Spindletop* made up for lost ground on the first reach, moving to twelfth and then eleventh at the halfway mark. With close quarters no more, Jessica drove the Flying Scot in and out of the separated fleet, holding the eighth spot after the fifth mark and into the finish line.

"Nice effort. Really nice effort," said Oliver Chambers. "In these conditions and given your relative inexperience, you get a battlefield promotion."

"And what might that be?"

"Did you bring a change of clothes?"

"I did."

"Good girl. Let's do this. Go into the ladies' locker room and take a shower. Get this spray off you. Then join me for lunch. Then," he said, looking across the horizon, "we can come out and do this again in worsening conditions."

* * *

Lunch came and went all too quickly. By 1:30, as sailors trudged to their crafts, the morning's drizzle had turned to steady rain. "You going to be able to keep that cast dry?"

"I'm going to double wrap it. What we won't be keeping dry are the sails, so just know you'll be having water shoot off them every time we change course."

"Will it impair my vision?"

"Not likely. You'll just have to keep wiping your face."

Fifteen minutes later, Lake Michigan was producing swells. "Steady as she goes, Jessica. Be extra careful. It's getting slippery here in the cockpit. Be patient with me if I can't scramble across the beam as fast as I need to."

"No worries. I practiced this all summer. I can handle sails during the changeover if you get trapped on one side or another."

The bumpy ride to the line produced one minor collision and one bruised ego. "I had the right of way, you son of a bitch," Mark Morgan on *Intrepid* shouted at the skipper of the *Liquidator*.

"Learn how to sail, Mark. Then we'll talk," responded Jerry Osborne.

"No, we'll talk at the protest meeting," Morgan hurled back.

When the race ended there was no protest meeting, just twenty-five soaking wet crews straggling to the finish. *Spindletop* battled the swells, wind, and driving rain and placed seventh. "I'm thrilled" capsuled Oliver Chambers. "I don't think I could have done much better as a healthy captain. You performed like a champ. Have you ever sailed in conditions like that before?"

"Never. I'll bet my dad did well, too. He loves this kind of stuff. Appeals to his macho, bring-it-on mentality."

"Results should be posted in an hour or so. Want to stay till then?"

"I need to get home. I've got company tonight. But call me with the results. It will get me thinking about tomorrow."

"About tomorrow. Take and dry these slickers. We haven't seen the last of this front. It is going to rain even harder tonight. I bet tomorrow will be beautiful. Sunny, no clouds, great temperature and high winds. We're going to get wet again unless I miss my guess. Noon start time. Skipper's meeting at 10:00. We'll want to attend that one for all the latest updates. I'm sure weather will be the main topic," he said.

"See you tomorrow then," said Jessica cheerily.

CHAPTER TWENTY-FIVE

After a shower, Jessica took a nap in anticipation of a family dinner that included yours truly. At the appointed hour I appeared at the front door after sprinting through a howling gale.

Erica Woolworth answered my knock. "Don't stand there, Looper. You look waterlogged. Weather not fit for man nor beast, is it?"

"Not hardly."

"Give me your coat. I'll hang it where it can dry."

"And people sailed in this stuff today?"

"Apparently. Jessica came home, took a shower and then a nap. Mr. Woolworth opted for a cold beverage before cleaning up. I expect we'll hear all about it at dinner. Come join me in the kitchen. The other two should be down shortly."

"Before they get here, I have a question."

"Yes?"

"Do these races ever have spectators," I asked.

"Sometimes non-racing club members follow the fleet from a distance."

"Really?"

"Would you like to go? For tomorrow's finale the club contracts a good-size excursion craft for onlookers. If you're free, you could be my escort."

"I managed to get the day off."

"What fun. We'll ride together. You probably ought to wear a blazer. And Eric's got some deck shoes I'll borrow."

"I was hoping it would be a surprise."

"I get it," she said, smiling slyly. "Mum's the word. Meet me here at eleven."

"Eric won't need his shoes?"

"He's off with Cynthia Cartwright and her parents for the next two days. We don't see a lot of him these days. He's more a member of their family than ours right now."

"I see."

"I guess love will do that to people." Mrs. Woolworth resumed skinning a squash. "When do you go back to school?"

"Friday. I'll pack Thursday night and head out first thing. It's about a seven-hour trip."

"You can pack all in one session?"

"I left eighty percent of my stuff with a family in town. Most of what I take will be clothes and sundries. Is there anything I can help you with? I feel useless just standing here."

"If the dining room table weren't set I'd tell you to prepare that, but since it is stay here and talk to me. These days I hear a lot about you, but I don't see you as much as I should, given the circumstances."

"What circumstances might those be?"

"Don't be coy, young man. I gather your relationship with Jessica is agreeing with both of you."

"This has been the best summer of my life."

"Go on."

"We seem to complement one another really well. She brightens my day. She challenges me. I need that and she has such a … a human way, about her. I feel really lucky."

"A mother likes to hear things like that about her daughter."

"What things?" said Jessica, prancing into the kitchen.

"That you're a good friend."

"Did you really use that term?" she said, looking at me.

"He did not," said her mother. "He said you brighten his day. You challenge him and you have a human way about you."

"That's better. I don't want to be just his friend," she said, giving me a playful peck on the cheek.

"What's for dinner?" said the man of the house, entering through the butler's pantry. "Smells good."

"Roast duck, rice, summer vegetables and a chocolate log roll for dessert. Jessica, be a dear and fetch the hors d' oeuvres from the fridge, please."

"Coming right up."

"Isn't a log roll a yuletide dish?" I asked.

"Traditionally, yes. But in this house we make it for special occasions, such as last meals together before returning to school," said Mrs. Woolworth.

"Here's the thing, Looper," said Mr. Woolworth. "Served cold, this is without a doubt the best dessert you'll ever have."

"I don't know. My mom's a pretty good cook."

"Son, if you play your cards right you could be eating well for the rest of your life."

"King," said Mrs. Woolworth sharply, "why don't you tell us about the sailing today."

* * *

In the high ceiling space of the dining room, the four of us sat together at the far end of what seemed to be an unending heavy Victorian flame mahogany table. Sixteen Victorian walnut balloon back dining chairs dominated a room complete with two side boards and two cherry breakfront china cabinets.

"I never realized how big this room was," I said.

"We entertain occasionally," said Kingston Woolworth, understating the obvious.

"I want to hear about the sailing. It must have been miserable out there."

"It was for the losers," said King. "But Jessica and I did fine, so there's no grousing from us."

"How fine?" said the wife.

"*Outcast* finished ninth and fifth; *Spindletop* eight and seventh."

"So you guys are pretty close then."

"Damn close. Going to be a gut check tomorrow."

"While you two are duking it out for family bragging rights, who's going to walk off with the Commodore's Cup?"

"Depends. Jerry Osborne, while not the most charming person in the world, looks to be showing the way. I think he's finished first, fourth, second and fourth. He's probably in the lead. Don Coolidge in *Summer Wind* is probably second and Webster Charles is likely third in *Whitewater*."

"Do either of you two have a chance at a ribbon?"

"We might. The field has been kind of scattered, particularly today with the foul weather. Corrected standings will be posted tomorrow morning. Then we can do the math."

"I can't imagine it was very pleasant out there this afternoon."

"A lot of chop and uneven swells," said Kingston.

"What did you think, Jessica?" Mrs. Woolworth asked.

"I thought a lot of the skippers seemed confused by the wind shifts. I saw some tacking when they should have been jibing, and several just took poor lines to the mark. Worked out OK for us though. I will say that's the wettest I've been since my last visit to the swimming pool. I'm glad it was eighty degrees and not fifty."

"Won't be that warm tomorrow. High winds, sunny, and 60 degrees if we're lucky," King interjected.

"At what point on the Beaufort scale do they cancel the race?" asked Mrs. Woolworth.

"The committee starts getting leery around thirty knots. Forecast calls for strong gusts most of the day. I'm sure it will be the first agenda item at the skipper's meeting."

"Would they consider cancelling it?" I asked.

"They might," said King, "but it's the most important late-summer race we have, and the club has never gone a year without awarding the Commodore's Cup."

"Still, there needs to be some concern for safety. People can get hurt when boats capsize," I continued.

"If there is enough concern, they'll put it to a vote. My guess is the race will go on because the traditionalists will want to see the cup awarded and those in the lead will want to vie for the hardware. Should be interesting."

"How would you vote, King?"

"You know me, Erica. I like to have winners. I'd vote to sail."

"How would you vote, Jessica?" I asked.

"Like you don't know the answer to that," she said.

"Changing the subject, what are your plans for the next school year, Looper? Jessica has shared some of them, but we'd like to hear from you."

I gave a long look across the table at Jessica who was desperately trying to hide an evil grin. "Go ahead, I didn't tell them everything," she said.

Over the next fifteen minutes I laid out chapter and verse on my plans for the next two semesters. I droned on longer than planned but kept getting peppered with questions I felt obligated to answer.

After what felt like an exhaustive interrogation, I concluded with, "I don't know what else to tell you. I think I might have a career in business, hopefully finance and marketing. I'm hoping an MBA might further define my career path."

"If I can help, let me know. Among other things I'm an investment banker. Bright folks with backgrounds in finance and marketing make great acquisitions people."

"Thank you, sir. That's very kind."

"That's the least we can do," he paused, searching for the right word.

"Don't," directed Erica Woolworth to her husband.

"For you," persisted King.

Gathering the dessert plates, she declared, "My goodness, it's later than I thought. You two sailors must be exhausted."

"Truth be told, I am," said her husband.

"Me too," said Jessica.

"Good thing the race isn't until noon," said King.

"I'll see Looper to the door."

Jessica escorted me through the front door and into the open-air alcove. "You were wonderful tonight," she said, before pulling my head to her warm lips. Imperceptibly, she leaned into my unsuspecting torso, letting her willowy frame linger against mine.

A minute, then two, passed with each of us enjoying the evening-ending moment. Suddenly a prolonged blast of wind broke our reverie. "Wow, I may have trouble going to sleep tonight."

Jessica laughed, "Me, too."

"Hey," I said, "thanks for a great evening. Thank your folks too, please. The dinner was fantastic. That log roll was out of this world."

"I'll tell her. Good night," she said breathlessly.

"Good luck tomorrow. Sounds like you're still in the hunt for hardware."

"More like ribbons. Sleep tight."

As I opened my car door, I saw Jessica quietly pause in the alcove before disappearing inside.

Once inside the lengthy front foyer she yelled, "Dad, it's blowing like crazy out there." Then added, "but the rain and lightning have stopped."

CHAPTER TWENTY-SIX

At ten in the morning the wind had not abated one iota. If anything, it had increased. The skippers were a jumpy lot as they crowded into the wide assembly hall. "Gentlemen, and lady," said Commodore Wessendorf, nodding toward Jessica, "the main agenda item is staging of the fifth and final race of the regatta. Before we move to that does anyone have any old business they want brought to our attention?"

Oscar Jensen of *Day's End* raised his hand. "What about the wind?"

"What about it?" responded Commodore Wessendorf. "Yes, gentlemen, it is blustery out there. About twenty-five knots. The race committee met earlier this morning. We have reviewed the weather forecast. The good news is that the skies are picture perfect. Unlike yesterday's dastardly conditions, ours are ideal – except for the wind. Several of you have spoken to me about postponing the race. We will not. We will conclude the regatta today either as a four" -- at this point a considerable murmur rippled through the crowd -- "or five-race competition. Others have asked that we delay the start, which is standard procedure. Gentlemen, and lady, the afternoon forecast is for continued breeze and a possible increase in velocity."

More murmuring.

"If we start the race, the TLE will be extended from thirty to forty-five minutes. We will continue to use low scoring as we have for the first four races. Those finishing today beyond time limit expired will be given the place number of the final finisher making the time limit, with an added two-point place penalty. Those abandoning the race will be designated DNF and will be scored with an additional two-place penalty based on the final finisher still on the course. Any questions?"

"That seems excessively penal," voiced Winston Wilson of *Far Reach*.

"Shorten the course," suggested Franklin Cox of *Deep Six*.

"We need to start the damn race at noon as scheduled," growled Harold Atkins of *Sirocco* from the front row.

"We'll not be bullied by some ancient mariner who just wants us deep-sixed in the briny," countered a wizened Wallace Clark of *Dire Straits*.

"You old pickle. If you learned how to sail like a true mariner you'd be pleading for this thing to go on. I say we take a vote."

"Aye, aye," came a semi-chorus of assent.

"Thank you, Harold. That is precisely the sentiment of the race committee. Is there any more civil discussion?" Commodore Wessendorf paused, scanning the room. "Any at all? OK. We will proceed by roll call vote. A vote, and only one, is to be cast by the skipper or owner of the craft in question. A vote of aye is to continue; a vote nay is to cancel the race. Need I remind you, in case of cancellation, by association rules, the Commodore Cup and associated prizes will be awarded based on the lowest four-race aggregate. Any non-finishing craft will *not* be eligible for any competition prizes. All right then, skipper of *Afternoon Delight,* what say you?"

"Nay."

The voting proceeded, with the abrasive sound of moving chairs reflecting the mounting tension.

"Armstrong," said an annoyed skipper, "you cannot abstain. Aye or nay."

"Nay," said the captain of *Blackbeard's Ghost*.

"*Liquidator?*"

Jerry Osborne rose, glared at his audience. "Aye, goddammit."

"No surprise there," murmured Oliver Chambers.

The roll call came to an emphatic close as a wind-aided shutter slammed the outer wall.

"What's the tally, Charles?" Wessendorf said to his vice commodore.

"The ayes have it, 13-12."

"We will race," said Wessendorf. Mixed cheers and assorted grumbling greeted the decision. "Gentlemen, gentlemen -- and lady -- come to order. If you decide not to race, state your position to me or a member of the race committee by 11:30. Otherwise we will assume you will be present in the run to the line. It is now 10:40. Down to the dock, gentlemen."

* * *

Dockside by *Spindletop* Jessica said, "Hey, you're moving better today."

"Yesterday was such a chore that I dialed my doc last night and asked him the shorten the cast. It's due to come off Wednesday. He came to the house and sawed off the top so I can bend my knee."

"That's good news."

"Jessica, I should have asked. Are you OK sailing in these high winds because I think Commodore Wessendorf underplayed the effect of the wind. I'll tell you this, there will be no spinnakers flying today. If someone sent one up, the shock load would send boat parts into the lake. Scary stuff happens when spinnakers are not done right."

"I like the adventure. Sure, this will be new territory, but with an experienced hand like you, I think we'll be fine. Besides, what else was I going to do today? My boyfriend is at work."

"Before we turn loose from the dock, put on your slicker and life jacket. Spray is going to be with us all day and if we get tossed, you'll want to be seen among the swells."

As they rigged the craft, Jessica kept peppering Oliver Chambers with questions. "What's this TLE the commodore was talking about? It sounded like it had something to do with a time limit."

"Precisely. The time limit for today's course is two hours. TL stands for Time Limit. TLE stands for Time Limit Expired. Today's limit is extended to 45 minutes. That's to account for the adverse wind conditions. Sometimes the limit starts after the first boat finishes, but apparently that won't be the case today."

"And what's with some of these boat names? I mean I get that *Chinook* and *Sirocco* are winds, but *Platinum Princess* and *Closing Bell*?"

"The owner of *Platinum Princess* is a crusty old fogey named Oscar Taylor. He is a jeweler, a wealthy one, by profession. Daniel Sparks owns *Closing Bell*. He's a stockbroker known for making last-minute trades in the market. Jerry Osborne has made a fortune buying vast quantities of people's moribund product and selling it overseas. Hence *Liquidator*. He can be a jerk sometimes, but he's awfully good on the water. He may be the best sailor out here. And when he says something, he means it. That compliment you got on Saturday, coming from him, that may be the nicest compliment you've gotten all summer."

"I don't think so," said Jessica giving thought to the young man in her life.

"A lot of the other names are nautical phrases. Terribly original," Chambers said with a bit of sarcasm. "But *Outcast*, your father's boat, that's a bit unusual. Initially he felt he wasn't accepted here until he began making some real money. He chose *Outcast* because he thought it fit his personality. Makes sense to me. Enough about names, let's push off and get acclimated to this wind. We're going to have our hands full today."

Classic understatement. After twenty minutes on the course the occupants of *Spindletop* were thoroughly drenched. Two minutes before the noon start Oliver Chambers said, "We only have a field of twenty-one. Four boats must have opted out."

"Some of the naysayers, huh? Who are they?"

"Can't say for sure, but I don't see the red and blue hull of *Fairweather Sailor* or the black of *Pequod IV*."

To the fleet's credit, for the most part, the individual captains gave a wide berth to one another in the run to the line. The obvious exceptions were *Liquidator* and *Forty Fathoms,* who barreled ahead. "I'm glad I'm wearing gloves," said Jessica, "I'd have no hands left after this weekend if it weren't for these."

"Oh, you'd have hands all right," said her mate, trimming the mainsail, "just no skin."

Even on the first leg it became clear that the competitors were in for a long day. The captains suffered from overboard lines, flapping sails, mistimed direction changes and unending spasms of inconsistent speed. Virtually every boat lost momentum more than once because of an inability to reef the sails. Thanks to winds that edged to forty knots, controlling sheets and lines became more difficult than ever. By the time the leader, *Forty Fathoms*, hit the second mark, the field was widely dispersed. *Spindletop* held its own but was admittedly sailing on the edge.

Aboard the excursion cruiser *Wayward Wind*, nose to outward glass, I surveyed the unfolding chaos. "Is every race like this," I asked.

"Heavens no," said Mrs. Woolworth. "This is extremely heavy weather. Usually it's sunlight, breezes and Bloody Marys on the foredeck, not foul-weather gear and confined quarters."

"I'm impressed with the sailors out there. They have to be more uncomfortable than I have ever been caddying in the rain. More courageous, too."

Aboard the *Spindletop,* Oliver Chambers, spray flying across his face said, "No day in the park is it, Jessica? "

"I feel like all we're doing is holding on for dear life," she said as she approached the third mark.

"It is all we're doing. Watch out for *Chinook* to port."

"What's with him?"

"Dead in the water. He's torn his sails. Oh, man, he's in deep trouble. Good thing he's fairly close to the harbor."

"Mr. Chambers, this wind has gotten much stronger. Our telltale is just blowing straight back all the time."

"You want to stop?"

"Definitely not. This is something I'll never forget."

"And never do again…?"

"I was going to say, 'always remember.'"

"I'll say this, we are actually outsailing people here. The usual suspects have left us in the dust, but we are definitely in this competition. Keep holding on, girl. We are a player," he said, as a healthy dose of lake water hit his slicker. "I've never sailed in winds this strong. An easy thirty-five knots or more. Truly brutal."

Afterwards in the common room, the race committee and survivors assessed the damage. Of the original twenty-five boats represented at the morning meeting, twenty-one started and only nine made the time limit. Six others completed the full course within the forty-five-minute extension; two others tarried after the extension. Four other Flying Scots abandoned the race at various stages, two from badly torn sails and one from a dismast. A fourth captain went swimming when a loose boom sent him overboard. The abandoned boats suffered added ignominy when they were towed back into the harbor by motorized craft. Later, more than one skipper swore that the hardest sail of the day was navigating a return to the harbor when he found his boat in irons.

It was a wet assembly that faced the blue-blazered competition committee. "Gentlemen, and lady," said Commodore Wessendorf in his most authoritarian tone, "we have identified the top six finishers and are still sorting out the rest of the field. Full results from today's race and the weekend series will be posted by 6 p.m. tonight. We intend to engrave the Commodore Cup and the silver plates for second and third. Those will be awarded at our season-ending banquet. Place ribbons for fourth through sixth will be handed out forthwith. Any questions?"

"Get on with the damn show, we're cold and tired," said Harold Atkins.

"Agreed, on with the show," said another.

To no one's surprise, especially Jerry Osborne, the Commodore Cup went to *Liquidator*. *Maritime Blue* and *Far Reach* placed second and third. "Fourth goes to *Day's End*, captained by Oscar Jensen. Fifth, by the slim margin of one point, goes to captain Oliver Chambers and *Spindletop*," said Wessendorf.

"Commodore, I would like the record to reflect that while I am owner of *Spindletop*, the captain this weekend was my mate, Jessica Woolworth." With that there followed polite applause.

"So noted, sir. And sixth place goes to Kingston Woolworth and *Outcast*. Well sailed, gentleman and lady. Thank you for a competitive weekend. Sorry I couldn't have ordered up more accommodating weather. Our next race in the summer series will be Sunday two weeks hence. Good day."

Oliver Chambers and Jessica stood and stared at one another in absolute disbelief. "You're kidding," said Jessica.

"Apparently not," said Mr. Chambers. "I may not believe it until I see the numbers."

"I think the numbers will only substantiate what we already know. You guys are fifth," intoned Jerry Osborne. Turning to Jessica, he said "I think you can credit that spinnaker move to the ribbon you're holding young lady. I said it before and I'll say it again -- the move of the weekend. Congratulations."

"And to you, sir, for the top prize. You earned it."

"I think we all earned battlefield promotions for enduring the weather the last two days. As rough as I can recall."

As he turned to go, a fourth person entered the conversation. "Jerry, well-deserved. You waxed all of us out there," said King Woolworth, extending his hand.

"That's some knot on your noggin, King. Is that an old war wound or did that happen today?"

A wry smile curled his lips. "War wound from two hours ago. I lost a line rounding the second buoy and got coldcocked by a wayward boom. Damn near deposited me in the drink. I lost my bearings there for a good five minutes."

"And you were solo out there, weren't you?"

"Affirmative."

"I would have thought a smart man like you might have tapped the other sailor in the family as your crew member."

"A smart man would have, Jerry. I was too late in asking and too dumb to recognize the talent and the person with it until it was too late. She was already committed to Oliver."

"That's not like you to miss an opportunity like that."

"Well, I think maybe it has been that way for far too long. I'm committed to not making that mistake ever again," he said, looking wistfully at his daughter.

"Thanks, dad," said Jessica, giving him a warm embrace.

From the periphery Erica Woolworth and I descended. "Mom, Looper, what are you two doing here?"

"We heard there was a race. We thought we'd check it out," said her mother.

"And look at you in your blue blazer and too large deck shoes. Are those Eric's? You two saw the race?"

"We watched from the excursion boat. You didn't think we'd miss this family moment, did you?" said the lady of the house.

"What did you think of the proceedings, Looper?" King asked.

"Scary stuff. Glad I was warm and dry."

"I'm glad you came." Jessica beamed and gave me a squeeze.

CHAPTER TWENTY-SEVEN

A busy Labor Day at Spring Willows turned into a quiet, almost somnolent Tuesday. The only holdover was a penetrating, cloudless blue sky and a welcome, dry seventy-degree temperature.

"The Titleist ball inventory coincides with your projected numbers, Mr. Starza," I said. "The only count that shows any deviation is in range balls. Since Spring Willows uses premium Titleist practice balls, I think a few members may be pocketing some for personal use. Range and short-game shrinkage is one thing, but this shortfall can't all be from errant shanks and slices. I think we can lay the rest to… and I hate to say this…"

"Say it," said the head pro.

"Pilferage."

"You'd think a practice ball would be the last thing these well-fixed members would steal."

"Maybe they think they're not getting enough for their monthly dues."

"Possibly not."

"I'm sure as hell not getting enough for mine. Where are my clubs and shoes? And where's my caddie?" came the raised voice of Billy Sauers. "By God, I've got a noon tee time and its 11:45."

"I'm on it, Mr. Sauers. I'll be right out with your clubs and shoes. Do you need anything else?"

"Bring your clubs too."

"Why's that?"

"We're going eighteen."

"I know that."

"This is a playing round. You and me. Didn't someone tell you to bring your clubs?"

"No, they didn't. My clubs are at home."

"Well, this is a golf club. There ought to be a spare set around here you can use."

Peter Timmons to the rescue. "Looper, use mine. They'll fit you perfectly. Might want to stroke a few putts to see if the putter is the right length. If not, grab a demo."

"So, we're all set. Hit the head and do whatever else is required, and let's go to the first tee," said Billy Sauers.

* * *

At two minutes to noon we sent our rockets off the first tee.

"Been playing much?" said Billy, as we trailed after our tee shots.

"Giving more instruction than playing."

"Playing with Miss Woolworth, I understand."

"Apparently it's the worst kept secret at the club."

"It's hardly a secret. Don't worry, I'm not going there. Long-term possibilities if you ask me."

I remained silent while thinning my second shot so badly that low flying insects headed for cover. "I can do better than that," I said.

"I know you can. Let's just play."

My game picked up considerably. On the par-3 fourth hole, I left my tee shot pin-high five feet right of the flag.

"That's more like it."

"Thank you. Not sure where that came from, but I'll take it."

"Muscle memory maybe," said Billy Sauers.

"I can only hope." As we walked to the sixth tee, I sought some clarity. "Mr. Sauers, I'm curious. Why this round?"

"It's almost the end of your summer vacation and I wanted to spend a little quality time with you before you returned to school."

"That's thoughtful of you."

"Son, I'm always thoughtful. My problem is that not everyone always appreciates my thoughts."

"Perhaps so, but you get results."

The older man smiled. "I do get my way a lot."

"What's the best round you've ever had out here?"

"Best round or best score? There's a difference."

"Both."

"Best score was a 74 about five years ago. I'm not playing as much as I did back then. These days my average score is in the low eighties. My best round, by far, was an eighteen with Kemmons Wilson, my guest from Memphis. He told me about a concept he was working on, a thing called Holiday Inn. I helped him with early financing and investment capital. Made some investments as a result."

"In the right place at the right time."

"Precisely. That's half the secret to business right there. You ever been in the right place at the right time, Looper?"

"I'm not sure."

"Well, I am. Your being here at Spring Willows these last three years seems like an instance of that."

"It's been a good run, I'll say that."

"It doesn't have to end, you know."

"Mr. Sauers, I have to go back to college. Then I'm going to have to get a job."

He chipped to within two feet of the hole. "Are you giving any thought to graduate school?"

"Recently yes," I said, as we moseyed to the seventh tee.

"The reason I ask is because you'd be more marketable with an MBA if you're still thinking about the business world."

"I am."

"With your intellect, I'd think you'd do very well in that environment. Any thoughts to where?"

"Probably east coast. Roll the dice and see if I couldn't get into Harvard or Wharton. If not there, Michigan or Northwestern. If I went to school in Evanston I could even live at home."

"Bad idea. Time to get away from home. All young men need to get away from home and see the world."

The grad school dialogue continued past the ninth green up the climb to the Halfway House and the elevated tenth tee.

"I forgot Brewster was going to be closed today," Billy Sauers said.

"No problem," said a third voice. "I figured you boys might be hungry. I rustled up some sandwiches and apples to carry us through the next nine. You guys are making good time. First nine in ninety minutes. That's some ready golf," said Carlisle Howard.

"Looper, I asked Mr. Howard to join us for the back nine. I thought he could add a perspective to our earlier conversations. I hoped his presence and shot-making ability might elevate our games. Lisle, why don't you take the box and show us how it's done?"

"Gladly," said the club champion.

"Young man," said Billy Sauers, "behold greatness." And when Carlisle Howard's ball came to rest four feet below the hole, I knew I had.

"Now, you do it, Billy."

"Lisle, I'll settle for the green." Two collective strokes later both Billy Sauers and I were putting for birdies, a feat achieved only by Mr. Howard.

It was on the twelfth hole that Mr. Howard began an animated stream of consciousness. "Without a doubt the ugliest hole on the course now that we've done something about Eleven, wouldn't you agree, Looper?"

"Having worked all eighteen holes as a caddie and a grounds crew member I would wholeheartedly concur. At the very least the club should put in some trees, or better yet shrubs on the left side, to offer golfers visual enhancement and psychic relief."

"We could do that, couldn't we, Billy? There's money in the budget, right? This is the one hole out here that I'm embarrassed to have my guests play. We're better than that. I'm surprised the State Am people didn't say anything."

"Actually, they did, as a part of their final report, but they were so pleased with everything else that they decided not to make an issue of it."

"Well, this twelfth hole eyesore needs to be addressed at the next green committee meeting. I'm going to make it an agenda item. Billy, have you addressed the other agenda item?"

"No. We only touched on it briefly."

After he poleaxed a 3-wood just short of the green Mr. Howard continued. "Looper, I was wondering about your plans following graduation."

"I've been wondering about them too," I said.

"You're a business, finance, marketing major right?"

"Yes sir."

"Fine. Any thoughts about graduate school?"

"Some, though it seems I'm not the only one with plans for me."

"And where are you thinking?"

"If I go, I'd like to go east, if I can get in. Boston or Philadelphia."

"Did either of your folks go to school in the northeast?"

"My mother went to Wellesley."

"That's a start. How about your dad?"

"University of Iowa."

"That's not east," said Billy Sauers.

"How about relatives? Any connections?"

"My mother grew up in Connecticut. Her father got an engineering degree in Boston. My three uncles earned degrees in business, English and medicine."

"Be more specific."

"Harvard."

"Bingo," said Billy Sauers.

"That would be a great line item on an application, wouldn't it, Billy? But it probably wouldn't do to have a family member write a recommendation."

"Agreed. I wonder if there is another source. Lisle, if I recall, didn't you go to Penn?"

"As matter of fact. And Billy, you have some connection with Harvard, yes?"

"Well, there is that law degree I got when not frequenting the bars on Charles Street."

"We're trying to paint a picture here, Looper."

"It's slowly coming into focus."

"I'm going to focus on getting a hole-in-one on Thirteen here," said Mr. Howard.

Whack went 4-iron on ball. "Lisle, unless the hole is in that trap there I think you'll have to wait another day."

"Maybe I can hole the sand shot." A game attempt left it five inches short. "The grounds crew must not have cut the green this morning. Otherwise that would have been in."

"You only wish," said Mr. Sauers.

After tee shots on Fourteen the sales pitch continued. "Looper" said Mr. Howard, "how many young men, say ages 19-24, are club members?"

"I have no idea. Thirty?"

"Forty-seven."

"How many of them do you think Billy and I would consider hiring for our businesses?"

"Ten?"

"How big a number is zero?"

"Pretty small."

"Correct. Zero is what we consider the applicant pool to be from club families."

"How so?"

"We don't see an inner drive that excites us. No hunger, no carpe diem if you will."

"If you're looking for good people, why not go to universities with whom you're well connected?"

"Why should we bother? We've already got a candidate we know, someone who has already been vetted, whose intangibles we admire."

"My way you'd have some choices."

"We don't want choices. We already have a candidate who has the intelligence, academic training and critical people skills necessary for success in business."

I knocked in my fifteen-foot putt. "Make your candidate an offer."

"I like the way this boy thinks, Billy."

"Looper, I have an opening in my firm, First Strike Investments. I need a young man with skills similar to yours, someone with the business acumen and understanding of the human condition, to join my very successful operation. To get that person I am willing to invest in their education by paying for their first year of graduate school and for the second if the candidate stays two years with my company. In addition, there is a paid summer internship."

"That sounds like a pretty good deal for someone."

"That's a very good deal by anyone's standards," said Mr. Howard.

"Let me be a little more direct," said Billy Sauers. "Do you want the job?"

"I still have to get into graduate school. I need to apply, get recommendations and the like."

"Yes, all that is a given," said Mr. Howard. "Young man, should you decide to apply to Wharton I will be more than happy to write you a recommendation. I'm on the board of the business school."

"And I'll write you one for Harvard," continued Billy Sauers. "With all your other sterling qualifications I have to believe that entrance to any of those four schools you mentioned is a fait accompli."

As we approached the fifteenth green, Mr. Howard said to Sauers, "He's kind of quiet."

"He's probably in shock. We laid a lot on him back there."

"Kind of like Christmas, actually. Did anyone ever make an offer like that to you?"

"No," Billy said, "but I didn't shine until law school. I got my break there. I could have benefitted from some more plebian training like he's gotten working here."

"Don't sell yourself short. You've done just fine."

"I have a lot of memories from this hole," I said, standing on the tee at Seventeen.

"Looper, if I may wax poetic here for a bit. It seems like what's happened for you here are more than just memories. You've had pivotal moments. You and I both lost a dear friend when Lucy Peck passed on. But I would submit you found a soul mate, someone who likes to triumph just as much as you do, when Jessica Woolworth hit her sand shot."

I smiled. "That clean fried-egg shot saved her match."

"Looper, there's a bonus I want you to consider before graduate school. What are you doing for spring break next year?"

"Mr. Sauers, I have no idea. I was thinking maybe some sun in Florida, but that's just a pipe dream at this point."

"I'm going to Italy next March and I'd like to take you with me, assuming we can come to an agreement here. What do you know about Florence?" he asked, waggling his 6-iron.

"Not much."

"Well," said Billy Sauers, directing his ball to the green, "during the Renaissance, the city became a banking center and was literally the continent's source of money. The gold florin takes its name from Florence, and was for years the most trusted currency in Europe."

"I'm not sure I knew that."

"Know this. I'd like you to come with me – to Florence. Based on some brief research I did; your spring break occurs at the same time as the international banking and investment conference I'll be attending. I also plan to take a side trip to Switzerland to check in with some banking friends. That would give you some days to yourself to knock around, travel, whatever."

"Really?"

"Take your time, we still have another hole to play," he chuckled.

Walking to the green, Mr. Howard turned to Sauers. "That's cruel, giving him a time frame like that."

"It's longer than that and he knows it. Just thought I'd ratchet up the sphincter factor."

"Still, kind of cruel."

"Lisle, it's just business, right?"

"I will say we have a funny way of doing it."

"No denying that."

The tee shots on eighteen were again dispersed in a radius of no more than eight feet. In the march to the balls, I turned to Billy Sauers. "It really is who you know, isn't it?"

A big grin crossed my mentor's countenance. "It's only taken you three years to learn that. Congratulations. Many people go a lifetime failing to understand that concept."

"And this round was never by accident, was it?"

"I told you back on Ten I asked Mr. Howard to come along. Life is a learning process, Looper. We're just trying to speed up your education. Everyone has a timetable. The hours pass quickly; you're leaving for school soon. We needed to plant the seed."

"I still think I need time to ruminate."

"With all due respect, Looper," said Mr. Howard, "kine ruminate. People on the go, like us, are men of action.

"Do you know who Cordell Hull was, Looper?" asked Billy Sauers.

"FDR's Secretary of State."

"Correct. He was also a lawyer and representative from Tennessee. He said, among other things, 'all decisions are made on insufficient information.' Have you ever had to do that?"

"I feel like I'm being asked to do that now."

"Life is just an unending maze where we are confronted with decisions every day. Our job is to make the best choices we can based on information in hand and gut reaction. No one is asking for a decision by the end of the day. But make no mistake, there is an offer on the table. Financial terms are negotiable but I promise you they will be fair and generous."

"Thank you, sir."

"Don't thank me. Thank yourself. You've been preparing for this moment for the last three years. You just didn't know it."

"Lookee here," said Carlisle Howard, spying three balls on the green just ten feet from the pin. "You're away. Looper."

"Not for long," I said, leaving my uphill putt three inches from the cup.

"Never up and never in," said Mr. Howard. "Let me show you how it's done," he said. He horseshoed his eight-footer.

"Amateur hour," said Billy Sauers, plumb bobbing the remaining six feet.

"For a guy who says he hasn't played a lot, you knocked it up there pretty close."

"Lisle, it's the competition. It brings out the best in me. Watch this."

It was in the heart all the way. Handshakes were exchanged all around as we exited the green. "Looper, call me before you leave," said Billy Sauers. "That's a live offer I made out there. I think you'd be perfect for our firm. You'd learn a lot and have fun doing so. Lots of opportunity with varied experiences."

"Me too, son. Let me know and I will write that letter to Wharton. I'm confident with your academic credentials and a favorable word from yours truly Wharton would find a spot for you."

"Thank you both. I don't know what to say."

"Your 'thank you' is a gracious plenty," said Mr. Howard.

"Can I take your clubs up to the bag room for you? I've got to turn in these borrowed ones."

"Son, you already have a bag."

"Yes, but I have two shoulders and two arms. I can take these up for you."

"Spoken like a caddie," said Billy Sauers.

"That won't be necessary. I'm going that way anyway," said Mr. Howard.

On the terrace outside the Pro Shop, the three warriors encountered two Woolworths and one Timmons. "How'd those clubs work out?"

"Just fine. The weight of those irons was just right, and the putter was well-balanced. Great clubs."

"Any course records today?" asked the assistant pro.

"Not today," said Mr. Howard. "We left a few strokes out there for the real players. The only disappointment was on Twelve and the lack of a buffer between the fairway and the road."

"We hear that a lot," said Starza, joining us.

"Stan, we're making that an agenda item for the next green committee meeting. You might jot down some thoughts about that. I know members have complained to you for years."

"Very true. I have some written complaints in a file somewhere."

"Gather them up," said Billy Sauers. "I'll use them as supporting evidence for the necessary environmental improvement. Timmons, be a pro and take these shopworn clubs from me and put them on the rack." Eyeing the group he said, "I best be trudging home. Lisle, thanks for joining us. I think the back nine worked well." Turning to me he smiled. "Don't forget what I said."

To Jessica and her father, I asked, "What are you guys doing out here today?"

"Settling a bet," shot Jessica.

"Really?"

"Tell him about it, Dad."

"Seems like I was challenged to demonstrate my prowess as a sand player. I think you are aware of the longstanding family offer. At breakfast this morning Jessica said that she was ready to prove that I was not the best bunker player in the family, so we came out to settle the issue," said Kingston Woolworth.

"It was not only an issue, it was a bet," Jessica said.

Looking at Peter Timmons, I asked, "And your role in this was?"

"I was a judge. They wanted an impartial source, so we went down to the practice area and had at it."

"And the rules of engagement were?"

"Forty-five bunker shots: fifteen shots from a fairway bunker, fifteen greenside and fifteen buried lies," said Timmons.

"And?"

"Mr. Woolworth won the fairway trap contest, 10-5. Jessica the greenside, 9-6."

"I knew I had her when it came to fried eggs," interrupted the father. "I've won a lot of bets executing that shot."

"And?" Looper asked.

"What do you think?" said the daughter.

"I'd like to have seen it."

"I got smoked, son."

"It wasn't even close," said Jessica.

"No," said a chagrined King Woolworth. "It was not. I thought I was good, but not anymore."

"You're still good, Dad. Just not as good."

"Was there money at stake?"

"There was," said Mr. Woolworth, "but she wouldn't take it."

"This is getting a little deep for me," said Peter Timmons, "so if you'll excuse me, I'll just mosey on."

"Thanks for the help, Judge Timmons," Jessica called to the retreating figure.

"Anytime."

"Now what?" said Looper.

"Here's what," said King Woolworth. "I'm going to give you these wedges to put back in my bag. I'm going to go home and have a talk with the other woman in my life. I think she can provide some context and maybe I can find out what else I've been missing all these years. As for you two young people, why don't you stay here and have a quiet dinner at the club."

"I'm hardly dressed for the dining room," I said.

"Neither am I," said Jessica.

"That's what the terrace is for. Eat out there. Soft breezes, no humidity, love in the air. Great night for it. Looper, see she gets home in one piece, will you?"

"Yes sir."

Turning to Jessica, I said, "I need to offload these clubs and wash up. How about we meet on the terrace in twenty minutes."

"I feel filthy. You'll just have to take me as I am."

"With pleasure. How about first person ready grabs a table?"

"Deal."

I put King's clubs up.

"You missed a show, Looper," said Peter Timmons. "I'm going to call it the bash at the beach. I mean those two really went at it. At the start it wasn't terribly friendly. That family is competitive. I'll give them this, they are both good bunker players, but when it came to the buried lies Jessica was in a class by herself. Of her fifteen shots I'll bet not more than three of them were longer than six feet from the hole. She almost holed three of them. Some display."

"Thanks again for the clubs. They worked out really well."

"Glad I could help. Will I see you tomorrow?"

"Briefly. I'm coming up around ten to pick up my check."

"Good enough. It's been a pleasure working with you."

"Same here."

* * *

Fifteen minutes later I found a table on the quiet side of the terrace. To my left I could see the green at Killer Ten. Rotating on an axis to my right I saw a twilight twosome trundling down the eleventh fairway. Their ambling evoked memories of my adventures at Spring Willows over the last three summers. Caddie, grounds crew member, Pro Shop staff, I wondered what was next.

"Looper, is everything all right? I've been standing here."

"Fine, just fine. I was just thinking," I said, as I rose to pull out an iron chair for her. "Wow, you look gorgeous. I thought you didn't have a change of clothes."

"I checked my mother's locker and remembered I'd put a dress in there at the start of the summer. Sorry I kept you waiting. I decided to take a quick shower to be more presentable."

"You're always presentable."

"You are so sweet, but I'm starving. Let's eat."

When the waiter arrived, Jessica grilled him on the evening fare and settled on rainbow trout, summer squash and blueberry compote. I opted for the Kobe steak salad, corn on the cob and lemon meringue pie.

In the waning moments of the meal Jessica teased, "You know, for a guy who is my boyfriend, you didn't handle that corn on the cob all that well."

"At least I don't have blueberry smeared on the right side of my mouth. Why do you think the people two tables away are staring at you?"

"No way," she said emphatically.

"Yes way. Go ahead. Ask the waiter."

Our server appeared to refill the water glasses. "I have a question," she said to him. "Is there blueberry on the right corner of my mouth?"

Looking at me and back at Jessica, he said, "There's no right answer here, is there?"

"The truth. That's all I want. Straight out."

"You're sure?"

"Positive."

"If there is anything there, I can't detect it. Will there be anything else?"

Jessica shot a look across the table. "You're a troublemaker." She made a menacing face, wiped the corner of her mouth, showed me the clean napkin, and said, "I knew it all along."

"If you were so sure, why did you ask the waiter?"

"Because I just wanted to make certain. And if this had been a normal meal out I'd have had a small purse with a mirror and that would have been the end of it." As the shadows grew longer and the fireflies began encroaching on the terrace Jessica mused, "Tomorrow's your last day here, right?"

"Actually, today was officially my last day. I'm coming up tomorrow just to get my check."

"I can't believe the summer has gone by so fast," she said. "Especially these last eight weeks. I can't tell if it's the end of a season or a harbinger of something else. Maybe something better."

"Speaking of which, I got a job offer today," I said. "Near the end of the round Mr. Sauers offered me a job with his firm after grad school. Said he'll pay my first year of MBA studies and if I stay with him two years he'll pay for the second year."

"Seriously?"

"Here's the best part. There's an international banking conference next spring that he wants me to attend." Reaching across the table, I tenderly grasped my dinner partner's forearm. "Have you ever been to Florence?"

"Florence, Italy?" Jessica said.

"Florence, Italy."

A smile settled softly on Jessica's lips. With her cloth napkin she lightly tamped the tear trickling down her cheek. "This has been the best summer ever."

"Yes, it has."